MORE SCOUSE, VICAR?

More Scouse, Vicar?

Billy Forshaw

JANUS PUBLISHING COMPANY
London, England

First published in Great Britain 2008
by Janus Publishing Company Ltd,
105-107 Gloucester Place,
London W1U 6BY

www.januspublishing.co.uk

British Library Cataloguing-in-Publication Data
A catalogue record for this book is available from the British Library

ISBN 978-1-85756-618-5

Cover Design: David Vallance

Printed and bound in Great Britain
Produced by Digital Book Print Ltd

Having a book published was one of my dad's dreams. He had many of these.

He was so excited this book was going to be printed, it was a dream come true. Though he died before the final printable copy, he had already enjoyed being involved in the tweaking, having a say in the artwork and telling his family and friends. Knowing this book would be printed meant the world to him at 69.

Dad you were a one-off. Your family, and all those that knew and loved you, will truly miss you.

All our love,
Louise Forshaw

to Amy and the people of Liverpool

Prologue

Part I

1 December 1940 – 55°30' North/11°03' West

The mighty Atlantic was placid, concealing its awesome power beneath a wide plastic sheet; oddly calm for December, only a curiously limp swell held sway.

'I never thought I'd see the ocean pancaked out like this,' thought Sub-Lieutenant Jimmy Jones, as the whaler headed across the flat mirrored ocean. 'Is it resting, Cox?'

'No. Be sure, it's not resting,' answered the coxswain. 'It's revving itself up and reviewing its options for tonight and swinging around to the north. There'll be gales by the morning.' The cox steered the whaler out towards the stricken liner, Pompeia. Blown apart by a handful of torpedoes, she was busy slipping gently down.

'Hardly any tilt on her.'

'Looks like the floating roadway down to Princes Dock,' said Jimmy.

'She's holed in three or four places.'

The whaler had left her mother ship, a corvette, HMS Swallow, when, through the telescopes, they observed the panic when the lifeboat launching gear had jammed, spilling the liner's passengers into the sea – not once, but three times. The ocean, ice cold and covered in a blanket of black oil, had gobbled them up. The passengers were dying; the crew needed to respond quickly.

'You can see the ship reflected in the water,' said a wag.

'Cut the piffle,' shouted Cox, concentrating on manoeuvring the whaler.

Nearer the liner the ocean was covered in glossy black bodies clinging to the murky wreckage and five unspilt lifeboats which were sitting in a morass of oil. Circles of passengers clung to each other, or a clutch of deck furniture – upturned chairs and loungers with the odd wooden crate or cabin door – and panic was rife in the overloaded lifeboats. A woman cried out for her lost children, who had been catapulted into the water when the launching gear jammed. She scanned the wide black ocean convinced that she'd spot them. They'd disappeared for ever.

The U-boats had sailed away, looking for further easy targets amongst the scattered convoy. HMS Swallow had happened upon the stricken liner in her role as 'sweeper-up' at the rear of the convoy. It was too late now, except for saving lives.

'Let's keep it steady, pull them up, one at a time. There's plenty to go at, so don't slack,' instructed the coxswain. 'Leave anybody that is definitely dead.'

They pulled in the survivors one by one and passengers who were clinging to an upturned lifeboat. One guy was dressed in his morning suit, as if heading off to the office. There were women and children in their nightclothes. The crying mother asked after her kids. She asked everybody for news; but there was no sign of her children. Even full-grown men were experiencing difficulty keeping afloat.

The mother's pitiful whimpers echoed across the sombre ocean, 'Where are you, darling?'

'Christ,' Jimmy whispered to himself, 'I don't know what I'd do if I lost my babies.'

They hauled in the survivors, like well-greased fish, wrecked bodies with broken bones, gasping for breath, all as black as death.

Back at the Swallow, there was an extensive medical check and a clean-up in full flow. Survivors were on the mess-decks, filling every nook and cranny, leaving black, stinking oil everywhere behind them. Some were flat out, asleep where they had landed, with no headrest or support. They sat on every available seat or bench, deep in thought or fast asleep with their heads in their hands, chattering on, scoffing food frantically or just staring ahead into space. The shivering and poorly clad were wrapped in blankets. There were black faces, like coal miners before a shower, and some surprisingly white faces; some crying, some trying to smile. Jimmy figured that these were off the upright lifeboats.

The medics busied themselves with the half-dead and dying, the cuts, the gashes, the broken limbs and enquired, rather belatedly, 'Any oil? Cough it up. Make yourself sick, if you can. Put your fingers down your throat.'

One man coughed up his guts instead and died minutes later. Some would die a painful death later from swallowing too much oil for their digestive systems to cope with.

There were survivors, still in their life-jackets, in the wardroom. The carpet was drenched in black by now. The sad souls were eating the ship's food as fast as they could lay their hands on it. They were dozing off in a selection of poses and attitudes; sometimes Jimmy thought they had died where they sat. The poor ship was a mess. Jimmy wondered when he would be relieved from his extended watch.

The storm promised by the coxswain duly arrived in the middle of the night. It was grossly uncomfortable, but it managed to convince the surviving passengers from the ocean liner, Pompeia, that maybe they were safe from further attack. Jimmy found his friend, Calum, his fellow sub-lieutenant, cursing the gale at the end of his watch.

'Bugger of a trip and the violent ocean comes to the rescue,' said Jimmy.

'Have you seen what they're using the PE kit for? The tops the football team play in?' asked Calum. 'Just look in the wardroom.'

Jimmy wondered what Calum was talking about. He glanced across and suddenly realised what he was talking about.

'You're joking,' he mouthed.

He couldn't believe his eyes. It looked as if the ship's football team were seated in the wardroom. The black oil-ridden clothes of the survivors had been replaced by the spare PE kit the footballers played in. Jimmy and Calum exchanged sulks because they were leading lights of the team, which managed a match ashore once every blue moon. It came as a shock.

'Oh, God! Calum,' moaned Jimmy. 'Thanks for the news. Just hope we don't get offered a decent game before we've re-stocked the kit locker.'

'Anyway, Jim. You missed the dancing. You should have seen the Boss jigging around when we were bogged down rescuing passengers,' smiled Calum. 'Fred Astaire has little to worry about.'

'I haven't heard,' said Jimmy. 'Too busy mopping up the oil,' he sulked.

'The Boss had a dicky fit. "Why are we clearing up the mess that Jerry has left?" he asked. "Why are we responding to their beck and call? Why aren't we taking the battle to them? We'll get nowhere playing the game on their terms. We should be hunting the bastards down, pursuing them, giving Jerry no rest. We should ferret them out and kill them before they wreak further havoc. We should wreak havoc first; stop playing their game and take the battle to them on our terms ... not theirs." We all just stared at him, with sombre faces, while he jigged about in frustration on the bridge. He's right, y'know, Jim. Picking up survivors is not going to win the bloody war for us.'

'I agree with everything you say, Calum,' Jimmy nodded. 'What we'll do for footy kit, I don't know. Given a match, that is,' Jimmy pondered.

'Bloody hell, Jimmy. Forget the kit. Certainly don't mention it to the Boss till he's in a better mood. Wait till we've spliced the mainbrace,' Calum suggested.

'Sorry, Calum. It just gives me something less horrible to think about. Losing our kit can never be the same as that poor mother losing her kids. I'd cry out loud if it was me.'

Jimmy felt like sobbing; but men don't weep. The tears welled up in his eyes and almost leaked out.

'Oh, by the way. White Rabbit!' Calum smiled.

'Is it still only the first of the month? God, at this rate it's going to be a bugger of a month, if today is anything to go by,' moaned Jimmy.

HMS Swallow was soon steaming through the North Channel and heading back home to the Clyde. Jimmy knew he'd survived a double watch when it was his turn to bunk down. He collapsed into the three foot of space in the tiny cabin he shared with Calum. Jimmy marvelled at the way his friend was able to curl his six-foot-plus frame up into a small bundle, supposing he'd spent his life fitting into confined places and trying not to knock his head. Calum slept like a baby. Jimmy soon fell asleep thinking, if I ever have another busy day at the office in Fenwick Street, just remind me about today, God.

Part II

2nd December 1940 – Bootle, Liverpool 20

In the dense darkness of a moonless blackout Emily Jones followed the older woman, Flo, down the street of terraced houses. Old enough to be Emily's mother, Flo nevertheless set a fast pace along the cobbled street. They carried all their gear in two white enamel buckets, which clattered enthusiastically even though their accessories amounted to little more than soap, a sponge, wet clothes and candles. They had each hung an assortment of towels over their shoulders. They strained their eyes to find a door number legible in the black empty stillness.

'Jerry might not see us; but he'll hear us,' Flo noted.

'That's 35,' Emily whispered, managing to read a clear number.

'Right, it's next door.' Flo pushed through the front door, which was only on the latch. It was gloomier inside than it had been on the street. Solidly murky, pitch-black, it was chilly on the ears.

'If you can't see ... feel.' Emily attempted to joke. Emily was nervous, even as Flo managed to light a candle. She'd never been on one of these nocturnal missions before. Then shivers ran down Emily's spine as the sirens bellowed out, warning of an air-raid. Emily was close to panic.

'We've plenty of time, Em,' said Flo. 'They've not been turning up till the small hours.' She took another candle out of her bucket, lit it from the first candle and thrust it towards Emily. Emily grabbed her candle and followed cautiously through the black. They were soon climbing the narrow staircase to the bedrooms.

'What's that smell?' asked Emily. 'There's a vegetable stench.'

'You'll soon see for yourself,' whispered Flo. 'Come 'ead.'

Emily brought up the rear, wondering what to expect. Flo could sense that Emily was afraid and starting to lose her nerve.

'Okay. I know it's your first time. But bear with me. You know he's such a nice fella. It'll be okay,' she said calmly.

Emily, despite Flo's motherly concern, was by now as white as a sheet as their feet clattered on the wooden bedroom floor. Flo's candle snuffed out as they approached the bed.

'It's all right. We'll use yours. Lead the way.'

Emily led the way across the room, her hands trembling with fear. The shaking candle fell out of its holder and tumbled to the bedroom floor, bounced and snuffed out. Pitch-black returned.

'Talk about the dead of the night,' was the best Emily could say as she bent down and re-lit the candle, which had hit her foot, so she knew where it lay.

In the first glimmer of light Emily saw Tommy's staring face, protruding from the pillow.

'Well done,' Flo acknowledged, just as Emily jumped up physically and let out a muted scream, her body miming violently. 'Well done, again,' she added. 'Good job you stifled the scream, or the ARP would be wondering what was going on. See, he's very happy. I told you so.'

Tommy was sitting bolt-upright in bed, very dead. The smile was hideous and straight out of a horror film. Emily wrapped her arms around her cold shoulders, horrified.

'Told you there was nowt to be scared of,' said Flo matter of factly, while lighting more candles which she placed around the room. 'Good job his blackouts are hung nicely; don't want them shouting to us to put the lights out.'

Emily found herself chattering about trifling matters. Flo chose not to respond, concentrating on the job.'

'I can smell gas,' Emily commented.

'It's cut off,' Flo said. 'It's probably Tommy.'

'Maybe we need a canary?' Emily's attempted joke misfired.

Flo inspected the body and tidied Tommy up a little, while Emily froze like a slab of ice at the fishmongers. By now she was sorry she'd ever come.

'For God's sake, Em, calm down. He's harmless,' Flo pleaded, while she organised herself and gradually removed the pillows from behind the dead man. Tommy slowly sank down into the bed as Flo retrieved all the bedding, sometimes slowly and sometimes with a slick heave.

'Right, we'll give him a quick wash', she announced, 'give the old bugger a clean send off, if nothing else.'

Emily watched, unimpressed and afraid.

'We'll lie him down,' Flo stated. Emily was shocked at the thought. 'Come on 'Em: you'll only lose your fear of the grass, when you piss in the meadow.' Flo moved to one side of the bed and beckoned Emily to do likewise at the other side. 'Christ, Em. What else did they teach you at drama class, besides how to move like a snail?'

Emily hadn't time to answer before Flo grabbed Tommy's shoulders.

'He won't bite,' Flo said.

Emily controlled her fears and held on to the other shoulder, guessing that was what she was expected to do. She followed Flo's lead as they lay Tommy out on the bed. He was still at the top of the mattress. Flo tugged swiftly at the sheet still under him and Tommy slid into place further down the mattress. Emily could see that Flo was pleased with the result.

'Trick of the trade,' she smiled. 'We'll wash him. There's plenty of hot water in the stove. I brought it down earlier. We can add cold from the tap to cool it.'

They retreated downstairs to the old back kitchen, where, true to Flo's word, there was a supply of steaming hot water. They half-filled each of the buckets.

'How long has the old bugger been dead?' asked Emily.

'Nellie found him yesterday,' Flo said. 'The midwife gave him his last bath seventy years ago when he was a babe in arms.' Flo smiled at her little joke. 'The smell will only go when he's screwed up.' They carried the warm water back up the stairs in their enamel buckets and set about giving Tommy his last wash.

'He looks happy with himself. Very pleased at something.' Flo noted.

'Maybe he's just glad to be leaving the Blitz behind,' Emily decided.

Flo rolled up her sleeves and said, quietly, 'Let's do the back first.' They turned the body over. 'Don't be too heavy-handed. You might fetch the skin off. See how the back is pink. His blood has already flowed downwards in the last two days.'

They washed his front and soon the old man was cleaner than he had been for many a year. The funeral directors wouldn't think that they had ventured into the slums. Not this street at least.

'Come into the world with nothing,' said Emily, inspecting Tommy's pockets. 'And he's leaving with two and eleven pence ha-penny in his pockets.'

'Can't take that with him,' Flo sniffed. 'We've given him a clean send off.' Tommy lay on the bed cleaner than he'd ever be again. 'We'll burn his clothes and the bedding,' Flo decided. 'His trousers stink. Old men don't half dribble.'

Outside, the night was livening up. They could hear bomb blasts in the distance, probably on the other side of the river in Wallasey.

'We'll make for the shelters,' Flo said, as they descended the stairs, snuffing out their candles before they returned to the street. There was another loud blast.

'They're getting nearer. Probably over the city.'

'Left it to the last minute again,' Emily gasped.

'Said the actress to the bishop,' Flo automatically added.

Chapter 1

Emily's Almanac

It had turned midnight before Emily had successfully negotiated her return to the Anderson shelter. It was pitch-black, but Emily's nose told her that she was back.

There was the musty smell of earth, paraffin and confinement that lingered day and night. Even though the sky was clear, ideal for star-gazing and enemy bombers, there hadn't been any bombing locally, just explosions from across the river in Birkenhead. Emily's mother-in-law, Ada, was sitting up waiting for her to return.

'Are the kids asleep?' Emily asked.

'Well on. They went out like a light; soon as their heads went down.'

'Good. I think I'll have a cup of tea before the all-clear,' said Emily.

Ada brewed up two cups of tea.

'What do you think of the new paraffin stove and billy-can I found in the old cocky-watchman's hut?' Ada was proud of her find.

'Looks just the ticket. So long as they do the job.'

'Well I brewed this tea up on it. It'll be handy if we are stuck in here.'

'Don't say that, Mum. Let's hope it doesn't get any worse,' said Emily.

'What was old Tommy like then?' Ada quizzed.

'Very dead.'

'No. I mean did he look after himself?'

'Y'know, he wasn't too bad for an old guy who liked his pint. He smelt of cigarette smoke and stale beer,' Emily enlarged and the conversation was as tired as the two women, who slowly supped their tea. It had been a long night.

1

'Suppose so. Only old spinsters look after themselves properly. Even though they've never had a man in years; but hope springs eternal,' Ada smiled.

'Don't know, Mum. Maybe they are just clean people. Some men are clean.'

'Not many that I've noticed. Usually they fall straight into bed, flat on their face, after their last boozing session. That's how they are found. Nose down in their own vomit and stinking like a tap-room ashtray.'

'With those pleasant thoughts, I'll try to have forty winks before the all-clear.'

'I think I'll drain the pot.'

When the all-clear sounded in the early hours the two women carried the two little girls back into the blackened house. Wrapped in their warm blankets they were returned to their own beds. Afterwards, Ada returned home. She was worried about Percy, her parrot. He had been left sleeping in his cage inside the Morrison shelter all alone. She need not have worried; Percy was full of life.

'Hitler missed the bus,' he chirped as soon as Ada uncovered his cage.

'You're a bit out of date, Percy,' said Ada. 'Hitler has planes now.' Ada smiled and went to bed with her hot-water bottle. People didn't appreciate that her clever bird was quoting Neville Chamberlain. I must keep his language clean, thought Ada.

The next morning, Emily walked up the hill to the church, looking around to see if there had been any damage overnight. She looked to see which shops had been bombed out or simply called it a day. There was little change and, likewise, the Victorian vicarage, sitting with the church in the trees, was as solid and commanding as usual. Ada looked after the kids in the morning, while Emily cleaned for the vicar. Cleaning was just one of Emily's part-time jobs. She sewed, she cleaned and she washed to supplement Jimmy's 'hostilities only' navy pay. In all, she scraped together four pounds a week, which was just enough for herself and the two girls to live on.

It was the beginning of what Emily would always consider to be her 'lucky break'. It started to unfold just after she'd cleaned the hallway and, seeing the vicar ascend the stairs, she'd decided that she would put the duster and damp cloth over his study before he returned. She worked quickly around the study from the doorway, making sure that nothing was disturbed. Everything was progressing according to plan until she tried to dust the black leather easy-chair in the far corner. There was a man, a clergyman actually, wearing slightly odd clothes, drinking a glass of red wine, sitting upright in the leather chair. Both Emily and the cleric were shocked.

'Good heavens!' he exclaimed, protecting his glass of wine.

'Wo-oooh!' Emily gasped. 'Sorry, I didn't realise you were there, sitting all prim and proper, like Eamon de Valera.'

'I'm not a bit like him,' the man seemed insulted. 'I'm from sound English stock. A Catholic, yes; but Dev is Irish-American. I'm from old-English stock and ... '

He never finished his sentence, because the vicar had heard the commotion and came rushing in.

'What is it, Emily?' the Vicar asked.

'I'm really sorry, Vicar, I didn't know you had guests. I'll finish it later.'

'It's all right, Emily. It is my old friend Father Deegan from down the road.'

'Emily reckons ... if I may call you Emily ... ?' the father asked.

'Certainly,' answered Emily.

'Emily reckons I look like Dev. I told her I was English. Just a local from Knotty Ash. I'm a fourth-generation Irish immigrant, long before the famine.'

'Suppose Knotty Ash makes you a scouser first and foremost, and you can't do better than that in my book.'

Emily was never slow to speak her mind.

'Brendan, you've got Emily's approval,' stated the vicar. 'Thanks, Emily. You'll have finished in here. Please may I see you later? I've a proposition that I'd like to put to you.'

Emily left the study and wondered what the vicar would propose.

A little later, Emily sat waiting for the vicar in the kitchen, wondering what he was going to suggest. Maybe she was going to be sacked. She had time to pour herself a cup of tea before the portly vicar, his full name of Reverend John Roberts was never used, came scurrying into the kitchen. Emily immediately knew there was something serious afoot and that there would be some purpose to the discussion.

'It's this, Emily,' started the vicar. 'You do three days a week at the moment. Well, next week my house-keeper, Mrs Lancaster, is leaving.'

He stood by the cooker and focused on the pots and pans, which Emily had just tidied up.

'Lily?' asked Emily.

'Yes, Mrs Lancaster. She's moving out to Southport. Ainsdale, I think. She says that she's too old now. What with Mr Lancaster being infirm, her nerves can no longer take the strain of the bombing. She's not slept for weeks. So she's going away, I'm afraid, and her position becomes vacant. So how would you like to become my house-keeper? It's a bit short notice; but there's a war on. It would be more than double what you earn at the moment. I suppose there's always extra food left over as well, which would help you survive the stringent rations we all adhere to these sad days. You would never be without.'

'Well,' Emily was taken aback, 'I'll need to think about it.'

While she thought the vicar continued, 'Only problem I can see, is that I need a cooked breakfast every morning so that I set forth on my rounds putting the right foot forward. Otherwise, the only other meal is the evening meal. I usually have sandwiches for lunch, because I don't know where I'll be. Every day is different; I'm here, there and everywhere. Of course, we'll have to find another cleaner to cover your hours. But basically the job is about looking after me and keeping the vicarage up to scratch.'

'Could a friend of mine have the cleaning job?' Emily asked.

The vicar wasn't slow to see that this was a sensible proposition coming from Emily, one that would save him hours of searching for a suitable candidate himself.

'Emily? You mean that this friend would come with your recommendation?' he asked. 'She would be a God-fearing woman and hard worker?'

'Of course,' said Emily. 'All of that.'

'Well, yes. She can have the cleaning job and as my housekeeper you can instruct her.'

The vicar was pleased that he'd solved his problem.

'Wait a minute, Vicar. I haven't said that I'll take the job yet; but rather than leave you in the lurch, I'll take it. Mornings and meal times are going to be difficult for me; but, I suppose, I can always adjust our meal times at home. My friend, Bessie, will cover for me at breakfast on occasions, if that's alright with you?'

'Splendid, splendid, Emily. I always knew you wouldn't let me down in my hour of need. I really am most pleased,' added the vicar.

'Suppose it's good that I've cooked for you before, when Lily was away on holiday. So you know what my cooking is like. So do I pass the test?'

'Most definitely; but Emily you'll need a diary to jot down where I'll be most days, especially the ones when I'm out and about. Every now and then, I invite some friends and colleagues for dinner.'

'Yes, I've helped out before, Vicar. I've a good idea of the menu.'

The Vicar looked through his cluttered bureau. Emily had no idea what he was searching for. A few minutes later, he reached into the bookcase and fished out a large foolscap-sized journal.

'There you are, Emily. All yours. Treat it like your own diary, so long as you know what I am about each day. It's all yours.'

Emily had never seen such a large diary in all her life before. There was one large page for each day. On the front in large letters it read: Page-a-Day Business Diary for 1941.

Emily always knew that when she returned home she would be faced with a backlog of nappies. The residue of the spoilt ones would be flushed down the outside toilet. Then the nappies would be put in a large bucket to soak overnight. After this, they would need a hot wash. There had been a line full of nappies blowing out all day on the clothes line. There would be almost as many cluttering around the fire to air out. She recalled the comments, "Well if you will have two babies so close in age, you should expect a conveyor belt of nappies." For now it was bucket, bucket, bucket everywhere in the house, particularly on washdays, which was most days.

Now she needed to return home from the vicarage and give Ada a rest from the kids. Gran would never admit it, but she would be tired out by now. On the way down the hill from the church Emily spotted the cake shop open. Although it had had its windows blasted out and been boarded up, it nonetheless opened most weeks on a Friday, when it had something to sell. Pies and cakes were strictly rationed. This week it was two pork pies, just tu'pence-ha'penny each, and a bag of cakes per adult. If you had a large family, then a few of you needed to take your place in the queue and if you had visitors then they would queue along with you. Emily bought her allowance, thinking that maybe Ada might like a pie and the little girls would love a piece of cake. Both of the little girls had scarcely started on solids, so most of their food needed to be minced up. Emily's little girls were just one and a half and two and a half. They were becoming a handful. Thank God that Ada, Jimmy's mother, was on hand to help out. Gran just loved being with her only grandchildren.

Back down the hill, she popped into Ada's. She had already fed the kids and they were both deep into their afternoon sleep. She'd call back for them later. She would make herself some tea, sit down and inspect her Business Diary. She needed to work out how she was going to organise it. For now, she ate her pie, washing it down with some strong tea. Looking at the formidable diary she knew that it was going to take some filling up. This only added to her enthusiasm for her new job. Maybe she could not only write about the events of each day, but she could maybe recall some of the happy events of the past.

She could write up her family history; at least the stories that her mother had told her about the 'good old days' and the 'not so good old days'. If the truth be known, there was more of the latter. Then she thought that maybe she could leave out the bit about living on dripping and bread during the Depression.

It was probably just steeped in folklore. She fingered her way through her tome.

Oh, good, she thought. They give you the last fortnight of the old year. So I'll be able to start next week.

She went to the cupboard and found the old dictionary in which she kept her marriage lines, birth certificate, medical cards, Jimmy's navy details, doctors' bills and such. From now on they would all have a new home in the huge diary. What else could she keep in there? There was her collection of recipes and two or three dressmaking bills with the prices of cloth, cottons and twines. From now on everything to do with her daily life, all her bills, messages, appointments, not that there were many, would all be found in one place. She thought that, maybe, it demanded a grander name than Business Diary. Maybe something special like 'Journal'... , Emily's Journal ... maybe Emily's Almanac.

Besides keeping a record of where the vicar was each day and a daily register of the household budget, food bills, laundry lists and reminders, she needed to keep a note of church festivals, high days and holidays, birthdays and anniversaries. Besides, the vicar had told her to use it as her own diary. She could use it to keep a track of food prices, tradesmen's prices and doctors' fees.

I'll try to record everyday life as I remember it; what's going on around me and my first impressions of people I meet up with.

I'll try my best on special days to record what I see and what it was like for me and the kids. I'll keep a track of the vicar's likes and dislikes, when it comes to food and meals. I'll make sure he eats mostly food he prefers. Make life easy for myself. Ask him if he just wants fish once a week on Friday, and, if so, what he prefers. Suppose it's good to know that he loves his scouse, like all Liverpudlians. Mind you, he can never complain about the spuds, because he grows them all himself in his allotment. I'll be able to keep a record and be able to refer back if I forget things. She finished her pie. Right, she thought to herself I'll go and pick up the kids. Wake them up if necessary; because they won't sleep tonight, otherwise. Gran has done well today.

Down at Gran's, Emily announced, 'Right, Gran. I'll fetch them down.'

'You don't need to, Emily.'

Ada tried to look happy; but she was yawning. Percy was now sitting in his cage on the Morrison. He'd pecked his way through the bottom of the cage and fortunately the Morrison was made of solid steel plate.

'Right, I'll be down before the sirens,' Ada confirmed.

'Put that light out,' chirped Percy.

Emily carried both girls back home. They were becoming extremely heavy. There would be time for a nice long play, then she would bath them and put them to bed. Ada would be down later before the sirens screamed out. The only thing for certain about the evening was that it would end in the shelter.

The oldest toddler, Margaret, was now walking and talking. The baby, Barbara, was crawling all over the place and proudly stood up a little. She could say a few words, mostly 'No' and 'Mamma'. It was pleasant to see the girls playing together, albeit separately. The age gap was wide enough to ensure that they had different interests and favourite toys. Emily looked at her new diary and thought that maybe she'd write something in it later. There may be a little time after the kids had been bathed and put to bed in their own warm clothes, ready for the move out into the cold Anderson shelter.

'Caught you at it. Doing nothing,' an over-large woman, obese and well-rounded, popped her happy, smiling face through the kitchen door. 'See you're back off your travels. Where were you last night? Don't answer that one.'

It was Bessie, Emily's best friend from her school days, twenty years ago. She ambled into the living room and flopped into the only really comfortable easy chair that Emily possessed.

'God, I'd love a cup of tea. Two sugars, now that you are asking.'
Emily smiled.

'I'll make a cup of tea. You must sing to the kids. Give us *The Dirty Old Woman* ... clean words only ... cut out the swear words. Think of the kids.'

Emily went into the kitchen and Bessie started to sing:

'On Hi-tiddley-hi-tie Island everybody lives in style.
On Hi-tiddley-hi-tie Island everybody lives a while,
The life is fast and swift and gay,
You live two weeks then fade away.
I'm sending the wife for a fortnight's stay,
On Hi-tiddley-hi-tie Island.'

'One of George Formby's,' noted Emily. 'The kids loved it. So how much do you get for singing in 'The Blobber'?'

'Just half-a-crown and five bob Saturdays and Bank Holidays.'

'Right, you know I said I'd try to get you some cleaning at the vicarage?'

'You haven't?' Bessie was amazed.

'Yes, the Vicar says you can have my job now that I'm finishing.'

'You finishing? What are you going to do? Bessie wondered.

'No. He's only gone and made me housekeeper.'

There was a long silence and Bessie breathed deeply now that her brain was in gear again.

'What has happened to Mrs Lancaster?'

'She's moving to Ainsdale away from the bombing. You know her husband is growing old and is in and out of hospital.'

'Oh good,' said Bessie. 'Not good he's ill. Good you've got the job. It's very nice living out there in Birkdale.'

'Ainsdale,' corrected Emily.

'Ainsdale,' repeated Bessie. 'Just along the electric line.'

'You'll clean just three days a week and I said you'll cover for me if I can't do the breakfasts and maybe some holidays.'

'Heck, that means I'm in for some early starts after late nights at the pub.'

'So do you want the job and the money?' asked Emily. 'Or do I tell him you can't be bothered getting out of bed in the morning?'

'Oh, of course. Yes ... Nice steady job. You'll be in the money now. Housekeeper? A real posh job,' Bessie felt she was free to suggest.

'Well, it's one of those jobs with status, responsibility and long hours. It's better money than some fellas take home these days.' Emily whispered in Bessie's ear. 'Four pounds ten shillings.'

'Heck, Emily, with Jimmy's navy pay you'll be rich and I'll be off the breadline, too, what with thirty bob extra in my purse.'

Bessie was happy at the thought.

'Great. You'll enjoy the vicarage and me as your boss,' Emily smiled.

'Oh! Aren't we superior already?' Bessie agreed. 'But is he easy to work for, the vicar?' she felt obliged to ask.

'Oh, yes. Not in the least like he is in church. Not in the least holier-than-thou. He's just a very ordinary fellow out of church. His main hobby is gardening. So do you think you'll be able to get up early in the morning, if called upon?'

'Well, I managed this morning and I was stuck in the pub air-raid shelter all night.' Bessie saw Emily fingering her new, impressive diary. 'There's a lot of space for each day. How are you going to fill it up?'

'I was thinking that maybe I could put down my personal thoughts,' Emily said.

'Don't you tell me everything as it is?' asked Bessie.

'Not everything. Maybe I could write to Jim.'

'He'll never see it,' decided Bessie.

'Course he will when he comes home on leave. I can put down some of the family history. Every little story my mother has passed on,' added Emily.

'It's going to be some diary. Just make sure nobody else reads it,' Bessie said.

'Bess, when you start at the vicarage, you're going to have to keep your mouth shut. Everything you see up there will be of a private nature. Try not to come out with ridiculous statements. Folk are often at a crisis in their life when they come to see the vicar. They are in deep despair, absolutely desperate. You just have to see all and never breathe a word about anything you see or hear. It's peoples' private business. You'll see all sorts; but everything will be strictly confidential.'

The bombing was heavy for the next three days and Emily virtually lived at the vicarage, from where she was able to return home with some hot food. They slept in the shelter as soon as it was dark. Ada's paraffin lamp was terribly useful at keeping the tea and soup warm throughout the night. During the day at the vicarage she was busy with preparations for Christmas. Life was routine and at times very tedious, but she was determined to see everybody safely through to Christmas and wondered what would turn up. Fortunately, the raids died down before Christmas week. Jimmy wrote Emily a letter home, saying that he would not be home before Christmas, but was hoping to be around in the spring, possibly Easter. There were no helpful signs on the envelope, which was brown, officially stamped, with no address and no markings. It meant that he could be anywhere on the ocean or in any port the world over.

Even though life was uncomfortable, the vicar had been generous, letting Emily take home any of the spare food. He let her have a weekly bag of his beloved potatoes. Along with the carrots, there had been a heavy crop that season. It was a good job, because there was next to nothing in the shops. Some of the main retail outlets had been bombed and many of the smaller premises had just given up the ghost. About half had been completely blitzed and were now just heaps of boarded-up rubble. Others gradually became depleted of stock, and goods arriving from the depot were distributed before the morning was out. A sign saying "Out of stock. Open tomorrow" would be displayed in the only unbroken piece of glass in the window.

The week before Christmas 1940, Emily quizzed the vicar about his plans for his Christmas dinner. She pointed out that turkeys were two shillings and fourpence a pound. She asked if he wanted a goose.

'No, Emily. I think I'll settle for one of the hens. One of the non-layers.'

'How will you choose the non-layer?' asked Emily.

'I'll lock them in the coal-cellar, one by one. We'll soon see which one isn't performing,' he reasoned.

'Will we keep watch over them?'

'No. We'll expect an "end product" in the morning.'

'I don't think we should joke about the poor creatures,' said Emily.

So each evening, during the next week, a different hen was exiled to the coal-cellar and would emerge when she had laid an egg. Usually they tumbled to the vicar's game and laid an egg the first night.

During the December raids the father seemed to pass through the vicarage at breakfast time, particularly after heavy bombing.

'Am I to cook two breakfasts?' Emily asked.

'No, no, Emily. I appreciate that you have to put up with a lot. I hope the extra food doesn't complicate everything. I'm aware that you keep our secret very well; but there's nothing untoward, Emily. It's just that we return up the hill from the mortuary together most mornings. We chat to grieving families and pray for the souls of those who have departed and comfort the living, of course. We've been friends for years, since we were young men together and played for the same cricket team. Now we have much the same interests at heart and are fortunate to have enjoyed an academic life during the same years, just after the Great War. Pity that Liverpool embraces such grotesque religious prejudices, which necessitate us hiding our old friendship away behind closed doors. Some people have the ridiculous idea that we should be at each other's throats.'

Emily was happy with the explanation as to why it meant extra eggs.

From now on, she was to make an extra breakfast each morning. Half-past six may be an early hour, but it was busy at the vicarage if there had been an air-raid.

One morning, she chatted to the father, while he was sitting in the Vicar's study, and mentioned the two clerics' joint interest in cricket.

'Was he much good?' she asked.

'An outrageous batsman. Always looking to score runs. Myself, I was a bowler, quick in my youth. Medium pace for much of my career.'

The conversation was cut short when the vicar returned up from the coal-cellar and announced that he had found an egg in the wood-shavings. The subject changed from cricket to eggs, hens and the Christmas dinner.

Since taking over as housekeeper, Emily had experimented with various wartime recipes from the *Bootle Times* newspaper. Sugarless fruit cake depended on how many tins of condensed milk you stirred into the mix. Sometimes Emily used too much dried fruit to make the cake edible. A chocolate potato cake was as ghastly as it sounded; even the hens refused to eat it. The best of the bunch was a sticky loaf that didn't need fats or sugars. It depended heavily on eggs being stirred in well and the fine balance between black treacle, syrup and fruit. The vicar, having a sweet tooth, didn't appreciate any of the sugarless cakes, especially those heavy on sugar substitutes with carrots or parsnips instead of fruit, despite Emily's efforts.

By Christmas, each of the five hens had survived at least three nights banished to the coal-cellar. Using every conceivable combination of hens, the Vicar finally decided upon the hen that he thought just didn't lay at all.

'That's the one,' he said, pointing her out. 'Shirley.'

'She isn't the fattest, Vicar,' Emily observed.

'She'll be a good meal. The potatoes are at their best and the spinach is still growing. The carrots have struggled a bit, but there is sufficient still edible. There is a fat, solid cabbage and the onions are as hard as rock. I'll let Shirley run around the pen for the last time.'

Shirley jogged off. Much later, Emily was called out into the hen-pen to help catch Shirley, who was becoming uncooperative.

'It's not a nice job,' Emily whispered.

'It wouldn't be difficult, if she wasn't so excited,' the Vicar said.

Shirley guessed that her time was up so she flew and half-jumped out of the pen before making a final bid for freedom across the vicarage lawn. Her surge of energy gave out on the top of the vicar's faithful, black car, parked by the garage. Feeling pleased with herself, she promptly relieved herself all over the car roof. The vicar sighed deeply and chased her back into the garden.

'She's iced the car especially for Christmas, Vicar,' chirped Emily.

At this stage Emily and the vicar were failing as a team. The vicar shooed the hen towards Emily, but at that moment Shirley took off and flew straight over Emily's head, landing on next door's fence. The vicar cleverly placed a handful of loose grain on the roof of his car and Shirley couldn't resist the prospect of a quick snack. She swooped straight back, nearly knocking Emily's head off, and was soon scoffing away. Having lulled her into a false sense of security, the vicar turned Shirley upside down and wrung her neck in a second. Emily was so shocked she cried buckets of tears and managed not to vomit in the spinach patch. The Vicar hung the bird upside down in the pantry.

'She knew she was destined for the pot,' said the vicar.

'How did she know?' asked Emily, who thought the vicar was joking.

'I told them, Emily, many moons ago when they were all pretty little yellow chicks. I used to tell them all about it by way of a bedtime story.'

By now Emily knew he was joking.

'Some bedtime story then. Was it *Hansel and Gretel* by any chance?' Emily asked, before calling an end to it all by saying, 'I'll peel the potatoes, Vicar.'

She worked away in the kitchen thinking, 'One thing is for certain, it'll be chicken scouse, soup and sandwiches till the New Year, that's for sure.'

Fortunately for Emily, Bessie was at hand to help pluck and clean the bird, which was healthy and a lot fatter than Emily had first supposed. She hadn't formed a false friendship with the bird, but had only made friends with Shirley when she advised each of the hens in the coal-cellar to try and lay before the morning, or it may be their last rumble in the coal and wood-chips.

'It's for your own good,' she'd whispered. 'Besides, eggs are worth their weight in gold these days. Each one makes a meal. It's your contribution to the war effort.'

Emily and Bessie discussed their own Christmas. It was agreed that Bessie would pop in to see Emily, Ada and the little girls on Christmas morning. Then Bessie tried to butter some bread, which was just like concrete.

'The fortified loaf gets worse.'

'It tastes of chalk this morning,' said Emily, before Bessie became carried away in her own special brand of the ridiculous.

'They're putting all sorts in it these days, so as we don't eat too much. Suppose if you fortify something you pour half a ton of concrete into the foundations.'

'As for the National Creamery Butter, I'm sure it's margarine,' decided Emily.

'I've heard that they are putting whale blubber in it,' assured Bessie.

'One thing's for certain, it's not butter,' said Emily. 'I noticed when I was trying to fold some of it into the Vicar's Christmas cake it wouldn't melt down. I had to buy in some extra eggs, because we can't count on our hens these days,' she added

'Fresh new-laid eggs are two and two a dozen,' noted Bessie.

'They're free here, after we've threatened the hens with the chop.'

'Have you heard from Jimmy?' asked Bessie. 'Will he be home?'

'Last letter said he wouldn't be home for Christmas. Maybe Easter.'

Chapter 2
Convoy Duty

The conditions were still stormy as the Swallow sailed up the Clyde to Gourock pier. The survivors from the Pompeia numbered two hundred and seven, nearly three times the size of the Swallow's company. There wasn't any part of the ship that had not been abused and exposed to thick black oil. The usual ship's smell had turned really foul before the end of the trip. A choice stench of heavy oil, over-used toilets, continual cooking of food and body odour hung in the air, even though four days of gales had dispersed much of it. They tied up alongside Gourock pier and unloaded their miserable cargo. The two hundred and seven were led away to the church hall and, as we are terribly British at times like this, they were given as much tea as they could drink and a bowl of very hot, thick broth, full of nourishment, and doorsteps of bread to help make a meal of it.

The ship's crew were left feeling miserable. One look at the widespread mess the army of survivors and their oil had created told them immediately what their duties would consist of for the next week. A giant clean-up.

'Let's hope we are not expected to go right out before Christmas. Or worse still, I bet we're back on the ocean for Hogmanay,' hissed Calum, as they rested together for a change in their tiny cabin.

'Good job we kept the tiniest bunk in the British Navy free from oil. We'll be able to hide away here, while they scrub down the decks on a regular basis,' said Jim.

'I never thought I'd be pleased with our wee bolt-hole,' said the Scot.

'I won't mention the football kit to the Boss just yet,' said Jimmy.

'Good thinking. I think he'd like a clean ship first, just in case we do a quick turn around. He's not a happy man,' said Calum.

After two days of constant cleaning the ship looked sparklingly new. It was oiled, watered, victualled and the wardroom carpet had been replaced. Glasgow was the best place to have a clean-up, being Britain's biggest workshop for new and refurbished ships. It was pleasant to smell the fresh air straight off the ocean with only new, fresh smells wafting about the vessel.

Back in their tiny bunk, which was becoming a habit now, even though Calum lay with his long legs hanging from the lights and Jimmy tried to make full use of the floor space to compensate, they made plans for after the big clean-up.

'Good news,' said Calum. 'But keep it secret. The Boss has got his hands on a few hundred quid. He's been told that he can claim five shillings per day for each of the survivors. So that's quite a hefty amount of cash.'

'Maybe it's a good time to ask him about the kit?' thought Jimmy.

'I don't think we'll be paying much for our drinks in the wardroom for a bit. Although I'd make sure the Boss has had a drink before you ask him about kit,' Calum said. 'Maybe it is your chance to ask after all.'

Jimmy plucked up the courage as soon as he had finished watch and judged that the Boss might have downed one or two drinks after his evening meal. He would be in his cabin under the bridge. Jimmy knocked on his door. He knew it would be okay, because the Boss was a team player and he looked upon every member of the crew as his family. His door was ever open.

'Sub-Lieutenant Jones?'

'Yes, sir.' Jimmy saluted, even though the Boss was taking time out.

'Is it another enquiry about leave?'

'No, sir.'

'Right, how can I help you?'

'It's the ship's PE kit, that doubles as football kit.'

'Yes, I noticed. It just came in too handy for the miserable wretches we fished out of the ocean. We'll replace it quickly. They'll stock some in Glasgow.'

'The other thing, sir, is about leave. If I manage to arrange a match, I'd like to play the fixture before some of the crew go off home.'

'If we are escorting the next convoy, we'll be straight out to sea and there won't be any leave. Maybe I'll let the local Scots nip home on Christmas Eve. However, I agree a few football matches over the holiday period may add something other than heavy drinking to the Christmas and Hogmanay celebrations. Yes, we'll need kit, whether we're stuck in port or not; we can't have the men looking badly turned out, whether anybody can see the kit or not. You can go into Glasgow and buy some. Use the station small truck. We can't be waiting for the navy to react pronto. It's not in our time-honoured tradition. Sometimes I think we should embrace "the snail" as a new emblem. I'm experiencing some difficulty nagging them at the moment to fully supply my ship and what do they do? They lose the victualling sheets, so we have to start all over again; fortunately the QM kept a copy. So right, Sub-Lieutenant, I want you to buy me new kit for every man on the ship. Don't spend too much money. Just replace the damaged and lost kit and we'll foot the bill. Make sure the sports kit is good quality; we don't want other ships suggesting that our gear is old and tatty. Let's look smart.'

Jimmy ventured to the door and was saluting, when the Boss added, 'Let's make sure the crew have a good run around in some healthy Scottish mud before they end up inebriated back on board the ship.'

The news came through that Swallow was indeed to be on standby over Christmas and could be away before New Year. Local lads could go home on a forty-eight hour pass on Christmas Eve, but had to be back by twenty-four hundred hours on Boxing Day, in case Swallow left port on the twenty-seventh. This didn't suit the Scots one bit, who would rather have had Hogmanay at home, but they accepted their passes gleefully.

Jimmy organised two matches in the run-up to Christmas.

The best player in the team was Calum, all six foot two of him. Calum played for Queen's Park Rangers in the 1930s and was still first-class at centre-forward or centre-half. Some matches he played both positions, depending on who was attacking. Jimmy captained the side at half-back and the cox was a tricky left-winger. The cox always thought that he was returning a favour when he recruited Jimmy to be junior officer on the whaler. This wasn't as grand a job as it sounded because of the number of gruesome sights to be seen, particularly when the assignment was to pick up evidence of a sunken vessel. The bits of evidence from a U-boat were often the human remains of a German officer still in his uniform. On another occasion a crew member was convinced a detached human heart was still moving. Probably turbulence beneath it. Jimmy didn't enjoy the job. Why couldn't they do what the Yanks did and recognise claims without physical proof?

The football matches were a great success, after they'd found a pitch free from barrage balloons. Light was another problem. It was dark by three o'clock in the afternoon near Christmas and, of course, the Germans didn't help by starting their air-raids before they'd reached the safety of the pub cellars. It made for a long night in the pub before the lorry or whaler turned up at first light.

Jimmy found another football pitch, a bit boggy, for the second match. It was away from the barrage balloons and anti aircraft installations. There was a decent pub down the road and the publican told Jimmy that there was plenty of drink, particularly whisky, in stock. It was a good night; they'd won the match against a local side, who complained that all their best players were in the services, and the Boss turned up to join in the celebrations with Number One. Next day was Christmas Eve and the Scots went home on their forty-eights.

There was a skeleton crew on the ship for Christmas. Some of the lads had been invited over by local Scottish lads. When they returned to the Swallow before midnight on Boxing Day, they were a lot more sober than the crew who had been on watch over the holidays. The food was edible and made a welcome change. The cook had tried hard to get his hands on some local produce, fresh fowl and vegetables. Jimmy thought of Emily and his two babies back home in Liverpool.

On the twenty-seventh they moved out into the Irish Sea and didn't hang about long before the Liverpool contingent came steaming up to join the ships from the Clyde and Belfast Lough. The convoy comprised sixty vessels of all shapes and sizes and each had its own individual speed and characteristics. They headed out into the North Channel, into the teeth of a gale and out into the mighty Atlantic.

Jimmy was glad that he had eaten well over Christmas, because eating wouldn't be his main pleasure until he reached America. He'd just eat the foods he knew kept down and drink lots of sugary tea and cocoa. The convoy scattered in the gale-force winds, so there was little by way of escort duty. The U-boats would be concentrating on staying afloat. Jimmy knew that the U-boats, because of their relatively small size, would be suffering even more than they were. Maybe they would be heading for the safety of the Scottish and Irish coasts and islands.

Off Halifax 44°03' North/62°30' West

The Swallow sailed for Halifax, where she arrived after thirteen days, a day behind schedule, having chased up smaller merchantmen who were lagging behind in the rough conditions. They passed through the Bedford Basin, where the eastern convoy was assembling. The Swallow's crew spent a week looking around Halifax, which didn't have much to offer, but, unlike Glasgow, was air-raid free. Jimmy enjoyed his new-found freedom and wondered if he could arrange a football match in peaceful surroundings.

There was another ship, out from Belfast, looking for an away game on Canadian soil. Everything was agreed; finding a snow-clear pitch was something of a problem but Jimmy was confident the game would take place. Then the port became snowbound and the Swallow was assigned the next eastern convoy. Next morning they were heading back out into the Atlantic. Service came first and the sea looked calm for a change; but it was freezing.

Off Cape Wrath 58°30' North/5° West

From Halifax they headed north-east towards Iceland, conscious that the calmer weather would bring the U-boats out to play. It wasn't until they were sailing down from Cape Wrath that they saw any U-boat action. It happened in a bizarre way. Swallow's role as escort was to zig-zag on the edges of the convoy, chivvying-up stragglers and offering help to smaller ships struggling in the heavy seas.

No sooner had *Cape Wrath* been spotted in the early morning mist, than a U-boat, probably in trouble of some kind, was spotted loitering near the entrance to Loch Laxford, one of Scotland's sea lochs. The boat was oblivious to Swallow patrolling the edge of the convoy. Something was obviously wrong; maybe she was just recharging her batteries on the surface. Swallow was able to sneak close before the sub dived below the water. Her position and speed were simply read. Instantly, Swallow was over the U-boat; which inexplicably resurfaced, took a look around and dived again. Top theory was that the U-boat skipper must have been drunk.

The Boss gave the order to ram to ensure that the U-boat didn't make good its escape in the confusion. The 4-inch guns were used on her and finally a machine gun on the bridge was used to pepper the conning tower. Just then the Swallow rammed straight into her and completed the job. She oozed out air and water and went straight down.

The survivors were taken aboard. Some were scared young men, happy to be alive, but some were proud Nazis, in smart uniforms. They were sure that they were going to win the war. The way things were going just then, they might be right.

In the collision the bow of the Swallow was split, just two feet above the waterline. Makeshift repairs were made and they headed back to their home port on the Clyde. The Boss was pleased with the sinking of the U-boat, but rather upset at the damage.

'Suppose we're lucky our next port of call is Glasgow. They'll have us repaired and as good as new in a jiffy.'

It was to take a month, during which time all of the crew managed some leave in rota.

Jimmy organised a few football games and then hit trouble.

'Why have we Fenians in the team?' he was asked out of the blue.

'Because it's the football team off the Swallow; nothing to do with religion.'

'We won't turn out again, if you have Celtic Catholics in the team.'

'Bloody ridiculous. We're fighting a war out in the Atlantic and you can't even play a game of football. I thought we were fighting for liberty and freedom.'

'I'm not playing with Catholics.'

Then later the other side joined in.

'I'm not sharing kit with the prodi-dogs.'

'Right, it'll be alright with me, if you can convince the team manager.'

'Why, aren't you the team manager?'

'No, I'm the PTI.'

'Who is the manager then? ... Calum?'

'No, the Boss is the manager. And I can tell you now, he won't like it.'

There was a hastily convened meeting in the wardroom. The team crammed in.

The Boss was at his sparkling best.

'What's this I hear about people not wanting to take part in PE? Every man has a responsibility to keep fit. I thought it was a good idea to let you men have a few kick-abouts rather than practise the boring deck-drill. I'd say we're pretty good at the ocean-going formats and attack drill. We don't need to practise for practice sake. So why can't you men join in a game of football?' asked the Boss.

'We do not mix with Catholics where we come from.'

The Boss met the problem head on and cut the discussion short. 'Maybe I should tell you exactly where I stand on this one. I'm in charge of this ship, I have the King's authority, and the football team is my responsibility. What I say goes. I have the power to stop leave if I want to. I can lock any of you up, if I so wish. See ... it's my ship. I am the boss of this ship. I think football is a good recreational idea and don't care what foot any of you guys kicks with; on my ship you are just my men. All of you are my responsibility. On my ship we all mix.

'We all pitch in. We do battle against Jerry together and we will play together on the football field. I know for a fact that Hitler doesn't play for Celtic or Rangers. He doesn't even play for Queen of the South or Heart of Midlothian.' Number One stifled a smile, while Jimmy hid a big grin and the non-committed felt pleased.

The Boss continued. 'So the crew on my ship fight together against Hitler and we play together on the football field. We drink together in the pub afterwards. Just because we're back on dry land in Glasgow doesn't mean we embrace local misplaced customs. And remember this, the Scottish lads were the last crew to get leave on Christmas Eve. Don't you forget that. The rest of us had to sit it out on the ship; because we couldn't reach home, even if we'd wanted to. What is your religion, Sub-Lieutenant Jones?'

'I'm Welsh non-conformist, sir.'

'I always thought you were a Scouser.'

'I am, sir. I attend Methodist church in Liverpool. I'm of Welsh descent.'

'Right, so there we have it. We are a ship's company and we are all together in this war on the ocean. Likewise, we are all together playing football. Catholics and Protestants all play in my team.'

'Leave won't be cancelled will it, sir?' Number One played the 'soft touch'.

'No, Number One, never on my ship; because we are a team. That will be an end to the matter. I don't expect to have to deal with it again.'

The boss turned and smiled at Jimmy and then spoke matter-of-factly, but out loud to Number One.

'Maybe in future, Number One, I'll only take on taffies on this ship. Have a full crew of Welshmen. What do you think, Number One?'

'Excellent idea. We'll have one hell of a male voice choir, sir. We could compete in the Eisteddfod, instead.'

'What a splendid idea, Number One,' said the boss.

Nobody had the courage to laugh at the suggestion, because they knew it was just a front to ease the atmosphere of contention.

'Very good, sir,' said Number One.

There was just one more game of football before most of the players went on leave. Jimmy tried to keep the fellows who had caused the fuss apart, in the beginning, but the problem never appeared again. Swallow was repaired and returned to her mooring off Gourock.

Jimmy went down to the engine room, where most of the Scots in his football team, apart from Calum, were to be found. The chief engineer was looking perplexed.

'No doubt, you've come about the football team, fitting a match in before we leave. Well, don't worry. Looks like we'll be heading back into the dock.'

'Why?' asked Jimmy. 'I thought they'd sorted out the bow. A decent job?'

'Yes, but look. Look at the hold. There's water. There's plenty of it.'

'Wasn't a good job then?' Jimmy asked.

'The job on the hull was okay. Looks like we ruptured the pipework in the collision. We've been trying to work out where it's coming from. Are you any good at tasting stuff?' he asked Jimmy. 'We've all tasted it.' He bent down and wet his palm and sucked it. 'Doesn't taste of salt to me. Have a taste?' he asked Jimmy.

'I'd rather not, if you don't mind. No saying where that's coming from. Could it be from the bilges or the heads?' Jimmy suggested.

'Could be, but not the sea. Maybe we need new piping. The Boss has booked her in again, so you'll be due for some leave after the football match.'

'Do you always taste the water like this?' asked Jimmy.

'It'll nay harm ya. Quickest way to tell where the water's coming from,' said the chief.

Jimmy remained unconvinced but the chief had twenty years' service. At least with the ship back in the shipyards it would cut down on the transport to the pitches near the port. There were plenty not covered by air defences.

Jimmy often wondered why he bothered with his team but it was simple really; it took his mind off more unsavoury matters, like survivors coughing up oil and horror trips out in the whaler.

Kicking a heavy leather ball around a soggy Scottish field was what civilised life was all about. After all the fuss about religion there were more Scots in the side than ever. They won the game easily. When you left the Scots to their own devices they came up trumps. Calum was outstanding as usual and the cox had an easy game on the wing against a lad who was scarcely out of short trousers. Jimmy knew that this was so much better than facing a Force 9 off Iceland.

Chapter 3

The Locals

The middle of December 1940 wasn't too bad for air-raids, but come the twentieth of the month there were raids on three consecutive nights. Emily was settling into her new job of housekeeper at the vicarage and was up and down the hill every day, keeping a note of her movements in her new almanac. Being busy kept her mind off the raids, even though long periods of time were spent in the shelter, as aircraft arrived overhead three nights on the trot soon after tea and the all-clear didn't sound till first light.

Bessie was singing in the pub every night and spent the night there. They'd have a sing-song some nights; other nights people caught up on their sleep, depending on how much they'd had to drink. Some people could sleep anywhere given a space and a blanket. There were those who couldn't sleep, while others would sing all night, given half a chance. Bessie would try out new local words to the latest popular songs, such as *The Nightingale Sang in Clayton Square* and *We got lit up when the bombs blew up in Liverpool*. She experimented, just to pass the time, and knew that often the words didn't really scan. About the only ones that did were *Mersey Docks and Harbour Board*, which she used in her act. Whatever she did to pass the hours away never really succeeded, because the nights were always long and there was always the chance of meeting your maker. The morning never arrived quickly enough.

Freddie, Emily's neighbour, was well known locally for all the wrong reasons. He decided that Hitler wasn't going to stop him enjoying his evening at the pub. Returning home during a raid, very drunk on 'fighting beer', he was ready for a fight with the first person to cross him. There was a mighty flash and he found himself in the gutter, looking up at the stars and the silvery pencils with wide wings flying overhead, glistening in the moonlight. Freddie managed to regain his feet, but another crash at the bottom of the road sent him back into the gutter. This time he landed on his back, looking up at the stars again and the offending bombers in the black sky.

'Come down, you bastards, and fight it out. Or are ya yella?'

He lay waving his fists about till they had disappeared out to sea. After he'd regained his feet, he looked towards his house. The front bedroom was well alight. He dashed to his front door, luckily it was on the latch, and raced up the staircase. The top floor was brightly lit up by an incendiary. Inside his bedroom a mass of heat and flames were coming from his mattress. He raced to the window and opened it as wide as he could. Then he returned to his bed, chose the only part not enveloped in flames, clung on and flung the flaming mattress out of the window in one manic effort. It landed in the middle of the road. Freddie hurled himself down the stairs, two at a time, grabbed hold of the stirrup pump and sprayed water over the fire till it finally gave up the ghost. The matt-ress was black and completely destroyed; Freddie had sobered up.

Geoffrey the local ARP warden was cycling past on an urgent call-out. He studied Freddie and the soaked mass of black mattress in the middle of the road.

'Can't stop. Two women trapped in a burning shop,' he announced, as he flashed past. 'Probably the hottest wash that mattress ever had,' he whispered to himself as he changed gear and headed up the hill. He knew Freddie from his job down at Huskisson Dock. He was one of the questionable characters that were often seen asking for goods, which they called 'samples', next to pubs near the dock gates. Geoffrey decided it was best to keep drunks at a distance. It was a dirty habit anyway.

Geoffrey Spencer was the vicar's church warden; he was also temporary choir master for the duration of hostilities, on the few occasions he was able to muster up a choir. He also played a leading part in the local ARP, which formed up outside the church, or in the church hall, if the weather was inclement, which was most of the year. At a time when social class still lingered in the background, Geoffrey was within his rights to think that he was a cut above the drunkard, who everybody knew as Freddie Mack. He vaguely knew the man, having seen him sober outside the dock and, otherwise, in a drunken state propping up the doors of the Blobber. The best policy was to steer clear and maintain some semblance of respectability. He had standards to live up to.

Geoffrey worked on the docks, checking cargoes in and out. It was a thankless task with all the bombing and destruction every night. Cargo was often stowed on a ship and it was bombed before it set sail. Likewise, goods were bombed before they left the dockside or the warehouses.

Geoffrey had a checking office, which had been bombed. It was as if all the German bombers were instructed to hit his office as a matter of priority. It had been hit seven times. The dock board gave him a tin hut, which he only used for brewing up. He preferred to carry the crucial dock papers around in a briefcase, which he carted home on the back of his bike. This way his 'office' was with him day and night. Every Saturday morning he would carry his briefcase down to the Mersey Docks and Harbour Board building at the Pier Head. Transport depended on whether the buses and trams were running. Some Saturdays he rode his bike, avoiding all the bomb craters in the roads. He found himself taking a different route each week. Craters were filled in by ancillary working parties and there was plenty of rubble close at hand.

The clerks at the offices issued Geoffrey with berthings for the next week, which were never correct. Usually, if ships turned up on time, in one piece, it was a miracle. Sometimes he had to return on Monday morning, usually after a heavy raid, to be redirected and have his berthing list amended out of all recognition.

On one Monday morning he was informed that his latest 'tin hut' had been incinerated.

'How have they done that?' he'd asked incredulously.

Then he'd seen it in the corner of the quay, just a heap of black metal without a speck of paint on it.

'It's a good job I keep everything in my briefcase then,' he'd mused.

Geoffrey amended his way of working thereafter. He wasn't going to deal in 'sight of paper' any more, he was going to record what he saw in front of his own eyes. Some ships didn't arrive; some goods didn't materialise; some goods sat waiting for a non-existent ship; some goods missed their train and to top it all, some goods and ships were bombed before his very eyes. So he tallied what he saw, without waiting for the paperwork from the office, which was usually a fiction when it materialised.

After heavy raids he found it best to walk to work, rather than cart his bike over the bomb craters and wrecked bridges. He was pleased to get away from the docks when he could because they were full of officials, dock-board, navy and army, all trying to look important but just getting in the way. Geoffrey would arrive with his briefcase, with all the important details inside, to be confronted by a petty official who knew 'bugger-all about the job', trying to move him on. He found it difficult to explain that all the movements were in his case. Some days he'd take one look at the bombed dock and knew immediately that nothing was making sense. He'd phone the dock office and they'd know less about the situation than he did. At this point he usually decided to return on the tide, if it was neaps, hoping that the air-raids didn't start too early. Sometimes the ships would stay out in the offings with their lights out and only come in after the raid, hoping they still had enough water.

Away from the docks, Geoffrey had two hobbies. Choir master was one of them, but it was difficult to organise with many of the male singers in the forces and the best choir-boys evacuated. He hoped to reform the choir as soon as hostilities permitted. His favourite hobby, however, was local history. Before the war he gave talks to local groups about the history of Liverpool and West Lancashire. He loved to regale about the times when William Ewart Gladstone went to school on Bootle Sands and picked wild roses along Rimrose Road. Why, indeed, was the biggest dock basin in the world named after him?

The vicar often showed some interest in Geoffrey's local history and one day asked him, 'Well, Geoffrey, are you recording the real history?'

'What history, Vicar?' Geoffrey asked.

'That which is thundering on around us,' the vicar replied.

'Is that history?' asked Geoffrey.

'Of course it is.'

Geoffrey was rather shocked. He'd never thought that he was playing a role in some real history. Surely history was about lovely thoughts of wild roses growing along Rimrose Road and early tales of Gladstone.

'Like it or lump it, Geoffrey,' said the vicar, 'this is the real history.'

'I still don't see it, Vicar. The docks, the port, the bombs are all part of my day job,' Geoffrey decided.

He wasn't going to be dissuaded from his nice, pleasant idea of what really should be. How could this miserable period be termed 'local history'?

Freddie Mack smiled back as Geoffrey sped away up the hill. He hardly knew Geoffrey. He had the impression that he was a big noise up at the church and he'd been the focus of his indignant looks when he rode his bike away from the dock gates.

He may think that he's a cut above me; but so what? thought Freddie, feeling as washed out as his mattress, which lay sodden in the gutter. He walked back indoors, went upstairs and shut the front bedroom window. He suddenly felt sober for the first time all evening. Shows what a bit of exercise will do, he thought. He walked back through the house into the kitchen, sat down in his favourite chair and fell asleep. An hour later, the all-clear sounded. Freddie snoozed on.

Freddie Mack was probably as well-known as Geoffrey Spencer but they moved in completely different circles. Chaos at the docks meant hard work for Geoffrey but for Freddie, it meant a better chance to get his hands on some decent stuff to sell around the pubs. Freddie dealt in the local black market outside the docks, in the nearby pubs. Easy stuff to store and sell were the canned foods from Canada, USA and Argentina. Tinned fruit from anywhere sold, tinned salmon from Canada and, of course, corned beef from Argentina. However, much of the tinned meats went straight to the war zones by ship, avoiding the North Atlantic. The British Army and Navy virtually lived on 'corned-dog'. It was easy to sell if he could get his hands on some. Sugar was golden, too, because it was rationed, while John West salmon just flew out of the door. The easiest goods to sell were cigarettes, nylons and Durex.

Lots of goods off the docks were damaged. A cargo vessel full of New Zealand lamb had suffered a direct hit and the carcasses had been blown all over the dock, in and out of the water; but after selling off a bit of meat, Freddie gave up. It was hard to find a butcher; bona-fide butchers wouldn't handle it because it was badly damaged and contaminated by all the nasty substances found in the docks. All the pre-war butchers' men and lads were in the forces, so Freddie could not find anybody to butcher the frozen carcasses. He gave up trying. Give me a case of tinned salmon or corned beef any day, he thought.

Freddie longed for the Yanks to come into the war so he could get his hands on quality goods. So far his best source of supply was the Canadians. British sailors wanted a bigger cut. Freddie spent long periods of time dodging the police and the port authorities, which was why he preferred to sell his goods in the pubs on the way back from the dock. He deceived himself into believing that was why he drank so much, being obliged to buy a pint in every pub he traded in up from the river. It was a good day if Freddie could acquire some goods near the dock that were easy to sell, then he could spend his evening wandering home, closing the door behind him with just the money in his pockets.

Freddie's main suppliers were the Brennan brothers, who seemed to know exactly where to acquire the goods. Trading with the Sligo family meant wall-to-wall Guinness drinking and he found it was a 'heavy evening' if he got caught in a round with them. The oldest brother, Mike, virtually lived on Guinness. He was once reputed to have drunk two crates of the stuff in an all-night session, celebrating his seventieth birthday. Freddie believed the story because he'd once seen him drink three pints straight off, after he'd bought the stuff in and his brothers hadn't turned up on time. The Brennan brothers were seven in number, using up every known Irish name including Ossie and Colly. Trading with the Brennans invariably meant that Freddie had to socialise at the same time, ending up very drunk. He took too much stuff off them and sometimes didn't get a good price. He knew that he'd been out with the Brennans when he couldn't enter his bedroom and tripped over piles of boxes. It was the Brennans who had given him Percy, the African parrot. He'd passed it on to Ada when he'd found feeding and cleaning the bird a bit too much like hard work.

It was the Brennans who had filled Freddie's hen-pen with Spam. The birds perched on the boxes till they gradually disappeared. Spam was another good seller, the kiddies loved it. When the Brennans partied they took over the pub. Everybody bought goods from them, so everybody knew them. They had friends from Ireland, friends from school, friends they'd dated and courted, and friends they'd produced children with and married. They were all young at heart, old guys, grandfathers and fathers. When the extended family turned up the pub was overflowing.

They had two claims to fame. The first was that brother Declan had played with Dixie Dean for Sligo Rovers. The second was that they had their own pub band. They didn't play folk, country or popular songs. They played Dixieland jazz, all the way from County Sligo. Some nights, after a session, Freddie didn't know what deals he'd struck or what goods he'd bought until they arrived on his door-step. This explained why, after Mike's seventieth birthday party, which went on into the small hours and through the air-raid, Freddie found his hen-pen full of soap the next morning. Two tons of soap that had come on a barge down the river from Port Sunlight and transferred to a Blue Funnel in Huskisson Dock for export to the Far East.

Freddie Mack and Geoffrey Spencer just didn't move in the same circles.

Chapter 4

Emily's Family

'Life is just one damn thing after another.'

Att. Elbert Hubbard

At the end of January 1941, Emily started to write more fully in her diary. She recalled most of her family stories. How her mother, Cathy, had come down to Liverpool on a sailing ship, a coaster, out from Stranraer, when she was an infant of five. She thought it was a white ship but it was probably the huge billowing sails. She'd been born in Kirkpatrick Durham, near Castle Douglas, in 1880. Life was extremely hard for the poor in the countryside, so the whole family headed for the City of Liverpool, which was growing in importance throughout Victoria's reign.

Emily's father, James, had left Welshpool, in the Welsh borders, at the turn of the century and walked to Liverpool. He had first headed for Shrewsbury and then Chester, sleeping out at night under the hedgerows, before reaching Birkenhead. Here he begged for the few pennies needed to catch the ferry across the Mersey to Liverpool.

Before long, he was an experienced handler of cart-horses, to and from the docks. Eventually, he ran his own small firm with just four horses in the yard. The stable was attached to the end of a terrace and James rented the end house, at the corner of Boundary Street and Commercial Road. James needed a wife and had met Cathy at the local non-conformist chapel. Cathy gave birth to six children. Emily was the youngest of four girls. The youngest and the oldest children were boys.

During January, Emily met Father Deegan many times as he passed through the vicarage on the way to the hospital and mortuary, or after a meeting at the town hall when civic acts of worship were discussed. It usually happened immediately after an air-raid and the two clerics had just returned from the temporary mortuary.

One morning, after a joint breakfast, the vicar felt he needed to explain how he and Father Deegan were such special friends, considering the religious divide in Liverpool. Emily revealed the little she knew to help the conversation along.

'The father said you were an outrageous batsman, Vicar,' she revealed.

'But did he say that he was just a mediocre medium bowler?' said the vicar.

'He said he was very fast in his youth,' remembered Emily.

'He may have been, but by the time I faced him, he wasn't ferocious.'

'So how did you meet the father then?'

'Suppose we both arrived in this area at the same time. We were each asked to read civic prayers at the cenotaph the same November. He was a soldier in the Great War, you know. Later, he became chaplain with the Liverpool Irish, although as he says, he is fourth- generation English. You know all about his cricket, and his love of Shakespeare. You see, he's a learned scholar. He has all the Latin languages and Greek. The only language I have over him is Inuit and, even when I speak it, he occasionally corrects me. He'll inform me on occasions that I'm not pronouncing certain words like I used to. He remembers every word I say, like it was a recording. He's even tried to apply classical parsing and analysis to Inuit. He keeps asking me, "But where is the verb?" I just say, "Don't ask me. You'll find the nearest Inuit speaker in Greenland." He just loves language. He's an educated man and I think that's why we get on. Dealing with so many dead has brought us close together.'

'So you never served in the war?'

'No, I was trekking around Northern Canada with the Eskimo. I spent most of my time with the Inuit at Resolute and York Factory.

'Is there a factory?'

'There was once. Most places in the Northern Territory were once forts, like Providence and Reliance.'

'So you were never a soldier?'

'No, that's where our paths diverge. I went straight into holy orders and wanted to work in the colonies. I wanted to work in the hot savanna, like David Livingstone; so the society sent me to the Arctic. I was the Bishop of the Arctic's right-hand man. Father Deegan went straight into the army at the outbreak of the war as an officer, and took holy orders after the war.'

'You seem to have a lot in common,' Emily decided.

'Well, yes. We have the ears of those who run the town, the docks and some of the navy and army establishments. We keep our mouths shut and listen. We read the national press and compare notes. They get it wrong so often. We love to read the *Echo* and see which information they censored out. Often the best bits.'

'Some of the stuff you talk about is never in the press,' said Emily.

'Most of it. So much is far too sensitive to reveal, so the censor just blanks it out. If it's too late they just leave a blank. It's either that or have people fretting hopelessly and sobbing like children. Every morning we resolve to forget what we have seen in the night. ... So what have we for cake these days?' he changed the subject.

'Cake is harder to find these days. You have such a sweet tooth. You've never really taken to any of the sugarless cakes I've baked,' Emily told him.

'Some of them were absolutely ghastly, Emily,' said the vicar.

'War recipes. Right. What do you think of this? First give it a try.'

She placed a plate full of sticky loaf on the table. It was the same cake the vicar had rejected previously but this time she had buttered it carefully. The Vicar tasted a piece and then swallowed it quickly, followed by a second piece, a third and finally a fourth slice.

'This is more like the cake I know, Emily. It's wonderful,' spluttered the vicar, with his mouth and hands full to overflowing.

'I have a confession to make. I served it to you and Father Deegan on Monday. The good Father quite liked it and you rejected it,' Emily revealed.

'So what's the difference?'

'I've buttered it,' Emily said in triumph. 'The recipe is supposed to be one that doesn't need butter, fat or sugar. Buttering the loaf seems to make it edible.'

'Emily, you are a genius,' The vicar decided. 'Delicious cake at last.'

'I couldn't be feeding the hens on cake for the duration, could I, Vicar?'

'We'll name the next hen Marie,' laughed the vicar. Emily looked confused at his suggestion. 'After Marie Antoinette.'

Emily knew he liked his own jokes best.

Nonetheless, the vicar's acceptance of the sticky loaf meant that she would cook all her sugarless cakes in future in loaf form and then spread a mixture of butter and margarine over the top, just before serving. People with less of a sweet tooth, like the father, could eat it without. This would save on the sugar and fat; but she'd still need to ration the butter and margarine. Fortunately, nobody could get enough of the sugarless cake and it proved to be a filler when there was a bread shortage. Ridiculously, parishioners would ask the vicar for the recipe, so Emily, after telling them it had been in the *Bootle Times*, would be asked to provide a copy of the ingredients.

'You are really so considerate about writing out these recipes for so many in the parish, Emily,' the vicar would say, after another list was copied out.

'It's alright, Vicar. I don't look upon it as an imposition. I look upon it as part of the war effort. Maybe you should print it in the parish magazine.'

However, she later confessed to Bessie that her hand was dropping off after so many requests.

On the breakfast front, Emily discovered that she could make one egg go a long way, by scrambling it and adding a little flour and finely-chopped onion. One egg did for both the vicar and the father, if he was at breakfast. If the vicar complained, she'd remind him that he'd promised to find some more good layers. Indeed, he had a dozen hens running around the chicken-pen. The manure from the birds came in handy when mixed with garden compost for the vegetable patch. Once a year, he purchased a load of horse manure from the local hay and straw merchant, which enriched the tomato crop and specialist vegetables. He grew almost everything in the garden with the help of cold frames, sheds and the greenhouse.

Home-grown produce wasn't too plentiful in the winter months but he had perfected the art of storing roots and there was always a hardy winter veg crop, mostly cabbages and sprouts. Come summer, even though he staggered the tomato crop, he would finish up giving many away. He grew a large salad crop, green and red tomatoes till the first frost which would make as much chutney as the availability of sugar and dried fruit permitted. He grew bags of potatoes from the earlies through to the lates. He preferred an autumn free from early frost and heavy rain, so he could leave carrots, onions and turnips in the ground till the last minute before storage. His favourite vegetables were leeks, spinach and celery. Sometimes, his spinach crop started growing in the cold frame in February, sheltered from the frost and snow, and was still alive come the Christmas dinner. He loved spinach. He enjoyed eating stews and hashes, which were essentially the same meal depending on the amount of liquid and baking or grilling applied. Potatoes were his main crop and his passion so they featured heavily in his diet. He loved potato stew, Irish stew or scouse. He pronounced himself the foremost expert on potato-based dishes.

Emily discovered a copy of *Mrs Beeton's Cookery Book* on the shelf in the study. She skipped the section on 'How to be a housewife'. I'm not married to a house, she decided, and moved on to 'Recipes for Mutton and Lamb'. According to the esteemed cook, you needed mutton for Lancashire hotpot and Irish stew. Emily smiled when she showed the recipes to the vicar. He became totally engrossed.

'Three pounds of neck of mutton, three sheep's kidneys, a dozen sauce oysters, four pounds of potatoes, one large onion,' the vicar read. 'Emily, run down to the butchers and buy some mutton,' he joked.

'The butcher by the post office was bombed out last week and the one up the hill has shut up shop and moved to Wales for the duration.'

'Precisely,' laughed the vicar. 'Wonder what she suggests we should do, if there's a war on,' he sniffed. 'She doesn't mention that the potato is the most important ingredient, and why you should use the freshest and the tastiest you have. Neither does she suggest fresh herbs and celery from the garden. She suggests only one onion. Ridiculous.' The vicar rejected the recipes out-right.

'The sauce has the crucial job of adding flavour to the potatoes,' Emily added.

'Exactly, but we make do with whatever meat is available, don't we? If the potatoes are good then they act like sponge on the gravy. That is why 1 grow plenty of sage, parsley, chives and celery. We've used every conceivable sort of meat that has been available.'

'We're experts at chicken hotpot, thanks to the non-layers,' Emily added.

'Exactly. Mrs Beeton doesn't mention the old lob or blind scouse,' the vicar noted. 'She doesn't understand the concept of making a beautiful potato dish with just a hint of meat.'

'Right, you can have blind scouse next week,' joked Emily. 'To be honest, you seldom have "meatless" scouse. I've chopped up a sausage or two before today to help with the essence of the gravy.'

'One of your best was the scouse you made with just bones and scratchings,' enthused the vicar. 'Mrs Beeton wouldn't appreciate that "blind" means you can't see the meat. She'd expect three pounds of mutton.'

'You are a lucky man, Vicar, to love spuds and veg.'

'And enjoy the thrill of growing them,' the vicar stuck his chest out. 'Yes, I try to grow the best quality food. The potatoes have to be the best-tasting varieties. Some of the tastiest are grown from Scottish seed. I'd like to get my hands on some.'

'Right, so blind scouse next week,' Emily decided.

The vicar paused in the doorway. 'Just a little meat, please, Emily?'

Then he looked at the smile on Emily's face and knew she was just joking.

Emily didn't know where Jimmy was stationed, but she'd written to him in one of her letters, explaining the vicar's love of scouse. Indeed, Jimmy was always on Emily's mind, so she found herself writing about him and how she first met him in her journal. It would have been when they were still kids at school. Or was it the church youth club? Was that before they used to see each other at choir practice? She remembered chatting to him when the choir went carol singing. He was always intensely serious and exacting. He wanted to get on in life and make something of himself. He was good-natured and ambitious. He had a steely determination and talking about working hard was his only conversation. He could be sharp-tongued on occasions about people who didn't give 100 per cent. This didn't make him popular, but he was so good on the sports field at all ball games that he was never short of friends and people wanting to be in his team. He was always happy and positive about the future. They all hung around in one huge gang and were happy and comfortable with each other.

She remembered that they had met up again as young adults when they had gone ballroom dancing. Apart from the expensive professional dance halls in the city, such as the Grafton and Orrell Park, there were the places that opened their doors on Friday and Saturday nights and were more utilitarian. The names of these places rather gave the show away as to their true function during the rest of the week, viz. Park Street Barracks, Litherland Town Hall, Stalmine Conservative Club and Johnston's Dye Works Social Club. They were part of the ballroom-dancing generation and every institution held dances to make ends meet and provide recreation for their employees.

The way to gain admission to a dance was to dress up cleanly, a decent suit, collar and tie, with polished black shoes for men, and tidy responsible ballroom dresses and dancing shoes for the women. It was best to not have the smell of drink on your breath and arrive early, long before chucking out time at the pub. The door stewards got to know you as a regular and never questioned your credentials.

Emily noticed Jimmy at all these locations, but he never asked her for a dance and she never indicated to him that maybe he should ask. They both considered the other too good for them; too nice a girl and too quiet and respectable a lad for them to even think of dancing with just them. They admired each other from a safe distance. This went on for over a year. Emily had developed into an attractive woman since her schooldays. She'd matured into the classic persona of a Gaelic woman with her long, dark-brown hair, and confidence oozed from her smart features.

It wasn't until Jimmy had moved up a grade at work that he plucked up the courage to ask Emily for a dance. He spotted her sitting with the wallflowers, with her dark hair cascading over her shoulders. She was so full of life and pleasantly smiling, wearing an elegant, long dress that made her look taller and turned the eyes, especially Jimmy's.

She accepted.

'I thought you'd never ask,' she said.

'I'm amazed you've said yes,' Jimmy sighed.

'You're a pretty useful dancer,' she said.

'Have I passed muster? I can dance a little bit better than this. Just hang on.'

Jimmy whirled around the floor and it felt so right, as if they'd always been partners and meant to dance together. They giggled as they spun around the floor.

'I went to Goodfellow's,' she said, naming the dance school on Breeze Hill.

'That's where I learnt the basics, too,' he said.

They danced nearly every dance together that first night and met up at all the other local venues in the coming weeks. When they were alone together they felt comfortable with each other from the very beginning. Conversation came easily and they seemed to have much the same outlook on life. The reasons for them being so compatible soon came tumbling out, woven into the conversation, the humour and habits of a lifetime. This concordance of purpose expressed itself in their joint attitude to dress, clothes, eating habits, aspirations and aims in life. They'd first seen each other at church and school and never wondered if they were both from Welsh stock, even though Emily was a Davies and Jimmy a Jones. They'd even lived a few streets away from each other along Hawthorne Road. Each seemed to know what the other was thinking and both felt that they had met their own true loves. Emily accepted Jimmy's commitment to his work and sport, coupled with his pleasant nature, high spirits, sense of fun and supreme confidence in the future.

Emily had worked in two factories since she left school. Her first job was in a paper mill that manufactured writing paper and envelopes for firms that used the postal services to convey their goods. Her current job was in the Dunlop factory, where she worked in a long line of girls fashioning plimsolls and deck shoes, which the locals called galoshers. Her main aim in life, like so many young girls, was to marry and bring up a family. It was the expected thing. Spinsters were frowned upon. Few women had successful careers and men were considered the providers.

They both received a limited education, leaving secondary school at fourteen and finding a job straight away. Although Jimmy continued with night school, Jimmy's parents wanted something better for him. His father had worked down the South Wales mines and after coming to Liverpool had laboured on the docks. So Jimmy's father managed to find him a job in an accountant's office on the top floor of one of the tallest buildings in Liverpool city centre. The job wasn't anywhere near as well paid as some of the men could earn with overtime on the docks, but there was a chance that Jimmy could better himself, if he passed his accountancy exams. For Jimmy, night school and correspondence courses were part of the norm. The idea was to eventually be offered articles and train as a chartered accountant. The firm of Ellis, Jones & Jones, although no relation, was filled with Liverpool Welsh; so Jimmy was in the right company from the word go. Jimmy's father, Gareth, would always say, 'It's amazing who you meet in chapel, especially if you are in the choir.' There was a route for Jimmy, if he worked hard, put in the hours and carried on singing in the choir.

Jimmy was always a natural at sport, particularly football and cricket. He could always run fast, playing on the wing at soccer, and when it came to cricket he was a fast bowler and enthusiastic fielder, particularly off his own bowling. He was an ever-present for all the teams that Ellis, Jones & Jones put out. This included the darts and bowls teams, if they didn't clash in the summer with the evening cricket matches. He also played in the I Zingari League at football. He was one of the thousands that could say they played for Everton, they had so many teams in the local leagues on Merseyside. The joke was that Everton had so many teams that they had run out of letters in the alphabet. Jimmy reckoned he played for the 'odds and sods'.

Jimmy was to find out, when he aspired to be a PTI in the navy, that being able to say he played for Everton at football and Bootle at cricket went a long way. Nobody outside Liverpool knew the standards reached.

It was while they were courting that Jimmy first met Bessie. She was singing in the local public house, the Blobber. They seldom went into a pub, because of their families being committed tee-total. However, one weekday evening when there were no decent dances on, nothing worth seeing on at the cinema and it was too miserably wet and cold to go for a long walk, they finished up in the local pub.

Emily immediately recognised Bessie, sitting at the piano, singing *An Apple for the Teacher,* as the girl she had gone to school with. She had filled out considerably but she was still a superb singer. At school she was awarded all the main solo parts. It was the first night that Emily had ever heard Bessie sing some of the local songs in her routine. The words were so disgusting that Emily didn't acknowledge her presence to Bessie initially, but in the end she relented and chattered to her about old times. They soon became close friends again, recalling old friends and pleasant memories. Bessie, like Emily, had only managed jobs in factories, and she currently worked in

Johnson's Dye Works and Cleaners. She was run off her feet during the summer months when everybody got something cleaned before the cold winds of autumn and the freezing winter months. Bessie was always good for a laugh despite her filthy pub routine. It was what the punters wanted to sing, when they topped up with 'singing beer'.

Emily and Jimmy popped into the Blobber a lot more after their first visit, but always left as soon as they anticipated that Bessie was about to go into her boozie song sequence. They'd wander off on their long walk home. They found themselves going to the pictures a lot more, preferring to visit cinemas which were that little bit off the beaten track to avoid acquaintances. They met up most week nights after work. They used to have tea with Ada and then spend the evening together. The time together seemed about five minutes long, while the time at work, during the daytime, seemed to last forever.

They developed a ritual of Friday night at the Stalmine and Saturday, into town and the cinema, after Jimmy had recovered from his football. In summer, cricket took up more and more time, but it managed to deposit Jimmy in some quiet places off the beaten track. If he found the place interesting then that would be their next trip out as a couple. This is how he discovered Hoylake, West Kirkby, Birkdale and Freshfield. The favourite two were on the Wirral. First, there was the lovely seclusion of Raby Mere and the other was the quay at Parkgate, where Nelson had once courted Lady Hamilton. Summers were cricket and long days out till dark. Winters were tough games of mud-splattered football. Saturdays, Jimmy sometimes played mornings and afternoons, before they would finish up dancing around the dance floor till late. Other times, if there was a good film on or if Jimmy was really tired out, they'd go to the cinema. It had to be a lively film to keep him awake.

Their lives were split into two parts. They would work during the day and be together evenings and weekends. They were a courting couple. They talked about what they wanted in life. Jimmy wanted to work hard for his firm and take every exam open to him, pass it and move up the ladder. He felt at home with Ellis, Jones & Jones.

He wanted to continue playing sport till he dropped. His father had been the oldest player to ever play in the Bootle JOC League, when he retired at thirty. Jimmy wanted to compete at a higher level. If the war came, he hoped to enlist in the navy and see the ocean. Ideally, he wanted to be a PT instructor. They both dearly desired to be married and start a family. Emily just yearned to leave the factory behind.

Jimmy had promised Emily that he would show her where he worked and one summer's evening when the weather was iffy, it had threatened rain all day, they caught the tram into the centre of Liverpool. The number 16 tram, which ran between Seaforth and the Pier Head, came trundling up Strand Road from the docks and stopped across the road from Woolies. They were soon viewing the liners moored on the Princes Landing Stage.

'One of these days I would like to be on one of those heading for Montreal,' said Emily, looking at the Empress of Canada.

'Sure you don't fancy New York?' Jimmy joked.

'No. I seriously have the urge to leave and live in Canada, maybe Vancouver.'

'Not before I've passed all my exams,' Jimmy said seriously.

'How do I know you work in the city? You are supposed to be showing me the offices and the high building you go on about,' Emily reminded him.

They walked up Mann Island, under the overhead railway, up the slope at the bottom of James Street and past the underground station. Opposite Queen Victoria's monument on the corner of Fenwick Street stood the National Bank Building.

'There you are,' Jimmy announced. 'I work on the top floor of this building.'

Emily looked up to the top of the building. It was certainly taller than Bootle Town Hall and the Dunlop factory. 'I think it is taller than Johnson's Dye Works.'

'Most definitely,' said Jimmy, proudly. 'And I work here all week.'

They wandered through Brunswick Street into Castle Street. Halfway along the street Jimmy pointed to the middle of the road.

'The Sanctuary Stone, I think they call it.'

Emily couldn't see what he was talking about.

'Wait till the trams have all passed,' Jimmy said, before grabbing Emily's hand and striding into the middle of the street. Jimmy was looking closely at the cobbled stones, just by the tram tracks. 'Look, all the stones are the same size and there's just one large stone that they have chiselled grooves across, just to match it up.'

Emily looked rather confused at the experience.

'Yes,' she said. 'What's so special?'

'That stone used to mark the centre of Liverpool market, years ago. They say it's the exact centre of Liverpool.'

'You wouldn't know,' said Emily, underwhelmed. 'It's hidden in the cobbles.'

'Emily?' Jimmy asked.

'Yes, I can see the tram coming,' Emily said.

'No, Emily. I want to ask you ...'

'Make it quick or we'll be knocked down by a tram,' said Emily. 'There's a tram. Oh, no, it's stopped at the bottom.'

'Emily. Will you marry me?'

'I thought you'd never ask,' she said. 'Course I will. If you hadn't asked me this week I was going to ask you instead.'

Jimmy grabbed Emily and they raced back to the pavement just before the tram trundled down the centre of the road towards the Town Hall. They paused and kissed.

'Maybe we should celebrate?'

They went into a small pub in Dale Street and ordered two halves of milk stout.

'Pubs have a use after all,' declared Jimmy.

Jimmy married Emily in 1936 and they had two children before Jimmy went into the navy in 1939. He was right in that he was considered suitable to be trained as a PTI. His all-round sporting ability made him suitable for the course. He had to do two extra months at Portsmouth. However, he didn't anticipate what was to happen next. Jimmy completed the assault course in a very fast time. When the instructor told him this, he offered to do it again because he hadn't been racing. This time, he broke the existing record. When the CO investigated, he found that Jimmy showed exceptional qualities of leadership and had performed well in all his written exams. Jimmy found it difficult to break his habit of studying well into the night. He was transferred on to the officers' course, which was physically less demanding but at the end of which he became Sub-Lieutenant James Jones (HO) in the RNVR, a temporary gentleman. He asked if he could still carry out some of the duties of a PTI aboard his future ships.

'Of course, you can,' came the answer. 'We expect officers to play a major part in all physical activities.'

Jimmy was hoping to be posted back up north to Liverpool; instead he was posted to HMS Swallow on the Clyde.

In the spring of 1941 there was a lot of heavy bombing, mixed with one or two incendiary raids, mostly over Birkenhead. Emily heard that Bessie had been bombed out. The vicar said that the Salvation Army had taken her in. Emily walked down to the army centre on Stanley Road. There, she was told that Bessie had returned home.

Emily figured that the best place to look would be The Blobber. Before Emily had entered the pub she could hear Bessie belting out her songs from behind the piano. She was very much alive and thriving on her predicament when Emily smiled across at her. She was singing *Colonel Bogey.*

'Emily.'

'Bessie,' shouted Emily, 'glad to see you're still alive.'

'I'm okay. I was around at the pub when it was bombed. I've moved back.'

'Yes, but how are you managing?'

'Its okay. I've just shut off the front of the house and they've boarded it up. I can manage with the kitchen, living room and one bedroom.'

'Won't it fall down?'

'No. Wait till you see the way they've faced it up with wood and concrete. It'll do. It's my own fault for living next to the station and goods yards.'

'It's not your fault. It's that madman Hitler's.'

'I know. That's why I'm singing *Colonel Bogey*. If you don't know the words you just whistle.' She started to sing: 'Adolf Hitlers only got one ball. Da, da, and the same to you. Da, da, and the same to you. Don't throw the lamp at me; you'll only waste the oil.'

She sang whole-heartedly and the punters whistled loudly.

'You can stay over with me if you want,' said Emily.

'I'm okay,' confided Bessie. 'I'm here most nights and most mornings I'm doing breakfasts at the vicarage. I'm okay for money. If I thought Hitler was winning, I'd join up. If they'd have me.'

Bessie played a few chords on the piano, then addressed the locals as she tootled over the keys.

'Listen up, everybody. If that little snake Adolf Hitler comes in here, just direct him over to me and I'll batter him.'

This warranted a round of applause. She continued.

'We may have been slung out of Dunkirk, we may be blitzed and, maybe, the ships are sinking fast and we may even starve. But I can tell you this – that Adolf Hitler and his gang of madmen have gone too far this time ... (pause and music) ... he's only gone and bombed me out of house and home. Well, I'm not disheartened, far from it ... he's bitten off more than he can chew this time ... because I'm back living in my own house already and ... if he comes in here... I'll give him a piece of my mind.'

Bessie changed the theme completely and sang *On the Sunny Side of the Street* and *Pennies from Heaven*. Then she sang an old favourite that they all liked to join in with, *A Dirty Old Woman*.

'A dirty old woman in Walton did dwell.
That dirty old woman I knew very well.
She didn't wash, she didn't bathe and stunk of stale scouse.
And the neighbours were all glad when she left the house.
Doodle eye, doodle aye.
And the neighbours were all glad when she went away.
Now the dirty old woman was in bed one night,
When all of a sudden she wanted to ...

God bless us and save us, oh, what a farce,
So up shot the window and out shot her ...
Doodle eye, doodle aye.
If you don't know the chorus, just doodle eye, aye
Now the old cocky watchman was passing by
When a ball of hot ... something hit him right in the eye
Doodle eye doodle aye and the neighbours were all glad
when she went away.
If you don't know the chorus just doodle eye, aye'

The drunks could just about sing 'doodle eye, doodle aye' and were happy with themselves; Emily wondered if the song had some clean words to it. Maybe it was getting to the time in the evening when the songs would get cruder, so she sought the sanctuary of the way out. She had soon reached the door and heard Bessie shouting after her.

'See you in the morning.'

Back in the street, Emily found herself joining in the chorus of 'Doodle eye, aye' pumping out from the pub.

When Emily reached home, she felt something strange about the house before she went in. She paused in the doorway, trying to work out what it was. The door was open and there was excited chatter and laughing out loud, all personal and familiar, coming from inside. She walked into the kitchen. Ada was there with the kids and Jimmy was standing there, beaming from ear to ear.

'Emily,' he beamed and said, 'Oh, Emily.' Ada marshalled the kids out quickly and Emily and Jimmy kissed and cuddled for ages.

'How long have you been home?' asked Emily eventually.

'Only just now,' he said. 'I caught the bus from Lime Street.'

'God, I've missed you, Jim. I've been lonely without you. The kids have grown up while you were away. They're both toddlers.'

'Yes, they are. They've grown so big in a year,' said Jimmy.

'God, I've missed you,' she repeated. 'Your mother has been great. Marvellous with the kids.'

They cuddled tightly in each others arms for ages.

When things had settled down a bit, Ada came back into the kitchen with the kids. Jimmy caught up on lost time, playing with the two girls. The oldest, Margaret, remembered him, due to massive prompting from her mother and grandma. The youngest didn't know her father but would seek attention from anybody willing.

'I received your letter,' he said, 'just before I left. I laughed at your comments about the vicar, his potato crops and the poor hen at Christmas. It was really funny. However, I noticed a sign outside a farm down the coast, where we often play football. It said "Best quality Seed Potatoes". So I bought some, with the vicar praising Scottish spuds and all that.'

Jimmy was on a fortnight's leave. The time just flew by. They made sure that they spent as much time together as possible as a family. They even managed to slip out once or twice, by themselves as a couple, after the girls had gone to bed. They had so much catching up to do. Jimmy finally got around to unloading his presents from America. The two girls were given beautifully clothed dolls and Emily received some lovely nylon stockings with Yankie-style underwear to go with them.

'I didn't know what to get you, Mother,' Jimmy told Ada as she opened her present.

It was luxurious soaps, scents, sponges and lavish toiletries.

'So what you are saying is that I need a good wash. Is that it?' said Ada.

They visited a photographer down Lord Street and posed for a family group photograph with Jimmy, Emily and the two kids. They collected the best copies at the end of the week; a traditional wartime portrait with the father in best naval attire. It was a happy two weeks, despite the bombing and the shelters. Emily introduced Jimmy to the vicar, who was filled with praise for the potatoes.

'I think they are called "something" Piper,' Jimmy said.

'Maris.' prompted the vicar, inspecting the seed potatoes.

'The farmer told me that they were best kept in a cold cellar till there were two or three good shoots. He said they would always be free of disease,' said Jimmy.

'Oh, excellent, James,' said the vicar. Emily had never seen the vicar so happy in all the years she'd known him. 'I was wondering when to dig up the front lawn for vegetable crops. Now I've received the answer.'

'God moves in mysterious ways,' Emily said.

'You'll find that William Cowper has already written a hymn about it, Emily!' the vicar prompted.

It was the first time that the Jones family had had the chance to function as a complete family, so they made sure they enjoyed every moment of the fortnight they spent together. The time just flew by, however, and soon Jimmy had to return north to Glasgow.

'Soon I'll be out of the navy and back home again. I'll pass all those accountancy exams and our little family will be well set up for the future. It'll be great. I love you so much, Emily, and our little girls are wonderful. I've loved being a father and having them on my knee for a change. I'll miss you all terribly. Just remember I'll be looking at my photograph of the three of you,' said Jimmy.

'I'm looking forward to seeing you again,' Emily stuttered.

'Yes, we've the whole, real future together,' Jimmy said, and he kissed Emily just about right. They embraced much longer.

'The Luftwaffe attacked Liverpool on eight successive nights in May 1941, killing nearly four thousand people and seriously injuring four thousand; ten thousand houses were destroyed and more than 184,000 damaged. Survival and ultimate victory rested on more than just the struggle at sea; this battle was being waged in the country's docks, shipyards, factories and shops.'

Andrew Williams, *The Battle of the Atlantic.*

Chapter 5

The First Week in May

'Liverpool suffered the most ferocious punishment of its
life, from a week-long series of raids which altered its
pattern and perhaps its spirit for ever.'

Nicholas Monsarrat

The first week in May 1941 was the week that saw the heaviest raid
ever delivered on an English city other than London; 70 per cent of
the buildings were in some way damaged and whole streets were
obliterated. By the end of April there had been over seventy air-raids
on Merseyside. On the nights of the twenty-sixth and the twenty-
seventh landmines were dropped along the coast as far as Southport.
Virtually everybody Emily knew had taken to trekking out of the
town into the fields, woods and hedgerows. Some would catch the
train out as far as Ormskirk. It was estimated that 25,000 people from
Bootle – population 50,000 – were on the move.

Emily and Ada started to make plans to camp out, figuring that
maybe going along the coast would be silly because of the bombing
and the minefields that were laid amongst the sand dunes. They had
the huge pram, which could carry the kids and most of the family
bedding, but there was no way it could be loaded on the bus. The
bombing on Thursday 1st and Friday 2nd, finally made them decide.
Bedford Road School had been hit by incendiaries, along with the
timber yards in Marsh Lane, and landmines were dropped on the
docks. The bombing was getting nearer to home, as the weather
stayed pleasantly dry. There was lots of sunshine during the day and

although the nights were chilly, they could always take thick blankets with them.

Geoffrey Spencer didn't have the opportunity to camp out in the country; he was completely occupied down at Huskisson Dock, as all the berths were full. In his briefcase was the classified information that two of the ships, Mahout and Malakand, were full of ammunition. The information he held in his case was secret, but everybody in the docks knew. Geoffrey would often sigh, 'Oh, well, thank God we're all on the same side.' He cycled down to the dock on Saturday evening. It was lovely weather; no wonder the Germans were making the most of the clear nights.

One thing was certain; all the berths were full. If it wasn't for the bombing, he thought that for once the information in his brief case made sense. He'd parked his bike near the gate, thought twice about leaving it there, and then returned to find it had been nicked. The only thing to do was to head back up the hill and home. He thought that maybe he could walk up to the railway from Huskisson and regain the road at Kirkdale. It wasn't as if there weren't any holes in the walls to take a short cut through. He followed the Lancashire line out of the city. He found himself intrigued at the way the tunnels and cuttings sliced their way through the suburbs. This was real local history, he thought; the dock railways in their time had been such massive feats of engineering. There were so many gradients and deep gorges to be admired. He was stepping out through the wall at Kirkdale when he saw a black figure on the line, emerging from the railway tunnel. Could it be a ghost?

'Who goes there?' asked Geoffrey, feeling rather military but a bit afraid.

'It's me, Geoffrey,' a slight, tiny old woman said. 'I'm looking for our Benny.'

'Little lad?'

'No. It's our tomcat.'

'I thought you were a ghost.'

'I've told him before.'

'The cat?'

'He never listens. He's so independent.'

'Yes; but keep off the lines, Suzie. Suzie Milburn isn't it?'

'Yes.'

'They bring ammunition trains through here.'

'I'll have to find Benny. Don't want him blowing up.'

Geoffrey left Suzie Milburn to it. Since taking over his job with the ARP, Geoffrey had found that trying to explain to some folk was a waste of his precious time. He needed to organise himself for his night out on fire watch.

Sunday morning before seven saw Geoffrey walking back down the railway cuttings to Huskisson to check on the night's damage. There were no ghosts, no old women knocked down by a train and no blown-up cat

It had been another night of devastation; Geoffrey lost count of the fires raging all over the city. It was just half-past seven when the most monumental explosion erupted. The blast sent Geoffrey flying backwards on to the track; bits and pieces of debris shot past. He was lucky not to have been hit. He crossed the dock road at the railway crossing. There was a private car sliced in two. He headed into the dock, wondering how the check sheets in his briefcase would measure up today, alter appearing 'okay' the previous evening. Large areas of the dock, the warehouses and cranes, had just vanished. The *Malakand* had exploded, with her cargo of bombs. Geoffrey's latest hut had just disappeared.

'Makes me feel responsible for it. Just hope it's not wrapped around some bugger's neck for a muffler,' Geoffrey sighed. 'Just when I thought I was getting this dock into some shape, they moor two ammunition vessels in it and one of them explodes and takes everything and everybody with it to kingdom come.'

He struggled to keep tears from forming in his eyes as he thought that it was still only half past seven on a sunny Sunday morning. Whatever next?

Saturday had been a lovely sunny day as Emily headed out into the countryside. Broken glass glistened in the gutters near the bombed sites and there was a heavy grey haze about the place. It had been decided that Ada would spend most of the day wandering out as far as the Cabbage Inn with the big-wheeled, black pram, conveying the tent, tarpaulin, heavy blankets, large piece of cardboard, newspapers, food and paraffin lamp from the shelter. Emily would feed the kids after their afternoon naps, dress them and then catch the bus out as far as the Cabbage Inn, where they would all meet up and head out into an open field. First, they needed to tell Bessie and the vicar. Bessie said she was staying in town as she was singing at the pub over the weekend. She was still convinced that she had a personal grudge match with Adolf Hitler and she didn't want him to think that she was about to take the easy way out; far from it. She'd look after the vicar.

'He likes my breakfasts. I give him loads of fried bread.'

'You can do omelette tomorrow, if there's fresh eggs. Or you could use the powdered stuff, disguise it with a little bit of egg shell and use the mushrooms and onions. There's plenty of onions. Fry some mashed spuds, if you're stuck. Sunday, he likes his sandwiches, 'cos he's in and out. There's plenty of tinned salmon and just the one tomato left. Unless he finds something else in his greenhouse.'

Emily told the vicar of her plans to camp out till Monday.

'If I was in the same position I'd be out camping, just like we did in the wilds of Canada. I need to be here for the dying and the poor wretches stuck in hospital, while the raids rage on.'

Before she left, Ada made sure that Percy had a three day supply of seed and water, before she placed him in the Morrison. When she was locking up she could hear him chirping inside, 'Jarmany calling. Jarmany calling.'

Ada spent the afternoon wandering with her huge load down to Litherland, and then along Gorsey Lane to Ford Cemetery and along the road to Sefton. The Cabbage Inn had hardly opened its doors when Emily arrived on the bus with the two babies.

'Just give us a minute,' said Ada, popping into the pub. She reappeared with four bottles of sweet stout. 'This'll help keep the cold at bay. Help us sleep,' she said.

They walked up Buckley Hill towards Sefton and knocked at the first farmhouse. An old man, who smelt of cows, answered the door. His towering wife stood guard, like a heavy-weight wrestler, in the background.

'Please could we pitch our tent and sleep in one of your fields, possibly till Monday morning? We've been bombed out in Bootle,' Ada felt the need to exaggerate. 'We need to get away for a few nights.'

'We understand completely,' the farmer said. 'Sleep as far away from the farm buildings as you can. We were hit by incendiaries last month, killed six of the cows and the grain silo burned for a week.'

His wife gave some practical advice.

'You can always use the old toilet at the back of the cowshed. There's a cold water tap there as well,' she said.

'Thanks,' said Ada.

They followed the advice and wandered down to the far end of the field and chose a flat piece of ground under the tallest bushes.

'Not that I think the bushes will keep out the bombs; but they'll be useful if a wind blows up,' said Ada. 'There's a nip in the air already.'

However, it was a beautiful evening and a clear night, to follow the sunny late-spring day.

'We'll need to pitch the tent before it's too dark for us to see.'

They had soon pitched the old army tent with the pram in position ready to be pushed into the entrance. The cardboard and newspaper were spread on top of the ground sheet and Ada soon had her faithful paraffin stove heating up some water.

'We'll see if we can get some milk at the farmhouse in the morning,' said Emily. 'I think I'll search out the old toilet.'

She walked around the back of the old cowshed and entered through a creaky old door, near what she supposed was the old tap.

Inside, the scene was one of rustic underused facilities, amazingly still clean with a current of water flowing through. Maybe they are over a stream, thought Emily. There were four seats in all. Suppose they use them all at harvest. Posh toilet paper lay lay at hand; a half-used Southport telephone directory.

Emily didn't tell Ada about the toilets, she thought it would be better to let her discover them for herself. Eventually, when she had returned, Emily just asked, 'Well? Did you find the tap then?'

They both had a good giggle.

'I wonder what they do if there is five of them?' asked Ada.

'Maybe they form a queue.'

'Must be very busy here at haytime.'

'Amazing that they have a stream running through.'

They enjoyed their salmon sandwiches and large pot of hot tea all the more. Then they opened a bottle of stout each and laughed even more. Life in the middle of a field escaping the bombing wasn't bad after all. They sat out looking at the stars, hearing the drones of the enemy bombers and seeing their silver fuselages shining over the river. The children were soon off to sleep, wrapped in the warm blankets.

'Some poor souls are getting it back down in town and here we are laughing at the old lavatory with a stream running through,' said Emily, feeling sad.

'It's one hell of a mess, but we'll come through.'

'You and Bessie are so sure about it, Mum. Who am I to doubt you both?' Emily found herself agreeing with Ada. 'Suppose we have to live through this lot, just to see Bessie slapping Hitler's face.'

'Is that what she's going to do?'

'Yes, she says she's going to batter him,' confirmed Emily.

The evening turned cold and the night was freezing, but the cardboard and newspapers helped the thick blankets keep them all as warm as toast. The kids were still piping hot in the centre of the tent in the morning.

'That's the last of the milk,' said Ada. 'I'll try later at the farmhouse.'

True to her promise, she walked across to the farmhouse at about ten o'clock.

'Nice quiet night, apart from the distant bombing,' said the farmer's wife when she answered the door.

'Have you any milk, please?' asked Ada.

'Certainly.' The farmer's wife took the jug away and returned with it full to the top with milk. 'The only other thing I can give you is carrots and onions. They're the only veg that's survived the winter; the cabbage has finished.'

Ada thanked them enthusiastically and returned overloaded with vegetables and milk. Fortunately, she had brought the makings of a scouse with her, but the new ingredients would freshen up the mix.

'We'll call this concoction "Carrot and Onion scouse",' she decided. 'What's more, it'll make some decent bubble and squeak for the breakfast in the morning.'

It was another sunny day and they sat out in the middle of the field munching away at their breakfast of jam and bread. The simple dish tasted delicious in the fresh-air surroundings of the large expanse of grass.

'Hunger's good sauce,' said Ada.

The little girls ran around the field all day long and they enjoyed looking at the cows and sheep in the next field.

'They'll be really tired out by tonight. All this fresh air and all the running about they're doing. It makes me tired just looking,' said Ada.

'I wish I was their age. They'll never fully remember these hard times, like we will,' said Emily. 'I felt safe last night for the first time in years. The bombing was so far away. It was as if it was in a different country.'

'I reckon it was the bottle of good Irish stout I bought you,' said Ada.

Back in town, Bessie was restricted to the cellars of the pub until first light Monday morning. She wandered back home, along the railway sidings. She turned the corner of the street and could see that the house had been hit again at the front. She ran around to the back and found that the back wall was completely missing. She peered over the rubble and could make out the remains of the kitchen. Some of the items were still intact. Geoffrey Spencer, in his job as warden, walked up and surveyed her with piercing eyes.

'The premises are too unsafe for anybody to venture inside. Could fall down any minute and we don't want looters in there,' he ordered.

'I'm hardly a looter, Geoffrey. You'll have seen me working up at the vicarage,' said Bessie, pleading her case.

'How come I never see you in church?' queried Geoffrey.

'That's hardly the point, Geoffrey, and you know it. It's my house. I'm hardly going to loot my own house, am I? When I was hit in March I moved out. When I moved back in, I carried all my worldly goods with me in two cases. I can see the cases under the window sill, or what's left of them. I never had a chance to unpack. Can I retrieve them? I can't see anything likely to fall.'

'Reclaim anything valuable, if you can see it, while you have the chance.'

Bessie reached in and lifted her two cases out of the rubble. She couldn't see anything else worth saving. She had replaced nothing in the shell of the house after the first raid in March.

'Take anything valuable in case there's looters,' advised Geoffrey.

Bessie looked around and thought that nobody would want any of the wrecked matchwood furniture with half the legs knocked off. Then she thought that she should maybe empty the gas meter, before anyone else had the chance.

It was under the stairs in the corner.

'Could I borrow your cutters?' she asked Geoffrey.

He went and fetched a huge pair of heavy-duty clippers. They were about four feet in length and very cumbersome.

'You couldn't get any bigger could you?' said Bessie, as she towed the clippers up the stack of bricks. She could make out the gas meter in the corner under the stairs. The huge clippers snipped the lock open with the first thrust.

'At least they did their job,' Bessie murmured and looked inside the meter cashbox.

She'd forgotten that the gasman had paid a visit as recently as the previous week. There was one shilling and tuppence and a selection of foreign coins in the box.

'I won't be dining out on that. Just my luck,' she said, as she returned the clippers to Geoffrey, who was busy working further down the street.

Bessie thought she would do her little bit for the war effort and carry on as usual. After all, Hitler was never going to win this war. She would do what she normally did at this time of the day and proceed to the vicarage to make the vicar's breakfast. She walked away from her home for the second time in as many months, carrying all her worldly belongings in two battered cases. There's nothing quite like being bombed out twice, she thought. I still wish it wasn't me.

The vicar was already up and about in his study. She put the kettle on and stored her cases in the pantry. Finally, she got around to taking him his first cup of tea into the study. Only then did she notice the father sitting in his favourite chair.

'Oh, right, I'll fetch another cup of tea,' she said. This she did. The vicar and the priest were in deep conversation. 'Will the father be wanting breakfast, too?'

'Bessie, if you wouldn't mind? We've both been down at the hospital all night with the casualties and their families. You wouldn't believe what we've seen.'

'Yes I would, Vicar,' said Bessie. 'I've just been bombed out again myself, only this time that horrible little man, Hitler, has made a perfect job of it.'

The vicar and the father were both shocked.

'Oh, Bessie,' said the Vicar. 'We didn't know. We're so terribly sorry. I feel so wretched being so unfeeling. Wouldn't you like to be off home and about your own business?' asked the vicar.

'Well, no, Vicar. You see the house was wrecked last time, so it's never been a real home for months. I'm better here, taking my mind off it, and looking out for some empty premises which I can rent. There's plenty of empty properties.'

'Yes, there is. What sort of house would you be looking for?' asked the father.

'Maybe, just another terraced house, as far away from the railway station and goods yards as possible.' She excused herself. 'I'll go and see if the hens have performed overnight, otherwise you'll both be making do with fried fortified loaf and bubble and squeak ... with more bubble than squeak, if you see what I mean.'

She went out into the hen-house and looked inside. The hens had had a busy night. There were three eggs, all decent sized. Probably the shock of the bombing, makes them lay like blazes. She smiled for the first time that day. She returned to the kitchen, pleased with herself, cleaned the eggs up and found the vicar.

'Vicar, there's three eggs this morning,' she announced. 'Is one of you going to have two or are the two of you having one and a half each?'

'Maybe you should have the third egg, Bessie,' the vicar said.

'Incidentally, Vicar, what have you named the latest hen in the shed?'

'I've named her Vera, after the singer,' said the vicar.

'You could have named her "Bessie", after me. I'm a singer, too,' she said.

However, the Vicar was already back in his study talking to the father. Bessie took the Vicar's advice and made herself some toast to go with her fresh egg, after she'd finished preparing breakfast for the two clerics. She was looking forward to Emily reappearing about the place in the afternoon.

At breakfast time in the country, Emily and Ada were just waking up to another sunny day and making plans for their long trudge home. They'd noticed the number 70 bus pass on the previous hour and Ada had noted the time on her ancient watch. So they packed up immediately, thanked the farmer and his wife, left the field behind and walked over to Sefton Church. True to form, the bus returned on the hour. They hoped to be able to ask the conductor if they could park the huge pram in the entrance, until the bus filled up. Their luck was in when they noticed the conductor was a 'clippy'.

'Sure,' she said. 'If you don't mind alighting at each stop to let the other passengers on.' They all agreed. 'Have you been sleeping out?'

'Yes,' they confirmed.

'Did you hear the huge bang on Sunday morning?'

'No.'

'Well, a ship full of ammunition blew up in the docks. There's hardly any of the city centre untouched. I'm one of the few still at home; because of my shifts.'

'So where do you live?' Emily asked the clippy.

'Fonthill Road.'

'So you're a real scouser then?'

The clippy just smiled in acknowledgement. They were lucky as the bus trundled all the way down through Ford before any other passengers appeared at the bus stop. For three or four stops, Ada would unload the huge, black pram on to the pavement, while the passengers alighted or boarded the bus. Eventually, they arrived at the Litherland lift bridge and the bus was filling up quickly.

'I'll walk home from here,' Ada told Emily and remained on the pavement with the pram. 'See you when I arrive home.'

It was late morning by the time they had all arrived back. The house was still standing. It had avoided the effects of the blasts and the white tape on the windows had done its job as they were still intact. There was heavy grey dust everywhere. The streets glistened, where the sun could get through, with the dusting of window glass and white plaster. Ada was overjoyed to see that Percy was still in one piece.

After a cup of tea, Emily went up to the vicarage to see how Bessie had got on at breakfast time. Bessie was relaxing in the kitchen, having found the comfiest chair.

'See you're run off your feet.'

'Emily, I've been bombed out.'

'What?' Emily found herself mouthing.

'This time that nasty little man, Hitler, has wrecked everything.'

'Where's your stuff?'

'In the pantry.'

Emily looked in the pantry.

'All your stuff in two cases?'

'Yes. I've perfected the art of moving lightly. I never really moved back properly last time. I've lived out of those cases. I've been here most days and the pub shelter at night. So, all in all, I've got what I'm dressed in and the contents of the two cases. Oh, there's my performing clothes at the pub.'

'Right, missus. You're moving in with me till you find a new address,' Emily insisted.

So Bessie moved in with Emily till she could find somewhere else. The truth of the matter was that Bessie was seldom at home. She spent her working days at the vicarage on Emily's days off and sang in the pub most evenings. She was great with the kids, so long as Emily kept a check on the words of her songs.

'So how did your trip into the country go?' she asked Emily.

'Great!' Emily said, and told her all about the farmhands' water closet, the four holes and the telephone directory for paper.

'So will you be heading out again on your day off?'

'Yes,' said Emily. 'The kids had some good sleep and it was a pleasant change. Not tonight, though. Maybe tomorrow night. By then we'll need to catch up on our sleep. We might go by train this time. Ada had to push the pram.'

'How far did she push it?'

'As far as the Cabbage Inn.'

'Christ, you're lucky. Just imagine all mother-in-laws being like that.'

'Yes. I'm very lucky.'

'How long did it take her?'

'She left at lunchtime.'

'Good heavens. Here's me finds it hard walking to the piano.'

Emily was fully occupied for the rest of the day at the vicarage, but Tuesday was her evening off. It was the vicar's quiet day. He liked to be left alone, to reflect, take stock and think about his sermon for Sunday.

So Tuesday saw Emily and Ada escaping again. Emily would have to be back on Wednesday because the Vicar had planned a hotpot supper for his friends and acquaintances, and people he was working with at the hospital and casualty centres.

'Doesn't it sound silly having a hotpot supper in the afternoon?' he said.

'Not at all, Vicar,' said Emily. 'It's the Germans who are silly.'

'Right, as always, Emily,' said the vicar. 'Enjoy your night out.'

The huge, heavy pram was the means by which they could convey the babies and the camping equipment out into the country. The main difficulty was pushing it there. It was too much to expect Ada to push it out to Sefton again. There just wasn't enough room on the buses, so this time they would try the train. If they couldn't board one of the newer electric carriages, then they could stow it in the luggage compartment at the rear. This time they thought that they'd venture out on the Ormskirk line as far as Maghull. They walked to Kirkdale station, past the still-smouldering Bedford Road School. At Kirkdale, they booked in and lowered the pram down the hundreds of stairs to the platform.

'How we'll haul the pram back up the stairs, God only knows,' mused Emily.

They didn't have long to wait for a train and, luckily, it was one of the newer types with wide double doors. The train was packed. Everybody was on the move.They managed to find two seats near the door, where they stationed the pram.

They were soon passing Aintree and alighting at Maghull, which had a friendly platform with just two steps to the road. Suddenly, they were in the middle of the countryside on a beautiful sunny day. The flelds were green, the hedgerows brimmed with life, and there was a radiance of flowers, flies and bees. The whole surroundings smelt all clean and drenched in the fresh scent of blossom time.

Emily sneezed. 'Just smell those flowers.'

'Is there a war on? Makes you wonder.'

They didn't have to wander far from the station before they found themselves on the edge of some deep thickets with the remains of an ancient spinney close by. There was a swath of meadow grass along the side of the road, presenting a wide area on which to pitch the tent. Ada entertained the kids, while Emily led the search for water. She wandered half a mile down the road before she found a public house. The publican willingly let Emily fill her bucket with water. She took the opportunity to enquire about the opening times.

'We open for just two hours in the evening,' he said.

Limited opening times were to be expected. Pubs were struggling to keep open in Liverpool. Many had been bombed, and others had been damaged or burnt out. Finding the staff to open up was a major problem as many had left town, been killed or called up. Supplies of drink for the premises were completely unreliable and one brewery had been bombed off the map.

'So is that seven till nine?' she asked.

'Yes, except Saturday, when we open all day. Sunday we are closed all day. Sometimes we open our doors if there are servicemen about, or when the Land Army girls are helping out with the local harvest. That's at the end of summer.'

Emily carried the water back and they enjoyed what was left of the sunshine. Ada brewed up and they fried up some hash on the primus stove.

'This stove of yours is a godsend,' Emily admitted.

'I knew you'd come around to it, after complaining about the fumes.'

'At seven, we'll take it in turns to visit the pub, buy two stouts each and pay a long visit to the toilets. Hope they have a wash basin in there,' Emily said.

Weatherwise, the fine week continued, enabling the two girls to play hide-and-seek amongst the trees and the long grasses. Most of the time they could be seen but as they had their own eyes covered, they believed nobody could see them. Later in the afternoon they wandered, as a group, down to the hamlet, which was just the pub, the church and the post office-cum-general store. They bought a loaf and some milk.

'There's even less food in that shop than the ones back home,' said Ada.

At seven o'clock they each visited the washing facilities at the pub and returned to pitch the tent under the trees. They each drank their milk stout and enjoyed an early night.

Next morning, Emily went along to the shop for some more milk and, on seeing the pub open, seized her opportunity and popped into the washroom. On her way out, she bumped into a disgruntled farmhand leaving the bar. Maybe, he's a gamekeeper or something like that, she thought, because he was carrying a bag.

'I don't know,' he gasped. 'I can't do right for doing wrong these days. That's what I get for being a faithful customer and servant all these years.' He was somewhat peeved.

'You're upset; but I'm sure they don't mean it,' said Emily.

'They do. They're miserable people. Tell me they'll buy anything if I fetch it. Now they are reneging on the deal,' the man growled.

'I'm sure they don't mean it,' consoled Emily.

'I've not been able to find any game birds, so I've fetched them two rabbits and they've turned up their noses.'

He opened his bag and showed Emily two fat rabbits.

'I'll buy them off you, if you want,' suggested Emily.

'You have a deal,' he said. 'Have you got half a dollar?'

'I haven't, but I've got two bob in change,' said Emily.

'That'll do, luv. You can keep the bag.'

He handed Emily the bag containing the two rabbits and surged off along the road, away from the hamlet. Meanwhile, the family were making their way to the station.

'What makes you think he was a poacher?' asked Ada.

'Nothing really. Could have been a spiv, if they have them in the countryside. It was just that he wanted to lose the bag as well as the rabbits.'

The train from Ormskirk pulled into the station. Emily thought that she saw somebody waving from one of the windows. She thought nothing more of it, as they succeeded in squeezing into another packed train. Passing through Walton and Kirkdale, they could see that there had been another heavy raid, leaving wide areas of destruction in its wake. They alighted at Kirkdale, wondering how they would manage to climb the hundreds of steps to the road. A fresh-faced young lad came beaming towards them. He looked vaguely familiar. It was young Colin Mack, Emily's next-door neighbour's lad. Colin had grown up and filled out since he was evacuated. He must be over eleven by now, thought Emily.

'Thought you had been evacuated to the country, Colin.' Emily said.

'Yes, Emily but I've come home now. I've run away. I've finished at junior school and I'd like to go to senior school in Liverpool.'

'Wasn't it nice and safe at night in Ormskirk?'

'It was, but I'm half starved, so I've come home,' announced Colin.

'You look fine on it, Colin, but it's not safe here with the bombs,' said Emily.

Colin provided two extra, willing hands to help them heave the huge pram up the mountain of steps and soon they had all reached the summit at Westminster Road. There was significantly more damage than there had been the day before. Colin walked back home with Emily and Ada, pushing the heavy pram enthusiastically. Emily looked at the lad, happy to be back home, and wondered how Freddie would cope with his lad just turning up on his doorstep like this. She wondered if Freddie had sufficient beds in the house.

Colin found his father outside The Blobber. Freddie was so pleased to see the only member of his close family still alive. He was filled with pride that Colin had been able to find his own way home and was longing to be back with him again. It had been a mixed week for Freddie. He'd managed to acquire a stack of beans, salvaged from a warehouse fire in Knowsley Road, but the beans didn't sell as fast as he'd hoped. He'd also taken a delivery of some cigarettes from the Brennan brothers. The cigarettes were called 'Passing Cloud', which he took to be of red-Indian origin and which

sold very well. Then, two nights before, fire bombs had rained down
and sent the cigarettes up in smoke.

'If ever cigarettes had been so appropriately named,' he'd cried,
as the lucrative batch had gone up in smoke.

It had indeed been a mixed week; but never mind, it was just
great to see Colin back home, looking fit and well.

'So what would you like for tea, Colin?' Freddie asked. 'Beans
on toast?'

Emily reported straight back to the vicarage to see how Bessie was
coping with the preparations for the afternoon's hotpot supper.

'So glad to see you, Em,' Bessie sighed. 'What a morning I've
had. I've been unable to find any meat of any description for the
hotpot. Even the hens are too tiny and full of bone yet,' Bessie
whined, 'I'm desperate.'

'It's okay, Bess,' reassured Emily. 'I need two shillings out of the
housekeeping.' She opened the bag containing the two rabbits. 'Get
them skinned.'

'Good heavens, Em. Have you been out hunting?'

'No; but the poacher who sold them to me had,' she whispered.

The ingredients of the vicar's stews and casseroles had always
been the high-quality fresh vegetables that he produced. Soon
Emily and Bessie had all the ingredients prepared and the thick
rabbit hotpot was baking in the oven.

'How many people are expected?'

'Most of the staff the vicar works with down at the hospital.'

'The feeding of the five thousand.'

'Somehow, rabbit doesn't have the same ring as loaves and
fishes.'

The vicar and Father Deegan had been down at the Bootle hospital
all night and were now in attendance at the temporary mortuary in
Marsh Lane Baths. One hundred and eighty bodies were laid out,

awaiting identification. It was a long, tedious job, because not everybody had relatives or neighbours still alive to perform the necessary process of identification. Sometimes, whole families had died in their houses, cuddled together in the Anderson shelter or under the table in a Morrison.

When they had ascertained the religion of a person, then the clerics spoke the appropriate words. They were assisted by the local doctor, Warren Golding, who signed all the legal papers after the formal identifications were completed.

'*Requiem aeternam donna eis. Domine et Lux perpetua luceat eis,*' recited the father.

'Heed my prayer, all mankind must come before the judgement seat,' the vicar continued along the line of bodies.

'We brought nothing into this world and it is certain we carry nothing out. The Lord gave and the Lord hath taken away. I am the resurrection and the life saith the Lord.'

Some time later, after Warren Golding had certified all the identifiable casualties, the vicar and the father decided to duplicate on the remaining bodies. It was a long and exacting task and took them into the afternoon. They had not expected so many. If there was a query, the vicar suggested the interdenominational form of words he'd used in the wilds of Canada, when there was no way of identifying a corpse. The father would then translate the words into Latin.

Just when they were ready for the off, they were confronted by a coffin with the remains of four different bodies, which would later be sent to the crematorium.

'It's a strong case for duplication,' suggested the vicar.

'Yes. Then Warren can complete the paperwork,' said the father.

'What a day,' sighed the vicar; but they were not finished yet. The agony was prolonged yet again by a further coffin, whose contents were so gruesome that the doctor suggested that they took his word for it and performed their task. They accepted his professional judgement and needed no further prompting. They decided on a form of words and spoke them over the coffin; English and Latin.

On the way out into the bright light of day, the vicar remembered that he had invited some of their co-workers in the hospital and the rescue services to come and join him for a hotpot supper at four-thirty. This way everybody got away before the bombing developed during the evening.

'Maybe we should invite Warren along for supper?'

'Maybe ... has he any special eating requirements?'

'We'll ask him.'

This they did, and were amazed when Warren said that he would come along. Most of the guests were sitting waiting in the lounge when the three men arrived late. They each entertained the guests in turn, while the other two disappeared for a quick wash and brush up and the vicar changed his clothes.

It was a specialist group of people that the vicar had invited. Most notable was the mayor, Alderman Kelly. There was a senior rank from the fire station, a ward sister from the hospital, a naval officer and the local ARP, including Geoffrey Spencer. It was an informal meal and all the guests related extremely well, having one topic everybody was deeply into – the Blitz. Warren Golding, the local doctor, knew most of the guests, and the two servers, Emily and Bessie, were his patients. Father Deegan performed wonders in finding some suitable wine in difficult circumstances.

Everybody loved the hotpot, particularly the browned roast potatoes which were tasty and in abundance.

'I make no apologies,' said the vicar. 'This may be called hotpot, but really, in my book at least, it's baked scouse. I'm a potato and veg man. I'm not sure about the meat. What is it, Emily?' he asked.

'Rabbit,' replied Emily. 'Gives it a pleasant flavour, don't you think, Vicar?'

'Yes, yes, delightful,' said the vicar. 'The wine is excellent, Brendan. What do you think of the meal, Warren? Are you glad you came along?'

'Certainly. It is wonderfully wholesome.'

'So you don't eat kosher then?'

'Yes, on special occasions and when I'm part of a large Jewish community. You'll know that we are rather few here in Bootle. We have to travel to Liverpool to be part of a larger group. I have to eat what is available. I would have starved in medical school if I'd only eaten kosher. I just had to eat what the rest of the students ate. In places like Leeds and Manchester, where there is a large community, it is possible to eat kosher. But this hotpot is delicious and, John, your spuds are amazing.'

'Thank you, Warren, growing vegetables is my hobby; but we must thank the cooks when they next come into the room.'

Eventually, Emily and Bessie carried in a huge dish of piping hot rice pudding, which was duly ladled out from the centre of the large dinner table by Bessie.

'We apologise if you have a sweet tooth,' said Emily. 'We've put the vicar's ration of sugar for the next week into it. So that's as sweet as we can make it.'

The vicar proposed a vote of thanks while Emily and Bessie were in the room. He then chatted with Geoffrey about the services coming up on Sunday.

'If we are all still here, Geoffrey,' said the vicar, 'we'll have a lot to thank God for.'

'I'm sure we'll still be here. I've been marvelling at the amazing construction of the railways to the docks recently. Tunnels and gorges cut through the very bedrock. Built to last for ever. Marvellous local history.'

'So have you started to keep a record of the bombing, Geoffrey; the history that is going on all around us this very week?' asked the vicar.

'Not really. I believe in building for the future, not destroying everything,' Geoffrey said emphatically. 'We'll probably just remember the bombers failed.'

The dinner party was a success and it prepared Emily for future dinners when the vicar invited a cross-section of the community. One thing was certain, the main dish would always be a variation on scouse, which was the vicar's speciality.

Most of the invited guests had duties to perform and had left before six. The nurses had returned to the hospital and the ARP had to ready themselves for another heavy night. Other guests had to decide where they were spending the night. Emily and Bessie made tracks home with the remains of the successful baked rabbit scouse.

Emily put the kids to bed already wrapped in a heavy blanket ready for the move down to the Anderson as soon as the sirens went.

Besides wrapping the kids up warm, Ada knew it was essential to have everything prepared before the blackout, when you couldn't see a thing. She always made sure that she had put tea in the pot; because she had once brewed what she thought was tea and poured out hot water. She always attempted to catch up on her sleep during the day, because she knew that she could be up and at it all night long. Some nights, of course, the outside was lit up with hundreds of fires and fire-watchers running around on adrenalin, trying to make the best of a bad job. Some of the fires burnt throughout the day. If the firemen knew there was nothing to be saved they would let the fire burn itself out and use the water for something they could save. Ada, for her part, concentrated on remembering to put the tea in the teapot and making sure she filled the kettle.

Thursday night, the 7th May, was the heaviest night of the Blitz in Bootle. So many local landmarks were to be bombed or burnt to the ground. Emily sheltered in the Anderson shelter with her two children and Ada. It was well into the raid when there was heavy rushing and running about outside along the pavements.

Eventually, Geoffrey, on fire watch, popped his head through the entrance to the shelter, and, after excusing himself, said, 'Emily, we need to evacuate you until we have extinguished the fires in the garage behind, just in case the petrol pumps are set alight. Wrap up warm, it's frosty out.'

At three o'clock in the morning, Emily and Ada, carrying a blanket-covered child each, left the shelter and walked down the road, looking for another safe place to lodge. They were going to return to Ada's house and sleep in the Morrison, when Geoffrey caught up with them and said, 'Its okay now. We've managed to extinguish all six of the incendiaries. Fortunately, most of them landed on the concrete forecourt and bounced; but we've extinguished them all.'

They returned to the Anderson, put the kids back in bed and put the kettle on for a cup of tea.

'Isn't it a bugger? When you need some light to brew a cup of tea, and there isn't any,' said Ada. She'd popped back to check on Percy. 'He's sleeping. Wish I could.'

'This proves the point that you should keep your day-clothes on in the shelter, in case you're called out. Big question is, whether to keep your shoes on,' said Emily.

'It's four o'clock after all that lot. The sun will be up in an hour.'

Bessie had had a busier night of it. She stayed in the pub cellars till three; after falling in and out of sleep, she found herself wide awake. It was time to wend her way back to Emily's. She wandered along Stanley Road, the main thoroughfare in Bootle. Suddenly, she became fully conscious, with the sound of activity and the noise of bombs exploding all around. At the bottom of Balliol Road she could see the boys' school alight, and further along the road, she could make out that the Metropole theatre, re-opened after damage, was now an uncontrollable furnace, with gigantic flames leaping into the night sky. She passed Ash Street, and was drawn into the chaos. People were being pulled out from somewhere.

She ran across the road and assisted the wardens pulling men and women casualties out from the rubble of, what she now figured, was a large community air-raid shelter. Wherever she looked there were people lying static on the red-sprayed pavement and roadway. Some sat on the kerb injured, covered in blood and in terrible desperation. She helped the ambulance men lift the living into two ambulances which had drawn up. She couldn't make out which people lying on the pavement were living or dying. She had no time to pause to sympathise with the injured and dying, there was too much to do in the whirl of frantic activity. In the madness of the situation there was no shortage of light from the nearby houses and the blazing theatre which illuminated the surroundings as if it were day. Bessie could see everything, the broken bodies, the dead, and people scarred for life in the bright, blazing light. The smell of roasting and burning flesh did not register. Bessie was too busy doing her utmost to help.

After an hour of helping as best she could, she realised that she was surplus to requirements, so she headed off homeward. Around the corner, the toffee works were ablaze. Everywhere was ablaze. Suddenly, what had happened to her registered and she started crying and just concentrated on returning to Emily's house.

Coming around the corner into the street she had the weird notion that maybe the kids might be up, so she had better stop crying. She dried her eyes and was met by Emily, who was sitting on the stack of coal outside the shelter. Now she was home, she started crying properly. Emily couldn't understand a word of what she uttered.

'Why, Bess? You look terrible.'

Bessie just cried hard and long.

'Emily, it was a nightmare. There were bodies strewn everywhere. Men, women and children. Some of the injuries were just terrible. There were fires all over the place. The Metropole has gone up again for good. It was lousy, Emily. Terrible.'

She cried her eyes out, like a big, spoilt child.

Ada joined them with two mugs of sweet tea. Bessie was back with her friends. Emily could see Bessie's tears falling into her cup.

'Wipe your eyes, Bessie.'

They sat outside till the sun shined brightly and Bessie regained her true self. Emily knew Bessie was on the mend when she constructed a sentence that only she could.

'I've lived a fortnight these last three nights and aged twenty years in all, less high days and holidays, that is. At least I can't be bombed out; I've no house,' she said.

The vicar and the father were together at the temporary hospital in Linacre Lane, comforting patients and supporting the staff. There was a huge bomb blast and all the lights went out. It was black because of the heavy blackout curtains on the windows. They managed to evacuate the patients outside, where it was considerably lighter as the raid progressed. They helped the staff load a double-decker bus with patients, who would have to be transferred to Walton Hospital. Later, a fleet of ambulances transported the less mobile patients to Fazakerley Hospital.

At first light they planned to make their daily visit to the temporary mortuary and were fortunate enough to be offered a lift down that way by the driver of an auxilary truck. The whole route was ablaze with fires, some small and some extensive, with the ARP, fully extended, running around all over the place. Everywhere was brightly lit up.

'Is this what you use to visit the mortuary?'

'Yes, I'm run off my feet tonight. I'm loading up all over.'

The vicar looked at the bins used to store the human remains that the auxillary driver collected during the raids and whispered a tiny prayer.

When the vehicle turned down Marsh Lane from Stanley Road, they could see that the old baths, the temporary mortuary, where they had said prayers only yesterday, were well alight. The truck pulled up and the two clerics alighted in the middle of the road. They looked up at the building engulfed in flames. Everybody was completely helpless to do anything about it. They said a quiet prayer before they were driven back by the immense heat of the flames.

'The whole place and all those poor souls still unidentified have been completely incinerated,' said the vicar, as they wondered what to do. 'The one hundred and eighty souls have left us for good, that's for sure.'

'We weren't to know, John,' said the father. 'Yesterday, we did the right thing and I think today we will do the right thing, if we concentrate on the living.'

'It's just that the living, the dying and the dead are all mixed up this week,' said the vicar, trying to come to terms with it all.

'Yes, John; but we'll be up to the test.'

'Yes, Brendan. I'm just worried about how tough the test will be.'

They wandered up the hill back to the vicarage, avoiding the huge rivers of water flowing from the damaged water mains and skirted the bombed buildings and fires burning themselves out.

'We will survive; but the Yanks have to come into the war now.'

'They'll come in late as usual. You'll see.'

They were both wondering where it was all leading. How much more of this could the people take? When would it all end? There certainly didn't seem to be any answers coming along.

Emily found the vicar slumped up over his breakfast, snoozing like a baby, tired and washed out. He awoke abruptly when Emily poured him another cup of tea.

'Where exactly do you think your husband, James, is?'

'Suppose he'll be out on the open Atlantic, between Scotland and America.'

'It can't be any worse than here.'

'Before the war total imports of food and raw materials, excluding oil, were close to 60 million tons. By the end of 1940 they had fallen to 45.4 million tons and the following year to just 30.5 million tons. McDougall remembers: "There was a risk that we would suffer such a dramatic fall in imports, we would have to cut our food consumption to impossibly low levels and morale would be very badly affected." Further reductions would also threaten the country's ability to prosecute the war. It was frightening all the time.'

Andrew Williams, *The Battle of the Atlantic.*

Chapter 6
Off the Hebrides

'It was not Death, for I stood up
And all the Dead, lie down.'

Emily Dickinson

58°30' North/6°10' West

Returning to the Clyde, Jimmy found the Swallow being made ready for another convoy across to the St. Lawrence and Halifax. Convoy duty occupied the group till mid-summer. In June, they were back on the Clyde re-grouping and he wondered how they would be deployed now that the boss was away on extended leave.

Number One took over the running of the ship and it was business as usual; particularly when the weather deteriorated and there was a batch of summer gales to be withstood. They were moored comfortably in the Clyde when they were ordered out into the gale to patrol the Outer Hebrides. U-boats were quite small craft and loved to sit it out somewhere safe, given the chance. The southern packs of U-boats could use the islands and lochs around 'neutral' Eire's shores, to hide away from the force of the gales, much to the disgust of the Royal Navy and the sea-going people of Liverpool. The northern groups of U-boats would use Iceland, while others risked the waters of the Minch, Hebrides and the north-west wilderness coast of Scotland. So these were the waters that the Swallow patrolled in the unseasonable and violent weather. They patrolled the leeward side of all the larger islands; particularly the 'bolt-holes' the U-boats were known to vanish into. The weather dictated how near the rugged coast they dared venture.

'In weather like this, you can't blame the Hun for seeking shelter,' said Jimmy.

'Yes, but not in my backyard, thank you very much. The thought of the bastards sheltering in Scottish waters,' said Calum.

Jimmy brought a modest cup of tea, to avoid spillage, to Calum in the radio-room, where he was entrenched. It was so rough Jimmy had forgotten there was a war on.

Enthusiastic flying-boat pilots, during lulls in the storm, came 'on the air' with reports of U-boats spotted ahead, astern or to the leeside of virtually every Hebridean island or sea loch. The Swallow would chase as hard as the weather permitted and then find a batch of discarded, black oil barrels, ancient wreckage or, in one case, a particularly vicious-looking skerry, which they needed to honour with a wide berth.

'Suppose those rocks look like a U-boat from up there,' said Jimmy.

'Probably wrecked as many ships as the U-boats,' wondered Calum.

'The idea is that this is a two-way process. If we see anything, we give them the position and they bomb it; but they'll never get into the air in this weather. If they think a skerry is a U-boat, what's to stop them bombing us?' asked Jimmy.

'Nothing,' confirmed Calum. 'Bloody amateurs up there, although I wouldn't like to be up there in this. Can you imagine having to come down in this?'

They found no U-boats hiding on their patch and saw little else out on the sea. They were the only silly so-and-sos out in the teeth of the storm. If there were U-boats 'holed-up' along the coast, then they were well drilled in the art of hiding. They knew the 'bolt-holes' in which to slide away from the prying eyes of flying boats and patrols.

'Miserable for the end of June, isn't it?'

'British summer is more like winter.'

At 8 a.m. the next morning, Calum was just about to take a shower, when the critical call came in. This gave definite co-ordinates, not the usual drivel that often cackled through. Besides, the asdic operator reported a definite submarine echo about 3,000 yards ahead. They increased speed to the limit in the winds. Alarm bells brought the crew to readiness and the depth charges were set to explode at 150 and 300 feet. Calum hobbled about in his bare feet, naked under his two navy towels, his huge legs protruding out. He was fortunate it was 'summer'.

The Swallow raced over the attacking position and ten depth charges exploded in a series of crashing roars. The U-boat plopped to the surface and amazingly dived straight back down. It was planning to make good its escape. The Swallow's guns opened up on the U-boat's conning tower before it disappeared from view.

'This must be the first time we've received the correct co-ordinates; they've sent us the position of Hampden Park and the Isle of Man before today,' said Calum.

The whaler was dispatched to collect wreckage and ample evidence was soon fished out of the water. Jimmy had once again been assigned duty in the whaler by the cox. Jimmy thought it was pathetic what he would do just to keep his place in the team. He detested the duty. There were locker doors marked in German, a burst tin of German coffee and various unmentionable parts of the body. Every time somebody said, 'Look at this.' Jimmy would look away, smiling as if he'd seen the monstrosity. He was glad he hadn't just eaten.

After two days of storm the weather abated and the Swallow was heading back to the Clyde, due west of Skye with the Isle of Canna to the east. Off Canna, the propeller shaft suddenly rumbled and clanged and then settled into performing at minimum efficiency. Number One figured they had picked up some fishermen's rubbish or war junk. He didn't want to limp back at this speed, they were barely making one and a half knots.

'It'll take till Christmas.'

The only thing to do is to heave to or anchor off Canna, he thought.

'The wind is in the right place, so we can anchor off Canna and send the divers down.'

It was a beautiful summer's day, the gales had receded and the wind was pleasantly light.

Off Canna 57°03' North/6°30' West

Canna has a small harbour between itself and the neighbouring smaller isle of Sanday but many rocks guard the entrance, so the Swallow anchored off, well-sheltered from the slight wind.

'Right, Cox, we'll make doubly sure and run a mooring wire out to the rock. It's called Sgeir Phuirt on the chart. Give you something to do in the whaler.'

Jimmy found himself back in the whaler as they carried the mooring wire out to the nearby large rock. They fastened a heavy warp around the rock, then, after the ship had taken up the slack, they tethered the whaler to the rock. They sat out in the sunshine. The world was peaceful and quiet, even though the war was being fought out on the ocean behind them; only the day before they had sent a U-boat to the bottom. It took the divers three hours to release the Swallow from the obstruction, which according to the chief engineer was 'nowt but ten tons of fishing tackle and, from the looks of it, a fishing boat attached.'

'The old chief is exaggerating again. Suppose Number One didn't want to take the problem back into port and let all and sundry gloat over it.'

The line was released, the warp retrieved and the whaler headed back to the mother ship, Swallow.

'Why do you always volunteer me for these trips?' Jimmy asked the cox.

'What? I thought you loved our trips out.'

'Well, I do, but preferably on dry land.'

By the end of the day the Swallow was back on the Clyde, awaiting the return of the boss, who had been on leave; but some said that he had been down to Liverpool, taking an extensive look around.

'Do you think they may be transferring him to Liverpool?'

'Well, I suppose we all have to go where we are posted in this bloody war.'

'Yes, I could think of worse places, like the desert.'

'Or the jungle, now the Japs are becoming a handful.'

'At least at sea, if you are killed, it's a clean death, if you avoid the oil.'

'Can you imagine the heat in the desert or the sweat in the jungle?'

'I'm not sure. The Atlantic is a cold hole. It's warmer in the desert.'

Once back on the Clyde the propeller was checked over again. The damage was only superficial, where the heavy jetsam had been clinging to the shaft. The Swallow returned to dry dock for another two days. The boss wasn't best pleased. He hadn't long returned from his leave and was eager to sail out to sea and see some action.

Contrary to this, Jimmy was hoping to play some football while the ship was out of commission. He thought that he'd better square it with the boss before he arranged any matches. The boss was back aboard, breezing about, yearning for some action against the enemy.

'Yes; but as soon as we are placed on standby, I'll expect you to cancel any unplayed games, so that we can sail at a moment's notice. Otherwise go ahead; as so long as the ship is out of the water, the crew are better off kicking a ball about than going into town, getting boozed and silly and creating all sorts of trouble.'

Jimmy's only problem was finding a pitch; the local field near the dock had been heavily bombed. It was impossible to play with the huge crater in the goalmouth.

'Makes you wonder what Adolf has against Scottish football.'

'Maybe the Jerries are just bad at aiming bombs.'

'Why? Were they aiming for the centre-circle?'

Eventually, Jimmy heard of a pitch that had no goalposts. He travelled out along the Clyde with Calum, wondering what to expect. There were plenty of playing fields covered in barrage balloons before they spotted the old football pitch. The grass wasn't too long and it wasn't too muddy in the penalty areas. There was an old pavilion and behind the pavilion there was a selection of discarded goalposts. Who was it best to ask? There was an old man walking his dog.

'Who should we ask about the football pitch?'

'It belonged to the old bakery; but it was bombed out. They've moved out of town to Larkfield, to avoid the bombing; but it's not safe anywhere just now.'

'Is there anybody we can ask locally?'

'There's the Presbyterian minister. He holds the kiddies' sports day on it.'

Fortunately, the church was close by and the minister was forthcoming.

'Certainly you can use the old pitch,' the minister said. 'You'll have to fish out a decent set of goalposts. Please will you return the goalposts behind the pavilion when you've finished? You'll need some white paint because they're past their best.'

'We'll just play two games before we are back at sea.'

'Are you boys on convoy duty?'

'We're not to say; but we are in the navy.'

It took Jimmy and a handful of lads the best part of a morning to sort out a decent pair of goalposts. There were some sturdy goal posts from years gone by, but never two exactly the same. In the end, they chose the two most complete goals they could find in the stack. One set was probably the last to be used before the war, whereas, the other set was clearly ancient, even to the least knowledgeable eyes.

'Suppose we explain the difference in the goals to the opponents and so long as both teams play exactly forty-five minutes each way, there will be no advantage.'

'I just hope the whitewash dries before the kick-off or we'll be covered in it.'

'I just hope they'll remain standing for the full ninety minutes. Suppose it beats playing in and out of a crater.'

After the extensive preparations they were rewarded with a decent competitive game against a team from a trooper heading out to North Africa. It was the best game the cox played on the left wing. Why did he need to keep in Jimmy's good books when he could turn in a performance like this? They won 3–1 and Calum scored all the goals. His own-goal proved unstoppable for the goalie, who only took off into flight when the ball was well into the goal. Jimmy discovered that he had been secretly drinking when the ball was at the other end of the park. So much for the boss's plans to reduce the amount of boozing taking place. The second game was at Dunoon and as it was the last day the Swallow was out of the water, almost all the ship's crew turned up for the drinking after the match. Jimmy put out his strongest eleven against a local side. Again, the cox and Calum were the stars, with Jimmy organising the middle of the field.

'I think they are playing some ringers,' one of the crowd shouted, when it became obvious how good Calum was in both penalty areas.

'That's right, mate. Queen's Park Rangers before the war and an officer in the King's Navy now.'

Calum stood out in size and ability.

This time they had to be content with a 2–0 win and headed into Dunoon for the evening's celebrations. It was a long night and, although most of the crew were back on board on time, the boss wasn't happy next morning.

'How are we expected to manoeuvre the ship out of the Clyde with all the crew drunk? Just let me put it this way: when we are called into action we better all be mustard and up to our jobs 200 per cent or I'll want to know why not.'

The Swallow was placed on standby in the Clyde, awaiting the expected call. None came. It's a good job; most of the men think they are still on leave, thought the boss.

We could have played a few more games, thought Jimmy.

'Much as I like football, Jim,' said Calum 'we're a ship not a bloody football team.'

They moored in the Clyde for another two days before they were given a menial task which the boss thought was beneath them and could have been carried out by any ship less equipped.

'A job they should give the Rothesay ferry.'

There had been a substantial build-up of flotsam in the Clyde after the heavy bombing, severe gales and the seasonal high tides. Much of the garbage was storm damage or the residue from bombed shipping or wrecked port installations. There was a wide area of flotsam floating into the Clyde, just west of Ailsa Craig. The cox's instructions were to go out to the mass of garbage and take a long look, study its course, ascertain how dangerous it was and report back. The port authorities would then decide what course of action needed to be undertaken.

The cox was pleased about his performance on the soccer field, how the spectators at Dunoon had thought he was professional before the war, so he immediately thought he would repay Jimmy by volunteering him for another duty in the whaler. They headed out into the Clyde, approaching Ailsa Craig from the east, round the stunningly beautiful rock and heading west towards the floating mass of rubbish. They didn't speak much on the trip, everybody was quietly thinking how pleasant it was in home waters; far better than the raging Atlantic. Jimmy was standing in the bows of the vessel.

'Keep an eagle eye out, Sub,' shouted the cox. 'Tell me immediately we near anything in the water.'

They sped towards the mass of flotsam. Jimmy looked out.

Within the next second there was a horrendous blast, accompanied by a mountain of water, and the whaler took off. The bow flew straight up into the air. The whaler bounced back on to the sea, still managing to remain upright as it bounced back on to the water. Most of the crew, apart from Jimmy, finished in the stem on top of the cox; others clung to the side.

The cox was amazed that the boat was still afloat and the crew, apart from a few cuts and bruises, were still intact.

'How are you up there, Jimmy?' the cox shouted.

Jimmy remained motionless, standing upright, clinging to the bow. There was no reply from Jimmy. The nearest crew member took a look.

'I think he is dead, Cox,' he shouted back to the cox, who didn't believe what he was hearing.

'Surely, he is just knocked out cold.'

On examination, they could all see that he was stone dead. There wasn't a mark on him. He had taken the full force of the massive blast and been killed where he stood in the bows, yet the whaler had survived in one piece. The boss was furious, particularly as reputations are made or lost over such small incidents. From the deck of the Swallow they were certain that it was a distant enemy mine, one of hundreds dropped on the Clyde. This particular one had nestled in the flotsam floating around the Clyde, after a busy period of aerial bombardment. Jimmy had stood open to the power of the blast at the optimum distance that would kill a man outright, while the rest of the crew and the whaler were protected by the mountain of water that went surging past. Months later, the cox would complain that the keel of the whaler had been warped when it shot up into the air and it no longer held a true course. The crew put it down to poor helmsmanship.

There was to be an inquiry, which meant that the whole affair was a complete secret. Jimmy's unscathed body was kept in the mortuary for a full fortnight, while the navy proceeded with the inquiry. Fortunately for the officers and crew of the Swallow, they escaped back out into the ocean. After a month, Jimmy's body was buried in a small cemetery near Gourock.

Even after the inquiry had reached a satisfactory conclusion, the details still remained wrapped in secrecy. The wheels of state moved slowly if there was the chance that details of an incident might upset the populace, when most of the time it was just rank inefficiency and red tape. Emily wasn't told of Jimmy's death till six weeks after the incident. To be fair, Jimmy could have been out in the Atlantic during this period; the Swallow did go straight back out to sea, so she wouldn't have been any the wiser. It was wartime and communications were difficult, mail went missing and never materialised. Often it turned up months later, after a home leave. The dates on letters made no sense, particularly as all the clues were censored out.

Emily wondered about Jimmy. She hadn't heard from him since before the Blitz, but that was quite normal.

> 'It sometimes seemed that the labour and the wounds were going to be in vain, as the old hymn cautioned us; that we had started a job which we could not finish, and the price of trying would bankrupt us, in blood and treasure, long before any westward sky brightened into daylight.'
>
> Nicholas Monsarrat

Chapter 7

The End of the World

'One can't live on love alone; and I am so stupid
that I can do nothing; but think of him.'

Sophie Tolstoy

It was the quintessential lovely summer's morning in August, just
like British summer days should be. Bessie was finally up out of
bed, just after Emily had returned from the vicarage. Bessie was
deep into relating the tales about the night before in the pub.
Who did what; who said what; who was miserable. The telegram
boy arrived. Emily signed for it and tore it open, half listening to
Bessie, who was working up to the punchline of her story. Emily
read no further than 'to notify the death of James Jones'. Emily
passed out on the floor. Bessie foolishly thought it was down to the
tale she was relating. She rushed over to Emily and lifted her on to
the sofa, before reading the telegram in her hand. Bessie had a
weep before Emily came around. She knew that she now had to be
the strong one.

'I'm so, so very sorry, Emily, love, so sorry, so hopelessly sorry.'

Emily cried uncontrollably like a baby. Bessie made a cup of tea,
deciding not to say anything else. The pub story she was telling was
a good one; but heck! Bessie put the tea on the table and tried to
think how she would tell Jimmy's mother, Ada, who was up at her
own house with the kids. She looked at Emily's face, awash with
tears; but Emily solved the problem for her.

'I'll go and have a lie down, Bess,' said Emily, bravely. 'When I
come down I'll try to keep it under control. I'll try my best.'

Emily went upstairs and Bessie could hear a loud wail followed by a long whimper, as she went out to see Ada, who was in her backyard playing with the two children in the warm sunshine. She figured it was best to tell her straight away, rather than attempt to choose an appropriate moment, when there wasn't one.

She told her straight out as the two of them watched the kids from the kitchen. Ada didn't cry at all. She went through all the symptoms of the physical shock. She sat down to relieve her legs, breathed in and out deeply, closed her eyes briefly, but did not make a sound. Her generation had come through the Great War; they were made of sterner stuff. She just said, 'I knew that bastard, Hitler, would get one of us eventually.' Tears appeared in her eyes. Then she added, 'It just makes me more determined to see the bugger hang.'

'Look, Ada, I'll look after the kids, you go down and see Emily. She's upstairs lying on the bed,' said Bessie.

'No, I'll stay here with the kids. Emily needs to weep it out of her system. She's got a harder battle ahead of her now. Just like I had when my husband died.'

Percy, of course, knew nothing of the grief as he chirped 'Jarmany calling, Jarmany calling', as Bessie walked back down to Emily's. She was amazed at Ada's fortitide. She wondered what she would be like in a similar situation, like Emily, crying out loudly, or whether she was made of sturdier stuff, like Ada. Bessie knew that she herself just had to soldier on, help out with the children and take on more responsibility at the vicarage. Emily needed some time to herself to aid her recovery.

Emily's mind was elsewhere for the rest of the summer. She thought of Jimmy constantly, just like she had when they had started courting. Ada and Bessie covered for her when she took to her bed to sleep whenever things got too much. The vicar came around especially to see her and prayed with her in her own kitchen, amongst the pots, pans and backlog of dirty nappies. It was the first time that Bessie had ever been impressed by religion. The picture of two grown people praying between the sink and the cooker in the kitchen, totally serious, acutely intense and yet feeling so honest and true about it. Bessie closed her eyes, clasped her hands and found that she didn't feel in the least embarrassed as uncontrollable tears rolled down her cheeks.

A week later, Emily received the official notification of Jimmy's death. She went down to the navy offices in Liverpool to find out the full details. They knew of the case but all the details were still secret. All that Emily knew was that she was now entitled to a widow's pension and no longer in receipt of Jimmy's service pay. 'It's a good job I have a decent wage coming in from my own employment.'

She couldn't understand why Jimmy's death was so secret? Why was it different? She asked the vicar all about it the next day. Father Deegan sat quietly listening to the conversation.

'So, Vicar, they say that they can't divulge the details, because there is still a Royal Navy investigation being conducted. Why does it take so long?'

'Red tape? Was he killed at sea?' the vicar asked.

'I don't know and they won't say,' Emily explained.

The father was most concerned and tried to explain from his experience as a serving officer.

'Official investigations do take a long time, because all the procedures have to be gone through rigidly and nobody wants to be left carrying the can. Maybe, your husband, James, died in unusual circumstances. Maybe, they think that there is reason to suspect foul play, wrong-doing of some kind, and need to point the finger at somebody or some authority. Possibly there were unusual circumstances, which they are at pains not to repeat in future, or at least want to make sure they can avoid a similar incident.'

None of this helped Emily.

'That's all well and good, but why does it have to be secret?' Emily asked.

When she returned with the breakfasts for the two clerics, the father smiled to reassure her and set her mind at ease.

'Emily, it must be wretched for you. I know how you feel. I lost my most dear friends and family members in the last war. I found that I got through it all by remembering that they would always be with me, for the remainder of my life. Their times with me would always be as clear as crystal. They will always be here, like they are now and I have the privilege of remembering them at their best and most brilliant. They are indeed, part of me just like your husband, James, will always be part of you and your lovely children.'

Emily took the two little girls into the park later and looked at them and could see Jimmy beaming back at her. It was another lovely day; a beautiful summer's afternoon. She watched the girls play on the grass, sometimes looking intensely serious, like Jimmy could be at times. She made up her mind that she was going to be strong for them. It was crystal clear, like the father said, that Jimmy was always going to be there with them in the future, whatever happened. Away from her little family it was difficult to accept that her husband's death warranted a secret inquiry, no detail of which could be revealed. Surely, one man working away quietly on one ship, could not be deemed a risk to national security?

She gradually fell into a routine of travelling through to Liverpool once a month to the navy offices and asking if there was any further news of her husband. Each time she received the same confused look from the clerk and the same empty answer. 'Secret information.'

Once she asked, 'Is that secret information on the file?'

'Secret information,' came the reply.

'Oh good,' she said. 'It must be secret then,' Emily beamed back.

The clerk looked as if he'd missed the joke. Emily wasn't going to explain it. The humour was in the total lack of any explanation at all. She started to wonder what ridiculous merry japes Jimmy might have been up to in Scotland or wherever. Could he, indeed, be a spy or a fifth columnist? She smiled at the thought. Certainly not. He only ever wrote to her about the places that he had been, which were often censored out. He wrote a lot about football matches and his friend, Calum. She often thought that, if the war had been a football match, Jimmy would have won it for us. But, it wasn't.

'Situations like this play silly-buggers with your mind,' she smiled. Each time she visited the navy offices she drew a blank. She knew it was her duty to keep trying. Her mind was alive with vivid memories of their years together, so she started to write them down in her diary, which was full to overflowing with stories that made less and less sense. The stories became part of a complicated mix of recipes, old wives' solutions to problems and the vicar's whereabouts, which became briefer and briefer as he settled into a routine that she knew by heart.

Towards autumn the air-raids were not as harsh as the first week in May. People were less inclined to sleep out as the weather grew colder and the nights drew in. There were fewer and fewer raids materialising and people remained in bed and were slower to seek shelter than had been the case in May. There was a heavy raid in mid-October that caught everybody napping. Landmines fell on the streets in the locality and there were one hundred and nine deaths in Surrey Street alone. Most of the casualties had not rushed to the shelters, having been lulled into a false sense of security by there being a string of occasions when raids hadn't materialised. Whole families were found lying in their beds or cuddled together in the Anderson shelter, without a mark on their bodies, just killed by the horrendous blast. Emily found herself crying more openly, when faced with other people's misfortunes. However, she was becoming more and more capable of putting Jimmy's death to the back of her mind and concentrating more on her two girls.

Despite the Blitz, life in the street carried on regardless. Never more so than when a neighbour, Milly, gave birth and, to a small extent, renewed Emily's confidence in the future. She thought of how the prospect of this 'new life' brought freshness into their gloomy world and pointed the way out, unlike death that offered nothing but endless unhappiness and desperation.

Colin Mack came running around to Emily's house.

'Emily, can you come? It's Milly.'

'Early is she? I'll get the stuff.'

Emily hunted about the house, collecting her specialist kit, and loaded it all into her white enamel bucket.

'Colin, get on that bike of yours and fetch Doctor Golding. Tell Bessie if you see her. Knock at number 7 Garden Lane and fetch the midwife. She's been expecting a call.'

Emily marched around the block as the huge form of Bessie appeared running up the street, hopelessly out of breath.

'How many is it this time?'

'Seven.'

'She'll soon have a full set of eight. Poor girl. Wear herself out.' Inside the house, the prospective mother held court. She was the most cool, calm and collected of the gathering; she'd been through it more times than anybody. Emily and Bessie fussed about performing the menial tasks for the medics.

'How did Eric manage this? I thought he was in a prisoner of war camp.' asked Bessie, subtracting nine months and trying to recall when Eric was last home.

'He is. He wrote to me last week.'

'Sex by post then.'

Lots of hot and cold water were made available before Doctor Golding, aided by the midwife, ensured that the birth went according to plan with as few hitches as possible. Emily soon had the baby in her arms.

'Gives the whole world a fresh sparkle,' she said, while Bessie sulked.

'You'll do anything to get first hold,' she said.

'Here, you have a hold, Bessie. Maybe you should marry and have some of your own.' Emily suggested.

'Not on your Nellie!'

Emily enjoyed nursing the 'newborn' baby in her arms and appreciating the fresh beginning and the simple happiness it fostered. Indeed, it put a skip into Emily's step as she walked back home.

The best means of escape from her cancelled future life with Jimmy was to bury herself in work. Now that she had less money coming in, she needed to make the most of every penny she had.

For his part, the vicar felt obliged to speak more openly to Emily and so did the father on his weekly visits. The two men discussed the war in her presence and welcomed her input into conversations. They even suggested there was the possibility that Hitler might starve the country out. From the information they had from a friend 'in the know', imports had plummeted and were about half the level before the war. Britain was heading for catastrophe. One morning, when she took two cups of tea into the study, the two men were holding a heated debate.

'Well, the USA just has to come into the war or we'll starve,' said the vicar.

'And I say, God help us then,' said the father. 'In the last war you always had to watch your backs when the Yanks were behind you. We always let them move out ahead of us. They fire at every moving object and ask questions afterwards.'

'If they don't come in before the year is out the U-boats will starve us out.'

'Jimmy used to chase the U-boats,' said Emily, and the study went quiet.

'Sorry, Emily,' said the vicar. 'I didn't mean to mention James.'

Before he could change the subject, Emily had already moved the conversation on.

'I've found an old book in the bookcase,' she said. 'It's called *Enquire Within*. It's dated 1863 and it is full of old fashioned hints for home comforts. Can I borrow it?'

'Certainly, Emily,' said the Vicar 'could do with some old fashioned comforts to take our minds off this blasted war.' Then he corrected himself, 'Blasted in the sense of bombs.'

'It only means "blighted" or "withered", John,' injected the father. 'It's okay.'

'There he goes again,' said the vicar. 'When it comes to words, Father Brendan remembers them all. He's a real academic; puts me to shame.'

Emily loved reading through her newfound book and tried to pick out items that might appeal to the two clerics. They met each

Monday in the study to co-ordinate the civic duties they jointly officiated at. They kept their friendship simmering with two or three glasses of claret and a humorous moment or two.

One week, she told them about a section on wine-making and ways to ferment rhubarb and gooseberry wine, both of which the vicar grew in the garden.

'I think we can discount those. We'd need tons of sugar, which is scarce, and our gooseberries are rather too tart.'

'I've a cure for corns. You boil some potatoes and then wrap the skins around the corn. Supposed to do them the world of good.'

'If you don't scald yourself in the process. Surely you have found something more interesting in this new tome of yours,' enquired the vicar.

'Well there's "Anagrams". Like Revolution. Anagram is "I love ruin".' The two men liked Emily's choice and chuckled away.

'Then there's "Parishioners".' They waited in anticipation. '"I hire parsons".'

'Well, they should pay us more,' the vicar howled.

'Next one is "Presbyterian". That makes "Best at Prayer".'

'Surely that should be "Last to buy the drinks"?'

'They're tee-total. Maybe it should be "Never buy a drink"?' The two clerics chuckled away and the Vicar replenished their glasses with more claret.

'Keep reading your book, Emily. Such a wonderful book,' chuckled the vicar.

The two men were constantly talking about the war these days, endeavouring not to mention U-boats, it being a sensitive issue. It became more and more difficult because more and more naval personnel appeared at the vicar's afternoon hotpot suppers. There was a build-up of Royal Navy servicemen and women in the city towards the end of the year. Naval activities were now increasingly taking place in the West to avoid the limitations of the Channel, caused by the mounting threat of the enemy off the French coast. The headquarters for Western Approaches had moved to Liverpool. It was rumoured that it was somewhere in town, by the Pier Head.

The hotpot suppers became lively affairs, with the locals enjoying the sailors' yarns, stories, jokes and, of course, love of rum. Far more spirits were consumed especially as the guests often brought a bottle as their contribution to the meal.

The mayor came along to the suppers occasionally, bringing with him the town clerk. It was through this connection that Bessie was offered another cleaning job, at the town hall, on a part-time basis. Staff were coming and going depending on circumstances, often relating to deaths in the family, being called up or being bombed out. Bessie was asked to cover when they found themselves short.

'Another nice job,' she said. 'I've three jobs that all sound grand, but don't pay well. The pub, the vicarage and the town hall. They still don't add up to one decent job between them, which is what I really need.'

The last hotpot supper before Christmas was on 10 December 1941 and it was a merry occasion. It was the day after the Japanese had attacked Pearl Harbor. Everybody was so happy at the prospect of the USA coming into the war.

'Thank God for that,' said the vicar, and they drank a toast to Uncle Sam.

'Churchill says, "Look to the West the sky is clearing," ' said the vicar.

Bessie couldn't hold herself back, ''Bout time, Vicar, the weather has been abysmal all week.'

Everybody laughed because the news was so welcome.

'I have to say, Brendan, that I told you so,' said the vicar.

'You did. You did. Albeit they're late again,' added the father.

Emily couldn't wait to see the old year out on New Year's Eve and welcome in the new year of 1942. She didn't want another year like the last one. She still had a home, a job and the remnants of a family. Life would never be the same. Maybe the Yanks coming into the war would change things for good. She didn't deserve Adolf Hitler and all his bombing and killing. He'd turned her life upside down and taken Jimmy, her one true love, away from her. Besides, Liverpool didn't deserve the battering that it had had to endure. She shed a tear for the old year and all the memories.

'Roll on 1942. Things can only get better,' she hoped and prayed.

Great expectations greeted the New Year but it was the same old story. The war continued in its downward spiral, even after the Yanks had belatedly entered the struggle and Roosevelt had started sending troops, ships and aeroplanes to Britain.

The first major catastrophe in 1942 was the fall of Singapore on 14 February. What would happen next? Only survivors would know.

Chapter 8
Andy Ritchie

In January 1942, Andy Ritchie found himself with another fresh start. It was something that he was well used to because his family had itchy feet. Since they first appeared in Liverpool at the turn of the century, his family had epitomised the unsettled, dissatisfied and restless Liverpudlians that gave the city a bad reputation. This, of course, was partly due to the thousands of people from the impoverished rural regions who sought refuge on Merseyside in the nineteenth century. They came to the port with itchy feet and still had them. No man can completely change his disposition and his personality overnight, let alone organise a pair of happy, dancing feet. So many of these incomers emigrated straight out to the colonies in the 1920s and 1930s. The Ritchies were never happy with Liverpool. Nothing was ever right.

The first attempt to change things was made in the 1920s, when the family moved from Vauxhall Road to Chester. Soon, the itchy feet reappeared and they planned their big move at the beginning of the 1930s. They emigrated to Australia, where, being such an easily dissatisfied family, they found it impossible to settle down. Andy's parents and brother settled in Brisbane, which was too hot for his sister who set up home in Melbourne. They were still disgruntled but well spread out.

Andy was still at school so he elected to live with his Aunt Elsie off Hoole Lane, Chester, while he completed his final year of study at King's School. He then won a place at Liverpool University, gained a degree in mathematics and completed a one year post-graduate course to qualify as a teacher of mathematics.

He was called up before he could start teaching and he finished his officer training at Plymouth in 1939. He was then posted to a supply unit on the Clyde, which organised the building and repairing of ships. He wasn't happy; he wanted to see the sea. He had to suffer the best part of two years as a general administrator before he was granted his wish of being posted to a ship. He was transferred to Liverpool, where he was due to arrive in October 1941; but official lines became crossed and he remained stuck in Glasgow feeling unsettled and generally 'pissed off'.

At the beginning of 1942 Andy began to grow a beard to hide behind. Maybe it would make him look less miserable, he thought. He kept it regulation trim but found it harder to smile, even after a pint or two. This wasn't helped by his naturally doleful disposition. The girls were attracted by his posh uniform but put off on closer inspection. So, despite the beard keeping cold Glasgow mornings at bay, he never felt completely awake much before lunch time. Shaving seemed to solve the problem; it woke him up much earlier in the day and put something of a smile on his face. His first shave had revealed a sad, hang-dog face. He nearly grew the beard back but vowed, instead, to practise smiling more. He put up with the 'Cheshire cat' comments and rationed himself. If people only knew his family background of grim, miserable, disgruntled existence they'd have appreciated his efforts to look less sullen and smile occasionally. Was it really too much to ask? He decided it was best to ration his impromptu smiles; folk didn't seem to understand. One night, he was enjoying a pint in the mess, feeling happy at the thought of moving to Liverpool behind a serious face.

'Why are you looking bloody miserable, Andy? It may never happen,' insisted one of his colleagues, with enjoyment beaming from his face.

'I'm feeling really good. I'm happy inside,' said Andy. 'Why must I gloat?'

Meanwhile, back in Bootle, Emily was still visiting the navy offices once a month, but in February they issued her with an appointment to see the commanding officer at the end of the week.

'Basically, nothing has changed, Mrs Jones. The inquiry still rumbles on; they are still investigating the details and hope to reach a conclusion by June.'

'That will be a full year,' said a stunned Emily.

'Yes; but the news is that you are free to visit your husband's grave.'

'Well, that's handy. I don't even know where it is,' Emily said.

'His grave is in Scotland. We can make arrangements for you to pay a visit. You'll have to stay overnight in an approved hotel in Glasgow, but you will be escorted to and from the naval establishments by our personnel.'

Emily was shocked; she didn't know what to say. She was bereft of thought.

'We'll send you details in the post and then our personnel in Glasgow will meet up with you when you arrive.'

'So Jimmy is buried up there in Glasgow?' Emily collected herself to ask.

'Actually, on the coast, near Gourock. You will be free to ask the officers in Glasgow questions about the incident, so long as it is not secret information.'

'That's good of you. When will I be able to go?' she asked.

'Probably the first week in April.'

After Emily had received confirmation of the trip, at the beginning of March, time flew by and it was soon April. She received a large brown envelope containing two train tickets, one Liverpool–Glasgow return and the other, Glasgow–Gourock return. There were also details of the hotel in Glasgow where she was to stay for two nights. These nights were 5th and 6th of April. She was booked in for full-board: dinner, bed and breakfast, luncheon or packed lunch, if requested. There were two meal vouchers, usable at a verified restaurant or hotel. There were also two travel vouchers for five shillings and a postal order for ten shillings to cover other expenses.

Ada helped Emily sort out her clothes for the trip, all black as far as possible, with three complete changes of clothes, just in case, besides the clothes she intended wearing on the train. Ada lent Emily her new utility black raincoat. 'It's always raining in Scotland and often very windy,' said Ada.

'That's what Jimmy used to say,' agreed Emily.

The vicar thanked God when he heard of Emily's trip to Scotland.

'When you visit the grave, tell him how well you and the girls are keeping. Tell him that you are progressing so well in your work and putting your own stamp on the job. You must tell him how wonderful the two little girls are now.'

Just as she was departing the father popped into the study and whispered a little prayer, before he spoke a little advice.

'Don't clutter the grave with too many flowers. Keep it simple and tidy. Maybe just a flower from each of you. Make sure he knows you still love him and he'll always be with you. God bless.'

Emily sensed that all her friends were taking part in her mission. She was representing the people of Liverpool and their sons on the ocean. She knew that everybody would be with her and Jimmy up there on the Clyde.

She set out from Lime Street Station on the 5th of April. It was a Sunday morning but it was as busy as any weekday. The station was crowded with servicemen and women, filling the departing trains and emptying the ones returning from far and wide. It was the busiest she had ever seen Lime Street. The trip went surprisingly swiftly and she read most of the way. After Carlisle, she changed her tack and wrote in her diary, making sure that she was up to date with the vicar's engagements for the week. She wanted to return and hit the ground running. The train arrived on time in Glasgow. She was struggling to carry her case off the train, when a naval officer approached and first excused himself.

'Excuse me, madam,' he said. 'Have I the pleasure of talking to Mrs Emily Jones of Liverpool?'

'Yes,' replied Emily. 'That's me, and yes, you can carry my case, if you want.'

The case was wrested from her hands, before she'd finished her request.

'I think it is this way to your hotel,' the officer said and led the way to the taxi bay.

The officer signalled to a black, unmarked car. After Emily made herself comfortable inside, she noticed that it was an official car, driven by a naval rating. They were soon entering a large hotel, much grander than any hotel Emily had ever stayed at before. Everywhere she looked there were red carpets and gold furniture. It was just like she had seen on the pictures; much posher even than the vicarage.

'So I'll leave you here for the night, Mrs Jones. The lady at the desk knows all about you. We've booked you in for two nights. I'll be back tomorrow morning at nine o'clock and then we'll travel to Gourock, visit the King's Harbour Masters and then later in the morning we'll visit your husband's grave.'

There wasn't anything Emily could say except, 'Thank you.'

The lady at reception chatted to Emily as if she knew her personally.

'We've found you an excellent room on the second floor. It's pleasantly quiet. Dinner is at seven in the dining room over there. Breakfast is from seven till nine in the same room. What time would you like?'

'I have to leave at nine.'

'Well, let's say eight o'clock. Will you be requiring a luncheon tomorrow or would you like a packed lunch?'

'I'll have a packed lunch.'

'You'll be able to collect it after breakfast. Will you be back before dinner tomorrow evening?'

'I certainly hope so. I've another busy day on Tuesday, returning to Liverpool.'

Emily took her key, Room 27, and found its location easily enough. It was on the second floor, looking out across the crowded streets of Glasgow. There were hundreds of servicemen walking to and from the station. She thought that if every major city like Glasgow and Liverpool was like this, busily chasing the war, then surely there would be some success coming our way before much longer.

She washed at her washbasin and felt immediately refreshed and wide awake. She spent the hour before dinner lying on her bed reading and making notes in her diary. At seven o'clock sharp she walked slowly down to the dining room. She was shown her own dining table for one in the corner, with her own white card on it.

What a lovely room I've been given in this spacious hotel, with such a gorgeous dining room, Emily thought. It made her wonder why the navy were making such an effort. It's as if Jimmy's service days were special to the navy. It was an enjoyable meal. There wasn't any choice and all the portions were skimped but this was war food. She ate a portion of meat entirely to herself for the first time since before the war. Succulent, but tiny, roast potatoes, peas and cauliflower. And there was a sweet, of all things. Steamed sponge pudding with syrup and custard. There was no choice but it was delicious. She made a point to ask the cook for the recipe. She confided in a thick Glasgow accent. 'Really, it's about finding a substitute for sugar. It's a mixture of condensed milk and syrup with finely chopped raisins.'

Next morning, at nine o'clock sharp, Emily met the same smart naval officer in the entrance hall of the hotel. She'd made a point of wearing her best black outfit, with Jimmy's favourite brooch on the lapel of Ada's new black raincoat. The officer led the way to the waiting car and they were driven to the station.

'Have you ever been to Gourock before, Mrs Jones?'

'No, officer. This is my first time in Scotland.'

They caught the train to Gourock and Emily was relieved to find that the journey wasn't as long as the trip up from Liverpool the day before. Upon arrival, they were delivered by official car from the station to the Royal Navy offices near the pier. Emily was shown into His Majesty's Harbour Masters office. She was asked to take a seat and felt relieved that, at last, she would know the full facts.

'First of all, Mrs Jones, we must offer you our full sympathy for the loss of your husband's life and apologise for the time it has taken us to reach a satisfactory conclusion to our investigations. The most likely cause of your husband's death would appear to be the late discharge of an enemy landmine in the Firth of Clyde. Your husband was in the company of a small detachment of men from HMS Swallow, sent out to investigate a large area of debris, mostly the result of gale and bomb damage. The debris exploded and killed him outright. We are sincerely sorry for the amount of time this investigation has taken.'

There wasn't anything that Emily wanted to say. She was asked if there were any questions she'd like to ask but she had long since accepted Jimmy's death.

In the outer room she was given a cup of tea and biscuits. The naval officer who had accompanied her to Gourock joined her.

'When will I be allowed to see my husband's grave?'

'That's next on the agenda.'

Emily remembered Father Deegan's advice about keeping tributes to Jimmy simple on the grave. She put her cup down and addressed the officer.

'Would it be possible for me to pop into a florist's on the way?'

'Certainly, Mrs Jones.'

The black car stopped at the only open florist's in town. Emily inspected the limited stock and then asked, 'Do you have roses?'

'Yes, madam, but they are out of season and very expensive.'

'I shall only want four,' Emily stated.

Emily paid the rather expensive bill and the florist was rather pleased with her sale.

'We don't sell many at this time of the year.'

The black car swept along the coastal road to the cemetery, which was fortunately not too far away. It was a clear day, with the sun trying to climb up through the low clouds. At the cemetery, the naval officer accompanied Emily to the graveside. It was a simple serviceman's grave, looking out over the Clyde towards Dunoon.

Emily smiled when she noticed that there was a football pitch in the adjacent field with a game in progress.

'Jimmy would have loved that,' said Emily to the officer. When he showed no understanding of her remark, she added, 'Football.'

She placed the four roses in the stone vase in the centre of the grave the officer moved away.

'Take as long as you want, Mrs Jones,' he said.

Emily spoke to Jimmy.

'You've probably been wondering why it's taken me so long to come up here to Scotland to see you, Jim? Well, I only found out two weeks ago. The four roses are just one from each of us. One from your mum, Ada, who is always talking about you. One each from your two wonderful daughters, who miss you, and one from me.'

She kissed each of the roses.

'I'll never forget you, Jim. We had a special life together and I know you'll always be with me and the kids.'

Then Emily whispered a little prayer to God.

'Please Lord, give me strength.'

She turned and walked to the gate. The naval officer met her just before the lodge and walked with her towards the black car.

'Was everything to your liking, Mrs Jones?' he asked.

'It's worked out a lot better than I thought. The delay had me thinking it was something really serious, when really it was just an unusual incident,' she said.

They climbed into the black car and were driven to the station. The naval officer smiled and Emily smiled back. They both appreciated that there was little that could be said. At the station they caught the next train back to Glasgow and were soon heading back to the hotel. It had been a simple straightforward trip and taken all day.

At the hotel, Emily said farewell to her naval minder, assuring him that she would be able to find the station by herself, next morning, using the vouchers in the brown envelope. The naval officer offered his sympathy again and then left the hotel. Emily went up to her room and considered having a long cry to mark the occasion but decided that now was the time to face the future by herself. She wrote in her diary about the events of the day and further thoughts about Jimmy and some other little things she wished she had said at the graveyard. It was soon seven o'clock and time for dinner. She washed and changed her clothes, before realising that she had only one change left in the case; her clothes for the return journey to Liverpool on the morrow.

She rode down to dinner in the lift for a change. She usually avoided lifts but there was a lift-porter.

'Ground floor, please,' she said.

Stepping out of the lift, she was apologised to by a tall, naval officer, in the sort of smart best clothes Jimmy wore on special occasions.

The officer just said, 'Sorry, I hope I'm not in your way,' in a detectable Liverpool accent.

Then he graciously stepped out of the way and out of her line of vision, as he took his place in the lift. She smiled to herself as she supposed it proved it was possible to have well-mannered, well-turned out men from the fair city. She found herself thinking that maybe, after working for the vicar for over a year, she was starting to like her own jokes best, too.

Chapter 9
The Train to Liverpool Exchange

'Time was away and somewhere else,
There were two glasses and two chairs
And two people with one pulse.'

Louis MacNeice

Emily was up and at it next morning, especially glad that she hadn't to find and make breakfast. She was packed, bathed and dressed before she went down to breakfast at eight, which somebody else had prepared. It was such a big change to be eating a whole egg and a rasher of bacon. Although tiny, it was such a luxury. She knew she should take the opportunity of having a further round of toast, when asked. The meal had started with a generous bowl of porridge. It was Scotland after all, she thought.

After breakfast the waiter asked, 'Will you require a packed lunch today?'

'Yes, please,' replied Emily.

Her lunch appeared, packed in a strong brown paper bag, as quickly as if it was on a conveyor belt at Dunlops. Clutching her bag, she climbed back up the stairs to her room to freshen up and clean her teeth. Ten minutes later, she carried her case to the lift and, from there, the porter carried it out to the first available taxi. Emily asked the taxi-driver if he took War Office tokens. He certainly did. She was soon on the platform at the station awaiting the Liverpool train at half-past nine.

When the train pulled in, she managed to climb in with her case and had a compartment to herself, before a tall naval officer climbed aboard. She thought she had seen him somewhere else before, although it could have been just the uniform.

109

It was quiet and chilly waiting for the train to set off and activate the heating. Just before the train was due to depart, four other passengers clambered aboard to fill the seats and the luggage racks. The tall naval officer moved down and excused himself for sitting next to Emily.

'Sorry, I hope I'm not in your way?' Andrew Ritchie said.

Emily knew it was the same officer who had stood waiting for the lift back at the hotel the night before. Despite an early morning bath and a huge breakfast, Emily was still half asleep. Nonetheless, she felt that she knew Andrew already, just because of the repeated considerate question. He looked at Emily in a way that expressed the thought that he was expecting the worst possible answer. He didn't look very sure of himself.

'That's all right,' she murmured, looking at him.

He was good-looking, ever so serious, and had long arms, as well as long legs. He had deep, watery blue eyes that seemed at the outset to be only fit for staring placidly out of. He looked too young for his uniform, but most servicemen in the war were young. He had sunken cheeks, smooth, white skin and thick, erratic eyelashes. She thought he'd be about twenty-five.

The train trundled out of Glasgow and headed south. Emily feigned sleep; she felt tired but wondered all the time about the sullen officer sitting next to her. She opened her eyes when the train rumbled up and down, crossing the points at Carstairs.

'Bit of a clatter,' said Andy, chancing a smile.

'Yes,' agreed Emily. 'I'm just waking up.' Then she added, because she had thought of nothing else since seeing him again, 'We met last night.'

'Yes, we did,' he said. 'I was trying to be a proper British gentleman.'

'With an accent like that?' she said. 'You're a Liverpudlian.'

'I was thinking that you were cool, calm and sophisticated,' he said seriously.

'Why, aren't I?' she begged.

'Just because I'm not from Liverpool, I'm from Chester,' he said, in a deep slow voice, letting his blue eyes light up for the first time.

'Well, you've got a Liverpool accent. You're just one of these toffs who say "I'm not from Liverpool but from 'near' Liverpool",' she said, excitedly, but he didn't mind. He was too busy registering her presence; he didn't mind being taken to task. She was wearing a white blouse under her blue cotton suit. Her face was pretty with a touch of pink lipstick and a quick dab of face powder. Her dark-brown hair was combed splendidly into place. He could smell the scented face powder, even in the crowded train, and, what's more, the attractive creature was talking to him, Andy. He found himself opening up and smiling back at her. He found her excited voice comforting.

'I've an observation about you and a question. You're obviously from Liverpool, aren't you? So my question is, what were you doing in Glasgow?'

'This is the Liverpool train, isn't it?' asked Emily. Then relenting, 'Okay, fair is fair, I'll answer your question briefly, if you tell me why you're up here in Glasgow. You'll understand my need to be brief. I've been up to the Clyde to visit my husband's grave. He was killed at sea. Right now, take my mind off it all and tell me why you're here in Scotland. I'm sorry for putting a damper on the conversation.'

'Oh, I am sorry,' Andy said, no longer feeling frivolous and looking dispirited.

'No, it's my fault. I just wanted to make the journey pass quickly,' she confessed, so Andy felt obliged to tell her all about his unsettled past, about his restless family emigrating to Australia and how his yearning for the sea had earned him a desk job in Glasgow.

For her part, Emily felt so relaxed with her new friend that she found herself instinctively pulling his leg after only having met him half an hour previously. It was his pessimism that did it for her. He was at his funniest when he was at his most miserable, desperate and despondent. She chuckled away contentedly.

'Oh, I don't know,' she said after a few minutes. 'Look on the bright side. I bet it was great in Glasgow, out on the town every night drinking.'

'No, no,' Andy sighed. 'The big problem was getting up at six next morning with a monumental hangover.' Emily looked at his doleful face and laughed. 'So I had to get out of it all,' he continued. 'When I took my leave I travelled up to Skye to see where the Ritchies, that's my family, originally came from. I'm Andy by the way.'

'Yes, I'm Emily; but tell me about Skye.'

'Well, it's beautiful but it rains and blows a lot,' he said, smiling naturally now, without having to think about it. He decided there and then that he liked Emily; she made him feel comfortable within himself. 'My Uncle Alex,' he continued, 'moors his fishing boat in Portree, sets his pots for lobsters and crabs and keeps hens.'

'So what do you do for a living back in civvy street?' asked Emily.

'I was training to be a maths teacher but before I could find a post I was press-ganged into the navy,' said the disgruntled Andy, conscious of Emily smiling away.

'So that's what you'll do when you go back to Chester; teach maths?'

'What do you mean "go back"? I've never started. Not one lesson!' He could see Emily chuckling away at his predicament, so he continued. 'I might not even like the job. Might not be cut out for it. Might not survive the war.' They both laughed as if getting killed was a laughing matter. 'So what do you do for a living?' asked Andy.

'Nothing as exciting as you,' whispered Emily. 'I'm the vicar's housekeeper. We keep hens, like your uncle up in Skye, but I don't like killing them.'

'Why, are you religious?' Andy asked, solemnly.

'Not really. I'm going through a bad phase at the moment, because of Jimmy being killed before we could realise our dreams. He wanted to work his way up and eventually become a chartered accountant. You see, it didn't take much to make me to stray on to my one and only subject of Jim.'

There was a pause. Andy took his cue.

'Look, we are approaching the Beattock climb .... and she's on time .... the one in the poem by W.H. Auden. We'll soon be at the top and then it's all downhill to England.' Andy had managed to change the subject; but poetry was never his strength. '"This is the Night Mail crossing the border ... bringing the cheque and the postal order". I think we all did it at school.' There was a silence. Had he failed to change the mood?

'Poetry?' she bubbled. 'You haven't even taught maths yet.'

'I shouldn't have told you about my predicament. You're a terrible tease.'

'No,' said Emily. 'It's my fault making you swiftly change the subject from Jim. My turn now. So have you ever been to sea?'

'No. Wish I had. I've been on the Admiralty launch out to a few battleships but I've spent my time behind a desk, making paper darts when I was fed up. I'm not supposed to talk about my job, it was secret.' This time Andy looked really serious.

'Aren't you the happy one? Glad it's secret so you can button up,' chided Emily.

Andy wasn't to know that the word 'secret' would open up Emily's inner feelings and, once started, he would be unable to stop them pouring out.

'You see, Andy,' she began, 'Jimmy was killed on the Clyde when a whole area of debris exploded. One of the officers said that there was not a mark on his body. He was killed by the massive blast. Fortunately, I understood what they were trying to explain to me straight away, because people in Bootle had been killed outright by landmines. I'm just left with only pleasant, happy memories of Jim.'

There was a long silence. Andy thought that he'd really put his foot in it. He was dumbfounded and couldn't think of anything to say. He'd tried to avoid the forbidden subject, but just one word had sparked an avalanche of detail from Emily. He frantically searched for something inconsequential to talk about. It wasn't easy but fortunately the train pulled into Carlisle. Stoppages could be long during wartime and there was plenty of activity on the platform, which was crowded with service people. Andy noticed a tea trolley serving tea. He jumped off the train and dashed towards it.

'Save my seat, Emily,' he shouted.

It was the first time he'd called her 'Emily' and, as it was shouted, everybody looked to see who 'Emily' was. Andy soon returned with two cups of hot tea in cardboard cups and two buns with white icing on the top.

'The cups are really hot,' he said.

Emily pushed her light day-bag under them. They sipped their tea, realised how hot it was and waited for it to cool. Emily located the lunch from the hotel. Inside the brown paper bag were two sandwiches, which they both could smell were cheese. They both mouthed 'cheese' together with a grin. Andy looked at her slender, smooth hands, unscarred by rough work, when she offered him a sandwich.

'A sandwich each before the iced bun,' she announced.

'Why not?' Andy agreed, enjoying touching her hands for the first time.

They'd finished the sandwiches before the train pulled away from Carlisle. The iced buns were not the crowning glory of the snack. They were stale.

'It's like the food in the navy canteen in Glasgow. Take it or starve,' said Andy.

'Never mind, you meant well, buying them,' Emily consoled.

'The tea was free for the services.'

'Did you say I was a wren on leave?' she asked.

'Let your tea stop your mouth,' he suggested, thinking of some smalltalk.

Maybe he should talk about himself. 'I'll be stationed in Gladstone Dock. Where do you live in Liverpool or where is your vicarage?' he couldn't avoid asking quietly.

She started to talk normally.

'Why whisper? It's common knowledge that the navy has taken over Gladstone. It isn't my vicarage, but the vicar lives at St Christopher's, Breeze Hill. It's in Bootle, near the docks.'

'I didn't realise there are any hills in Bootle.'

'There aren't. It's just what we call a "brew". It's at the top of Merton Road that leads up from the docks. I'm pretty sure it is not top secret. Hitler seems to be able to find it regularly,' said Emily, now talking normally.

'I was just avoiding using that dreaded word "secret". It starts you off,' he said.

'Oh, I see,' said Emily, pausing. 'If you only knew the problems I've had with secrets you'd have a bee in your bonnet, too. But I won't start this time.'

'So would you mind if I paid you a visit at St Christopher's?'

Emily found herself thinking, no but saying, 'Can't see why not. Come up on Sunday. I could see you there. Bearing in mind, of course, it's only a year since Jimmy was killed. You'll understand, being a navy man.'

There was a considerable pause, then Andy asked, 'Can we be friends, Emily?'

'Of course. You're my friend already, aren't you? I don't share my cheese sandwiches and rock-hard iced buns with every Tom, Dick or Harry,' Emily smiled.

'So there's other guys as well?' Andy smiled at his own joke, while Emily felt a really pleasurable sensation in the pit of her stomach; the like of which she had not felt since Jimmy had left Bootle a year before.

It wasn't Andy's fault. It would be all right, if they just remained friends. She was Jimmy's widow for goodness sake.

'Yes,' she said. 'It'll be good to be friends, if we keep it under wraps till you sail off again, like sailors do. It'll be long enough to stop people pointing fingers.'

'I'll always respect your wishes,' Andy said seriously.

'Indeed, you will,' she smiled.

At Preston the station-master and his staff walked the length of the train popping their heads into each compartment.

'This train will no longer terminate at Liverpool Exchange but Aintree.'

'The stations and bridges have been bombed,' the station-master added.

There were plenty of buses taking passengers into town at Aintree. However, Andy hailed a taxi. He was going to pay the fare but Emily produced the last of her vouchers from out of her brown envelope and said, 'Use this. I've no further need.'

'I'll drop you near the church and then I'll know where it is next Sunday.'

'That's a good idea, Andy.' Emily felt really cosy in the taxi next to him.

The trip had flown by and even though Emily wanted to know much more about him, she thought he hadn't put a foot wrong since they had first met. She needed to be careful though, most people believed that marriage was for life and widows melted into the background, never looking at another man and suffering in silence; particularly if they had children and family to support.

They alighted outside the church on Breeze Hill. Andy suggested that he should carry Emily's case around the corner to her home.

'No, Andy. No. Maybe yes much later in the year, after you've been away to sea for six months. You'll appreciate where I've just returned from in Gourock.'

Andy understood and didn't want to ruin his new friendship. They shook hands and the taxi headed down the road towards Gladstone Dock.

Emily continued down the road with her case and turned the corner into the street. She wasn't thinking of her visit to Scotland at all. She was thinking of Andy and how she felt so comfortable with him. Yes, he was too serious, just like Jim, but he was somewhat more vulnerable. She couldn't feel any weight in the case and bounded towards her front door with a gleefulness and optimism she had thought no longer existed in the dark world. She felt as if she'd always known Andy. She certainly wanted to see him again. She'd have to be careful and make the most of the friendship before it blossomed into something special. She had to think of the kids and Ada first and foremost, whatever the others might think.

Ada met her at the door.

'The bombing has been bad. All the stations and bridges.'

It was back to the war.

Chapter 10

Just Friends

'Fare thee well, for I must leave thee. Do not let this parting grieve thee And remember that the best of friends must part.'

Anon.

Back home Emily concentrated on her job of keeping the vicar. She seldom went to morning service. She was too busy planning and providing food, particularly if there was a hotpot supper coming up. She usually went to evensong. She loved the closing hymns because they meant so much to her. *Now the Day is Over, The Day Thou Gavest, Lord, is Ended* or *Abide with me.* They always reminded her of Jimmy on the other side of the ocean, particularly the line 'As o'er each continent and island the dawn leads on another day'. She imagined Jimmy was still away on the other side of the world and wasn't dead for those few moments at least.

Some Sundays the vicar only required a breakfast and sandwiches for lunch, depending on where he could slot it in. Bessie had now moved out after Father Deegan had found her a house to rent off Rimrose Road.

'You can tell how close I am to the sea, by the names of the nearby streets: Atlantic, Pacific and Baltic. I'm in Atlas Road,' she said.

'So you don't need a map to get there?' asked Emily.

'It's quite a hike walking up to the vicarage but it is handy when I'm cleaning the town hall. It's near the pub, too.'

Emily found herself telling Bessie about Andy. It just slipped out. All about the journey down from Scotland, the packed train and them sharing a taxi from Aintree Station.

'So when will you be seeing him again?'

'I've no plans. It's all too early. Besides, he's probably back on the ocean.'

'That's the trouble with sailors. They sail off into the sunset most mornings.'

'One of your better lines, Bess,' Emily noted. 'Nearly as good as your next door-neighbours who live over the road.'

She wasn't going to confide completely in Bessie but she might need a friend in future because she needed to see Andy again.

She need not have worried. Andy came to evensong the next week. He was sitting near the front, looking like a tall, navy blue column when the congregation stood up for the hymns. Emily remained in her seat near the back. She wondered what it would feel like when they met again. How would she feel? Would it be over?

At the end of the service he came walking out and it was as if they had never been apart since the train journey. He looked just as natural and relaxed as he had been on the train. They beamed widely at each other.

'So nice to see you again, Andy,' she said.

'Oh, there you are, Emily. You've been sitting at the back. You should have come down and sat by me. Couldn't promise iced buns this time,' he said, pleased.

'So you are still in town?'

'Yes. I'm staying at the naval billet, till I get posted to a ship. The group is expected back in port soon. So I'll be off into the thick of it at last.'

'Nice of you to keep your promise and come up to the church.'

'I know what I was meaning to ask you,' he said slowly, 'will you let me take you to the cinema or something before I head off?'

'The answer is no. You know why. I'll certainly say yes in future, when next you are in port.' She wasn't expecting his question. She didn't want to ruin it all.

'What makes you so certain I'll be back?'

'You will be. I'm sure of that. Like I'm so sure of you, Andy.' Andy just smiled contentedly as he walked away. 'Besides, you've finally got to see the sea,' she added.

She could see he was really pleased now. She thought it was down to him achieving the wish he had always wanted. Andy knew it was because of Emily.

It wasn't long before Andy was posted to his new ship, a corvette, HMS Buzzard, which had returned to Gladstone after escorting a convoy back from Gibraltar. He decided that he was going to save himself for Emily, be patient and wait for at least six months before he asked her again for a date. With a bit of luck, time would soon pass by, especially if he was involved in convoy duties across to America. The North Atlantic in 1942 was in the thick of the sea battle. In June of that year one ship was going down every four hours and there were four hundred U-boats in service.

Life in the dock wasn't too bad. There was the 'Flotilla Club' in West Gladstone, cheap beer and plenty of rum. There was a small seamen's chapel, in which the boss usually read the lesson, when he was on base. Just out from Gladstone there were two pubs, famed for all the wrong reasons, the Royal and the Caradoc. The latter, on the Crosby road, revelled in the nickname 'The Bucket of Blood'. Both pubs had a reputation for providing all the comforts that visiting sailors sought ashore.

Andy was granted a twenty-four hour pass, the day before he was due to sail out of the Mersey on convoy duty. He went with the other lads into Liverpool for a drink and was heading off with them to the Grafton ballroom, when he realised his heart was not in it. He needed to see Emily, for just one last time before he went out into the ocean. He caught a taxi back to Bootle and knocked on the door of the vicarage. Amazingly, the door was opened by Emily.

'I've come to see you. I'm sailing off tomorrow,' he said.

'You're lucky to catch me, I was just leaving to go home. Just give me a moment to tidy up and put my face on.'

Emily dashed inside, leaving Andy standing at the door. She was soon ready, however, and rejoined Andy outside. Emily was carrying the remains of a meal in a large tureen.

'This is for Bessie. We'll pop into the pub on the way home,' she explained. They reached the Blobber and were soon inside. Bessie was at the piano singing *Underneath the Arches* before she noticed Emily walking over to her at the piano with her dish.

'Is that Andy?'

'Yes.'

Emily was sorry she'd said yes because this was the signal for Bessie to break into *If You Were the Only Boy in the World and I Were the Only Girl* with little comments such as 'Especially for my friend Emily' and 'They're new together' littering the piece. The old song always attracted drunken singers to join in, and this occasion was no exception. Emily nearly walked straight back out on to the street. She was totally embarrassed, but supposed she should expect it in Liverpool with a sailor in tow?

'So you gave him a date, after all you said?' asked Bessie.

'No. I didn't. Would I be off on a night out with a casserole dish full of scouse? I wouldn't, would I?' Emily complained.

'Oh, I don't know. You could put it in the middle of the floor and dance around it,' Bessie suggested.

'Besides, Andy is just showing me home and any more clever comments from you and you'll have this basinful of scouse over your silly, smiling face.'

'Sorry, sorry, Em,' said Bessie, enjoying the success of her tease. 'So this is Andy. Pleased to meet you, Andy. I've heard so much about you.'

Andy wondered what Emily had disclosed, while Emily closed her eyes in frustration, afraid of what Bessie might say next.

Andy and Bessie shook hands before Bessie turned to Emily and asked, 'Can I have my supper now?'

'I'm not so sure,' Emily smiled before she passed the dish over to Bessie.

'Ladies and gentlemen, if we have any in tonight, we've a real seaman in our midst, one who goes out on to the Atlantic, so suppose I have to sing *Maggie May*,' she announced.

'I'll let you buy me half a sweet stout; but only one,' Emily whispered to Andy, as she sat at the nearest table to the performing Bessie.

Bessie sang:

'Come all ye sailors bold, and when me tale is told,
I'm sure you'll all have cause to pity me,
For I was a Goddam fool, in the port of Liverpool,
When I met up with a girl called Maggie May.
Oooh, dirty Maggie May; they've taken you away
And you won't never walk down Lime Street any more.
For you robbed full many a sailor
And also a couple of whalers
And now you're doing time in Botany Bay.'

Bessie played on the keyboard as Emily and Andy chatted.

'Does she do this for a living?'

'One of her many jobs.'

'What else does she do? Chuck out the drunks? She's built like a wrestler.'

'No. You're talking about my friend. Friends since school. She's always been big like that. She's a cleaner at the vicarage and part-time at the town hall.'

'Do the vicar and the mayor know she sings in here?'

'The vicar recommended her to the mayor. They think she is marvellous. She's an extremely hard worker. Always cheerful. They say she's a "joy".'

'Is she in the choir?'

'No, but she's been asked often. She works most evenings and would not be able to get along to practices,' Emily told him. 'That's what she says.'

'Right. What night is that?'

'What?'

'Choir practice night?'

'Tuesday night. Why do you ask?'

'I used to sing in Chester Cathedral.'

'So you are thinking of singing here?' Emily smiled. 'Good grief.'

'Yes, probably, when I return. I'd have to see the vicar and the choir master.'

'I'm amazed,' Emily gasped out loud.

'It'll give me a better excuse for knocking at the vicarage door. Rather than feel like a rag and bone man or a destitute seeking a free meal.'

Bessie pounded on the keyboard, chatting to the punters. 'This job's killing me, but it's for life.'

A wag shouted from the back, 'It's killing us, too, Bessie.'

'You aren't listening to what I'm going to tell yer. I'll play some decent songs now, but I want you all to join in. Even the sailors.' So Bessie went into her popular song sequence. 'This is the army Mr Jones, No private rooms or telephones, You had your breakfast in bed before and you won't have it there any more.' Then she launched into *We'll Meet Again* and couldn't resist having another go at Emily.

'This song is especially for my old friend Emily and my very new friend Andy, who is shortly leaving on a slow boat to Birkenhead,' Bessie said, just as Emily and Andy were slipping away. She managed to sing a few pertinent lines to Andy as he walked out into the street. 'We'll meet again, Don't know where, don't know when, But I know we'll meet again some sunny day.'

'I need to rush back home. I was only popping in to see Bessie. Doesn't time pass quickly when you're having fun?' They walked home. 'It isn't bad this just being friends. No date. No pack drill. It was okay, wasn't it, Andy?'

'It was great in a weird sort of way,' admitted Andy. 'I've never had the performer sing to me like that before. The words were appropriate, too.'

'It's just the way Bessie performs. She's very personal and it get the drunks laughing and eating out of her hand.'

'So that'll be it. Till I see you again,' said Andy. 'It's been an enjoyable evening. Like you said, time just flew by and I wondered what to expect next.'

'We'll see how it goes on your return. Are you serious about joining the choir?'

'Course I'm serious. And I'll be patient and not even ask you for a kiss. I won't spoil it, if you promise to take me seriously on my return.' Andy smiled.

'Who says I don't take you seriously already. I just need to do things in a respectful way for the memory of Jimmy, for his mother, Ada, and for me and the kids. And for you, Andy.'

Andy was already walking away. At the end of the path he just said, 'Friends.'

Emily turned away, all mixed up and confused inside. It was the right course of action for them to take. They'd come through it.

The morning after Andy sailed away, Emily endeavoured to remove him from her mind. Maybe, she would never see him again. Besides, he may lapse back into his previous depressed state. Life was complicated enough without fresh items creeping in before long-term problems had been put to rest. Family came first.

The most important item on her agenda at that moment was the forthcoming hotpot supper for the servicemen in the town. It was to be mostly naval personnel. However, there was an army officer from the Liverpool Irish. Father Deegan engaged him in conversation all afternoon and nobody else could get a word in.

'It's such a pity that we can never make an evening out of these suppers, but we'll wait a year or two and hope the air-raids disappear completely,' said the vicar.

'Major Saunders here is stationed at the Liverpool Irish depot at Formby,' the father said after a time.

'You'll know all about Brendan's time as chaplain with the King's in the Great War. He was on the Somme and finished up at Lille,' offered the vicar.

'Yes, I've suggested to him that he comes out to Formby and takes a look around at his old battalion,' the Major said. 'You'll be amazed at the changes.'

A week later, Father Deegan caught the train out to Formby, after he had travelled down to Seaforth by bus to catch it; Marsh Lane was closed for repairs after another fire. At Formby, he was met by the battalion padre. After being shown around the quarters and the small chapel, the padre escorted Father Deegan along to the dining rooms for afternoon tea. Here, he found himself back on familiar territory, completely at ease, and all the memories came flooding back. The old army smells, some pleasant, some not, reminded him of his days in the ranks at the front. He felt for a time as if he had returned home after a long holiday.

Chapter 11

Father Deegan Goes to War

Father Deegan had enjoyed his day out visiting the Liverpool Irish depot at Formby. The whole episode brought back all the happy and sad memories of his time in the trenches. He had immediately felt in tune with the regimental values and camaraderie. He had always felt that the British were going to win the war; now, after visiting his old regiment preparing to play their part, he was completely sure.

Midway through October 1942, he received a telephone call from the adjutant at Formby asking him to meet him in the Needles, a public house on the corner of the dock road and Miller's Bridge. He was asked to treat the telephone call and the meeting as strictly top secret. It seemed to be a distant phone call and he hadn't had the opportunity to ask questions. Why the Needles, and why such a brief, hurried request? It couldn't be a hoax? People pedalling falsehoods in wartime usually finished up locked up in Walton prison.

He decided to play along with the request and walked down the hill towards the docks, managing to cross Miller's Bridge, despite the reconstruction works after repeated bombings. He entered the Needles. It was full of seamen and dockers. Any difficulty he thought he might have had in recognising the person he was to meet was immediately dispelled, when the only army officer in the pub approached him.

'Father Deegan?' he asked the father.

'Indeed, yes,' the father answered.

'I'm liaison officer out at Formby with the 8th Irish Battalion King's Liverpool. If we could meet over here in the corner. Will you require a drink?'

'Yes,' said the father. 'It's a bit early. I'll just have a cup of tea.'

So they both ordered tea at the bar and were given two large mugs of strong tea and asked to add their own milk and sugar. The officer explained himself.

'We've been advised that you were an efficient chaplain in the Great War,' the officer opened, sipping his hot tea, expecting a long response from the father.

'I carried out my duty. I served as an officer in the trenches, where I found myself carrying out a series of pastoral duties, looking out for the men. At times, I felt like their mother. Some of them were so young, it was the first time they'd been away from home. So when a vacancy arose with the chaplains, clerics were being killed too, you know, I willingly filled the post. I served for three years as padre.'

The officer listened and then spoke earnestly. 'Maybe I should cut all the corners and explain the predicament in which we find ourselves. You see, the chaplain services have become overstretched at a time when the 8th Battalion King's find themselves being somewhat depleted. The latest request is that a detachment of the regiment be absorbed into the 6th Battalion of the Royal Inniskillings, who are serving in North Africa. Basically, the two situations coming together mean that we are short of a padre to send with the men to North Africa. I realise that this is going behind your back somewhat, but the commanding officer has recommended you for the post. We've already had a long conversation with the bishop, who respects you as a soldier, a friend and distinguished priest.'

'What did the bishop say?'

'He left the decision to you.'

'I'll need to think about it,' said Father Deegan.

'Yes, you can have time to think about it overnight, but you would need to come out to the depot at Formby tomorrow to get kitted out, if you decide to go ahead.

'So why is there all this rush?' asked the father.

'Well, you need to sail the day after tomorrow, Thursday.'

'It's all a bit of a rush. I've scarcely got over the surprise,' said the father.

'You know war is like this, one surprise to stomach after another. I'm as surprised as you, but then I deal in them daily,' the officer said.

'So, if I was to decide yes, what will I do next?'

'The first thing would be to parade at Formby tomorrow at nine o'clock, talk it over with the CO, then have your medical to check your fitness for the task and then, if everything is okay, you'll be kitted out in desert gear.'

The officer ran through the procedure, as if, in his own words, he did it daily.

'So when will I get to see the men?' asked the father.

'You won't till you arrive in Africa. You see, the regiment has already sailed from the Clyde on the liner Strathallan.' The officer knew his brief.

'When do you need to know my decision?' asked the father.

'Yesterday; but tomorrow when you parade at nine, or by phone if you decide against it.'

The officer packed up his things and paid for the tea. They walked back to Stanley Road together, where, after paying his respects to Father Deegan, the officer vanished into the Merton Hotel.

Probably another poor blighter in the Merton due for a shock next, the father thought, as he scurried back up the hill to the vicarage. He would run his situation past his friend, John, the Vicar. He would try to dissuade him but it would help him decide whether or not to go on the adventure.

Fortunately, the vicar was in his study and the staff had all long since gone home; Tuesday was the vicar's evening to contemplate. He was sitting in front of a blank sheet of foolscap, pencils sharpened and India rubber cleaned, praying for inspiration. Father Deegan's plight came as a welcome relief.

'So, the regiment have asked you to do a bit of covering for them. Mind you, you always were a soldier at heart, Brendan. Enduring those long years in the trenches means that, even now, you still feel the urge to return. Despite all the misery, you still have unfulfilled dreams, knowing far better than me what that entails.'

The vicar thought hard and long to come to terms with his friend's dilemma.

'No, seriously, do you think I should go?' the father asked, and the vicar could see that he was really serious about it all.

'It's come as rather a surprise,' said the vicar, while he thought.

'It was a huge shock to me.'

'I bet it was,' said the vicar. 'Now you expect me to be helpful, to join you in kicking it around a little? My first thought is your age. You are still in your forties.'

'Late forties.'

'But you're still fit. Do you feel fit and well, Brendan?'

'Course I'm fit and well. I run about all day. Never see a quack.'

'That was my next question,' said the vicar. 'You reckon you are in good health, but are you eating and sleeping well?'

'You're sounding more like a doctor. Course I sleep well, every night.'

'Good. All the right answers so far,' the vicar said triumphantly. 'Now, they'll have your records and know about you being able to handle French and Italian, so are you prepared to work with the enemy, if assigned the duty?'

'Certainly, certainly, John. Please don't ask any more questions.'

'I need to, Brendan. I don't want my current best friend to come to any harm and I certainly don't want him to be killed, when he needn't be. Right, the last question, Brendan. Do you feel guided by God? Is it the wish of the Almighty?'

'Yes, John. Indeed, yes. I felt his presence there in the public house.'

'Well, that's good but, tough as the pubs in Bootle are, I think you'll find the battle front a lot tougher. God might not be there. You, of all people, must know what to expect. Will you be up to the final call ... if it comes?'

The father didn't answer the question. 'Thanks for your help, John. I'll turn it all over in my mind overnight and then wake up with the solution. I'll decide whether to make that phone call or parade at Formby at nine o'clock.'

'Go with God's love,' the vicar said gently. 'I'm sure we will live to continue our friendship.'

'Thanks, John. Thanks for not asking am I afraid about it all.'

'Rubbish, Brendan. You are the bravest man I know. I'd certainly never go to war. It would be completely chaotic for me to contemplate.'

The father left to return to his presbytery, while the vicar continued writing his sermon. It was one of the best sermons he'd ever composed. It flowed straight from his sharpened pencil and he never had recourse to use the clean India rubber once. It was about how he advised a friend to go to war, when he hadn't the courage himself. The congregation would never know who the soldier in question was.

At nine o'clock next morning, Father Deegan paraded at Formby, having run his dilemma through his mind over and over again. The argument that had finally decided him was not duty to the regiment or service to God but simply, whether he was still a young fit man? If I am, then I've no excuse for not going. It was all so simple in the end. He was shown in to see the Commanding Officer, who shook his hand over-enthusiastically.

'Well done, well done,' he said, forgetting that the only thing the father had 'done' was turn up. 'I should first like to thank you personally for volunteering to plug the temporary gap which we seem to have incurred. We are making every effort to ensure we don't make the same mistakes in future. Indeed, as soon as we have bridged the gap, so to speak, you'll be free to return to your parish.'

'How long would I be required?' asked the father.

'Who knows in wartime? However, the main concern is the post in North Africa which is just a three month assignment.'

'Short and sweet then?' asked the father.

'Yes. You'll be back in January,' said the CO. 'However, as soon as I read through your file, I knew you were our man. I have to be honest with you, one of the items that stood out was your ability as a linguist. You see, the French are still involved in North Africa, on

129

both sides. So we may need your skills. Then, of course, there are the Italians. So if you are still completely committed to the task ahead, we'll have the medics check you out, then get you kitted out. Oh, and good luck.' He reached forward over his tidy military desk and shook the Father's hand again.

After a short medical, which was no more thorough than the vicar's old one-two assessment, Father Deegan was led away to the quartermaster's store. Here he was kitted out in the full kit afforded one of the King's chaplains and issued with tropical gear. He was fortunate to meet up with the liaison officer he had first met at the Needles pub in Bootle, the man who dealt with 'daily' surprises. He suggested to the father that he should return home that night with just his basic chaplain's clothes, leaving the bulk of his kit with the quartermaster. The liaison officer would meet him down at Gladstone Dock the next morning with his full kit. A clothing van had to meet up with some of the men boarding the trooper, who needed to be issued with extra tropical gear.

Father Deegan returned to his presbytery for the night, wondering if he had made the right decision. Suppose there were easier ways to find out if I was still up for it. But, like all good Catholics, I chose the hardest. So I'll soon know if I'm still a man, let alone still a soldier. God help me. I wish somebody else had decided for me.

The next morning, Father Deegan stood on the dark grey cobbled road outside Gladstone Dock gate, dressed in his chaplain's uniform and carrying two cases. One held the instruments of the job and the other contained his civvy priest clothes. He checked his watch and found out he was half an hour too early. He was amazed at the goings on around the dock basin. Every tram in Liverpool must have been parked along the length of the dock road. Whole regiments of soldiers were jumping off vehicles and leaving in organised platoons. They marched through the dock gates, carrying their personal kits with kitbags across their shoulders. The father realised that he had volunteered for something big. He never knew that the city had so many trams. The last time he had seen such a large volume of men was on the Somme in 1916; but he knew he had to forget those days and concentrate on his new role. Fortunately, he was saved by the liaison officer and two trucks from Formby carrying tropical kit.

'The regiment has been stationed all over the country, some men have come straight to the dock from the south coast for embarkation. So they will need extra kit,' he said, deep into co-ordinating activity. 'You can see your kit on the back, father,' he added.

Father Deegan made a swift grab for his kit while he had the chance. He soon had a handsome stack of kit on the dockside. Soldiers were now coming up and asking his advice. He just had to smile and explain that he was joining the trooper himself, when he found out which one. The liaison officer was rushing around frantically dealing with his 'daily' crop of surprises, issuing extra tropical kit to the troops. The father was amazed at how much desert gear he required; after all, he wasn't a combatant. He received an additional water bottle and some sun-shades. Each man was issued with a light sun-helmet (Anglo-Indian–topi). Nobody liked the look of them. None of the men could see themselves wearing one.

'It's getting more and more like the "Four Feathers".'

The father watched as the troops were kitted out on the cobbled roadway and found it rather absurd, but he knew it was always like this. At least they weren't being shelled at the same time, he thought. Eventually, the chaos subsided and the liaison officer appeared at the father's side and they headed towards the liner Calgary Bay, which was the largest ship in the basin.

Father Deegan was scarcely on board before the Calgary Bay was nosing her way out of the Mersey into Liverpool Bay. The father's last memory of the Mersey was of seeing hundreds of troops throwing their white topi overboard; none of them wanted to be seen wearing them. The mass of white floated off towards Waterloo and Blundell sands. The father wondered whether to keep his or not. He understood the joy of the men throwing away a symbol of a bygone age, then he murmured, 'I'm not going to be the odd one out,' and threw his topi as far as he could, watching it bobble its way towards New Brighton.

One of the deck officers showed the father a small common room area which he would be able to use for services on Sundays and other activities. His cabin was not only for sleeping in; it was used for storage of everything to do with his job. There was a stack of body bags, which he thought were rather unpleasant, particularly as the ship was nowhere near the battle zone. He managed to get them removed and stored in a hold. He soon figured out that his cabin wasn't a cabin at all but a store room that they had pushed a bunk into at the last minute.

Admin on the trooper was all over the place, there being so many different units travelling to Africa on the same vessel but heading in different directions when they got there. The members of some units, like himself, had only really met up on the liner. The liaison officer from Formby was still rushing around and dealing with his fresh batch of 'daily' surprises, the first of which was that there were not only few men from the King's on board but there were no troops from the Inniskillings at all. The main body of the regiments had sailed from Glasgow and Belfast. He had very few men with whom to liaise. The father knew that this was his opportunity to take things steady. He knew what he was doing and he'd managed to survive and minister to troops in far more difficult circumstances.

The Atlantic was true to form and was rough. They were part of a huge convoy, comprising some three hundred ships from anchorages on the Clyde, the Mersey, Belfast Lough and Milford Haven. The convoy zig-zagged its way down the middle of the Atlantic till it reached the coast of Morocco. Father Deegan could not have perceived that a similarly sized fleet had set sail from the east coast of North America at the same time. The rendezvous was Algeria.

The father helped organise the boxing contests, which took place on deck, weather permitting, but indoors in the largest of the common rooms-cum-saloons, if the weather was impossible. The father found that if he refereed in his dog-collar, his decisions were accepted more readily. He noticed that the port-holes on the lower decks were crossed with bars. The Calgary Bay was still in the garb of prison ship from a previous life. Returning to his own cabin, he revised his theory that it had been a store room and decided after examining the thick doors and peep-holes that this had been a special cell. The cabin/cell was on an upper deck and was probably used for officers or VIP prisoners.

The Mediterranean wasn't as rough as the ocean but there was action off the shore most of the journey. The Calgary Bay headed for Oran to unload its cargo of troops, who weren't too happy at the amount of action along the coast. It was then that the father heard about the Strathallan; it had been sunk by two torpedoes. Over 5,000 servicemen and crew had been taken off successfully before it plunged beneath the waves. Arriving at Oran, the father was told that the King's Liverpool Regiment had been transferred to the Duchess of Richmond and the Duchess of Athol. Conditions aboard these two liners were much more comfortable than the father had experienced on the Calgary Bay. They had disembarked American troops who had headed off into the desert.

The father soon got into the swing of things, doing the rounds of the three troopers. After two days in port he was allotted headquarters in a bombed-out chapel. The clergy had upped and gone, leaving the ruined church, living quarters, vineyard and orangery. It was easy to see why the priests had vacated their beautiful location; a battle had taken place in the vicinity and the dead still lay all about.

After tidying up his new quarters, the father was called upon to help organise the burials that were still outstanding from the landings along the Algerian coast. Corpses bobbled to the surface for weeks along the coast. They were wrapped initially in blankets and stored in a variety of unsatisfactory locations. Fortunately, Father Deegan was up to the job and, in the absence of a mortuary team in the original landings, set about pulling one or two strings. There seemed to be some disagreement as to who would bury the dead. The father talked to all concerned and then located just the unit of men he required; engineers with digging equipment.

There were three hundred bodies in all, of which twenty-nine were still unidentified because of limited clothing. The father visited a neighbouring hillside and watched as the engineers cut out a long trench in the ground. He wondered how long the trench was going to be, considering that they had over three hundred soldiers to lay to rest. The trench went on forever along the same contour, so once they had started it was just a question of continuing in the same direction. Burying the dead was a talent the Father had learnt on the Somme, where he had buried hundreds. He was tied up with this assignment at Oran for most of the month. Meanwhile, the King's Liverpool Regiment were absorbed into the 6th Battalion of the Royal Inniskillings and were soon scattered throughout the desert battle zone.

The father continued doing what he did best at Oran. Sometimes he said mass from the tailboard of a fifteen hundredweight truck and, more often than not, on an altar made of four 'compo boxes' covered in the faithful vestments he'd fetched in the case from Liverpool. After one such service, he was walking away wondering how he could cadge a lift back to Oran, when he was asked to help with some Italian prisoners. There was a group of men and one officer trying to help two miserable Italians. One was crying out loud and seemed to be having a fit.

'Padre,' asked the officer, 'do you speak Italian?'

'Of course, I do.'

'Tell him that we are not going to kill him. Tell him that he is okay, so long as he doesn't make a run for it.'

The father spoke to the men and soon found out that both thought that they were going to get a bullet in the head.

'Ask him where he got that idea from?'

The father asked the Italian and wasn't amazed at the answer. They'd been told to fight to the death or they would be shot by their officers or the British, who took no prisoners.

It proved to be the father's first encounter with prisoners of war, which was to be his next assignment, after he'd cadged a lift back to Oran. The original job of burying the dead had petered out and moved along the coast with the battle zone. Oran was a different port now and the father's faithful old ship, Calgary Bay, had come into its own. It had been converted back into a prison ship. For a fortnight or so, the cells were systematically filled with Italian prisoners of war. The father went on board to see if the prisoners needed an interpreter, particularly if it was a religious or family matter. He was amazed at the number of French soldiers on board. The French were fighting on both sides depending on which general commanded them.

The father became more and more regarded as the interpreter whom the military could trust for accuracy. He found himself conducting interviews on the top deck of the liner and each day he would take a look at his old cabin 'cell', just to see who was imprisoned in it. He was more often than not strangely pleased at the high rank of the officer incarcerated in his old bunk. Eventually the floating prison was filled. Father Deegan paused to think why he never wondered why such a vessel was making its way to the front. It was simple, really; but it never crossed his mind.

The Commanding Officer of the harbour at Oran asked to see the father at his HQ on the quayside. He left his quarters at the ruined chapel on one side of the harbour and walked almost the full circuit around to the headquarters. He was invited straight into the COs office.

'Right, Father,' the CO announced. 'No beating about the bush. We want you to sail on the Calgary Bay as a full member of our staff.'

'Where will the ship be sailing to, sir?'

'Canada. Somewhere like Montreal, I expect. The main reason for our request is your ability to be able to communicate with both the Italians and the French. We know you came along here with the King's Liverpool but they are scattered widely in the desert. Since you arrived in Oran no task has fazed you, particularly when you organised the cemetery on the hill when all others weren't up to the task in the early days after the invasion. What we are suggesting is that the original crisis your regiment encountered is now well and truly over. So you could help us one last time by assisting us in the delivery of these prisoners to Canada. And after that ...' he paused searching for suitable words but failed to find them, 'you are free to go home.'

'Back to Liverpool?'

'That's the idea. You'll be sorely missed but one can't help feeling that it is not your war, as brilliantly as you have performed in the circumstances.'

'So from Canada, I'll be free to return home?'

'Certainly.'

'Maybe it is time to go home when I've finished on the Calgary Bay. I came out here with my old regiment. Few regiments seem to stay together in this war. I was just responding to a temporary crisis they had,' the father said.

'Yes, Father. You are right. In this port I've men from all the major regiments, some are square pegs in round holes but basically you can't change the numbers you require, so you have to recruit from whoever is on the next trooper out. I have to take what I am given like everybody else.'

Oran was a different port now and the Father's faithful old ship, Calgary Bay, had come into its own. It had been converted back into a prison ship. He felt a lot happier this time, holding a much more superior cabin on the top deck. He had a beautiful, wide view of the ocean on good days and felt just a little wind blown on the rough days as the Calgary Bay gradually moved into colder latitudes and climes. Being a priest was certainly an advantage when refereeing the boxing matches on the way back; the Italian and French prisoners respected him so much.

His principal job, however, was to act as the chief interpreter for the senior French officer, who was imprisoned in his old cabin. The proud Frenchman was filled with some handsome dilemmas, principally because he detested Charles de Gaulle.

'If I were you, when the call comes to join de Gaulle, I'd banish all my misgivings and join the Allies,' the father advised, after listening to the officer's long tale of woe. 'It is time to let bygones be bygones.'

'Yes; but you do not know de Gaulle. I can't trust the man.'

'Yes; but if you join de Gaulle you will be out of prison tomorrow.'

'I couldn't face the man. He looks upon me as a traitor.'

'Just throw your weight behind the Allies.'

'Really, I am no traitor. He is the traitor.'

'Let me just say that you have a voyage and a prison term to think it over.'

The voyage to Canada was uneventful and finally they sailed down the St Lawrence to Montreal. The prisoners were taken in hand by the Canadians and disappeared from the quayside in long trains with nearly as many guards aboard as prisoners, heading off to prison camps out on the prairies. By this time, Father Deegan had come around to the view that perhaps he had done everything expected of him.

He'd seen North Africa for the first time in his life and he'd performed all the tasks asked of him to the best of his ability.

He left on the next trooper out from Montreal for Liverpool. He had difficulty explaining why he had so many cases of Algerian red wine, but there was a war on and they accepted his explanation that they were all for church use. Back in Liverpool he was thanked again for filling the breach and demobbed within the week.

Chapter 12

Newfoundland

'The ice was here, the ice was there,
The ice was all around.'

S.T. Coleridge

46°04' North/52°30' West

Andy Ritchie spent most of the winter of 1942–3 in the North
Atlantic aboard his newly assigned ship, HMS Buzzard. He was the
most junior sub-lieutenant and filled the role of general dogsbody,
above and below decks. He filled in whenever the most specialist
officers were eating, showering or taking forty winks. He was
enthusiastic about all his jobs, and it meant he visited all parts of the
ship and knew where everybody performed their duties. Much of the
winter was a succession of gales, one after another. It was normal to
expect hurricane-force winds and to be hove-to for the best part of a
week. The convoys would be scattered in all directions. Most of the
ships were damaged. Seaboats and whalers were wrecked; wooden
boats' fixtures and fittings would be smashed to smithereens and
guard-rails would be flattened. It was cold so there was plenty of ice
floating on the sea off Newfoundland and covering the
superstructure of the ship. The extreme weather limited U-boat
activity, fortunately.

Andy started off sleeping in the bunk he shared, but was thrown
out of it four times in the rough seas. On the last occasion, he
finished up in a foot of water on the cabin floor. After that, he slept
in a hammock immediately below the bridge. It was more
comfortable in rough seas and he was nearer the action when it

came. He became accustomed to the Buzzard hoveto off Newfoundland. The seas were gigantic and menacing, day in, day out. The ship's leaks became larger and the crack in the quarterdeck became wider and wider. Andy soon became used to the rushing rollers. Water was everywhere but Andy managed to keep out most of the cold, using a few tricks from Liverpool, like 'don't think about wearing it – put it on'. The name of the game was to expel cold and wet at every opportunity. It was the North Atlantic, after all. Salt water could penetrate anything and this affected the crew's ability to laugh at themselves. Few laugh when they are cold, wet and miserable. Eating became a test of strength and tenacity; drinking soup and tea was a finely tuned skill. A lid on the cup became useful, unless the ship lurched and shook the contents and lid to the wind.

Andy tried to be sensible in what he ate apart from 'easy to eat' food and hot cups of beverage. Anything heavy constantly tried to escape from his stomach so he tried not to over-eat or eat for comfort. Eating sensibly meant that he could grab some sleep in his hammock, once his body had attuned itself to the sways, long, short, quick and slow. So long as his food lay cosily in his belly he was able to sleep. He was much better off than the gun crews, who would stumble off watch and lie down anywhere, completely exhausted. Often, they were like a counted-out boxer, flat out on the nearest table or crumpled up in a dry corner, still wearing their soaking clothes. Andy swung back and forth in his hammock out to the world.

Inevitably on these voyages they would finish up at Argentia, Newfoundland, or Halifax, Nova Scotia. On one particular occasion they sailed into St Johns. The crew set off on a shopping spree and bought food and goods not seen in Britain since before the war. Andy shopped for Emily, if he was ever to see her again. He wondered if she would accept his silken underwear and long nylon stockings. 'Let's chance it,' he whispered to himself at the counter.

During the ship's stay, the snow fields were replenished. Andy borrowed a set of skis from the harbour master's office and showed off his 'teach-yourself' skills down the slopes of the bay. His crewmates were amazed at how quickly he picked it up, but were unimpressed and showed their disapproval by snow-balling him heavily.

'Good moving target practice.'

Nonetheless, Andy enjoyed being ashore at St Johns. He liked looking around the multitude of shops, even though he couldn't afford most of the merchandise. It was a great feeling just to be able to walk over firm earth and hear the birds singing, after they'd weathered the snow storms. Even the smell of street traffic felt wholesome and real. Far better to be here than swaying up and down endlessly on the Atlantic with no land in sight. It was so comforting to sleep in a steady bunk with no hint of tossing or rolling. The ship was strangely quiet, no longer creaking or groaning. Life moored up in a safe harbour with as many trips ashore as you wanted somehow felt like a different world. It was, of course, being away from the Atlantic and Liverpool, where the war was being waged.

Bungey Connaught was chief officer in communications. Andy had often as not covered for Bungey on the trip out, when he was ill. His stomach had almost given up the ghost. He was in constant pain, losing weight, and his face always conveyed the thought that there was something wrong inside, probably an ulcer. However, at St Johns he managed to wangle a chitty from the medical officer, booking him into the navy hospital for a full examination. Andy went along with Bungey into town and arranged to meet him afterwards, about two hours later. Andy wandered through the shops, spending all his loose change and inspecting everything he couldn't afford. He nearly bought another present for Emily, only hesitating when it occurred to him she could have found another man.

He returned to the arranged meeting place at the corner of Main Street and found Bungey sitting on a low wall crying his eyes out.

'What is it, Bungey?' he asked.

'The medics reckon that I've got a stomach full of ulcers and need immediate attention in the nearest British naval hospital,' said Bungey, collecting himself.

'What's wrong with that?'

'Not here in Canada but back home in Seaforth. The pain's killing me, Andy.'

Bungey sat on the stone wall with his head down by his knees, weeping like a child.

'Never mind, old man. We'll soon be home. Just one more convoy back to Liverpool. Most of the ships need to go in for repairs and a boiler clean on our return.'

'I'm not sure I can hang on that long,' said Bungey.

'Of course you can. Tell the boss everything. He's got a good idea of your condition. Ask him for light duties and say you'll be on duty when the shit hits the fan, keeping me and the others up to scratch,' pleaded Andy.

'Maybe, I should. He asks me about my health. He knows all his men and so long as I work hard during the high-jinks, like he expects ... I'll ask.'

It did the trick. Andy found himself working mostly in communications and navigation, making a point of referring to Bungey before taking decisions. The older man's experience was worth its weight in gold when it was required. Invariably, Bungey found the most comfortable places to hang out, while his weight fell away and he sucked his bottle of white medicine like an infant.

The trip back home to Liverpool proved to be quite normal in many respects. There were estimated to be at least nine U-boats poking about. Some were sunk without much fuss, while others vanished from the scene as soon as they fought back.

Andy was able to observe the activities of the boss at closer quarters in the radio room, where he needed Bungey's expertise to make sure he gave the boss the information he wanted 'mustard' quick. His keenness and enthusiasm went down well with the senior officers, who had a soft spot for Bungey. Andy's only problem was that the boss was so terribly fast when calculating distance, speed and direction in his head. Andy could see the boss's brain calculating even as he delivered the relevant information, before Andy had had a second to study it.

'I thought you had a degree in mathematics, Lieutenant?' he once asked before returning to the bridge. Andy was again given scant time to respond and had to be content with looking stupid and hoping not too many of the crew heard the comment.

The second night out they made contact with a huge supply U-boat. Andy helped the asdic team find the range and bearings. They recognised the decoy echoes and by a process of elimination worked out the location of the sub. The boss decided to stay in contact till daylight, when they would attack. For the rest of the night they jogged along behind the submerged U-boat. At dawn, three sloops converged on their target and then swung over the spot where the U-boat was expected to surface. A barrage of twenty-six charges tumbled through the water and exploded at six hundred feet. A few minutes later they heard breaking-up noises from below as the U-boat disintegrated. Bubbles of oil spurted to the surface along with a selection of U-boat rubble. Andy was pleased with his minor role in the action.

The boss ordered 'Splice the mainbrace' to be hoisted. Andy had heard all the stories about the boss, as he was a continual source for discussion. He took the opportunity to take a closer look in this action, making sure he followed Bungey's advice to be 'mustard' quick. The Boss had shown his ability to be able to anticipate the movements of the opposition. He seemed to be able to locate the U-boats, just by taking into account the projected convoy route and what he would do if he were the enemy captain. His mental arithmetic was often more accurate than all the ship's instruments and Andy's slide-rule put together. He only had problems when the U-boat commander was new to the job and not full of old tricks, just like 'beginners luck' often pays off in a game of cards or dominoes. Andy kept himself in the background. He didn't want to hinder 'greatness' and knew that when the boss was around something significant was sure to happen.

The convoy sped on its way, while the Boss tried to send each of the accompanying U-boats to a watery grave. Andy concentrated on covering for Bungey in as efficient a manner as possible. He found Bungey a mine of information about the instruments on the ship and in dealings with the boss. Besides, Andy felt so safe at his side.

'Basically,' he said, 'no pissing about when the boss is around. Pleasant gentleman as he is normally, he's absolutely ruthless in action.'

'I've noticed,' agreed Andy. 'I'm a mathematician, but his mental calculations are just too fast for me.'

'Don't tell him that.'

Before the group reached Liverpool the boss had booked six dry docks to take all the ships for repair, a general clean-up and boiler clean. There would be some leave so all the crew were interviewed to make sure that they knew the exact time and dates of their leave and duties during the period. Andy found himself singled out for special interview by the boss.

'Sorry if it comes as a bit of a shock, Lieutenant. It isn't, however, a dressing down. You'll know Lieutenant Connaught has been admitted to the navy hospital; appalling stomach. What I'd like you to do is to go back to school for three weeks. It's based at HQ. There you will learn all the ins and out of the lieutenant's job. All there is to know about radio, radar and asdic. On your return, you'll be able to take your place in the team. Don't get too carried away with some of the new-fangled equipment. We have the best equipment in the fleet when it comes to U-boats. It's called my nose. Having said that, I've lost a few bets in my time when it comes to the deviousness of the enemy. You can stay in the naval hostels while you're on the course. Number One will see to it. Mention it to him.'

'Will there be leave, sir?'

'See Number One. He'll fit it in before or after your course.'

Andy was back in Liverpool and his thoughts turned to Emily.

Chapter 13

Spring 1943

It wasn't till the end of March 1943 that Father Deegan and Andy reappeared upon the scene in Liverpool. Emily and Bessie were working at the vicarage preparing the vicar's latest hotpot supper. Normally, Sundays were avoided because both of the clerics were fully engaged.

'Y'know, Bessie, 1943 isn't much different from 1942 when there's a war on.'

'Not that different from 1941, either,' said Bessie.

'Oh, I don't know; at least, touch wood, we won't have another Blitz.'

'There's still rationing and fathers and sons getting killed.'

They worked away chopping the vegetables and filling the pans. The vicar popped his head through the door, so Emily repeated herself, just for his benefit.

'Every year is the same when there is a war on,' she reiterated.

'You're right, Emily. Mind you, I've had two remarkable potato crops since war broke out. Ever since your beloved husband, James, brought the seed down from Scotland. What's more, the seed potatoes in the cellar are sprouting already. I'll soon be able to plant them out.' The vicar paused before retiring to his study.

'Father Deegan will be joining us this afternoon. Suppose we can eat later as the evenings draw out,' the vicar informed Emily.

'How's the father coping with life back here in civvy street?' asked Emily.

'He's struggling to find his land legs. He's finding it hard walking about the city, like he used to do. There's nowhere to walk on a ship,

145

particularly if the weather is foul and wretched. He's having to build up his stamina again.'

'Everybody thinks he is a war hero,' said Bessie.

'Quite right, too. I'm immensely proud of him, Bessie. I'm still amazed that he went. He did his bit in the Great War, you know.'

Emily sat in her usual pew near the back of the congregation and watched as the choir walked in during the processional hymn. The choir were few and rather tiny in stature, due to the congregation gradually dribbling back from evacuation to the countryside. In the centre of the choir was one huge man, towering above the rest. He was six foot plus. Emily was a little confused. When the choir took their places in their stalls, between the altar and the organ, Emily strained her eyes and took a longer look. The huge chorister looked familiar.

It wasn't till the choir wandered down the aisle at the end, leaving the church and disappearing into the vestry, that Emily was able to take a quick close look. It was Andy. Hand it to him, she thought, he did say he was going to join the choir. She followed the choir into the vestry out of curiosity, feeling thrilled inside.

'Hello, Andy. Great to see you back,' she said, excitedly.

'Emily, I was going to call around. I only arrived in port yesterday.'

'You look like a bean cane with all the tiny choir-boys around you,' she smiled.

'The problem is that the best lads have been evacuated. We take anybody who volunteers. Including me,' confessed Andy, happy with life.

'The wee lad must be about seven?' asked Emily.

'He's six, I believe,' smiled Andy.

'What are you doing this afternoon?' asked Emily.

'Nothing. I was planning to call around to see you.'

'Right, I'll save you the trip, 'cos I'll be here serving the hotpot supper.'

'In the afternoon?'

'It's the tradition we started during the Blitz, so we could finish before the raids started. I'll ask the vicar to invite you. Where are you staying'?'

'At the navy billets along the Crosby Road.'

Emily walked through the vestry to catch up with the vicar, bumping into Geoffrey, the choir master.

'Nice to see you, Geoff. Makes a change from the middle of the night. It's a bit quieter these days,' Emily chatted.

'It is indeed. We can only hope it stays that way,' said Geoff, pleased to be enjoying some respite from his ARP duties.

'See you've a new chorister. Is he much use?' asked Emily.

'Yes, Emily. He'll be a valued member when he's in port,' said Geoff. 'He used to sing in the choir at Chester Cathedral.'

Emily could see that Geoff was impressed. She wandered into the vicar's cloakroom. The Vicar had disrobed and was now back in his normal daywear.

'Would it be possible for Andy, the naval officer in the choir, to come to the hotpot supper this afternoon?' she asked, simply.

'Certainly, Emily, so long as you can squeeze out another portion. My aim is to invite as many servicemen as possible. The meal binds us all together at this time.'

Emily returned to Andy, who was joking with the young choir-boys in the main vestry as they scampered off home as soon as they had disrobed.

'I was a choir-boy like that once myself,' said Andy, turning away.

'Andy,' said Emily, 'the vicar says you can come along. I need to go home now and spend some time with the kids. The meal will be at about half past four.' She turned to leave, had second thoughts, and turned and asked Andy, 'Would you want to come and see the kids?'

'I thought you weren't going to ask.'

They strolled down the hill to Emily's terraced house. The streets were beginning to liven up in 1943. Children were gradually returning home from far and wide. The trickle back home after the Blitz had become a steady flow by the summer. The smaller kids were now playing street games, using chunks of white plaster from the scattered debris as chalk. The pavements were laid out as hopscotch and London to Paris courts. The street ends had goalposts and cricket stumps chalked with Liverpool and Everton at opposite sides. Skipping ropes swirled on the paving stones and tennis balls were booted, caught and thrown. The gang were back; well, most of them. Street games rang into the night with shouts of 'Lar-lee-o-co-co, lar-lee–o-co-co' and 'Coming ready or not.' Emily and Andy walked through a game of hopscotch, excusing themselves and then making a bee-line for the door when close enough. The door was on the latch; there was nothing worth nicking. They were soon inside. Ada wondered why all the light from the open door had disappeared so suddenly after Emily had entered. Then she saw the size of Andy standing there.

'I thought storm clouds had blown over,' she said. 'So who is this?'

'Mum, this is Andy.'

'I've heard all about you, son,' said Ada, shuffling across.

'This is my mother-in-law, Ada. She's like a mother to me. This is Margaret and this is Barbara,' said Emily.

'So are you on convoy duty?' asked Ada.

'Yes. I'm doing much the same thing as your son did.'

'So you are the fellow I thought Emily might have hidden away in secret,' said Ada, pleased that her guesswork had been proved correct.

'I've been crossing the Atlantic for six months, so if it was me, I was well hidden,' confessed Andy.

'There's been nobody at all, mum, and you know it,' said Emily, as Ada smiled at her little leg-pulling.

'More importantly,' said Andy, 'I'm here now on dry land.'

'So when will you be back out at sea?' asked Ada.

'People always ask that as soon as you get home, but I should be in Liverpool for a month or so. I'm enrolled on a course in town and the ship is in dry dock. Now you know all my business,' said Andy.

'Where are you staying?'

'In the naval billets on Crosby Road.'

'Enough questions for now, mum,' insisted Emily. 'Andy will tell you everything you need to know. He's honest and true.'

Andy sensed that he'd spent enough time for his first meeting with the family. It would be for the kids, Ada and Emily to decide whether to accept him into their small tightly-knit family.

'Emily, I need to return to my digs, have another shower and tidy myself up for dinner. There's one or two things I'll need to do before evening.'

'That's alright, Andy,' Emily said. 'I'll see you later at the vicarage. It isn't dinner, Andy. It's just the best food we can lay our hands on. Hotpot.'

'The girls are delightful,' Andy whispered, as Emily showed him out. 'See you later then.'

Andy strode down the street towards the docks. Back at the house, Ada was most impressed with Andy.

'He's an excellent navy man. You've been lucky finding him like that. He's back in the thick of it, just like my Jim,' said Ada. 'We'll understand each other.'

'Yes. He's lovely, mum. I must try to be friends as long as possible,' said Emily.

'It'll be difficult for you to remain friends. You look too well together.'

'What makes you say that?'

'Well, he's waited almost a year since you first met. You're well suited.'

'Thanks, mum. I was just so worried that he would never return.'

'I don't think he'd ever do that. He thinks you're wonderful.'

'What makes you say that?'

'I can tell by lots of things; but really it's the way he looks at you.'

Emily didn't see Andy till much later, when she walked into the main lounge at the vicarage carrying a tray of small glasses of sherry. The vicar attempted to chat with all his guests before they assembled at the dining table. He spoke to all the first-time diners and felt that he had gauged just the right mix. The gathering was mostly civic dignitaries, local parishioners and men and women from the services. There was no end of topics to be discussed; the war, of course, the shortages, the losses and the Germans coming to a halt at Stalingrad. Was this the beginning of the end?

Andy fitted comfortably into the group. Emily joked about the number of glasses of sherry she was serving up. 'Good quality for wartime.'

'Dish it out, Emily. Legally acquired. No black market here,' said the vicar.

'No, Vicar. I just want the guests to taste the herbs in the dish,' said Emily.

'They will, Emily. The food will be delicious,' stated the vicar.

'Don't count on it, Vicar. Their taste buds will be numbed,' chided Emily.

The vicar felt obliged to reassure his guests, so he turned to them and said, 'Emily is only joking, of course.'

The diners trooped into the dining room and soon the conversation was loud and happy around the wide vicarage table. The diners asked Father Deegan about his trip to the desert.

'How was your trip to North Africa, Father?'

'I'm afraid it was top secret,' was his first quip. Then he added, 'Extremely hot.' Then, when pushed, he said, 'I spent most of my time in Oran, Algeria. My quarters were in a disused church near the port, surrounded by beautiful vineyards. The war raged just over the garden wall. I shall spare you details of my work.'

The father remained centre stage for most of the meal, even though he refused to be drawn into details of the job he had undertaken after the initial assault at Oran. The vicar tried to draw Andy into a discussion about Canada, once the father had mentioned that he had docked at Montreal. Andy felt rather shy in such ebullient company. He didn't relish entertaining the entire throng, unlike the clerics. The father repeated his story about the vicar's poor Inuit dialect and how, on occasions, he felt obliged to correct his grammar.

'So, Lieutenant?' the father addressed Andy. 'During your repeated visits to Nova Scotia, did you encounter the Inuit?'

'No, Father. I seldom left the ship or the harbour,' admitted Andy.

'It doesn't matter,' said the father. 'John here was fifteen years in the Arctic and Tundra, living with the Inuit, and he still mixes up his tenses.'

'It's because, Brendan, you are a linguist and I am a gardener. Is everybody enjoying the meal?' the vicar looked to the diners for praise.

'All the veg is extremely fresh and tasty, John,' came the reply from the town clerk, which was the answer the vicar had wanted to hear.

'See how John skilfully changes the subject,' whispered the father.

The town clerk genuinely loved the meal and made sure that he shook the hands of all the auxiliary workers.

'Thanks for keeping the town ticking over,' he said. 'We've to thank you men and women for keeping the docks open during the Blitz, when Hitler tried to close them down and sink every ship in the Mersey. Thanks, John, for bringing us all together. You are an excellent host.'

The vicar's rotund chest shot out still further with pride.

Soon, as the early evening turned to twilight, the gathering dispersed and split up in all directions, heading off to their ancillary jobs and families. There had been fewer raids recently, but everybody was still aware of the possibility.

Andy sat waiting for Emily, after having his offer of helping with the washing up declined. He sat in the study talking to the vicar. They could hear the clanging of pots and pans from across the hallway.

'Such a successful evening, vicar,' Andy felt obliged to record.

'Yes, it's one of my few wartime responsibilities, but an enjoyable one, to bring the community together. Make us all feel part,' said the vicar. 'I believe you will be staying ashore for the next month or so?'

'Yes, my ship is being given the once over in Harland's. I'm lodging down in the naval billets at Seaforth. I catch a train to town each morning to my course.'

'What sort of course is it?'

'Navigation, I suppose. All the methods of communication and detection of the enemy at our disposal. Basically, it's understanding all the instruments on the ship.'

'Are there many new gadgets these days?'

'Yes. Too many and all secret.'

'You are certainly welcome to come here for a meal any time you are up this way. You'll notice we pride ourselves on the best food in town,' said the vicar.

'That's an immense boast, Vicar,' said Andy.

'Yes; but it's true. All the vegetables are freshly grown.'

Emily appeared at the door. 'And scrubbed for hours by Bessie and me. We have gallons of black water to show for it.'

The vicar smiled and couldn't conceal his pride as Andy thanked him all over again.

'The meal was delicious, Vicar.'

Emily and Andy set off home. Emily waited until they were well clear of the church before she turned to Andy and amazed him by saying, 'And don't offer to do the washing up again.'

'I thought I was helping.'

'No, unlike me, who draws a salary, Bessie is paid by the hour. So we don't want your goodwill reducing Bessie's money do we? She's on the breadline as it is.'

'Suppose not.'

'If you do offer to help in future, work slowly. Hold a plate for ages in your tea towel and chat to me. Let Bessie get on with it.'

'Right, I'll dry up just like my sister does then.'

They reached the house. 'Are you coming in for a cup of tea then?'

The house was empty. The kids were still at Gran's. The fire smouldered in the grate; she placed just a shovelful of coke on the top. When she stood up again Andy handed her a box, which she opened to revealed the silken underwear that he had bought for her in St Johns, or was it Halifax?

'This is too good for me,' Emily said, saying the wrong thing.

'So you won't want these then?' he said, handing her a bag with six pairs of nylons inside.

This time Emily was excited, like a child given a bag of sweets.

'I don't know you well enough to be receiving stuff like this.' Emily kissed and hugged Andy for the first time. It felt so natural. It was as if they had been kissing and cuddling each other like this since they had met in Glasgow.

'Everybody gets nylons from sailors, don't they?'

Andy kissed Emily strongly on the lips. It was the first time after all.

'I'll come around as often as I can, now I'm in town. How about coming out to the cinema on Saturday night?' he suggested.

'That's an idea. Yes, I'll make the effort and go out for a change.'

'Tuesday evening is choir practice. We finish early, so I can come later. Why don't you join the choir?'

'Don't you think I see enough of the church? I'm tone deaf, too,' stated Emily.

'You can't be that bad.' He queried her assertion.

'The choir master used to tell me not to sing, but look as if I was.'

'That's ridiculous,' said Andy. 'Don't sing, but look as if you are. Is that yet another one of those ridiculous Liverpool states of affairs?'

'Afraid so. The choir master was ridiculous. I'll get the girls involved when they're old enough. Anyway, start your course and when you've settled into it we'll work on your social life. Your course may be exhausting,' said Emily.

'Suppose I've navigated a ship across the Atlantic. So I've some idea.' Then he thought about what he had actually made claim to. 'Okay, it was very much a case of following the rest of the convoy, with a genius breathing down my neck, pre-empting every move.'

'Andy, I'm sure you'll do wonderfully well on your course.'

Chapter 14

Back On Course

'and heard great argument about it and about:
but evermore came out the same door wherein I went.'

Omar Khayyam

Andy was looking forward to his course when he boarded the train
for Liverpool at Seaforth. The train was a mix of services and civilian
workers on their way to work in the city. Liverpool had started to
bubble with fresh life after surviving the heavy bombing of the Blitz
two years before. There were sailors on leave, office workers
heading into the centre and tired-looking factory workers returning
from night-shifts. The streets between Exchange Station and the
main HQ had been heavily bombed. Some buildings had completely vanished, others were burnt out and a few were down to just
their steel girders. There was a selection of pre-fabricated premises,
boarded up gaps in walls and displayless shop windows. People were
still eager to get on with life and ignored the shortcomings as they
went about their daily lives.

Most of the lectures on Andy's course were practical hands-on
experience of new instruments, which took place in a purpose-built
complex of Nissen huts, near the centre of town. There was further
heavy equipment in one of the warehouses in dockland and the
lectures on strategy took place on the top floor of the Western
Approaches HQ in Derby House. Andy looked upon the course as a
chance to better himself and hoped something would come from
the three weeks of his involvement.

The first week was mostly radio. All the standard techniques were studied and the lecturer, although probably the most miserable fellow Andy had ever encountered, knew his stuff. His lectures were repetitive, but the hands-on experience was first class. He was able to make Andy understand for the first time where all the bits and pieces fitted into the chain of command. He realised that in future he should choose his words carefully when transmitting messages, just in case there were people listening secretly to him. Everyday the general public were ear-wigging into many supposedly secret messages that flowed around the port and up and down the estuary. The staid lecturer would refer to the loose chatter as 'material for ITMA'. It was his only joke.

During the first week they visited the dock; Andy was hoping it wasn't his ship, Buzzard, that would feature in the scheme of things. Fortunately, they were invited aboard another sloop, Swallow, freshly down from the Clyde as a replacement for one of their heavily damaged ships. The radio officer was a huge Scot, nearly seven foot tall and almost as broad in build. He certainly knew his stuff and Andy noticed that his equipment wasn't as good as the equipment on the Buzzard. It was great to get out of their Nissen hut and see how other ships organised their radio rooms.

Tuesday evening saw Andy making sure he didn't miss choir practice at seven o'clock. The choir master, Geoffrey, was referred to as 'Mister Spencer' by the choir-boys. He listened intently as each hymn was sung, then he endeavoured to make sure that the phraseology and meaning were successfully conveyed by the choristers.

The first hymn was a favourite, *My Song is Love Unknown*. The choir sang it with relish, before Geoffrey took it apart, making sure that the meaning was not lost in the general love of the melody.

'The first verse includes probably my favourite phrase in a hymn, lines three and four,' Geoffrey announced as all the choir members looked at their hymn books.

'Love to the loveless shown that they might lovely be.' They all read it to themselves. 'At the moment you are all enjoying the beautiful melody and are losing the meaning. So this time sing, just sing "Love to the loveless shown".' The organist played the sentence and they all sang it.

'Now this time sing "that they might lovely be" and mean it ... and mean it. Don't just croon it, like Bing.'

They sang the line and then the whole verse, attempting to convey Geoffrey's insight without sounding like Bing. After repeating the hymn Geoffrey was satisfied that he had pursued his objectives as far as he was able and moved on to the next hymn, *The Day Thou Gavest , Lord, is Ended.*

'Now, Andy, you will understand the sentiments in this hymn better than most, such as verse 4, "The sun that bids us rest is waking our brethren' neath the western sky". Now, Andy, you must feel as if you are singing about your family in Australia on the other side of the world.'

Andy could see the young choir-boys hanging on every word, so he verified Geoffrey's observation.

'Of course, Mister Spencer. The words do make me think of home and also my sailor friends over the other side of the Atlantic.'

The children were impressed with his answer. Andy was a real sailor after all.

Come the next Saturday, Andy went with Emily and her two girls to Southport for a day out of the city. He pushed the pram with both kids aboard down along the front. Most of the entertainments were closed, with slot machines that had been empty since before the war, but there were still one or two cafés struggling to keep open. The beach stretched out as far as the eye could see in every direction, with no water in sight. They wandered through the fairground, which was mostly shut; some kiosks looked as if they'd never opened. There was a small café which was selling sandwiches, so Andy joined the queue. The choice was cheese sandwiches, take it or leave it.

Emily whispered in Andy's ear, 'Go to the woman at the end with the big heavy knife,' which he did.

When he returned he asked Emily, 'Why that particular woman?'

'She looked as if she enjoys her food, so you'd get a better sandwich.'

'Oh, I'm not so sure,' he said before they opened the sandwiches to eat and saw the cheese just ooze out of the sandwich from the café.

'God. There must be about half a pound of cheese in this sandwich,' he said.

'You're kidding,' said Emily.

'Well, almost,' decided Andy.

'I told you who would give the most generous portions,' smiled Emily.

Monday morning saw Andy back on his course. This week it was asdic and radar. The two lecturers were in complete contrast. The asdic operator was quite chubby, covered in sweat and smelt of rum, while the radar man was tiny, rather scrawny and white-skinned, even though he had lived in Bombay for most of his life. Neither man had a sense of humour. Andy noted that none of the lecturers so far had told a joke; except just the one from the radio lecturers. Maybe it was the requirement of the job to be deadly serious. Both men knew their stuff and Andy learnt that it was best not to ask questions as the answers other people received were often very complicated and confused them still further.

Towards the end of the week they visited the Swallow again, in Gladstone. The huge Scottish radio officer was on hand to answer questions and show them around so they could develop an understanding of how the instruments were installed in the different vessels. Later, they were taken to the partially bombed warehouse now used to train up sailors from the merchant fleet, and spent many hours gaining hands-on experience of the instruments. At the end of the session they were introduced to some of the new tracking devices that would be installed soon in the latest additions to the fleet. Andy found them a lot faster than the old gear, because they cut out a lot of the personal calculations, usually made on the faithful slide-rule.

'Some of these instruments make your equipment as effective as the "bow and arrow".'

Andy couldn't see the boss falling over with enthusiasm for the 'newfangled gadgets'. He had his own rule of thumb techniques and basic instincts, which seldom came unstuck. Andy could see why the boss always insisted on speed and accuracy. Andy would choose the boss over the new gadgets every time, purely on confidence.

Choir practice on Tuesday was special. The young lads loved singing *Eternal Father Strong to Save,* and looked across at Andy when they sang out 'for those in peril on the sea'. Andy wasn't going to dispel the myth and say 'Actually, it's calm'. Afterwards, Andy was invited to Emily's for supper. He had Emily laughing at the thought of all the humourless tutors, the boss's take on 'newfangled gadgets' and who he would rather be at sea with in a force 9. Then he mentioned the trips out to the dock. How he'd manage to avoid his ship and how they'd found the huge Scot on the Swallow more use at times than the stuffy tutors back at the course centre. Emily didn't hear him first time; she was preparing food.

'Anyway, this huge Scot, I think his name is Calum, comes from my family's happy hunting ground of Skye.'

'What did you say the ship was called?'

'The Swallow. It is berthed at Gladstone.' Emily was speechless.

'What is it, Em?'

'That's Jimmy's old ship, the Swallow. I think that's his footballing friend.'

'He's a massive guy. Loads of knowledge of the instruments.'

'He played for Queen's Park before the war. I'd love to meet him.'

'Maybe I'll talk him into coming over.'

The final ten days of the course were the busiest part of the scheme. There was the Specialist Navigation section, when students on the course were expected to have reached a certain level of mathematics. Those who hadn't spent the evenings doing extra maths to catch up. Andy was pleased that at last there was some credit given to his degree. Some days there were only himself and a fellow from Manchester sitting in the lectures, as they were the only ones capable of performing the trigonometry.

The tutor was full of simple advice, such as, 'Make sure your slide-rule is always functioning and at night, make sure you can read off the calculations in whatever light is available.' With this in mind, he inspected each of the slide-rules in use and advised Andy and his Mancunian colleague to purchase a better model. 'Your life might depend on it. Larger numbers, sharper lines and try reading it in the dark.' However, when it came to suggesting where they could purchase a better model he was less forthcoming. 'Try Philips, Son and Nephew,' he just said.

Andy smiled when the Mancunian said, 'Sounds like a family firm.'

Andy guessed that Philips was still in Whitechapel if not bombed out. With this in mind, he sought out a local sailor. The most social place to ask was 'Smokers' Corner', which was a moveable feast, because, even though everybody smoked, it was frowned upon. Some lecturers would use the expression 'you may smoke' almost like a Christmas present or year's bonus, so most sailors smoked behind turned backs.

Andy was lucky. He walked straight into a ginger-headed scouser, who seemed to be always with a bunch of wrens, which were his main interest in life.

'Where would I purchase a slide-rule in Liverpool?'

'Philips, Son and Nephew.'

'Is it still in Whitechapel or have they been bombed out like everybody else?'

'Yes, just on the corner. They're still doing business,' said the smoker.

'You seem to be okay with the wrens.'

'I'd like to say it's my life's study, but it's Cynthia. She's in the wrens and we're not supposed to socialise, on duty at least, but we find ways around it. Mostly getting as far away as we can, out of sight, out of mind, out of hours, out of uniform. Cynthia's my girlfriend,' said the ginger-headed sailor.

Andy felt more comfortable with his new, clearer slide-rule. He'd had difficulty in the shop, trying to test it in dark conditions. The assistant thought he was trying to thieve it and couldn't understand why he needed to be able to read it in the dark. The main disadvantage was that the tutor could read off the sharper numbers over his shoulder at a distance. What's new? he thought. The boss is just as bad. It did, however, sharpen up his resolve and accuracy. The tutor, true to form, lacked a sense of humour, even when defining the opposite side of a triangle.

'It's quite like Tarzan in his latest adventure. He props open the croc's mouth with a stick and has all these crocodiles swimming around the river with their mouths propped open. Well, the stick that Tarzan has wedged inside is the "opposite side" in relation to the open mouth.'

It was certainly an easy way to remember it, but at no time did the tutor show any indication that he saw any humour in a situation that had sorry crocodiles swimming around a river with their mouths propped open. Andy smiled to himself behind a straight, serious face. The man's too serious for words, he thought.

Andy was growing in confidence and started to realise why the boss had sent him on the course. The tutor concentrated more on accuracy and showed how the tiniest angle could lead to such a large deviation in distance. They measured minute inaccuracies at distances of a yard, ten yards, one hundred yards and a thousand yards so they could see how a very tiny difference led to such a huge inaccuracies.

'The two essentials are speed and accuracy.'

Andy was beginning to enjoy his mathematics, appreciating afresh why he had always enjoyed the subject. He decided there and then, in the middle of a navy lecture in Liverpool, that he would try to start teaching mathematics after the war, if he was still around, because it was his thing. At least after all this lot, with the boss breathing down my neck, I'll be able to think on my feet.

Later in the week they were assembled in the technical unit on the top floor to listen to the boss give a one-off lecture on the tactics to be used in convoys and in the location of U-boats. To say he knew his stuff would be an understatement, because a lot of the methods outlined were invented and practised by his group. In these lectures they used small wooden blocks in the shape of various ships. Andy knew that it was not so much a case of him not asking questions, it was more a straight fact that he should 'button it' completely when the 'old man' was on his feet. The boss covered the general overview of operating in convoys. How to locate the enemy; how to destroy the enemy. Avoidance techniques, while you planned your next move. Much of his talk was about instinct. How to develop it and second-guess the enemy; what to always be on the look out for. He even divulged one or two 'rules of thumb' in mental arithmetic, at which he was much quicker than anybody else in the room. Nobody was left in any doubt about his knowledge of the subject.

After the lecture the boss whispered to Andy as he left the room.

'Lieutenant Ritchie, thanks for not asking any questions. I think you must have been tempted to put me on the spot, because I don't always follow my own principles. You'll know that I often just sniff the enemy out. So far I've failed to think of a way of teaching that skill. Thanks for not disclosing that you've seen me lose a few bets in the past. Don't get too carried away with some of these newfangled gadgets, they are not worth a place on my ship. I use tried and tested methods, mostly my instinct, and it's never let me down so far. Our results are second to none.'

Later the same day, members of the course returned to Gladstone and visited the Swallow again. Andy wasted no time in seeking out Calum.

'You'll have known Jimmy Jones, of course?' Andy said.

'Jimmy? Our favourite football coach? How do you know him?'

'He used to live in Liverpool.'

'Yes, he did. The team have never been as good since he was killed in that stupid accident on the Clyde.'

'His widow, Emily, would like to meet you,' Andy said.

'That's right. She was called Emily.'

'She works for a vicar. So she suggests that you could come up to see her at the vicarage. Maybe this Sunday?'

'Certainly. What time?'

'Let's say around lunchtime. You might be lucky and get some lunch. Do you like scouse?' Andy asked.

Calum smiled, 'I'll look forward to it.'

On the Saturday before Calum's visit, Emily and Andy set off for a day out by themselves without the family. It was to prove a good opportunity to talk about everything. They talked about his family in Australia and how 'itchy feet' were in his genes, and Emily told Andy all about the plans she and Jimmy had to emigrate to Canada as soon as he'd passed all his accountancy exams. Andy concluded that maybe it wasn't just his family, maybe it was their generation who were restless.

They caught the number 70 bus to Sefton Church, because it was the nearest stretch of country to where they lived. Fortunately, the Punchbowl was open and had some beer on tap.

'That's great,' said Emily. 'Last time I was in a country pub they only opened for two hours in the evening and they were rationing the beer.'

'Things must be looking up,' said Andy.

'Well, it was during the Blitz,' said Emily.

'You were lucky if the pub wasn't on fire,' added Andy.

They drank half a mild each at the bar and set out on their planned long hike, past the farm where Emily had spent a few nights camping two years previously.

She pointed out the trees under which they had sheltered from the wind. Then they tramped across country to Thornton on the road to Southport and cut through Little Crosby, before finally following the road to Sniggery Wood.

At the edge of the wood, Andy asked Emily for the first time, 'Will you marry me, Emily?'

Emily was half expecting it from the way they behaved together.

'I hardly know you,' she lied. 'Besides, there's a war on.'

'I just thought that we'd be better to emigrate to Australia or Canada together rather than do it separately,' said Andy.

'But we can't emigrate in the middle of a war,' said Emily.

'You always wanted to emigrate to Canada. I can't go to Australia with my family spread all the way along the east coast, so maybe I should go to Canada too.'

'What's the sudden rush?' asked Emily. 'It's as if the war will finish next week.' There was a long silence as they walked deeper into the woods. Emily turned and faced Andy. 'It doesn't mean you can't kiss me, though,' she said.

They kissed long and strongly before Andy repeated his plea.

'Please marry me, Emily.'

'Please wait and have a bit of patience,' Emily muttered. 'We'll get the war out of the way first. We can plan the future later. I love the idea of escaping to Canada. The vicar talks about nothing else, apart from gardening. "If I was a young person etc". The two of you can't be wrong.'

'So you do think about it?'

'Of course I do; but only as unfinished business. We always wanted to emigrate for the kids' sake. Give them a better start than we ever had. We were never really sure whether it should be Australia or Canada. Jimmy reckoned it would be where he could find a decent job.'

Emily pondered as they followed the path out of the wood and finished up at Hall Road railway station. They looked over the sand dunes towards the sea and shared a sandwich perched on a concrete wall.

'Just one guess what the sandwich is.'

'Cheese?'

'Yes, national cheese and the vicar's beetroot, specially pickled by me.'

After their tiny lunch and cup of tea from Emily's tired old flask they waited on the empty platform for the next train back to town. When it arrived they squeezed inside another packed carriage just inside the sliding doors and stood up all the way back along the track to Marsh Lane.

Calum appeared at the vicarage at lunchtime the next day. The vicar, who was just returning from matins, answered the door. He thought that Calum was one of his guests arriving rather early for the hotpot supper.

'Sorry, you are rather early. The hotpot is at four.'

'I've come to ask after a Mrs Emily Jones,' Calum explained.

'My housekeeper,' noted the Vicar. 'Who do I say?'

'Lieutenant Calum Kennedy.'

'Is she expecting you?' the Vicar asked.

'I think so,' said Calum, as Emily came rushing out.

She looked at the mountain of a man and knew, immediately, that it must be Calum off the Swallow. She led him through to the kitchen and sat him in the comfy chair all visitors occupied near the door, looking out over the extensive kitchen garden.

'Those are still from the same potato seed that Jimmy fetched back two years ago.'

'I remember seeing him struggling to carry the sack to the train,' said Calum.

They were soon deep in conversation about Jimmy. Calum told her all about the difficulties they had locating a suitable football pitch near the port.

'The main problem was craters and barrage balloons. We once had to erect some goalposts ourselves before we could play a game,' Calum said.

'Were you with him when he died?' Emily asked.

'No, I wasn't. He was out in the whaler. He never liked the trips. He didn't like some of the disgusting jobs they were expected to perform,' said Calum.

'Was he happy before it happened then?'

'Yes, I think he was happy. We were planning a few matches and he was pleased with the way we were playing.'

'No. Was he homesick? Was he lonely?'

'We're all homesick most of the time. I'm homesick for Skye at the moment. It's all this sitting around on a ship just waiting at the other end of the country. We think of home and shed a few tears. We just find something to occupy our minds. That's why we played football, it took our minds off the war,' said Calum.

'So you spent some time together?'

'We spent lots of time together; good times and bad times. I miss him terribly, Emily,' said Calum, with a tear in his eye. 'I miss having a friend to confide in, to enjoy a laugh with over a drink or two. I've been lonely aboard ship ever since. Organising the team without Jimmy just isn't the same. He used to write my name down first on the team sheet. I've nobody to share a joke with. He's still somewhere in the cabin.'

Emily was overcome at the thought of such a hardened sailor, like Calum, being so sensitive about her man, Jimmy. A tear spilt down her cheek, when she noticed Calum's eyes filling as he said' 'He thought of you and the girls every day.'

'I still miss him every day,' she whispered.

Calum was going to agree, but the tears in his eyes said it all and no further words came out.

Much later in the afternoon, at the hotpot supper, Calum was the centre of attention. He was a born and bred Highlander, so this brought the other Scots out of hiding and they let rip with their mature lowland accents. Father Deegan noted the distinct differences in their dialects and the absence of a Glasgow tongue.

'This is excellent. There are many Scottish dialects but nobody confessing to be from Glasgow,' said the father, fuelling an argument as to who spoke most like a Glaswegian. Nobody wanted to be accredited the distinction.

'We can't complain,' said the vicar. 'Who confesses to being a scouser?' There was a silence before Father Deegan owned up.

'I'm from Liverpool,' said the father.

'So am I,' said Warren Golding, the doctor.

'Neither of you speaks thick scouse,' said Calum.

'Wot yess mean by dat?' asked Warren.

'Don't get Warren started on his Frisby Dyke impersonation or we'll be here for the duration,' warned the vicar.

Chapter 15

The Street

'There's a tavern in the town.'

Anon.

Colin Mack was walking past old Flo's backyard when he heard groans and crying coming from inside the outside WC. This was followed by soft pleas, 'Help, help me somebody'. He didn't know what to do so he knocked on Emily's door.

'What is it, Colin?' asked Emily.

'I think Flo is in trouble in the lavatory.'

'What makes you think that?'

'She's crying inside. I think it's her. She said "Help me".'

'Where did you say, Colin?' asked Emily. 'In the outside loo?'

They ran around the corner and then back up the back entry passageway, concentrating on their footwork. 'Watch out for dog muck, Colin. It's like a minefield.' There wasn't a sound coming from inside the toilet. 'Was it this house, Colin?'

'Yes Emily,' Colin confirmed.

Emily tried the door tentatively. 'Flo! Flo! Are you alright in there?' There was no answer. Emily tried to open the door but it was wedged solid. 'Help me, Colin.'

They pushed and Emily managed to glimpse Flo lying down flat on the floor of the toilet.

'I think she's dead.'

Just then, Bessie came running down the passageway.

'Good job you've come.'

They both forced their way inside and managed to sit Flo back on to the toilet seat. 'Flo! Flo!' they took it in turns to plead.

'She's dead,' pronounced Emily, with tears in her eyes.

Bessie was experienced at raising a gang, she knew everybody who lived in the neighbourhood. So she recruited a band of keen, and not so keen, helpers to come and put their shoulders to the wheel. At first the recruits stood peering into the toilet, watching Emily and Bessie making the best of an awkward job, covering Flo in a respectable blanket.

'Stand back everybody, you're missing nothing,' which only made them think they were missing something and peer in all the more.

The bookie's runner, Leonard, was standing out in the street with a face on him like a battered arse, because a small crowd had by now assembled in his favourite spot for sheltering from the wind and rain. Nonetheless, within the half hour, Flo had been carried into her house and laid out on the bed upstairs, awaiting the doctor. Doctor Warren Golding soon arrived and was dressed in a long black coat and what looked like a black cowboy hat, the sort worn by the 'baddies' at the flicks. He examined Flo, sighing a great deal, before making a few notes and returning downstairs.

'Was anybody with the deceased when she died?'

'Hardly, Doctor. She was in the outside toilet,' said Emily.

'What did she die of, Doctor?' asked Bessie.

'She died of old age, probably a weak heart,' Doctor Golding said simply.

'Bessie and I will do the necessary, Doctor. She was a spinster.'

'That's good of you, ladies. Is she a relative?'

'No, we are all good neighbours around here.'

'We give everybody in the street a good send off.'

Warren Golding buttoned up his black coat, touched his hat and said, 'Good afternoon, ladies.'

He then placed his black case in the passenger seat, started up the car and drove off down the street.

'When I die, I hope I've lived a full life like Flo,' said Emily.

'Behopes you have, because you'll be in sheer agony if you are still alive,' said Bessie.

Emily made no attempt to try to make out what Bessie was trying to say, so she gave up and settled on watching the black car turn right at the end of the street and move out into the traffic.

'The doctor's nice,' said Bessie.

'Showing an interest in men at last. Warren Golding? Keep your eyes off him; we don't want any mixed marriages here,' said Emily.

'I'm only looking at his handsome black cowboy suit. He looks like a sheriff.'

'Besides, he's Jewish.'

'Is that Catholic or Protestant?' asked Bessie.

Emily ignored the comment.

'I think Flo had a good innings, didn't she?' said Emily. 'By now they'll be signing her in at the Pearly Gates.'

'That sounds like a pub along Scottie Road.'

The black market was thriving more and more as the war progressed and luxury goods became harder to acquire. There was a shortage of almost everything and rationing restricted honest endeavour. Liverpool had many undercover activities flourishing and spivs abounded. Liverpool had the extra facility of imports from the USA, trafficked in by traders wanting to make larger profits, merchant sailors on the make or just simply organised thieving from the docks or warehouses.

Locally, trade fell into the latter category. Freddie Mack operated at the lowest level in the chain. He stuck to just cheap nylons, contraceptives and clothing coupons, counterfeit or stolen, and made enough money to keep himself in drink and cigarettes and banish poverty from the door. Every now and then he would receive a batch of goods from the Brennan brothers, who traded at a much higher level than the locally restricted Freddie. The old problem remained when receiving goods from the Brennans. There was always far too much to move in one shift and storage was impossible for Freddie. He had limited floor space and lacked the muscle to manhandle it any distance. He had to sell the goods overnight.

All the locals would point Freddie out to whoever asked. He was the one who would have the latest gadget or most unusual brand of American cigarettes. Freddie used to swagger and wander around casually as if he was a Yank. People used to joke, 'Look at Fred with his posh cigarettes, he thinks he's Edward G. Robinson.'

Bessie loved to bait him in the Blobber whenever she had a chance in her songs. It always earned an enthusiastic response from the punters, so Bessie figured that she was right to keep it in the act. She was just finishing the *Ball of Kerrymuir* when she saw Freddie come in with his batch of nylons, so she added a few lines to her song. She sang:

'Oh Missus McInty she was there sitting at the back.
Knitting contraceptives for sale by Freddie Mack.
Singing I'll do yer noo sir ...'

She continued singing through her usual lewd programme with her shrewd and irreverent comments on life in the local community.

'Two old queers in a fold in the bed
One turned over to the other and said
"Yes we have no bananas. We have no bananas today"
Two old queers in a fold in the bed
One turned over to the other and said
"I've got a lovely bunch of coconuts."'

Bessie continued her melody of lewd songs. At this juncture, young Colin Mack, who had a part-time job in the bar collecting glasses, turned to his father and asked, 'Dad, when are we going to buy a new bed. They'll be singing about us next.'

'Shut up, stupid,' Freddie scowled.

Bessie carried on singing, ignorant of the offence caused.

'There's six in a bed at the old Pier Head and it's Liverpool town for me.'

Freddie left the pub with young Colin, looking disgusted. Gordon, the publican, came across to Bessie as soon as she'd finished her session at the piano.

'What's wrong , Gordon? Am I emptying your pub?'

'You've upset Freddie Mack and young Colin. Freddie lost a bed in the Blitz, when he had an incendiary through his roof.'

'Hasn't he replaced the bed yet? He's plenty of money from what he sells stashed away in that house. I was bombed out twice in the Blitz and I replaced my bed. Some can take a joke. People call me "fat arse". I don't cry.'

'Yes, but Colin's getting a big lad now and since he returned from evacuation they've been sleeping in the double bed together.'

'Why should that affect my choice of songs? Fred's got tons of money hidden away in his house; burglars can't find it. He should buy a bed for the lad. How am I expected to know he is sensitive? He probably doesn't know what a queer is. I was just singing the old sailors' shanty *Six in a Bed at the Old Pier Head*.'

'What about Mrs McInty?'

'She shouldn't be knitting them and he shouldn't be selling them.'

'And you shouldn't be singing about it, either.'

Freddie's house lacked a woman's touch; it was dog rough. The curtains were old, full of moth holes and hung appallingly. The walls were plain colour-washed; the bedrooms and backyard lime-washed. The unwashed linen on the bed could be smelt at a distance. It was an all-male establishment and looked rather like a barrack room in appearance. Tasks such as dusting, washing and ironing were never performed.

There was just one double bed in the house. Freddie had never got around to replacing the bed incinerated in the Blitz. Freddie and Colin slept back to back.

Father and son communicated a lot with each other as they only had each other in the world. They rejoiced in vehement discussion, particularly when they lay back to back, looking out at the white walls. Debate was often heated and quarrelling was expected and regarded as the norm for dealings within their minute family.

'When are we going to buy another bed?' Colin asked.

'When I get fed up of feeling like Stan and Ollie,' said the inebriated Freddie.

'They're singing about us in the pub now.'

'That's only Fat Bessie. She's plain ignorant. Sing anything for six pence.'

'Everybody laughed.'

'When you get older I'll tell you what an old queer is. We're not like that.'

'I need my own bed,' pleaded Colin.

'Earn the money first. Be told and be satisfied. How much does Gordon pay you for doing glasses?'

'A shilling a time and one and six if I do all day Saturday,' said Colin.

'Daylight robbery. Gordon Penn is as deep and dirty as the Mersey. I was at school with the thief. Even in those days he could fetch a ciggie out of his pocket already lit.'

Memories came flooding back with the beer inside him.

'Why would he want to do that?' asked Colin, after thinking about it.

'Suffering kids. S'pose it's my job as father to explain things,' he conceded. 'He was too tight to pass the cigarettes around. So he lit one first, when nobody was looking.'

The booze did the explaining.

'Oohhh,' said Colin as the penny dropped.

'Now he's got you running in and out that bar washing every glass because he can't be bothered buying more glasses. Tight bastard,' decided Freddie.

'Gordon says there's a war on.'

'I had noticed.'

'Is it difficult?'

'What? Buying glasses?'

'No. Lighting a cigarette in your pocket.'

'How the hell do I know, stupid?' There was a silence, followed by a question. 'I hope you're not thinking of trying it.' Then another silence. 'You'll burn your balls off next.'

'You know you sell Durex, Dad. Why do they call them rubbers?'

'Jesus wept,' said Freddie in exasperation.

'Why did he weep, Dad?' Colin wondered.

'Jesus, Mary and Joseph,' said Freddie now at the end of his tether.

'The Holy Family? Why them?' asked Colin.

'Okay then, try this for size. Jesus cried his friggin' eyes out.'

Freddie needed to relieve himself, so he went to the front window and peed out into the front street, shutting the window when he'd finished.

'Why do you do that, Dad?'

Freddie paused to think.

'Suppose it's the force of gravity. Maybe we need a guzunder. Besides, it's a long way to the khazi when you've a weak bladder. Besides, get some sleep. You'll be running in and out of that pub tomorrow, like the ARP with his arse on fire, earning every penny of your one and six.'

Emily's young daughter, Margaret, had learnt her first hymn at Sunday school. She was sitting on the back step singing away. Repeating the same line over and over.

'Yes, Jesus loves me. Yes, Jesus loves me. The Bible tells me so.'

'Is there another verse, Margaret? Or is that all you know?' asked Emily.

Freddie was ear-wigging over the backyard wall, inspecting his hens.

'It's nice to hear you singing away like that, Margaret. I used to go to church a long time ago,' he shouted to the little girl. 'After I became a Catholic there were less hymns, more Latin and many more priests and brothers.'

'Didn't know you were a Catholic, Fred,' said Emily.

'Yes, I'm left-footed, Emily,' he said. 'Changing the subject, I won on the horses yesterday. Got you a nice large tin of salmon.'

Emily gazed over the wall at Freddie toiling in the hen-pen.

'Yes, please, Fred. Is it that Canadian stuff?' asked Emily.

'And some pineapple for the kiddies.'

Freddie handed the two bulky tins over the wall to Emily. It was just like Christmas. Emily placed the two luxury items in the larder. Looking at the labels she could see the salmon was indeed from Canada and the fruit was from Florida, USA. It never crossed Emily's mind as to how Freddie came about them. Maybe he was just lucky on the horses.

Outside, Freddie continued with his task of feeding the hens, while Colin propped up the wall of the hen-pen. However, he did move his feet so his father could rake the floor of the hen-run and scatter fresh ashes from the kitchen grate.

'Colin, you are neither use nor ornament. Here, feed the hens.'

'Dad,' said Colin. 'Gordon Penn calls you a denizen.'

'Gordon Penn?' said Freddie. 'There but for the grace of God, goes God.'

'Churchill said that,' added Colin.

'Be told, Colin. I had enough of your intellect last night.'

Does denizen mean you wear false teeth?'

'For crying out loud. It means "alien". If you want to know that's what tight-arse, Gordon, used to call me at school, 'cos I was a new kid down from Glasgow. The last time Gordon put his hand in his pocket, it was to play pocket billiards.'

'How did he .... do ... that?' Colin was confused.

'Suffering tantalising, suffering duck. Why the buggeration of the vestal virgins do you need to know?'

Later, in the living room, Freddie was organising his stocks of Durex and nylons. Both sold like mad to the Yanks, although they sold easily to the servicemen. Local girls were always looking for cheap nylons. Freddie was currently counting his stock of contraceptives, which he sold around the pubs.

'And, Colin, don't accept any clothing coupons on the cheap. They're a waste of time and effort. Somebody is on the fiddle.'

'It was Gordon Penn who gave them to me!' said Colin.

'Certainly not from him. They were obviously forged. Nobody would accept them. I could make better ones with a kiddies' John Bull Printing Kit,' stated Freddie.

'He said they were the genuine item,' said Colin.

'They were the wrong colour. The stuff they use for bus tickets. Even you know clothing coupons were never purple and orange.'

Freddie lost count and had to count his stuff again. He'd get Colin to check through.

'Tell me how many in that pile.'

Colin counted. 'Twenty-six, twenty-seven ... No twenty ...'

'Colin. You are like a fart in a trance. Count them properly.'

'Charlie came into the class late,' said Colin, 'and said to Mister Porter, "Can I do you now, sir?" Everybody laughed. Mister Porter caned him. Gave him two of the best on the bottom.'

'I'd cane him, too, if he couldn't count,' stated Freddie.

'Mister Porter didn't know it was Mrs Mopp off ITMA. Said he didn't listen to such rubbish and didn't find it at all funny. Charlie didn't find it funny, either.'

'Is that the end of your story?' asked Freddie.

'Yes.'

'Thanks for that. How many nylons in that pile?' he watched his son counting.

'Twenty-four,' said Colin.

'Twenty-four?' Freddie was amazed. 'There's about a dozen.'

'Yes,' said Colin. 'Enough for twelve ladies. Two each.'

'Haven't you been counting them in pairs?' asked Freddie

'No,' said Colin with confidence. 'You counted the Durex singly.'

'I wish I'd used a packet of these.' Freddie brandished a packet of contraceptives across the table at Colin's face.

'You wouldn't have had me.'

'At last we are on the same wave-length,' stuttered Freddie.

'So can we tune in to ITMA on the radio after all?' asked Colin.

Chapter 16

The Mayor's Parlour

'An dreamin' arl the time of Plymouth Hoe.'

Sir Henry John Newbolt

Bessie was carrying out her duties as a cleaner in the town hall, unaware that she would soon be playing a tiny role in the history of Liverpool. She'd spent the morning cleaning the council chamber, before moving over into the mayor's parlour, just to give it the once over. She thought that she would start by replacing all the furniture in its correct position. The furniture in the far corner was completely scattered all over the floor. She walked across and found a naval gentleman with his legs resting on the coffee table, snoring away, fast asleep. Must have been a good night, she thought, just before he opened his eyes.

'Sorry if I woke you,' she apologised.

'No, I was awake already,' the officer jabbered with a yawn.

'So, you are the naval commander that they all talk about?' asked Bessie.

'No, I've just spent days without sleep, hunting U-boats.'

'That's good. I'm glad somebody does it. My friend Emily's husband was killed at sea,'

Bessie cleaned around the officer.

'Oh, what ship?'

'I don't know. She's on widow's pension now; but she has a good job as the housekeeper at the vicarage, where I work. What sort of ship are you on?'

'A Royal Navy sloop.'

177

'See, that was a waste of time asking. I don't know one boat from another.'

'Most people don't.'

He studied Bessie polishing the coffee table. He was so intent on watching her work, she thought she'd give him one or two hints.

'You see those white marks? They're left by wet glasses. I'll have to find some Brasso for them. It cleans the white off.'

'Don't you use Brasso for the brasses?' he asked.

'Yes. Do you use it on your ship?'

'Just a bit these days. Most of the decor is strictly utility. We keep polish away from the delicate instruments. We are a destroyer, out to kill U-boats. All our equipment is in constant use. It doesn't need bulling-up.'

She changed the subject.

'When we see sailors coming ashore they always walk as if they've just stepped off a banana boat. They wobble all over the place,' she said.

'That's true, of course. It takes some time to accustom yourself to the solid ground. Land legs have to be acquired gradually. The ocean can be extremely rough.'

Just then, the mayor popped his head into his parlour to see how his guest's little nap was progressing. He was amazed to hear Bessie chattering away.

'Bessie, I told you not to disturb the commander,' he said.

'She didn't, Stan,' said the officer.

'No, Mr Mayor. He woke me out of my stupor,' said Bessie.

'Don't tell me that you have been grabbing forty winks on your job?' he asked.

'No, Mr Mayor, when I said stupor, I meant in the sense that you've got to be stupid to work here.'

Bessie was at her inarticulate best; a subtle cross between plain ignorance and humour.

'I'm just in a trance.' Listeners either laughed or gave up.

'I love the Liverpool sense of humour. People looking for a laugh,' said the officer, smiling at Bessie's wild use of language.

178

'Either it's a sense of humour or we are all just loopy.' said the mayor.

Bessie cleaned around them while they talked and then, finally, she was introduced to the officer and they shook hands.

'I'm sorry for preventing you getting on, but I haven't slept for thirty hours.'

'Good heavens. It was like that in the Blitz,' said Bessie.

'Bessie works at the vicarage, where we'll be dining later,' said the mayor.

'It'll probably be chicken hotpot again. The vicar rears the hens for the pot, because they are such bad layers. We give the chicken scouse a long bake in the oven, add extra gravy and brown the potatoes up,' Bessie enthused.

'It sounds delicious,' said the mayor.

Bessie neared the door and turned around to address the officer.

'Mr Mayor is easily pleased,' she said.

Bessie could not wait to tell Emily all about her morning's work down at the town hall. Emily was just glad to see her back, because the panic was on.

'Thank God you are here. The vicar is rushing about all over the place. We've a very important visitor this afternoon. The mayor is bringing some big-wigs from the Royal Navy along. I've never seen the vicar so happy since Jimmy fetched the spuds.'

'I wonder if one of them is the fellow I saw sleeping in the mayor's parlour?'

'Hardly. Not going to be one of the most famous sailors in Liverpool history is he? Can't be one of the top men, can he?' said Emily.

'Suppose not, because he was hard on; not been to bed for thirty hours. He was tired out; kept on yawning. Said he went out chasing U-boats,' said Bessie.

'Well, that can't be them then. The big-wigs don't go out on to the ocean. They just stay at home here in Liverpool in big, posh offices and contact the ships by radio. The special guest is coming along with the mayor. So we'll be able to tell from that,' Emily suggested.

The vicar popped his head into the kitchen to check that everything was going to plan.

'Have you told Bessie about the special guests?' he asked.

'Yes, Bessie has met one of the officers coming this afternoon.'

The dinner party got underway. There were more guests than usual. It was the largest hotpot supper the vicar had ever arranged. The evenings were drawing out and there was less fear of the meal being foreshortened by an air-raid. All the guests were still eating and talking after eight o'clock. It was beginning to be like old times, where people were able to relax in the evening. Emily and Bessie were run off their feet, but they'd prepared double the normal amount of food, so there was little chance of them running out.

Father Deegan brought out some of his own special vintage red Algerian wine.

'I brought it with me from Oran and encountered the most difficulty getting it out of Canada. The grapes grew in the vineyard next to my accommodation, oblivious to it being a battlefield.' He paused for thought. 'A lot of our lads perished in the vineyard. We should remember that, when we say grace. It's really a unique wine. The vintner said it was so sad that such a rich crop of grapes was grown when everybody was at each other's throats. I used to look at the grapes maturing and be thankful that nature carried on as if nothing was happening.'

'This isn't this season's vintage?'

'Of course not. I believe it's 1940 vintage.'

The vicar talked about Canada as was his custom on such occasions, particularly if some of the guests had connections overseas, and these days there were more and more Canadians attached to the navy. He tried to draw Andy into the discussion; but he remained politely quiet. He was sitting three places away from his boss and he was endeavouring to be invisible except in body.

The town clerk thanked all the guests who were serving in the town and asked the Vicar about his preparations for the civic service on Sunday, when all the army and the navy units in the town were due to attend.

'Yes, I'm still looking for somebody from one of the services to read the first lesson about the sea. The Acts of the Apostles, Chapter 27.'

He was amazed to hear the commander quoting the passage from the Bible.

'And when the south wind blew softly, supposing that they had obtained their purpose, loosing thence, they sailed close to Crete. But not long after there arose against it a tempestuous wind, the Euroclydon. And the ship was caught ...'

The vicar was most impressed to hear the commander quoting the words.

'You know the piece then, Commander?' he asked.

'Yes. It is often used as the reading in naval church services. It's one of the earliest records of a storm in the Mediterranean. It's the chapter about Paul being shipwrecked off Malta.'

'You wouldn't like to read it, would you?' the vicar asked shyly.

'I've read it a thousand times. Lieutenant Ritchie would do the honours.'

The vicar and the commander looked towards Andy.

'If you did read the lesson, Lieutenant, you could parade here at the church by yourself and be excused the mass parade up the hill from the town hall. You'll find the text will become familiar after you've read it many times during your career.'

'Yes, sir. Thank you, sir. I've read the passage before down in Portsmouth,' Andy stuttered, trying to appear excited at being specially volunteered.

'So there you are Vicar, Lieutenant Ritchie is familiar with the passage. I'm sure he will perform it well and uphold your high standards.'

'That's excellent, Andy. Will you need a copy of the Bible?' asked the vicar.

Andy nodded and wondered how he'd managed to become the centre of the conversation, while keeping his mouth zipped and trying to hide under the table for the major part of the evening.

The sweet was served and was steamed treacle pudding with custard.

Emily was delighted that most of the guests loved the dish. She knew they would, because sweet things were a real treat, with sugar and jam being strictly rationed and other preservatives hard to come by.

'Delightfully sweet, Emily.'

'Nobody like my scouse then?' asked the vicar, not missing an opportunity to blow his own trumpet.

Emily smiled and was very pleased with herself thinking of the night that she'd obtained the recipe off the cook in the hotel at Glasgow, where she'd first seen Andy waiting for the lift.

'You know I'm only joking about the scouse,' confided the vicar. 'The meal has been a tremendous success.'

After the meal, Andy was chased out of the kitchen, where he was attempting to help with the mountain of dirty dishes so he could avoid more embarrassing moments with the top brass.

'Go and join the big-wigs in the lounge,' said Bessie. 'Who is the highest ranking officer of them all?'

'The fellow you found asleep,' confirmed Andy.

'Really?'

'Yes. He's also my boss. So please don't shame me in front of him. I've already been "volunteered" to read half a chapter at the civic service on Sunday.'

'It's not so bad. At least you won't have to march,' Emily tried to console.

'Marching is easy. I'll have to be word-perfect in front of all the men from the fleet. Besides, the boss knows the chapter off by heart, so he'll notice any mistakes.'

Andy joined the guests in the lounge. The father was still serving up his excellent wine from Oran. The navy men had not come empty-handed and had fetched some rum along. The commander excused himself and went into the kitchen to thank the cooks. He presented Emily with the biggest piece of cheese she'd ever seen. It was just like one of the large slabs she'd seen in the shops.

'With the compliments of my chief cook,' he said.

'You shouldn't have bothered,' said Emily, wide-eyed.

'Nonsense. If we are going to win this war we have to pull together and your meal was excellent,' the Commander said.

'We're lucky here. The vicar is so handy in the garden,' said Emily.

'Yes, but the pudding was beautiful,' said the commander.

'I got the recipe from a hotel in Glasgow,' Emily whispered, sheepishly.

At the end of the evening, after they'd finished the washing-up and Bessie had clocked up an extra two hours overtime, they brewed up a cup of tea.

'The commander was a real gentleman.'

'Just shows you how appearances can be deceptive.'

'How was I to know that an officer slumbering on the couch in the mayor's parlour would be guest of honour at our hotpot supper?'

They found themselves gazing at the huge piece of cheese.

'How are we going to organise the eating of it, before it goes off?'

'Well, I reckon there's so much that we'll all get fed up eating it soon.'

'It'll be one taste, even with onions and tomato. So we'll start with Welsh rarebit for breakfast. Save the eggs. Followed by cheese potatoes for lunch and cheese and beetroot sandwiches for pack-up and tea.'

'We can have plenty of cheese in the bubble and squeak.'

'It looks like national cheese. So it'll taste like a cross between Cheddar and Cheshire, with the cheese taken out,' suggested Bessie.

'You're at it again.'

'It's thoughtful that he should contribute to the meal like that.'

'Suppose we could have served it up with the tea and coffee,' suggested Emily. 'But, and it's a big "but", we've never seen a cream cracker in years.'

They started the process of eating the mound of cheese by taking some home. 'Maybe I should ask the vicar if he likes Welsh rarebit? If he says yes, then I'll serve it up to him till he's sick of it. Save the eggs,' Emily concluded.

'One thing is for certain. It'll have gone off or he'll have gone off Welsh rarebit,' Bessie made sense for a change. 'Won't last long in this weather.'

'I think he likes his cheese,' said Emily. 'I'll feed him it in sandwiches.'

'Bad news; it's all one taste. Good news; there's plenty of it.'

So, the vicar had plenty of cheese in his diet for the next fortnight, while the huge cob of cheese diminished in size and went off faster. Fortunately for everybody, the vicar brought matters to a close.

'Emily, sorry for sounding like Oliver Twist in reverse, but please, Emily, can I have no more. It's all one taste. Even with onions and tomatoes. No more cheese for at least a month.'

So Emily gave the final piece away.

The following Saturday, Emily and Andy spent a day in the country with the two girls. They caught the bus to the Pier Head and the boarded the ferry for Birkenhead. They trudged up the gangway and out into the green bus station at Woodside. They folded up the children's pushchair and climbed aboard the bus for Bromborough, which cruised along the road to Chester. They alighted at Bromborough Cross and wandered down the road towards the station, walking enthusiastically through the country lanes. Emily asked directions from a man who was perched up a ladder outside a round white house.

'Excuse me, please, but could you direct us to Raby Mere?'

'Certainly. Straight on. You can't miss it.'

'The round house looks like a sea captain's house,' said Andy.

'He doesn't look like a captain,' said Emily. 'More like a window-cleaner.'

They were soon out in the fields and sitting close to an appealing mere, surrounded by trees and shrubs. In the field there was a set of fairground swings. Andy climbed aboard and took the kids with him. They swung up and down till they were exhausted and the picnic beckoned.

'Guess what's for sandwiches.'

'Cheese.'

'How did you know that? Not to mention beetroot and tomato.'

They sat out in the field amongst the cowpats and Andy remembered all the jokes about people losing their hats and trying on half a dozen before they found the right one. The girls raced across the field after their ball and Andy opened a piece of exercise paper that he had tucked in his shirt pocket. He started to read.

'What's that?'

'It's my reading. I've copied it out from the good book.'

'You're not supposed to know it by heart. It's in the Bible in big letters.'

'Funny you should say that. The boss knows it by heart so I'll have to be word-perfect. Otherwise, he'll ask me again about my degree,' said Andy, settling into an afternoon of mugging up for his examination by the boss and the entire fleet.

Next day was Sunday, the day of the big civic parade in Bootle, when the mayor walked to church. The parade formed up outside the town hall and marched up Merton Road to the church on the top of the hill. At this time a quarter of the men in Liverpool served in the navy, while another quarter worked on the docks and river. Bootle Docks were the home for many of the ships that comprised the North Atlantic fleet. The coats of arms and flags from all the vessels were hung with pride in the council chamber in the town hall. There were so many ships in the port that the whole of Merton Road from the bottom to the top was crowded out with ship's companies marching up the hill to church. They all fell out in front of the church, removed their headgear and filed respectfully inside.

The mayor, lady mayoress. town clerk, chief constable, fire chief and port officials all sat in the front pew with the commander and some of his leading officers. Andy occupied the nearest seat to the lectern, where he collected himself, preparing himself for his reading from the Acts of the Apostles. His legs felt like jelly, even more so when he recognised the Admiral i/c Western Approaches.

I've really gone and got myself into a whole load of bother this time, he thought. It was so much more scary than tracking a torpedo under fire. He placed his notes on the lectern before the service got underway. It would look as if he was reading from the good book. He'd just have to remember to retrieve them before he returned to his seat. He was sitting with the leading players in the port. He anticipated that he would be asked by somebody why he was seated where he was. One of the officious stewards, Andy couldn't make out whether he was civilian or military police, asked, 'By the way, officer, do you realise that you are seated with all the dignitaries?'

'Yes, thank you, officer. You can read the first lesson if you so wish.'

The steward melted away into the background.

The start of the service was majestic, when the flags from all the units serving in Bootle were delivered up to be placed near the altar by the vicar and another visiting cleric. Andy smiled back at his young colleagues in the choir, who saw him in full naval dress uniform for the first time. They thought he was one of the top brass.

The choir-boys found themselves out-sung by the booming voices of the sailors when the congregation bellowed out the words 'Will your anchor hold in the storms of life? Fastened to a rock, which cannot move.' They were deeply impressed by the sheer earnestness of the sailors, believing in what they sang.

Andy found the anthem of the sea hard to follow, but he endeavoured to put some real feeling into his memorised words, even though fear had reduced the power of his voice. The church had suddenly become icy cold and silent, while he read the story of Saint Paul's arrival off Malta. Fortunately, the reading went according to plan, without a hitch, and he was soon reading the last stanzas.

'And when they were escaped then they knew that the island was called Melita.' After adding, 'Thanks be to God,' Andy closed the Bible and, placing his notes in his pocket, escaped to his seat next to the big-wigs. He felt as if he had been reprieved from the death penalty.

Better was to follow. The vicar was on top form. The only reference he made to the reading was to say, 'And, of course, today

Melita is known as Malta.' Then he launched into a heartfelt sermon, which said that if the people of Bootle were going to suffer so much, then surely we were going to win the war. The mood of the congregation was such that they knew he was right. He praised all the services and all the men and women who had been valiant. He told them how he had checked the meaning of the word that morning in the dictionary. He didn't want to use the sort of words used in films at the pictures, starring Clark Gable.

'Valiant means, quite simply, brave, courageous, heroic, gallant, fearless, bold and intrepid in danger. And I'll tell you this. I've seen you men and women performing your courageous deeds day in and day out, at home and on the ocean and, I'll tell you, I know one thing, one thing for certain. It is that we are going to win, without a shadow of a doubt, make no bones about it. We will win. In victory we will be benevolent, compassionate and far more decent to our enemies than they ever were to us.' There was a silence in the church. 'Now we will sing the hymn *Eternal Father Strong to Save*.'

The hymn boomed out and was probably heard miles away. It was rendered even more strongly than *Will Your Anchor Hold?* The men of the fleet wanted to believe in something positive and the vicar had provided it. He knew he was right. So they applauded him with the might of their singing. You couldn't hear the voices of the choir-boys.

The service ended with the singing of the national anthem and the colourful flags were trooped back out of the church. Andy went around to visit his friends in the vestry. The choir-boys were impressed with his uniform.

'Is it yours?'

'Yes.'

'Why don't you wear it more often?'

'Because it's Number Ones. I only wear it on important occasions like today.'

'So is this service today important then?'

'Yes. The naval officer in the front row is an admiral.'

'Which one?'

They strained their necks to peep.

The top brass had all filed out of the church by then for the parade back.

Christmas Day 1943 saw Andy being invited around to Emily's for the festivities. He'd passed on to Emily two lovely dolls for the girls, which he had picked up in Canada. Each of the dolls had her own little bed with sheet, blanket and pillows. The girls spent hours putting the tiny dolls to bed and getting them up again, so they could be put back to bed again. It occupied them over the holidays.

Andy thought at first that he would be back on the ocean before the New Year. Then he thought mid-January; eventually, the group were not to leave port until 29 January 1944.

During the brief stay ashore, Emily was finally convinced that she would be emigrating to Canada with Andy at the end of the war or soon afterwards, when Andy's career and family matters were sorted out. Meanwhile, all Andy's proposals of marriage were rejected and there were no plans for a wedding on the horizon. They made plans for Andy to go on ahead, come demobilisation, so he could find somewhere they could live. Where they lived would depend on where Andy could find a suitable job teaching mathematics. After one particularly long chat about setting up home and managing a house overseas, Emily asked Andy not to propose yet again.

'Why? Do you plan to live in sin?' he asked. 'Anyway, what makes you so sure I'll ask you again? I've already asked four times. I'm beginning to get the message.'

'Don't sulk about it,' Emily noted. She looked him up and down. 'I've noticed how you have changed for the better,' she observed. 'Yes, much for the better.'

'What do you mean?'

'You've become so much more positive since you came to Liverpool,' she said. 'Must be all the time you've spent sailing with this boss of yours.'

'Suppose it does rub off. He believes we are invincible,' Andy reflected.

'Which has to be good in the middle of a war,' said Emily.

They kissed long and hard. 'You know it isn't about me being sure of you. I have to put my two little girls first and foremost; I'd like the war to end, too,' she added.

Chapter 17

Six of the Best

'We must take the offensive against the U-boat and the Focke-Wulf wherever we can ... the U-boat at sea must be hunted, the U-boat in the building yard or the dock must be bombed'

Churchill, 6 March 1941

Before he sailed out of the Mersey, Andy visited his old colleague, Bungey Connaught, who was still occupying a bed in Seaforth Naval Hospital. Andy walked down the centre of the ward to find the gaunt-looking Bungey, almost a stone lighter, on his feet, batting a table-tennis ball thrown to him by another pyjama-clad inmate with half a brush handle.

'Bungey, nice to see you up and at it,' he said.

'It's the drugs I'm on. They make me feel frivolous.'

'Playing cricket?'

'Yes. You didn't know I played cricket once, did you?'

'No.'

'Down at Portsmouth,' Bungey was serious.

Andy laughed at the thought.

'Are you fit to get out of here?'

'No. You see, Andy. I can hardly eat. They inject me with drugs because I can't digest them. I've had more arrows in my arse than the dartboard.'

'We'll be back out at sea in a few days,' Andy told him.

'Don't be too sure of that, there's a gale blowing up,' Bungey said.

'I'll see you, Bungey, sometime about Easter. Good luck,' he said, finally.

On his return from the hospital, just down the Crosby Road, Andy was introduced to the new sub-lieutenant who was to be Bungey's replacement in communications. The new man was called Ginger Hardy and Andy recognised him as the ginger-headed sailor he had seen chatting to the wrens at HQ.

'I know you. I saw you at HQ. You directed me to Philip, Son and Nephew,' said Andy, as soon as he saw him.

'That's right, you were the guy on a much superior course to me,' said Ginger.

'Oh well, we both finished up in the same ship, slide-rule or no slide-rule. Are you still going out with that wren? I think you called her Cynthia?' asked Andy.

'That's right. Cynthia is still my girl; lives locally,' confirmed Ginger.

He was to brighten up Andy's life at sea, even in the first few hours they worked together. Ginger was a complete novice and an expert at misfired, inappropriate comments, lame jokes and excuses. The crew always referred to complete novices as chocolate teapots – no use at all. However, as soon as they discovered Ginger's name was Hardy they had a field day and decided that his first name was Oliver.

Before the Buzzard sailed they were inspected by a boffin from the Admiralty, Mr C. K. Smith, who was in weapon development. The boss was away and Number One was in charge. The man was obviously not a military man but a brilliant scientist with an acute mind. Number One missed the point of the inspection in that he chuntered on about the man's dress and demeanour.

'Bit of a bad show. How are we expected to keep the men up to scratch, if the Admiralty top brass can't wash their neck occasionally? It's a disgrace.'

Andy was given the job of showing the guy around the ship.

'Keep him away from the men. We don't want them seeing his dishevelled hair and lame deportment.'

Andy followed Number One's orders and concentrated on the instruments and the weaponry on the ship. After all, the boffin was only interested in the technology in operation on the Buzzard. Andy could tell by the way he applied himself to the task that he knew every nut and bolt on the vessel. He even made one or two fine adjustments to some of the instruments and explained the workings of others.

'Did you design any of these instruments?' Andy found himself asking.

'No, I specialise in designing carriers,' came the reply. 'What's your job?' the boffin asked Ginger Hardy, who was caught by surprise.

'Travelling salesman, sir,' Ginger replied, thinking he was still in civvy street.

'No, on this ship.'

'Navigation and communication.'

'Where have your journeys taken you to?'

'Glasgow, Liverpool, Stoke-on-Trent, Leeds, Sheffield,' Andy and the boffin realised that Ginger had misheard.

'No, ports, Sub,' Andy said.

'Well, I've been to Southport and Stockport.'

Thankfully the boffin stopped asking questions. Andy knew that the only way out of the shambles was to walk the boffin away from Ginger, who was just not communicating on the same subject.

He did his best to stifle a smile, before the boffin gave a knowing look and said, 'It's always good to get out of the office and meet ordinary, decent, everyday fellows at the sharp end. They are a complete joy.'

North Biscay 47°02' North/ 6°02 West

When the Buzzard sailed out with the group at the end of January, the sea was performing normally after a month of gales. Andy knew he was going to be experiencing events that would play a significant part in the war at sea. It was inevitable that anything involving the boss took on immediate relevance and importance. Andy just felt he was seeing history unfold at a distance and he was a tiny cog in the wheel; a privileged observer with a minor role to play.

The Boss had confessed in his lecture that he broke his own rules on occasions by not trusting his attuned instinct. The group were assigned to protect a convoy with aircraft-carriers in prominence. The boss always considered carriers to be sitting ducks for the U-boats; easily seen from a distance with the naked eye. They attracted U-boats like flies, but limited the range and movement of his ships; the difference between defence and attack. The group's role was thus changed to protection, instead of all out concentration on killing U-boats.

True to form, the U-boats couldn't resist a pop at the carriers. An asdic contact that was doubtful at the outset was changed into a 'probable submarine' signal. The U-boat was slipping between two of the ships in the group, working its purposeful way towards the aircraft-carriers. The skipper of the Buzzard thought that the U-boat would soon get his torpedoes away and then make good his escape. The Buzzard let him have a pattern of depth charges, just as he was about to release his torpedo. The huge explosion ensured that the carriers turned in unison and offered their sterns to the action, presenting a smaller target. Then all the ships in the group released their depth charges in what was to prove a successful attack.

'How come the boss didn't use all your information?' Ginger asked Andy.

'Because his instinct is finely tuned,' said Andy.

Ginger wasn't so sure. Then a mass of debris and black oil appeared on the surface, enough to signal the end.

'I see what you mean,' Ginger admitted.

Andy had viewed the whole episode from the centre of the action. He had an excellent, if precarious, grandstand from which to view the entire operation. Much to the delight of the boss, the convoy was soon escorted into safe waters and the group was free to roam and seek out U-boats. They headed for the killing fields of North Biscay.

What followed was ten days of looking, listening, watching and waiting. Andy thought it was a good opportunity to brush-up on his mental arithmetic so that he would be up to the mark when he lectured after the war. He need not have bothered. The boss was so quick with his mental calculations that he just had to concentrate on keeping up to the break-neck speed expected. Now the boss occasionally asked, 'Isn't that so, Lieutenant?,' to which Andy would reply, 'Yes, sir,' just hoping like blazes that the boss had got it spot on again because it was too late to check it out on his slide-rule. His fingers had long since gone numb.

Andy spent most of his time, when not on watch, sleeping as comfortably as he could, eating and preparing for his next duty. He seemed to live with a mug of cocoa or tea in his hand and a sandwich, often corned-beef. His brain had to be alive when on duty. He seemed to form a relationship with his screen, his earphones and an organised scan of the horizon every half-minute or so, in case he spotted something not on the screen but blindingly obvious. More information these days came from radio. Aircraft spottings became more accurate, added to perfect information from HQ. They seemed to have access to the enemy's plans and may even have broken the enemy code. They were often able to point the group in the right direction to intercept packs of U-boats, freshly out from French ports.

On the tenth night the weather was clear and the officer of the watch spotted a U-boat sitting on the surface about a mile and a half away. This came on the back of news by the radio that a pack was working on a convoy to the north.

By the time the guns had opened fire, the U-boat had dived. The asdic team did their stuff and it was not long before there was a contact. The U-boat made no attempt to shake the group off and didn't increase speed or violently change direction. Instead, the U-boat put up her periscope just twenty yards from the ship. The U-boat commander had a good look around and probably had a bigger surprise than the crew of the Buzzard.

The skipper didn't want to drop a pattern of depth charges so close because the ship would have her stern blown off. Instead, they retired to a decent distance, followed by the U-boat, attempting escape. The Buzzard could not get away from her. Eventually, the ship was joined by another member of the group and they each set off a pattern of depth charges. This signalled the end of the operation and, as a mass of U-boat wreckage and oil bubbled to the surface, the boss signalled the skipper to say, 'Just look at the mess you've made.'

Three hours later an able-seaman on radar watch detected another U-boat on the surface. Events followed the same pattern as before. The U-boat dived before the guns could be trained on her. Then the asdic contact told all the members of the group what was happening. However, once located, the skipper got off two 'Extra Specials' with help of other members of the group. The first one burst her and after that she left a trail of oil behind her. The second completed the job, wreckage bubbled to the surface and no survivors appeared in the water.

Little time was wasted before the group made off to another incident. The commander of this U-boat proved to be tougher and more experienced than the skippers of the two previous boats. An organised plan of attack was essential, with much patience and fortitude forthcoming. The boss enjoyed the challenge and approached the task vigorously. The opportunity was there to be taken. The U-boat avoided attack after attack of depth charges but eventually even the skilled U-boat commander succumbed to the constant hammering from the group.

The action continued without break. Andy knew he had to be on the ball with his work but he knew he was experiencing something special when a fifth U-boat was discovered just before midnight the next night. The attack was launched at such a short distance that the explosion lifted the stem of the Buzzard. Remarkably, there was no damage and all the instruments still worked. However, the U-boat slid away in the encounter. Eventually, the asdic team announced a firm contact, and the battle with the U-boat recommenced. This time, a successful batch of charges produced the desired effect and, before long, 'breaking-up sounds' could be heard down below. At first there was an extensive patch of oil on the surface with a splattering of debris just to help confirm.

The boss signalled, 'The U-boat is sunk. You can splice the mainbrace.'

The ship's crew enjoyed drinking the king's health.

Nothing more happened for a week or two when the group were attached to another convoy. U-boats had been reported about but none had sunk any ships in the convoy and the group had failed to catch any U-boats. After the convoy had escaped into safe waters the boss decided to search far astern for any U-boats still lurking about. Andy was concentrating on the minute accuracy of his figures and shutting everything else out of his mind while they searched. Eventually, a U-boat was caught that was leaking like a colander. The skipper used the last of his high-pressure air to lift the U-boat to the surface. The whole crew were rescued by the ships in the group.

Chasing up after the convoy was a seventh U-boat. However, before it could be attacked it managed to damage one of the ships in the group. The boss took on the responsibility of towing the damaged vessel, until a tug arrived from Falmouth. Eight days of towing took the ship as far as the Scilly Isles, where a storm blew up, and during the night she capsized and sank.

The final score for the trip was 6–1. Andy felt really sad about the loss of the ship, even though all hands had been saved, including the prisoners from the U-boat. The group now set sail for Liverpool Despite the ferocious action all about, Andy had loved the sea, ever since his first glimpse out from the Wirral across to Wales. He loved long-range views of distant shores, the incredibly slow approach with the land growing larger and more acute, until you were upon it and it was larger than the ship.

During the humdrum days, which were few and far between on this trip because of the constant chase and instinctive action, he found himself trying to remember the lines of a poem written by Emily Dickinson:

Exultation is the going
Of an inland soul to sea,
Past the houses – past the headlands
Into deep Eternity –
Bred as we, among the mountains,
Can the sailor understand
The divine intoxication
Of the first league out from land.

Yes, the sea was incredible. He remembered the lines as he stared across the empty Irish Sea, with the occasional sight of Ireland to the west and, every now and then, a glimpse of the mountains of Wales, through the low white clouds. To the south, the sea and the sky were clipped together, like a smart seam on a bespoke tailor's new suit of clothes, bluish-grey merging into silvery white.

Andy's end of voyage musing was interrupted by Ginger Hardy's latest bloomer as they steamed into Liverpool Bay and New Brighton appeared in the light-grey mist. There was a general chatter about the place as shore leave loomed. Crew were suggesting suitable taverns to meet up for a few bevvies, including The Caradoc.

'Why "The Bucket of Blood"?' asked Ginger, innocently, just as the cox, whose mother-in-law ran the place, appeared in the galley.

There was an embarrassing, prolonged silence while Ginger tried to figure out why everybody had suddenly become dumb. His face was a picture. His nickname of 'Oliver' would stick.

JOHNNIE WALKER

'Walker was self-effacing and spoke the slightly unreal language of a modest hero. "I do not think that I am an ace U-Boat killer, That formidable character is one thousand British tars".'

Chapter 18
Gladstone

'They secured their beauty to the dock ...
after long months of water and the sky.'

John Masefield

News of the sinking of six U-boats in one trip had got out. First there
was a signal from the Admiralty saying that the prime minister and
the war cabinet wished to convey their congratulations. Running up
the Mersey, the First Lord of the Admiralty passed aboard the
Philante and signalled his personal congratulations. The group
finally arrived at nine o'clock on a dull morning at the end of
February. They steamed up the channel into the Mersey and turned
left into Gladstone Dock. The other ships in the river and docks
sounded their sirens and a crowd of thousands lined the quay.
There were sailors and wrens lining each side of the dock and a
military band playing the boss's signature tune *A-Hunting We
Will Go.*

There was a small group of dignitaries, naval and civic. The First
Sea Lord gave a speech which compared the Battle of the Atlantic
to the Battle of Trafalgar. There were rows and rows of sailors from
the escort vessels and the battleship King George V. Andy was
amazed at the reception; he'd never seen thousands of cheering
sailors and wrens before. A few seconds later he was completely
flummoxed, when he spied amongst the civic dignitaries the vicar
and Father Deegan, who were with their friend, the town clerk.
They waved to him, after the vicar had pointed him out. He waved
back just once so they could see he'd seen them.

Later in the day, when he was congratulated about his achievements, the boss just said, 'I do not think that I am an ace U-boat killer. That formidable character is one thousand British tars.'

The prospect of leave loomed and Andy knew where he would be spending most of his time. For the first time in his life, he felt as if he'd achieved something of note, even though most of the time he'd watched at a distance the genii of the group getting to grips with the situation as a team. All the skippers of all the ships were formidable in their own right. The boss brought them together as an effective team and every ship had contributed to the group's huge record of thirty-one U-boats sunk. Andy just felt so proud to be able to witness them performing brilliantly and making history out in the open Atlantic.

During the first three months of 1944, fifty-four front-line U-boats were lost; while in February only two ships were sunk and seven in March. Most of the U-boats were bombed in their bases or sailing to and from their ports in Western France. The information now coming from the code-breakers was spot on and wolf packs were bombed and hunted before they got anywhere near the convoys.

Ginger Hardy was amazed to see Cynthia waving madly amongst the wrens who had welcomed the group back to Gladstone. This leave was a chance for Ginger to meet up with Cynthia's family who lived along the Newport Road. The name of Newport went back to the previous century when this section of the docks was built. It was the area at the end of Boundary Street, near where the Leeds and Liverpool canal reached the river in the Stanley Dock. There wasn't much new about this part of the port in 1944; indeed, the heavy bombing experienced in the Blitz had made sure of that. Ginger and Cynthia had always got on like a raging torrent, ever since they'd met up at HQ. She was one of the troop of telephonists who operated the extensive telephone systems, ship to shore radio and intercom between shore establishments. She loved her job, was more than competent at it, and was an attractive girl, full of life. She lit the place up with her enthusiasm and was good for Ginger. He often complained that she smoked, because few women did in 1944.

Cynthia would ask, 'But how would we ever have met up, darling, if wasn't for Smokers' Corner?'

Nothing was to prepare Ginger for meeting her mother and the family down near the docks. Cynthia made no attempt to hide the full facts. Her mother, Cissy, was still a young woman; she had given birth to Cynthia very early. She dressed twenty years younger than her true age and carried it off because she was physically glamorous. She'd kept herself in trim by smoking heavily; a habit she'd passed on to her daughter. She had a heavy smoker's cough that ruined the image.

She attracted the Americans very easily and had all the money and trappings of having a string of wealthy boyfriends from the other side of the Atlantic who stayed a short time, paid up and moved out and on. Eventually, with the money she'd come by from her rich Yanks, she'd invested in the old whorehouse at the end of the street, next to the dock gates. She became the madam and attracted business racketeers, big-time crooks and simply rich guys, because she was still attractive to men. The brothel mainly attracted seamen of all nations from the ships in the line of docks. The vocabulary of pidgin English used in transactions had a few key words. The business thrived in an old four-storey tenement building with rooms on every floor, which posed as a sailors' doss house. The family had always had an interest in the place; Cissy's mother, Cynthia's grandma, had worked there and was still on the game. She had her own list of clientele. It was quite normal for a foreign sailor to only have a few choice pidgin English words, 'Get me Grannie.' Grannie knew them all and spoilt them rotten and they returned time and time again. She was doing something right.

Ginger was shocked at first, because he'd arrived during a monumental argument between a foreign seaman, his captain and Cissy, which looked as if it would never subside. Each of the rooms in the brothel always had a huge chamber-pot, in which the prostitute would relieve herself heavily immediately after the act. The pots were always full because the girls and clients all drank heavily. The seaman tried to explain the incident to Ginger, while asking him to peer into a bedroom that was ankle deep in urine. Ginger tried to say, in as many languages as he could, that he didn't understand. It seemed the seaman had tripped over the pot and soaked his best togs. He had returned to his ship half naked and stinking of urine. His captain hadn't believed him. Cissy said that her girls didn't do things like that.

Ginger soon understood that Cynthia was trying to get away from there and start a life elsewhere. She wanted to be a telephonist after the war and move away. They spent much of Ginger's leave dancing at the Grafton and drinking in a pub near his digs in Lark Lane, near Sefton Park.

Completely oblivious to the horrors at sea and the local difficulties down in the brothels of the port, Emily and Bessie wandered back from the vicarage. A middle-aged woman passed on her way home, heavily loaded up with shopping. Bessie smiled sheepishly to the woman as she passed. She returned the greeting.

'So you know Mrs Summerville?'

'Yes. The lady walking her dog without.'

'Why not just call her Mrs Summerville?'

'She's always walking her dog, isn't she?'

'Well, yes.'

'Except today, she's without it,' insisted Bessie.

'It's as bad as "your next door neighbour that lives three doors down".'

'I think it's a pretty good description,' said Bessie with pride.

'So what about the window-cleaner over there with his ladder?'

'Y'mean Ben?'

'Yes, why isn't he the guy with the ladder?'

'Cos it's Ben Seddon and everybody knows it's Ben,' said Bessie.

'I've never really understood your expression "One of the six that walk seven abreast". What are you trying to say?' asked Emily.

'Cos some of them do, don't they?'

They shuffled along past the pub and walked straight into the rituals at chucking out time. One guy didn't want to be shown the door. The barman, in a rather embarrassed way, tried to explain that he was always like this, never wanting to go home.

'Maybe his missus wipes the floor with him'

Meanwhile, there were the local drunks walking smartly along the pavement, with their heads held high and chin pointed to the sky, failing to navigate a straight path, looking as if they were afraid of spilling their beer. They'd spend the afternoon sleeping it off.

'Families starving yet they can always find money for beer and smokes,' said Emily.

Back home, the two women played with the little kids till bath time and Bessie helped with the chores. Bessie sang a few of her own words to nursery rhymes, which brought a smile to Emily's face. After a short story the girls were carried upstairs to bed.

'Will Andy be around soon?' asked Bessie.

'Yes, the vicar was invited to a big home-coming for the ships down in Gladstone. He said he'd given him a good wave,' reported Emily.

'Do you think Andy would take a part in my little concert in the mission. It's for Holidays at Home. He's a good singer, isn't he?' asked Bessie.

'Says he is. You'll have to ask him. He doesn't sing dirty songs. Besides, you won't be able to sing most of yours in the mission,' said Emily.

'Do not fret, Em. I've got it all under control. It's just that I need one or two men in the sketches. Young men, that is. All the men are overseas and we can't have the old codgers and young lads in the sketches,' said Bessie.

'See what you mean. Well ask him. You've a tongue in your head. Ask him as nicely as you've mentioned it to me,' said Emily.

'Suppose he can only say no,' Bessie thought out loud.

'Anyway, we're off to Chester at the weekend. Andy's old stomping ground. Where he used to live before his family all emigrated to Australia. Where he went to school and sang in the choir. We'll probably just go down to the Dee,' said Emily.

'They don't call it the River Dee, they call it the Roodee,' said Bessie.

'No, that's the racecourse,' said Emily.

'I'm pretty sure they call it the Roodee,' said Bessie, while Emily sighed and thought, here we go again; maybe it's the riverbank that's called "the Roodee".

'They never call it the River Roodee.'

'They do,' repeated Bessie. 'They say we're off to the Roodee.'

Andy had been delayed in a scramble for leave passes and had then been invited for a drink on the way up from the dock by Ginger. When he'd entered the pub he was surprised to see not only Cynthia at the bar but what turned out to be her mother, Cissy, plus a large entourage of middle-aged men who liked their drink and cigarettes. Fortunately, the drinks were free as soon as Cissy's friends saw the uniforms. There was a large, hairy Belgian seaman, called Henry, occupying one end of the bar and creating a big fuss. Andy thought nothing of it, thinking that the man looked remarkably like Bluto of Popeye fame, and this was what was causing an overflow of drunken camaraderie. The huge sailor kept smiling at Andy and inspecting his body at a distance with his black hairy eyes. Andy didn't get the joke.

Out of the blue, Ginger said, 'We'll drink up and go to the next pub.'

This they did and left amongst some confusion and laughter at the bar.

'What was all that about?' asked Andy at the next pub.

Ginger was going to explain but left it to Cynthia, who felt rather guilty and blushed a little.

'It's my mother,' said Cynthia. 'Ever since she found out that Henry, the Belgian seaman, was a sissy she's baited him. Likes to put ideas into his head. Tonight, she thought it was a good idea to suggest that both you and Ginger were queers.'

'Weird sense of humour,' said Ginger.

'Just that Mother thinks that absolutely everything is about sex,' said Cynthia.

'I'm glad Cissy and her friends found it all highly amusing,' said Andy.

Later than intended, Andy arrived at the vicarage looking for Emily. The vicar answered the door and seemed to be using his words precisely.

'I was wondering, Andy, if you'd like to stay at the vicarage, bed and breakfast, while you are on leave this time. I've plenty of unused rooms, which I've always kept furnished for emergencies, but it's never come to that. So would you like to stay here, away from the ship and docks? It would be more comfortable than the hostel,' suggested the vicar.

'Certainly, Vicar. I'd need to arrange some leave first but having been away from home since 1939, I'm never short of leave. It's always a question of where I spend it. I could return to Chester and stay with my aunt but I've already leant on her far too much in the past. The ship has been my base. I'm always owed leave.'

'Well, yes. Sort out your leave. Then we'll decide what you should pay. Maybe the same rates as they charge at the naval hostel. Dinner would be extra but optional, just in case you get invited out.' The vicar was expounding just as Emily appeared in the door so he turned to her and said, 'Andy has accepted the offer of a room, Emily. We'll sort out a key for him after he's had his leave pass signed.'

After the vicar had disappeared they sneaked a kiss and a cuddle in the kitchen. Emily brewed up a cup of tea and Andy tried to explain why he had been delayed, but arrived at the conclusion one does in situations like his – if only he hadn't been talked into going for a drink. He found it impossible to explain to Emily what the Belgian seaman or Cissy were about, as they lived in a totally different world to Emily; so he gave up. She'd never understand. It was difficult enough for him. So Emily told him of her plans for a day out to Chester, and Bessie wondering if he would volunteer for the concert party.

'So go on, tell me off for saying I thought you'd consider it.'

'No. It's okay. I've nothing to do while I'm here and learning the lines for the concert will make a change from remembering messages word for word during a Force 9 gale. It's fine; it'll be fine,' he assured Emily, as she vanished into the pantry.

On her return, she was completely flummoxed because Andy was fast asleep where he was sitting. Bessie arrived and was told to tip-toe in by Emily.

'He's only been cat-napping for two hours a night since January,' said Emily.

Half an hour later he was awake and, when pressed about his sleeping habits, he said, 'The boss never sleeps.'

'I don't believe that,' said Bessie, 'I caught him sleeping in the mayor's parlour.'

She turned away, expecting a reply from Andy, and found him asleep again.

'Let's measure him for a suit, while he's asleep,' said Emily. 'He's no civvies. I don't want to be walking about with a sailor while he's on leave. He's my man, not the property of the King's Navy.'

'His jacket's over there,' said Bessie. 'The inside leg will be difficult.'

They thought for a moment about how they could obtain the measurements. Emily inspected the clothes he was wearing and noticed that there was one or two years of wear and tear, loose buttons, a pocket with a little hole and an unmended blemish. That's what she'd do. When Andy woke up he accepted Emily's offer of instant repair to his uniform. She said it would take a few days; just a little white lie. After she'd repaired the minor blemishes in half an hour of honest endeavour, she took his uniform down to the tailor, who was always looking for work because few people had the money or the coupons for new clothes during hostilities and made do with old. The suit was knocked up within the week.

'Now I can walk the streets with a civilian,' she said to the tailor.

'Except for the navy hair-cut,' said the tailor. 'He's a tall customer.'

'Six foot two in his stockinged feet,' said Emily, proudly.

The following Saturday was their trip to Chester, followed by the Holidays at Home concert. The kids were looking forward to their day out. Emily presented Andy with the new suit on the Friday before the trip.

'Aye, Mr Andrew Ritchie, civilian,' she said. 'Wear this tomorrow.'

On the last Saturday before Easter they caught the bus down to the Pier Head. The kids enjoyed the ride downtown on the top deck, thinking it was so grown-up. The real pleasure was to come. The tide was out so the gangway down to the ferries was the lowest it ever went and was really steep. The eldest girl ran all the way down the slope at the Princes Landing Stage and Andy had to rush to catch her up. They boarded the Royal Iris and sailed across to Birkenhead. There were ships in the river, some of which Andy remembered seeing in convoys. An endless supply of goods and troops were pouring into Merseyside from the other side of the Atlantic. At Woodside, they walked up to the station. Emily was pleased that the train for Chester was filled with servicemen and women and she was seated next to one of the few civilians. Okay, so he had a sharp haircut. The services dominated the station at Chester, the city centre along the main street and around the cathedral. In the spring of 1944 there was a build-up of troops throughout the country. All military establishments were full.

They stopped at a tiny café just inside the wall and Andy asked Emily to marry him again, with the offer of a long engagement.

'We could get married after my next tour of duty,' said Andy.

'And ... Andy you've made a complete bore of the subject. Are you really sure that you want to marry me? I've nothing but my two girls,' she said, 'not to mention endless woe. Are you sure?'

'Of course I'm sure. Yes. This is the fifth time,' said Andy.

'I'll say yes then. For persistence. You'll have to wait for a kiss till we're out of the public gaze,' Emily said, as they packed the kids up and headed down to the gardens along the riverbank.

Andy pecked Emily on the cheek while the girls became fascinated by the activities of the ducks and swans in the water and on the riverbank. Later, Andy produced an empty two-pound jam jar, which he'd acquired from the café, and showed the girls how to collect fresh-water life from the river's edge. He was excellent at it, while the kids were hopeless. Besides, Emily didn't want them in the water. Eventually, they had a jar full of tiny creatures and tiddlers to show for it.

'Well done, Andy,' said Emily. 'You're really good at collecting stuff.'

'Local knowledge,' said Andy. 'You forget I'm local.'

'Won't the fish eat the water creatures? Wash your hands before your food.'

After lunch, they rolled down the small slope, which proved fun, before they wandered along the riverbank until it got too muddy underfoot.

Andy hadn't found much time to memorise his words for the concert. When he looked at them he knew they would be easily memorised.

'I seem to be in all the sketches,' he said.

'Bessie is short of men,' said Emily.

'I'm in everything.'

'I hope you're not going to make a fool of yourself,' said Emily.

'Surely the idea of sketches is to make a fool of yourself.'

They bought a pot of tea and finished up their special treat of strawberry jam sandwiches. Emily felt that she had a family again for the first time since Jimmy's departure three years ago. Maybe they should get married. It was a thought.

Bessie's concert for Holidays at Home took place in the old mission. The concert hall was packed out with the local people starved of live entertainment. It was very much one of those concerts where the leading light directs operations from the piano stool because she is the only competent pianist. This was Bessie's role. She accompanied all the dancing and singing acts, directed and encouraged events from the side and then sung one or two of her favourite Gracie Fields and George Formby numbers.

The show opened with the tiny tots from the local tap-dancing school hoofing away on stage to 'Happy Days are here again. The skies of grey are clear again. So we'll sing a song of cheer again. Happy Days are here again', a very relevant song, which mirrored the mood of the moment because the Allies had certainly started moving forward on the battlefield. The grandmothers were in a state of ecstasy, watching their little grandchildren hammering it out on the stage. All the costumes were make-do and mend. The audience clapped the dresses and outfits they'd helped make themselves. True to form, there was one little girl who went to pieces completely on the stage and had to be carried off by her mother, crying, but once back in her mother's loving arms, she felt secure all of a sudden and couldn't understand what all the fuss was about. She warranted a special round of applause.

This was followed by Andy's first sketch: The travelling salesman arrives at the hotel and is shown to his room by a beautiful chambermaid. She leaves him and a little later he decides he would like her back. He rings down to reception and an ancient geezer appears and asks, 'You rang, sir? Can I help?'

'Not you,' the travelling salesman says, 'where's the chambermaid?'

The old geezer staggers across the room, reaches under the bed and pulls out the guzunder, peers inside the pot and says, 'Stoke-on-Trent, sir.'

The audience fell apart laughing. It was quite a rude sketch but the audience couldn't stop laughing and considered Andy a comedy genius. Bessie, at the piano, was helpless with laughter, even though she'd seen the sketch many times in rehearsal.

Emily was pleased with Andy's performance as an old geezer and beamed with pride. The next item was three singers from the choir singing *All Through the Night*.

This was followed by the tap-dancers, still intent on drilling a hole through the stage to the cellars. Bessie then sang George Formby's *When I'm Cleaning Windows*.

Andy's next sketch was the one about the father waiting in the hospital for his new baby to arrive. He's told his wife has already had a baby but he needs to wait a while for further news. This is repeated until the fellow decides to wait in the pub and is given the phone number 12345. The final scene is the one where he is phoning the hospital using the number 54321. He has inadvertently phoned the local cricket club at Wadham Road. A cricketer answers the phone, 'Hello!'

'What's the final score?'

'Seventeen all out,' comes the answer, 'and the last three were ducks.'

The father passes out on the stage. Andy was most realistic. The audience applauded when Andy was helped back on to his feet by Bessie, who was laughing herself silly. The choirboys, of course, were beginning to see Andy as a real actor from Hollywood, particularly as he was so convincing in the way he collapsed. Emily was impressed.

The choir sang three choral numbers and Andy was clapped when he came on stage to take his position on the back row. Bessie used the choir as backing when she sang *We'll Meet Again*. Then the little dancers danced to music from the *Wizard of Oz*. There was just one little clod-hopping boy out of step and bobbing about in front of the girls. He'd obviously been taken to lessons by his elder sisters, under pain of death from his dance-crazed mother.

Bessie sang *Blow the Wind Southerly* unaccompanied. She sang it so full of feeling and emotion that some people were close to tears. The audience were in raptures when the concert came to an end. The vicar stepped forward at the end to thank everybody, especially Bessie, for the excellent evening's entertainment.

'Beautiful, beautiful, beautiful. I'm going to ask you, Bess, in front of these people, all assembled ...'

Ada whispered in Emily's ear. 'He sounds like he's going to propose.'

'... in front of these people, all assembled ... will you join the choir?'

Nobody could hear Bessie's answer because the mission was filled with masses of applause. Everybody had enjoyed their first concert for years. Then the entire audience sang *Land of Hope and Glory* and the evening ended with *God Save the King* being sang really loudly with feeling, as if it would help end the war a bit quicker.

The vicar thanked Bessie again and repeated his plea.

'It was a truly excellent concert, Miss Prescott. You should really seriously consider joining the choir. Don't you think so, Emily?'

'I'm always telling her, Vicar.'

'Maybe you could persuade her?' said the vicar.

'I've too much on each evening, Vicar,' said Bessie.

'Well, think it over.'

'I will,' repeated Bessie.

When they had discovered a little privacy, Emily told Andy how pleased she was with him for joining in with the concert party.

'You were really exceptional tonight, Andy. Trust me to be the one who is so slow about marriage, but somebody had to be. It was never going to be you. I'm really so pleased.'

Emily was really happy with herself and life. Andy was just pleased he'd stayed the course.

Chapter 19

Neighbours

Emily's immediate neighbours, Freddie and Colin, usually played just a pastoral part in her life. The only time there was ever any disagreement was when Freddie had had too much to drink and, in the absence of upstairs plumbing, he relieved himself out of the front bedroom window. It was just too bad if you were returning home late from the cinema and everybody else was tucked up in bed asleep.

Freddie had a heart of gold and gave away many of the eggs his hens had laid and also many of the tins of fruit and salmon from America. Emily was keeping her diary up to date after another busy week, when Colin came running in through the backyard.

'Me dad's ill. Can y'come, Emily?'

'Still drunk from last night, I expect?'

'No. He's dying.' Colin said. Emily thought she had better check and followed the upset lad back home. He's probably exaggerating, she thought. Freddie was sitting up in bed looking pathetically ill. The bedding smelt appalling; the linen stank of damp sweat, beer and cigarettes. The sheets looked as if they'd fall apart in a wash. There was a strong smell of urine.

'Look at you,' Emily said, ruthless to an easy target.

'I lost a bet,' gasped Freddie.

'So then you said, "Great, I'll drink myself to death"?'

'No, it's me waterworks,' said Freddie. 'You know that, Emily.'

'Just let's say, some places have pavement artists who work in chalk and crayon. We have the original piss-artist in our midst.'

'It's not like that,' Freddie pleaded, a little hurt.

'It is like that. All over the pavement for all to see. Figures of eight, shamrocks, loop-the-loops; all artistic stuff, it has to be said.'

Freddie was obviously acutely ill because he couldn't take a good wholesome scouse rebuke in his stride and started to blubber. Soon he was weeping gallons of tears down his old crinkled cheeks. Emily was amazed that her rebuke had had such an effect.

'I'm really very, very sorry,' Freddie wept.

Emily thought she should continue telling him off; it would save her time and energy in future. Save all the nagging.

'You're sorry? I'm sorry; he's sorry; they're sorry. What's a few wet feet and the occasional spray between friends?'

'It's not like that,' Freddie cried like a child.

'You can't blame old age. You're only in your fifties, for God's sake,' Emily continued.

If she was going to make him see sense and do what he was told in future, she needed to be ruthless.

'Emily, stop sounding like a foghorn on the river.'

'What's the problem then, Freddie?' asked Emily.

'It's the hawk.'

'The what? What hawk? Which hawk?'

Emily hadn't a clue as to what he had said. For his part, Freddie just wept and stuttered, which didn't help matters.

'The h-h-haw-k.'

'Oh, come on, Fred. This is getting too far-fetched. God bless us. Are you bewitched?' she asked.

Emily why she was bothering to discuss it with a man who was still drunk from the previous night. 'Right, I'm fetching Doctor Golding. Yer losing your marbles.' She retreated to the door. 'Great headlines this'll make in the *Echo*. "Local Piss-Artist Blames Witches". That'll shove the war off the front pages.'

'No–no, no,' Freddie cried.

Emily paused at the door.

'Witches did it, indeed? I'll fetch Doctor Golding.'

Fortunately, Emily met Bessie outside. She had heard the commotion.

'He's as mad as a hatter. Thinks it's witches. He's feeling very sorry for himself, crying buckets of tears, like a baby,' reported Emily. 'We'll send for the doctor.'

'Pathetic to see a grown man cry. I'll fetch him some freshly made scouse. We'll feed him some wholesome food, even if we have to force it down him,' said Bessie, before she went to fetch the meal across.

She fed Colin a generous portion of scouse in the kitchen and then they returned to the bedroom.

'Right, so you haven't eaten for a week. Just drinking on an empty stomach, Colin tells me,' stated Bessie. 'The poor lad is tucking into his first square meal for a week downstairs. He's fed up of baked beans.'

'Right, get this down yer. Eat it,' announced Emily. 'Hold his nose, Bess.'

Bessie held Freddie's nose and Freddie struggled with the little strength he had.

'For God, sake, Bess. Don't throttle him.'

'Wish I could. He won't stop struggling.'

'Get yer knees off his shoulders then.'

Bessie's obese body was perched like a human mountain on top of Freddie lying spreadeagled on the bed.

'Are you sure the bed will take the full weight, Bess?' asked Emily.

Freddie spluttered. 'Get off my chest. You'll fracture me rib-cage. God, woman, once around you, twice around the gasworks.'

'If you don't shut up, we'll fetch Father Deegan.'

'A bottle of whisky would be better than fifty priests.'

'Your problem is that you've nothing in your stomach and yer body can't absorb the drink. So eat some food and we'll be off. Come on, be a good boy.'

Meanwhile, downstairs, Colin had finished his plate of scouse and been awarded another heaped plateful by Bessie, which hadn't touched the sides of his mouth on the way down to his stomach.

'How long's yer dad not been eating, just drinking?'

'He never eats. There's never any food in the house, only drink.'

'Where's he keep his money? We'll need three and six for the doctor when he comes,' asked Emily.

'There's two large earthenware jars at either end of the mantelpiece,' Colin said.

Emily looked inside the jars. They were both crammed full of cash, mostly half-crowns and two-shilling coins. It would be money from Freddie's lucrative trade in contraceptives and nylons. The money spilt out as Emily counted out three and six.

'These jars are bottomless pits of cash,' said Emily.

'There's more money in the hidey-hole,' added Colin.

'No, this'll do. Just shows, you can starve in a house full of money. It's easy to see where the half-dollars come from,' said Emily, as she inspected the dilapidated living room.

There was the metal tail of an incendiary bomb on the mantelpiece between the two jars of cash. The room could have been bombed just yesterday; the thick grey dust of the Blitz coated all the furniture and the lampshade.

'With so much cash, it's almost like Aladdin's cave; but I think Aladdin tidied up occasionally,' suggested Emily.

'Everything in place and the piss-pot on the dresser, they say,' Bessie surmised. 'Here it's nothing in place and an incendiary on the mantelpiece.'

'Isn't it amazing how dirty men are when left to themselves?' said Emily, blowing the grey dust off the mantelpiece, before she found a bottle of whisky tucked behind the clock. She showed it to Bessie. 'Half empty,' she said.

'We'll keep drink out of the place while he's confined to bed,' said Bessie.

Meanwhile, Doctor Golding had driven up outside in his car and used the black knocker on the front door. They showed him up the stairs to Freddie's bedroom.

'This way, Doctor.'

It wasn't long before the doctor had examined Freddie and asked him a few questions, showing a stern disapproval of his diet and eating habits.

'You realise that you are killing yourself,' said the doctor.

Freddie nodded and was near to tears but managed to hold them back. The doctor collected up his stuff and then went down the stairs to the kitchen.

'Apart from the defective liver through his drinking, he's still shell-shocked.'

'The Great War has been over twenty-five years and Freddie isn't a coward,' Bessie decided to point out, in his defence, she thought.

'Shell-shocked men are not cowards; that's old thinking. He's still a bag of nerves from being one of only twenty survivors. Terrible experience, watching your friends drown off Jutland. Men turned to drink after the war. Helped them face up to life; but it ruined their insides. Freddie has cirrhosis of the liver.'

'Yes, Doctor,' the women said in unison, to suggest they knew what he'd said.

'He's feeling guilty because he knows he's killing himself. I take it he has a weak bladder.'

'Yes, Doctor, like April showers. Except that there's no flowers.'

'Is there anything else?' asked the doctor.

Colin, who was on his third helping of scouse, came to life. He spoke, restricted by a mouth full of food.

'He jumps out of his skin, if there's a loud bang near him,' he said.

'We all do,' said Bessie. 'It's what the Blitz did to us.'

'He quakes and quivers for nothing and stammers, like the king,' he added.

'Did he tell you that he was on H.M.S Hawk when it went down off Jutland?'

'Nothing to do with witches?' Emily asked, feeling stupid.

The doctor continued. 'Nothing. The Hawk was a frigate. I'm trying to remember the story. A fellow called Jackie Parnell. Ask him to tell you about Jackie Parnell.' The doctor moved to go but paused at the door. 'And don't forget to pray for me.'

He smiled as he went out but Bessie asked, 'Why do you say that, Doctor?'

'It's just my attempt at mischievous humour. My response to the Catholic prayer "Let us pray for the perfidious Jews",' he smiled.

'That's okay, Doctor. We're C of E.'

The doctor smiled back and climbed into his car and had soon left the street.

'The cheek of it.'

'I think the doctor thinks we look like Catholics,' said Bessie.

'There you go again, Bessie. What exactly do Catholics look like?'

'Probably Bing. He always plays a priest in films.'

'Besides, what does a perforated Jew look like?'

Next day, Emily took Freddie some breakfast in. Some of his own eggs, boiled, and some thick toast with lots of butter and strawberry jam, which was like gold.

'There you are, you old bugger. You don't deserve it but you've got to eat. Anyway, the doctor says I've to ask you all about Jackie Parnell,' she said sheepishly.

Freddie was sitting up in bed eating his breakfast and was stunned at Emily's question. She knew she had hit home.

'So what's all this about Jackie Parnell?' she urged.

'Another Liverpool lad. The bulkhead landed on his foot and we heaved him out. We swam away from the Hawk before it took us down with it.'

'Is that it?'

'No. You see Jackie was built like a shithouse door. Should have seen the shoulders on him. When we got to the recovery ship we discovered that he'd swum all the way across with no foot.'

Emily felt shocked and rather sorry she'd asked.

'Yes. He'd swum all the way and he even helped me, 'cos it was bloody tough for me with two good feet.'

Emily was impressed.

'We asked him before he passed out, where his foot was. He said, "Under the bulkhead, and don't think I'm swimming back for it." Then he conked out.'

'Something of a hero, then?'

'Yes. Jackie was. Big man; big heart.'

'Not him. You, you silly bugger.' Now she knew the full facts, Emily had a lot more sympathy for Freddie. 'Now that I've made you better by making you eat properly, I want you to look after yourself and young Colin much more sensibly in future. You should be up and at it again by the end of the week.'

Emily told the vicar all about it as he ate his breakfast and she was laying a fresh fire in the dining room. He listened intently.

'He was one of only twenty survivors.'

'I'll mention it to Father Deegan, next time we meet.'

Bessie was performing in the pub when Emily happened to be passing. She could hear the tune of *Mairzy Doats* being hammered out on the piano. It could only be Bessie. She opened the door and casually peered inside at Bessie singing away.

> 'Mersey Docks and Harbour Board and Wallasey and New Brighton,
> Eye diddly, eye-dee-doo wouldn't you ... Oh
> Catch the boat to Birkenhead, visit the one-eyed city,
> Eye diddly, eye-dee-doo wouldn't you.'

Bessie caught a glimpse of Emily in the doorway and changed her lyrics to just a repeat of the last line of the chorus. She signed off and then chatted away to Emily.

'Basically, the vicar has told Father Deegan about Freddie, so he's going to pay him a visit. Didn't know Freddie was at Jutland,' said Emily.

'I'm not surprised. Nobody knows I'm at Bootle,' she said. 'Not a soul.' She added, 'Maybe the priest will help him sort himself out.'

'You make out that living in Bootle is like a life sentence,' said Emily.

'Well it is. You don't come out alive. Maybe Freddie will give more of his time to poor Colin, now he's had all the warnings,' suggested Bessie.

'The poor priest has got thousands like Freddie to help out,' noted Emily.

'Maybe that's why so many Catholics emigrate to America,' mused Bessie.

'What's that got to do with it?'

'Well, it's always priests in films; never a vicar,' confirmed Bessie.

Something might have come out of a visit to see Freddie Mack by Father Deegan, if he'd counselled him before he'd returned to his drinking ways. However, he arrived too late. Freddie had been drinking all day at home and had topped it up with ten pints of mild at the pub. The father timed it badly and arrived just as Freddie was relieving himself of his excess liquid out of the front window. No prisoners were taken. A deluge of urine descended from the top floor just as the father was knocking on the front door. Freddie didn't hear the knock as he collapsed back into his bed. Father Deegan walked purposefully out of the street, as wet as a duck in mating season.

A week later, Freddie was studying an official letter, which had been dropped through the letter box by hand; that told him it had not travelled far.

'They can't even afford a postage stamp,' said Freddie.

'So what does this mean? Does it mean you won't go to heaven?' asked Colin.

'That's the gist of it. I've been banned from taking Mass or entering the church. They think I won't go to heaven.'

'They should know,' Colin decided.

'How do they know? None of them's been there. And I'm pretty sure they didn't clear it by phone, before they penned this letter.'

'So you're not excommunicated?' asked Colin.

'No. Only the Pope has the right to do that. They're hardly going to tell him it's because I haven't got a WC on the top floor, are they?'

'I thought it was because you sold contraceptives.'

'That, too, maybe. But really, Colin, it's because they don't think I was married to your mother. Your mother was Protestant. I married out of the faith. It's not a new ban. I've always been banned.'

'So why the letter, Dad?' asked Colin.

'Well, basically, they don't want to face me. The letter is "talking at" me from what they consider is a respectable distance. Sort of making sure that I know my place, which isn't in their church.'

'And my mother was a Protestant?'

'Yes, Colin, but I loved your mother and we'd have made a go of it, if she'd lived; but pneumonia isn't choosy. Only last week a fourteen-year-old girl died from it in the next street.'

'So why don't they like you?'

'It's probably because I'm from Glasgow. Anyway, who wants to go to heaven, if it's full of Englishmen playing cricket and speaking all posh like "it's a farce sitting on the gr-ar-ce, all by yourself in the moonlight". Besides, they sent all the best things down from heaven. The Scottish pipes and whisky are things of heaven. So I'll have a good case to argue on Judgement Day when the Archangel Gabriel asks me what I did with my life. I'll tell him.'

'What?'

'I'll tell him, I was there when they crucified Liverpool.'

'Who?'

'The Germans. They thought they were bombing the fleet and the convoys; but they were killing scousers and driving them out into the fields.'

'So they will let you into heaven?' asked Colin.

'Never more certain. The guy at the gates is called Archangel Gabriel; that's a good old Scottish name, if ever there was one. The Gabriels owned the corner shop in Govan.'

'So have they opened a shop in heaven?'

'Who said anything about a shop?' Freddie thought for a time and then delivered the most condescending rebuke he could muster. 'Y'know, Colin, sometimes you come out with the most unadulterated drivel. I'm ashamed to ... I'm ashamed to ...' He was lost for words.

A week later Colin collected his father from outside the pub, where he was throwing up all over the pavement. It would have embarrassed any adult but Colin just walked him home and put him to bed, where he went straight off to sleep like a baby. Emily counted out another three and six from the money jugs on the mantelpiece. Emily was amazed that the amount of money never decreased. Both jugs were overflowing on to the fireplace. I wish I had just one fountain of cash on my mantelpiece,' thought Emily. She sent Colin off to collect Doctor Golding and he was soon parked out in the street. He slipped inside; he knew his routine by now.

'It's his liver,' he told Emily afterwards. 'It's worn out. He shouldn't be drinking.'

After the doctor had departed Emily talked to Colin in an attempt to explain the situation.

'You can see that your father is very ill. Why have you been fetching him whisky?'

'He's been asking for it.'

'It's killing him.'

Freddie lay in a coma for days at a time. He seemed to be in a world of ships and swimming to safety, or he was having dealings with the Brennans and selling nylons in the pub.

'Look at your father in bed now. He's out to the world. How long has he been as ill as this?'

'He's been throwing up for a week and blacked out yesterday.'

'Colin ... Colin. I wish you'd told me, son,' groaned Emily.

Emily decided that she would scribble a note to one of her long time associates. She wrote in large letters on the envelope, 'Father B. Deegan.

'Take this around to the Catholic presbytery. Just say Emily sent you and you've to give him this.'

In the letter, Emily pleaded with the father to come around and say one or two words for a member of his flock who had strayed, adding that the letter was being delivered by his son, Colin.

Colin knocked at the presbytery door and it was opened just a fraction. The father peered out and saw the young lad bearing the letter.

'The letter is from Emily,' said Colin.

'Ah, yes, Emily. One of God's mothers. Thank Emily for me.'

The father closed the door and Colin returned home. When he arrived back home Freddie was looking pale and emaciated. The doctor had just paid another visit.

'Keep trying him with food. Miracles happen,' suggested the doctor.

'He can't keep anything down,' Emily confided.

'Try your best. Who knows, the worst may have passed.' The doctor turned at the door and added, 'Pray for me,' smiling.

Emily appreciated his joke now and smiled back as he made his way out and Bessie appeared on the scene.

'Every time I do another show it's another sixpence. How come the doctor gets three and six a time?' asked Bessie.

'You can't cure the ills of the world, only prolong the agony singing,' said Emily, brewing up again.

'Thanks, Emily. Nothing like a round of applause,' said Bessie.

'Here, have a cup of char instead.'

Emily handed her a cup of tea. She'd just taken a sip when there was a heavy knocking on the front door. Outside, there was a furniture van and a fellow in overalls looking for the 'Macks'.

'It's this house,' Bessie announced, not knowing what was being delivered.

Soon, they all could see it was a new single bed for Colin. It was lified upstairs into the empty room with the bomb hole still in the ceiling. Colin was extremely happy at last.

'Just shows you what a little letter will do occasionally,' said a pleased Emily.

'Thanks for getting me a bed at last,' said Colin, thanking Emily. 'You are like Mrs Miniver on the pictures.'

'It's okay. I think you should thank Father Deegan rather than me. You need to be by yourself, with your dad being so poorly.' Emily was pleased and pondered the Mrs Miniver tag. 'They'll never name a rose after me. The "Emily Jones",' she laughed.

'You do help bring most kids into the world, nurse the sick and see the old dears into the next,' said Bessie. 'And you don't even get a sixpence for it.'

'Still smarting, Bess, because I said your singing wasn't worth three and six?'

'No. You are a sort of Mrs Miniver,' decided Bessie.

'I'm never that posh. What will you do when I leave for Canada after the war?'

Bessie was caught unawares. 'You're not emigrating are you?'

She was rather shocked and completely amazed. Emily didn't say anything further on the subject but she had started to plan for the future and think seriously about going to Canada.

Chapter 20

To Russia

In the middle of Emily's toing and froing from Freddie's sickroom and her work at the vicarage, Andy went back to sea. He had had an extended leave and he was looking forward to marrying Emily in a year's time. Life aboard the Buzzard was much as it had been when he had left in the huge glow of success in March.

Now he had two places where he felt at home, the ship and Liverpool. Emily hadn't told him that she had started thinking about moving with him to Canada at the end of hostilities. He still thought that it would be down to his powers of persuasion.

Out in the open Atlantic the first U-boat was spotted by one of the aircraft out from the aircraft-carrier the group were working with. One of the ships in the group made the contact but it was the Buzzard that carried out the first attack. Amazingly, the U-boat was sunk with the first pattern of depth charges. Ginger Hardy was growing in confidence and playing a larger role in the action.

Indeed, it was he who spotted the merchantman's rowing boat in the sea, three hundred miles west of Ireland. The skipper didn't think twice about picking up the survivors in the boat.

'We've cleared the area of U-boats.'

They took the twenty men aboard. They were all shocked, concussed and some were ill, near to death; others, notably the senior ranks, were really drunk and out of this world. They'd probably been torpedoed by the same U-boat that the Buzzard had later sunk. The last poor wretch aboard caught a sudden lurch by the vessel, hammered his head against the gunwale and fell like a rock beneath the waves. They couldn't find him.

'Three days in the ocean and now this,' said Andy. 'Poor bastard.'

Being merchant seamen they were no longer in receipt of pay because their ship had sunk under them and now, of course, they had no job.

'No wonder they are drunk,' said the skipper. 'When I see guys like this I know why we are fighting this war but how long must this bloody war continue?'

The group were ordered to Scapa and issued with cold-weather gear. It was called Eskimo clothes. The new gear was windproof, chill proof and waterproof. The crew spent a day ashore at the Home Fleet's HQ. There were some smart facilities with a huge canteen and a cinema, which could take Ensa shows. There were no famous entertainers there at the time and the lack of a decent grubby, Liverpool dock-road pub was a distinct disadvantage. It was left to Ginger to put his foot in it, when the group were looking around the facilities.

'Wouldn't you think that with all the money they've spent on this place they might have built a decent pub,' he scoffed.

'What do you mean by that? This is the best British base in the world,' said the officer showing them around the base and taking exception to Ginger's comments.

'I can show you a dozen pubs in Liverpool with more heart and soul and better facilities than up here,' said Ginger. 'There's not even a lady of the night.'

The officer was really upset. He'd never heard the base criticised before in this way. He threatened to place Ginger on a charge, when Andy interrupted the discussion.

'Ginger, catch up with the other lads in the mess, please,' he pleaded.

'I didn't mean it like that,' said Ginger.

'Please, Ginger. Follow them to the mess.'

Andy eventually got his own way and explained to the officer that Ginger was a bit of a new boy, who didn't know what he was talking about.

'He's lucky he isn't a new boy on a charge,' the officer commented.

However, Scapa and Eskimo clothes meant only one thing – Russia. Despite the warm kit, nobody was happy at the promise of ice and the prospect of the violent Arctic storms; but it would have to be faced up to one way or the other. The convoy set off for Russia and, from the beginning, German air patrols from Norway were continuous, so the convoy was spotted early in the trip. This gave the wolf packs lots of time to work out where the best place was to attack. The convoy was heading for Vaenga Bay and, whatever the zig-zag employed, the end result was the same; the convoy had to round the north of Norway.

It was bitterly cold and Andy worked hard at keeping warm. He worked out the driest place to swing his hammock; keeping it low meant he reduced the ice-cold draught. It was dark for only five hours each night, which limited the time the enemy could be active, but aircraft from the convoy were busy during all of the nineteen hours of daylight. This was with the exception of when there were snow storms, and they were frequent. Andy could set his watch by them and arrange for a hot cup of whatever was going and a thick, healthy sandwich, usually corned beef, as soon as the snow fell.

Early on in the trip they stumbled over a U-boat in the path of the zig-zagging convoy. Obviously, the vessel was full of raw recruits on their first trip out from the new U-boat bases in Norway. Applying the straightforward tactic of keeping quiet was reasonable enough but with the boss as your adversary it was a little too obvious. The wreckage of the U-boat was soon on the bottom of the cold Atlantic. Air attacks from Norway never materialised and soon they were anchored in Vaenga Bay.

Vaenga Bay 68°02' North/33°10 East

Some time was spent larking about in the snow but Andy, ever mindful of his exploits in St Johns, declined the offer of another skiing display. He could see the smiles hidden behind straight faces when they dug out some skis for him. They fancied another snowball fight, with him as moving target. He caught up on his sleep instead.

The trip back was a nightmare. They spent the whole voyage fighting against their strongest adversary – the North Atlantic hurricane. The only good thing was that the convoy was protected from the enemy, who were guarding their own safety.

Andy didn't know if this was good or bad. They were sitting ducks in the ocean because they were going nowhere for days on end. Andy concentrated on keeping himself warm and fed with easy-to-eat food. He'd perfected the art on his trips across from Nova Scotia. Now it was cruelly put to the test. After five days, the ship was still roughly in the same place; insignificant progress had been made; finding a passage around the top of Norway was impossible, but they struggled on. This was the worst weather that Andy had ever experienced on land or sea.

Ships just bobbed up and down at all points of the compass and were now miles apart. Forget the war, the whole sea was covered in struggling ships. The gale, which Andy concluded was from the south, had swept the length of the Atlantic. The storm was in a depressing rage about something. Maybe it's the war, thought Andy. We're all pissed off about that.

Some of the waves must have been a mile long from crest to crest. Sometimes, if there was a slight variation, the irregular edge tossed any ship in its path into the air.

The landing was soft but there was a lot of it. Tons of water oozed in and out of the vessel on a mission to wreck. Boats on the deck, although tightly lashed, were smashed mercilessly and the ship's funnels were buckled. The whole superstructure of some ships was hammered out of shape, like a piece of cardboard.

The wind screamed through the rigging and sounded like an overture composed by Neptune. Fearful nights slipped into hopeless days. It just went on and on relentlessly. Andy concentrated on keeping himself together. It was difficult with the ship cracking up around him, and the yudderings and shudderings were uncomfortable. He just wanted them to desist. Normally, the Buzzard could help out other ships in distress in a storm, but not this one. It was every ship for herself. Day after day the battle continued with the ship going this way, that way and back again. Andy wondered where they would be at the end of the storm.

Everybody was struggling to eat without emptying the food all over the place. Andy sandwiched everything and kept each sandwich in a separate pocket from which he would munch it quickly, when the storm wasn't looking. Being thrown about the deck was the hardest part of the day or night, making sure you weren't injured or swept overboard. Paying a visit to the heads, the toilets, was a major trial to see if you could remain in place to deliver your residue, standing up, or sitting down. The whole facility stank of vomit, stale food and human waste. It was good to get back outside after you had clung on for dear life, while the ship swung mindlessly.

There were no aids to navigation. There were no stars at night and no sun during the day. The navigator guessed where they where, noting exactly sunset and sunrise, and from this he could work out a northern position. The only east-west position was principally derived from the conclusion that they hadn't hit Norway yet. Basically, they were near the Arctic Circle and in the middle of the Atlantic, between Iceland and Norway, and not far removed from the previous day's guessed position.

The mess deck was a shambles and there was no hot food. Andy's pocketed corned beef sandwiches kept him alive. His clothes were best kept dry on his body and he looked out for himself, while the Buzzard survived every assault from nature. She was built for it. She pitched, swung about and struggled her way through the ocean; but she was up to it. Some ships gave up in weather like this but the Buzzard rode the waves.

The day came when the wind dropped to just a reasonable force and the sun dried the decks. There were only four ships where the convoy should have been. Over the course of the next three days the ships of the convoy were located; the weather was still wild but most of the convoy was intact. They headed for Scapa, hoping that the enemy would be slow off the mark.

By mid-1944 there was less purpose to the enemy attacks and the U-boats seemed to be less courageous than before. The Buzzard went straight into preparations for the D-Day landings. The ship was to perform her usual role off the Normandy beaches, keeping the area free from U-boats. It was a very quiet affair. The nearest action came over three hundred miles away, when an American escort was torpedoed. The Buzzard chased after the U-boat and three days later the U-boat was located. She was then chased for another twelve hours. Just after midnight, the U-boat was spotted on the surface but heading off with an amazing burst of speed. It zig-zagged and fired torpedoes and wasn't going to give up easily. Every gun let fly and, eventually, the U-boat turned and decided it was going to try to ram one of the group. The ships of the group kept firing, even when she came very close in. Eventually, all the activity paid off and there was a huge explosion and the U-boat slid beneath the waves.

The German survivors were picked up. Their captain had been killed in the action and this had been the signal for the rest of the crew to abandon ship. The battle had lasted a full day. Andy was knackered. The group headed off to patrol the beaches off the landing zone.

After the landings the group returned to Liverpool for repairs, an oil change and boiler cleaning. Some of the jobs dated from the trip to Russia. Andy knew he was home when he saw the white concrete end to Gladstone Dock jutting out into the channel. It was absolutely exhilarating to be on the Buzzard, wending her way in from Liverpool Bay with the prospect of at least a little leave.

Chapter 21

The Big Fall Out

Liverpool was very busy, with armaments and explosives being loaded on to trains and sent down south for the build-up in France. Andy was tied up with the ship in dry dock, while repairs were carried out. The shipwrights listened in disbelief as he explained that the severely dented superstructure was not down to enemy action but to a week's heavy pounding from the North Atlantic.

It was a miserable, wet August and Emily was engrossed in her work at the vicarage and in watching out for her irresponsible neighbour's decline in health. Emily and Bessie had been chatting in the kitchen, fixing up a decent square meal for Colin, when they heard the front door close ever so quietly. Freddie had slipped out, unnoticed. He walked away from the street dressed in just his overcoat, pyjamas and flat cap. It was misty and wet but he was on a mission. He headed along the Stanley Road towards Bankhall. Eventually, he reached his destination, the Commodore cinema. He sat outside on the white-tiled art-deco steps. He was well wrapped up, except for his carpet slippers. The one person he didn't want to see came out of the cinema: Colin.

'What are you doing here?' Colin asked responsibly.

'Getting away from you and those mad women.'

'You're killing yourself, Dad,' rapped Colin.

'That's the idea,' answered Freddie.

'Anyway. I need you to write me an absence note for school.'

'Ruined my bit of peace and quiet then,' said Freddie.

'They need a note,' stated Colin.

'Didn't you say that I'm ill?'

'Mr Cook reads out the absence notes to the class to shame us, and says that our mothers will never go to heaven, if it goes by the lies they tell on absence notes. And, if it came down to spelling, they'd never get into hell, either.'

'Didn't you say that your mother is in heaven already, looking forward to seeing me in a week or two,' said Freddie, unmoved.

'You'll be okay, Dad, won't you, Dad?'

'Course I will y' soft bugger.'

That satisfied Colin, who loved his dad.

'What are you doing here, getting cold?' asked Colin.

'I'm just irresponsible, one last time. It's here that I first met your mother.'

'Sitting on the steps?'

'Well, queuing up for *The Jazz Singer*. And that is why I'm here.'

'She's not here now.'

'She is, Colin. She'll always be here. I can feel her about me. We'll get back home now. I just needed a chat with your mother.'

When Freddie and Colin returned, the dark-suited man from the Pru was sitting on his bike outside the house, waiting. He smiled at Freddie; now they would get down to business. Freddie was one of his few customers with money.

'There's something for you inside,' Freddie said.

All three disappeared into the house, where Freddie handed the dark-suited man a list.

'That's what I want. You've got all those policies I've been paying off all these years,' said Freddie, proud of his list.

The agent scanned the long list.

'I'll keep it somewhere safe for the time being,' said the man from the Pru.

Meanwhile, Ada discovered that Percy had escaped from his cage. She went down to see Emily, and was just explaining when they heard a large commotion in Freddie's hen-pen next door. They raced around and entered Freddie's backyard. They could hear the tell-tale sounds of 'Jarmany calling, Jarmany calling'.

Percy was in the pen eating his way through the hens' food of mostly corn and seed. The hens cowered in the corner. Ada approached to reason with him. Just then, Maurice, the wildest dog on the block, shot into the pen, barking loudly.

Ada, anticipating danger, shouted out loudly, 'My poor bird. My poor bird. Help. Percy. Help.'

Percy coolly stopped chewing the corn, turned around and pecked Maurice viciously in the face twice, mid-bark, drew blood and calmly returned to his corn. Maurice performed a standing jump into the air in complete agony, and howled and whimpered, as if dying. He turned and raced back down the back-entry much faster than he had run up, sobbing his heart out.

Ada tried to retrieve Percy but he just took to the wing and flew straight up on to the nearest roof and looked down on the gathering throng shouting 'Jarmany calling, Jarmany calling'. Here, Percy continued his meal. Everybody laughed.

Colin borrowed a window-cleaning ladder from Ben Seddon and climbed up on the roof and talked to Percy quietly about a variety of subjects suggested by Ada, who was craning her neck to shout up. He calmed down and after such a good meal he just wanted to rest a while. He'd had enough fun for one day, so Colin was able to carry him down the ladder. Ada carried him back home triumphantly, placing him back in his cage, replenishing his dish with more of the food he liked from the hen-pen.

'My poor bird, my poor bird,' sighed Ada, before Percy started to sing 'Yes, Jesus loves me. Yes, Jesus loves me'.

I'm proud of my bird, thought Ada. First he quotes Chamberlain and now he's singing hymns. He must have learnt it off little Margaret.

Next morning, Freddie was up bright and breezy and out in his yard feeding his hens, dressed in well-worn pyjamas.

'What are you doing out in the cold?' Emily asked over the wall.

'Feeding the hens. Nobody else will.'

'Have you been taking your medicine?'

'Yes, Colin's been fetching it for me.'

Just then, Colin appeared carrying a bag, which looked suspiciously large to Emily. The object inside was much bigger than a bottle of medicine.

'Your medicine, Dad,' Colin said, as Emily grabbed the bag off him.

Inside the bag was a bottle of whisky and a bottle of cider.

'Sometimes you behave like the silly old reprobate that people think you are.'

'Don't hold back, Emily. Give it to me straight.'

'Get back to bed and we'll send some food up. I was expecting better of you, Colin,' Emily said.

Colin looked ashamed as he led the weak Freddie back indoors.

'You're drinking yourself to death.'

'That's the idea,' he said, before adding, 'I just need the freedom.'

'You'll get as much freedom as you want up there in heaven. An eternity.'

'Oh, good. Will I get a wee dram of whisky with it?' smiled Freddie.

'You'll get a kick up the arse if you carry on,' said Emily, annoyed.

'For Christ's sake, Emily, let me die in peace,' pleaded Freddie.

'Seems to be the object of the exercise,' sighed Emily.

Just then, the cavalry in the form of Mike Brennan arrived. The still sprightly, white-haired, Guinness-drinking septuagenarian appeared through the back door and assessed the situation as soon as he saw Freddie out in the back in just his pyjamas.

'Giving you grief is he, Emily?' he asked.

'Yes, he's killing himself and not thinking of Colin,' said Emily.

'Right, I'm ordering you back to bed you stupid old reprobate. I had come to ask you to put all your goods in my hands to make sure Colin gets a fair price, but first things first. Get yer arse back up those stairs, you worthless bastard,' said Mike, but Freddie was already pulling himself up the stairs with the help of Colin, protesting on every stair.

'Now the Brennans are lords in my own house, are they? Who put the Irish in charge in this green and pleasant land. It would never happen in Glasgow, I'm telling ya. If this is freedom, you can stick it up yer arse,' complained Freddie.

'Shut up complaining. I only came to tell you that I'll make sure Colin gets all your worldly goods. Me and me brothers will handle it for you,' said Mike.

Freddie stopped complaining and went back to bed. 'Oh, good, you will? Mike, thanks very much, I know I can trust you lads.'

About this time, the vicar was visiting Father Deegan over at the Catholic presbytery.

'You'd better come into my study, John,' the father suggested.

Once inside, the vicar was offered some claret as was the usual habit. They both sipped their wine slowly, savouring the thick taste of the sun. The vicar tried his hardest to taste the wine properly. This he found difficult because he knew the father would ask questions and he wanted to at least present some semblance of an answer. The father didn't ask a question but gave the answer.

'It's the same claret we enjoyed at the last civic dinner at your place.'

'Is it?' asked the vicar. 'My tastebuds aren't as well tuned as yours, Brendan.'

'What brings you here?'

'Emily has been nagging me silly,' sighed the vicar.

'What's new? If you are so easy-going with staff, they'll take advantage.'

'No. It's about her neighbour, Mr Mack. He's very ill. He needs prayers.'

'You know, I can't help. The man is no longer in my flock. No longer my responsibility or worry. Maybe you could minister something along the lines of the interdenominational stuff you used to deliver to the non-believing Inuit, John?'

'When it was three hundred miles to the nearest Catholic mission?' the Vicar sighed.

'Yes, just make sure you are wearing first-eleven kit, number ones only,' said the Father.

'Now, you're just being sarcastic, just because I've done it and you haven't. You know I possess just as fine vestments as you, when I can be bothered wearing them. You think I won't look the part?' queried the vicar.

'No. You're just too jolly; too easy-going.'

'And Christ wasn't,' commented the vicar, swigging the remainder of his claret.

The vicar returned to the vicarage, wondering what he could suggest to Emily, who was cooking the dinner in a heavily steamed-up kitchen.

'Emily, I've been to see Father Deegan and he won't say prayers for Mr Mack,' the vicar announced, quietly.

'What about you then?'

'I can't. I'm not of the faith.'

'You are not willing to be there, either? Well, thanks for nothing, vicar. It's true what the locals say about you,' Emily found herself saying.

'What's that?'

'You're so friendly with the priest that you must have gone over.'

Emily searched throughout Bootle looking for a parson of some description from any religion who was willing to say a few prayers for the dying Freddie. She explained the problem as best she could but either all the various sects lived in fear of each other or there was a closed shop when it came to heaven. It was a cold and miserable enterprise and, despite her efforts to find some denomination willing to undertake the job, she returned home unsuccessful. Bessie went out later, asking a few clerics she knew as an accomplished pianist, but even she returned empty-handed.

Back home, Emily's irresponsible next-door neighbour was in a terminal coma. Emily and Bessie spent the time socialising, while Freddie slept in the background and tracked through his fantasies and nightmares.

'How long have I got?' he asked, coming around.

'How long do you want?'

'Who are you kidding? I feel terrible. Another clean shirt and that'll be me. When I was in hospital after the Hawk went down, when your time came, they'd sing you out with your favourite hymn or song,' Freddie giggled. 'Fat chance of that here. Bessie can only sing filthy songs. Now that my ball's on the slates, I think I'll have *Count your Blessings.*'

Freddie went back to sleep, out to the world, into his dreams, as Emily and Bessie started to sing 'Count your Blessings While You May'.

'I wish I had my piano,' said Bessie.

'Why? Does your piano sing for you? Hang on a minute, I'll lug it up the stairs for you. Stop complaining and start singing. He's nodded off back to sleep.'

They sang the song as best they could. Suddenly, Freddie sat bolt upright in bed and asked, 'What's going on here?'

The women didn't know what to say. They couldn't very well say, 'You are supposed to be dying'. Freddie solved their dilemma.

'It's like a morgue in here. Can't you sing something by Al Jolson?'

Bessie started to sing *Sunny Boy*. 'Climb upon my knee, Sunny Boy. Though you're only three, Sunny Boy ... When there are grey skies. I don't mind the grey skies. I'll still have you.'

Before they had sung *Sunny Boy*, Emily said, 'He's gone.' Bessie stopped singing and Emily continued. 'Maybe I should say a few words. Seeing as there is nobody else here to do the job. Hands together.'

They both did.

'Oh, God, please accept Freddie into heaven with you. He'll make an excellent next-door neighbour.'

Then they both wept.

'Or one that lives three doors down,' added Bessie.

They walked back to Emily's house in the dark.

'You didn't have to say the "three doors down" thing.'

'Why? So God hasn't got a sense of humour? Miserable git is he?'

The next day in the kitchen at the vicarage, Emily collected her belongings. She was always ruthless with an easy target and, in this instance, the vicar was a sitting duck. She detested anything that she considered to be injustice and she thought that the vicar had been rather unfair and inconsiderate. He was returning innocently from the church wearing his cassock and surplice.

'What is going on?' he asked.

'I'm leaving. That's what, vicar,' said Emily.

'Why?'

'Andy wants me to go to Canada with him as soon as possible after the war is over. So I'm off with somebody who appreciates me.'

'But why this minute?' asked the vicar.

'Because you didn't turn up.'

'I couldn't.'

'Why? Because your intellectual friend behind closed doors said no?'

'All right, I'll be honest. Brendan talked me out of it.'

'Has it ever occurred to you that we women do all the slopping out in this life? Have all the babies, do all the shovelling and all the filthy jobs. We handle all the drudgery, while you men get all the cake.'

'It's not like that in the Church,' said the vicar, regretting his love of cake.

'You deceive yourself. It is. In the Church, men even get to wear the frocks.'

The vicar, besides feeling gulity about his love of cake, now felt even more guilty for wearing his vestments back from church, even though it was part of his job.

'That's not fair,' he muttered, without forming an argument.

'It's not unfair. Just a few simple words for a simple man and you can't do it. It's always left to us, the women, to pick up the pieces,' said Emily.

'It's the Pope's fault,' muttered the vicar, realising it was a silly comment.

'I knew you'd bring him into it. How can you blame the Pope? He plays outside-left for Italy,' said Emily without pausing.

'I can see that you are really upset, Emily,' decided the vicar.

'I'm sorry, Vicar, but you've really let me down. The church talks a lot about good neighbours but when a really good neighbour dies, none of you wants to know.'

Emily finished packing and made her way to the door.

'What am I going to do for tea?'

'You've plenty of tins of salmon in the pantry and some national loaf. Better still, go and ask Bessie. You'll find her singing in the Blobber.'

Emily left abruptly, hoping she had conveyed to the Vicar just how upset she was.

Bessie was at the piano in the Blobber, and well into her routine, when she noticed the vicar standing by the door.

'Now that dirty old woman was in bed one night ... Good evening, vicar. Won't you come over? I've just had a request for ...'

She asked around the punters quickly, attempting to change her material mid-song. *Count your Blessings*, wasn't it?'

So Bessie, not to be out-faced, sang the song in as straight and non-commercial a manner as she could manage. Her beautiful voice sounded even sweeter than usual and she won the day. The vicar listened, looking and feeling miserable, standing alone in the corner.

'Another show; another sixpence,' Bessie said to the vicar, who whispered something about it being teatime, and Bessie twiddled away at the keyboard before launching into *Breath of Life*. The vicar allowed her to sing the first verse, before he intervened again.

'Wonderful, Bessie, but can I have some tea? I'm starving. I've hardly eaten all day.' Bessie hadn't finished.

'*Breath of Life* was written by another Bessie. A lady called Bessie Porter Head, back in the 1920s. But I can see you'd rather I came with you to the vicarage,' she said.

The vicar led the way out of the door and Bessie mimed to the drinking customers, 'I've to go and put the kettle on,' and followed him into the street.

Emily was back to being an ordinary housewife, with all the chores. She black-leaded the grate for the first time in months. She set her own fire at home, rather than at the vicarage. Ada usually helped Emily at home, so at least she was enjoying a well-earned break. Emily had a full washday on Monday, trying to wash everything because it was a good drying day, a steady wind off the sea, with no rain about. Fortunately, Ada had already sandstoned the steps but she scrubbed the kitchen floor.

'This is harder work than my chores at the vicarage. Back to being a mum. Heck, I wish I was still working. This is pure drudgery. What's even worse is I don't get to see and talk to anybody passing through, 'cos nobody save Ada passes through.'

Chapter 22

The Funeral

Emily moved from depression into fantasy when Bessie popped in to tell her what had happened to Johnnie Singleton, who used to sit next to her in class in the 1920s.

'Well, he came into the pub,' Bessie began, with her usual opening words. 'He looked like a coloured. He was so brown. His skin was dried out. If you remember he has been missing, believed dead, for three years. Well, he's been marooned on an island in the Caribbean. He said off the Grenadines. Lived with the natives on fish and fruits like paw-paw, guava and different types of banana. Finally, he was rescued by some fishermen who took him to French Guiana. A place called Cayenne. The French there were Vichy, so they locked him up for over a year.'

'Are you making this up?' Emily asked.

'Bear with me. He escaped and stowed away on an Elder Dempster ship and arrived in Liverpool last week. He's found out about his wife, Annie, remarrying and moving to Newcastle. Now he has plans to go up there and save his marriage.'

'Does he know that she has twins by her "new" husband?'

'I didn't have the nerve to tell him,' added Bessie. 'It gets better. The navy police, just like the Yanks shore-patrol, comes into the pub and arrests him. Now he's locked up in Seaforth for desertion. He asked the officers, "Would I make up a story like that and live on a beautiful tropical island, just to avoid the war?" "Yes," they said.'

Emily had a nightmare that same night. Jimmy reappeared, clear as if he was standing in the room. He'd been marooned on an island

241

since 1941. He wanted to know just why she was planning to marry Andy. It was so real that it took a lot of snapping out of when she came around. It was all a nightmare; but what if Jimmy was still alive? Could just be red tape about him being dead. Then she recalled visiting his grave and his footballing friend, Calum, had told her all about his death first hand, as they wept together. That wasn't red tape. Face up to it. Jimmy is dead, she thought.

Andy must never know she was depressed. Times had changed. Andy was confident about the future, while she was the worried, miserable one. How was she going to get married now she had fallen out with the vicar? How would they pay for the wedding? She better not tell Andy. His head was just full of the war at sea. However, if, before too long, matters did not change, then she'd have to own up and find another job, preferably with good money.

'People will think I've lost my mind,' she confided in Bessie.

'I lost mine at Lewis's.' Bessie had misheard. 'Join the party.'

Emily was in her kitchen struggling with a pair of laces, which kept snapping.

'I bought these laces from a beggar. Took pity on him. "Strong laces," he said.' The laces snapped again. 'God they're strong,' she said sarcastically.

'Tie two pieces together,' suggested Bessie.

'I have done. There's three pieces already,' moaned Emily.

'I've got a pair you can have.'

'Suffering tantalising,' she cursed. 'Really strong laces.'

'Emily, I think the vicar is at the door. I'll be on my way,' said Bessie making to leave.

'Are you joking or something, Bess?' said Emily, still upset about the laces and not realising Bessie had purposely made a swift exit. 'If it is the pompous old vicar, tell him to take his hook and sling it.'

Just then, the Vicar slipped in through the door through which Bessie had departed. Emily was standing in the middle of the floor with two broken laces in her hands.

'I've come to say I'm sorry, Emily, and I'll do the funeral,' said the vicar, who, in all sincerity, was terribly upset.

He hadn't anticipated the response he was to get. Emily stood on her shoe laces, broken in four places, and tripped up. Then, losing her balance completely, she cascaded from one side of the kitchen to the other, landing in an ungainly heap in the corner.

'Emily, are you all right?' asked the vicar, helping her back to her feet.

'Other than wondering if I've broken my leg ... yes.'

Emily struggled to regain her poise, before taking her shoes off completely.

'That's better. Never buy goods out of pity, Vicar. You think you are helping out but your generosity is misplaced, you could end up in hospital. Poor laces.'

'Real rubbish,' the vicar agreed.

Emily was feeling more herself now after being soundly shaken up. Returning to earth with a bump had mellowed her.

'It isn't for me to stand my ground, Vicar, but I truly believe that sinners, and let's face it, Freddie was a sinner, should be loved by the Church, if not by everybody.'

'Yes ... yes, you are right, Emily. I didn't want to stand on Father Deegan's toes.'

'You see that table,' she spoke her mind. 'Freddie put food on that table at the beginning of the war, when I was struggling with the two kids, when Jimmy was called up. Freddie was a wonderful neighbour.'

'Emily, I've thought of a way to proceed with the funeral,' said the vicar.

'It's what I've always wanted all along. I'm really sorry about what I said. I was upset and tired and the words just spilt out.'

She wanted to make her peace.

The happy vicar left, full of thought. The friendly vicar-housekeeper relationship had been re-established, but it was too early to ask Emily to return to her post. Instead, Emily just picked herself up off the floor. There were no bones broken, just a little scrape. She saw a man with a dark suit propping his bike up against the outside wall. It was the man from the Pru. He knocked on the outside door and Emily answered tentatively.

'I've been holding Fred's will and policies for over a week. He's left ample money to do the job. Then there will be money from the raffle.'

'What raffle?'

'I think you'd better read the will.'

There was a look of genuine disbelief on Emily's face as she read the document presented to her by the man in the suit.

Next day Colin, his Auntie Milly, a small group of neighbours, one or two drinkers from the Blobber and the Brennan brothers, out in force, joined Emily and Bessie in the procession up to the church. The vicar had promised an interdenominational service, guaranteed not to upset people of any religion or faith, which covered 'all eventualities'.

'I see what he meant about his service,' Emily whispered to Bessie.

'You mean it's very simple?'

'Yes. He's not mentioned anything religious at all. He doesn't want to offend anybody. Nobody seems concerned. It's just a funeral to them.'

'It is for us.'

'Don't start.'

Outside the church, the procession trooped to the cemetery, where a lone piper, especially requested by Freddie in his will, played over the grave.

'Where did you hire him from?'

'Liverpool Scottish.'

After the burial they all walked down to the Blobber for a brief get-together. There were sandwiches and drinks all laid on. Emily addressed the mourners. They were surprisingly attentive.

'Freddie requested a piper in his will and then he suggested that we have a sing-along in the pub.'

Bessie positioned herself at the piano and led the singing. She played *There's a Tavern in the Town, Kiss Me Tonight Sergeant-Major, Show Me the Way to Go Home* and *Auld Lang Syne*. They all linked arms, which steadied most of the drunks and the elderly. Most of the mourners were openly weeping by now, aided by the free drink. Emily felt like that herself but she hadn't finished reading out the items on the will.

'Next item on the will. Freddie requests a raffle. Don't ask me why? So we have some tickets. The proceeds go to Colin to help him along. The prizes are donated by Freddie. First prize is a bottle of whisky; second prize is a pair of nylons; and the third prize is h ... h ... h ... err ... clothing coupons and Durex. Oh yes, I'm told there is a fourth prize from Mike Brennan, a crate of Guinness, which he's promised not to drink all by himself. So, you tee-total, bare-legged Catholics, this is the draw for you. The last request is for the whole proceedings to end up in the gutter, but we'll overlook that one.'

Most of the mourners understood Freddie's will was just the desire to be outlandish to the end. Others understood his frame of mind in the last few months, when he'd drunk himself to death.

Everybody was now happy after the free drink, and the Brennan brothers brought out their jazz instruments and played all the standards. Bessie was pleased when they let her jam along with them, especially when they let her sing.

China, one of Freddie's drinking partners, was really drunk before the end.

'"See yer later, Fred," I said. "See yer later, China," he said. That's all I know. "See yer later, Fred," I said. "See yer later, China," he said ... See yer later. Now he's gone. People said that Fred was a gob-shite; but he was always good to me,' China sobbed.

Much to Bessie's relief, Emily returned to the vicarage next morning. There was a backlog of work, although most of it was simple 'know-how'. Emily had caught up on herself by lunchtime, leaving Bessie to cover while she paid all the bills, cleared the paperwork, organised the laundry and planned the menus for the week ahead. The vicar was smiling again and even more so when Emily congratulated him on the funeral service, where he'd endeavoured to seek a delicate balance.

'You see, Emily, I haven't used that form of the service since my days in Canada, when there were so many different religions, varieties of Christian faiths, native customs and beliefs. I learnt how to bury them with the minimum of fuss, without stepping on too many toes. It's man returning to the good soil of the planet from whence he came.'

Emily was most impressed and the vicar was pleased with his work for the first time in many drab months of the war. They never mouthed the words 'forgive and forget', they just did and set about working together again.

Chapter 23
The Wedding

Apart from one or two meals at home and at the vicarage, Andy stayed well out of the way while Emily settled her differences with the vicar. After spending most of the time down at the dock, while belated repairs were made to the Buzzard, Andy had then sailed off to North Biscay with the group. There was only one subject at meal times and that wasn't the proposed wedding, which was on hold; it was the dispute. Indeed, even the dispute had got to the stage of never being discussed because the positions of the parties remained fixed. Father Deegan seemed to have vanished from the scene altogether, which was a slightly better way of handling the situation because the vicar had spent his time bumbling about the place wondering where his next meal was going to come from. Emily had inadvertently hit home by affecting the vicar's eating habits; every other activity at the vicarage had been placed on hold.

In the middle of the Bay of Biscay, Andy was helping the group fish for U-boats. It wasn't quite the same without the boss, who had been taken into hospital the week before they sailed with exhaustion, brought on by overwork. He had been taken ill at the end of the previous trip and told to rest. Years of staying awake for hours on end had caught up with him. A week into the trip the boss died in Seaforth Naval Hospital, where Andy used to visit Bungey Connaught. It came as a severe shock to everybody. The group returned to Liverpool long after his funeral had taken place and he'd been buried at sea, out in Liverpool Bay. Andy visited Bungey when he was next in port.

'It made me feel guilty,' said Bungey. 'I've been here for months. The boss comes in, full of life, and is dead after a few weeks. I'm an impostor. I keep chugging on. I've had so many second chances. I'm like a cat with nine lives.'

Back in Liverpool, Andy wanted to get the proposed wedding for 1945 back on track. Everything looked rosy when he called around to see Emily and discovered that she was at work. Thank God, for that, he thought, as he walked up to the church, seeing one or two of his fellow, youthful choristers on the way. He could see that they'd grown since last year. They loved to see him back from the sea in his uniform; he was a real sailor.

At the vicarage Andy hugged and kissed Emily. The vicar and Bessie vanished through the nearest 'get-out-quick' door, after glowing smiles and happy greetings had been exchanged.

'Choir practice tonight,' the vicar reminded him.

'Everything is on track for the wedding,' Emily said. 'Just three things. The Vicar thinks we should both come for special prayers for Jimmy the week before. That should be okay, shouldn't it?'

'Yes, certainly. Maybe the kids should come, too.'

'They're still too young to know what's going on. Then there is your best man. Have you any idea?'

'Probably Bungey Connaught, if he is still alive. He still looks distinguished in uniform.'

'I thought he was clinging on to life by a thread?'

'Well, he is, but he's still my closest friend. Ginger Hardy would make a pig's ear of it. Say all the wrong things to people.'

'Can't have that. Bessie will be my chief bridesmaid with my two girls.'

'Of course.'

'The third thing is my dress. Wartime makes the "Something borrowed, something blue, something old and something new" rather ludicrous. It'll all be old and borrowed. About the only thing "new" will be my handkerchief.'

'It'll be okay. I'm sure you'll look wonderful.'

'I'll have to make my little girls their first long frocks. Ada reckons she can find some material,' Emily revealed her thoughts.

'How is Ada?'

'My rock, Andy. She's my mother not my mother-in-law. She just wants the best for me and her granddaughters. She's helped me survive the war.'

'So have you seen Father Deegan lately?'

'Yes. He and the vicar have made up their differences.'

'More like old times then?' asked Andy.

'Yes. They had to arrange a joint service at the cenotaph and rediscovered that they were men of like minds. I went down to the cenotaph with the kids, wearing our poppies. They both had a few words with me and the girls about Jimmy and it was back to normal.'

'So they've learnt to beg to differ?'

'Yes, old Freddie asked questions of us all,' said Emily.

'I'm amazed you accepted Freddie for what he was.'

'He helped me feed the kids, when I was broke just living on Jimmy's navy money before my "posh" job,' said Emily. 'The vicar wants to chat to us before we formalise the marriage. He was just concerned about the need to pray for Jimmy, particularly as he was serving his country when he died. Then we need to be able to provide for the two girls and respect Ada's wishes.'

'We'll do all that and more,' said Andy. 'You forget that your mother-in-law has been like a mother to me as well.'

'She's like that with everybody.'

'We'll leave the honeymoon till after the war.'

'I was thinking we could spend the night in Southport.'

'At least it will get us out of town for a night.'

'The food for the reception, if we bother?'

'Don't let's break with tradition; let's have cheese and beetroot sandwiches.'

'You are being impossible now.'

They kissed and shared a giggle.

Andy was back at sea over the Christmas of 1944. When he returned in February 1945, Emily arranged for them to have their chat with the vicar. All the points Emily had made previously were discussed. At the end of it all she told the vicar all about their plans to live in Canada after the war and was soon conscious of having strayed on to the Vicar's third favourite subject, after potatoes and cake.

'You are wise, Emily. You are very wise. Canada is a young country and the country is for young families. It is indeed the place to bring up your two young girls.'

The wedding was fixed for April. From now on it would be a battle to find the money for the reception and the wedding clothes. Ada set out to find some material for the children's bridesmaids outfits. It became a case of 'who do you know?' Bessie met a woman in the pub, who knew a guy who sold cheap material. It proved to be the quickest way to solve the problem. Ada and Emily ran the dresses up themselves. It was only when they had almost given up hope that Bessie found an old sky-blue evening dress that provided enough material to make Emily a plain, blue wedding dress. The bodice of the dress displayed intricate needlework. Once Ada and Emily had readjusted the arms, waist and length, the old dress came together and the needlework stood out in bright light.

'There you are, Em. Looks like new.'

'I wouldn't go that far, but it solves three of the requirements, borrowed, blue and old. What will I do for new?'

'You'll have a new man.'

'Yes, but I can't carry him down the aisle,' said Emily.

'Few people could.'

Emily tried not to mention the month of April too much to Bessie, because she'd start singing *April Showers*. Emily and Andy made sure they heard the banns being read out at least once together, even though Emily had to leave the service before the end, to put the oven on.

The two clerics still discussed the state of the war over breakfast on the occasions they met up. Each was now predicting when he thought the end would come. The vicar couldn't see it ending before Christmas but the father reckoned on the summer months. The war in the Pacific was another matter and could trundle on for years, if the invasion of the Japanese mainland proved to be bloodier than the present fighting in Germany. Emily listened to their deliberations at a distance.

'The only thing I know, Vicar,' she said one day, when drawn into the discussion as she brought the tea and biscuits into the study, 'the only thing I know is that the Battle of the Atlantic has been raging since 1939 and it is still being fought as we speak and they still haven't starved us out.'

'Well, starvation rations have made John a much better gardener, Emily. His fruit, vegetables and salad are better every season,' the father said.

'I may be a better gardener but it's scant consolation for the poor souls who have perished in this terrible war,' said the vicar.

'It'll be good to see an end to it all this summer,' decided the father.

'Certainly before Christmas,' added the vicar.

Next morning at breakfast the news from the battle front was even better.

'Just look at this, John. Mussolini has been strung up by his own people,' said the father.

The vicar hastily looked at the photograph in the newspaper of Mussolini, his mistress and an aide.

'We've seen gory stuff in Bootle but this is disgusting,' said the vicar.

When he was at home on leave, Andy spent as much time as he could with the two children. He would take them regularly to the park. where he would push them incessantly on the swings. He would continue until the pleas of 'again, again, again' died away. Then there was the see-saw, which, fortunately, they could operate themselves, so long as he positioned the heaviest child nearer the fulcrum. After this, there was the slide and ensuring that they didn't fall off when climbing the steps to the top. The girls had so much more confidence than he had, racing all over the playground.

Dressing up day arrived. Andy was down at the dock putting in the hours before his week's leave after the wedding. Emily, Bessie and the two girls dressed up in their finery. Ada pronounced them all 'just beautiful'. And wept.

Later, Emily asked Ada, 'Why are you so upset?'

'Jimmy would have loved seeing the three of you all dressed up to kill.'

'He would but he is happy for us all and very proud, I'm sure.'

Father Deegan wished Emily all the best for the future. Emily thought about Freddie and his marriage that was disapproved of by the Church. She found it difficult to accept that personal life was rather different than the requirements of the various religions of the world. She valued her relationship with both the clerics, so long as religion didn't get in the way. When it came to Emily's two children, both the clerics believed that Andy would prove to be a responsible stepfather.

Wedding day came along just after Easter. The weather was warming up at last and, despite Bessie predicting 'April Showers' for the big day, none materialised. Everything ran according to plan. Andy spent his last night as a single man down at the dock, attempting to stay sober despite all the plans to get him drunk. He left an hour before the ceremony was due to start and picked up Bungey Connaught from the naval hospital, who graciously paid the taxi fare. Bungey looked extremely smart in his senior officer's uniform. Ginger Hardy would be travelling across from Lark Lane.

'Heck, it looks like you are the one getting married, Bungey,' Andy said. They arrived at the church well before the designated time. The bride's party arrived and paraded down the aisle. Emily was to be given away by her Uncle Ted, whom she had seldom seen, particularly during the war, her family being widely scattered and mostly deceased. Uncle Ted was her father's twin brother and lived in Ormskirk.

It was a wartime wedding and as a consequence there was only Bungey and Andy on their side of the church, apart from a few well-wishers who had crept in. The lopsided congregation fell in love with the two pretty bridesmaids, obeying Auntie Bessie's every command. The vicar was wearing first-eleven kit, as his friend would have it. Two hymns were sung. They needed something about the sea so they chose *Lead us, Heavenly Father, Lead us O'er the World's Tempestuous sea.* and *O Perfect Love, All Human Thought Transcending.*

It was a harmonious wedding. The wedding party were extremely happy and the vicar enjoyed performing the ceremony for two dear friends. Ada sobbed, particularly when nobody was looking. Bessie felt like weeping but she was in the limelight with the two little girls to look after and couldn't look silly.

When they walked out at the end, it was in triumph. They'd survived the war unscathed and stayed together, first as friends and then lovers. Now they were together as bride and groom, looking lovingly at each other. The little bridesmaids were delightful, the best man looked distinguished and the vicar paraded as if he was happy with a job well done.

'Such a lovely day,' the vicar said, looking at the sun slipping behind the harmless white clouds. 'Maybe I could get a line of spuds in.'

The wedding breakfast had been arranged at the vicarage. Emily had persuaded Mrs Silverton to look after the proceedings because both she and Bessie were centre stage. It was a quiet affair with few guests and the food was restricted. After the little get-together Emily and Andy withdrew early as they wanted to be in Southport before nightfall; a night away from the family. Doctor Golding drove the couple down to the station and wished them good luck.

After the breakfast, Bessie invited some of the guests along to the pub for a few drinks. She was asked to play the piano but she decided against it because she wanted to wear her bridesmaid outfit for as long as possible. Bungey Connaught amazingly watched what he drank, not wanting to suffer later, and was soon on his way back to Seaforth. Bessie was left with just a few old friends with whom to socialise. Before long, the guests drifted away gradually to all parts of the city. Bessie consoled herself in the knowledge that it was, after all, a quiet wartime wedding. Often at such weddings there were only the bride and groom in uniform at the registry office. At least this time there had been a proper church.

She was heading off home herself when a ginger-headed sailor arrived looking for the Ritchie–Jones wedding party. He was accompanied by an attractive wren, who was giving him earache as he spoke to Bessie.

'You're a bloody idiot,' she said.

'This is Andy and Emily's wedding party, or what's left of it,' confirmed Bessie.

'You see,' said the wren. 'Another right balls-up.'

'I'm a bit late,' said the sailor. 'I got the wrong week. It was only when I saw old Bungey Connaught all kitted out that I realised I'd managed a major cock-up.'

'So were you invited?' asked Bessie.

'Of course we were,' shouted the wound-up wren.

'We could have done with a few more on Andy's side of the church,' said Bessie. 'Anyway, Andy and Emily have long since gone off on honeymoon to Southport. Who shall I say finally turned up?'

'Just say Ginger Hardy,' said the sailor, deciding he would buy a few drinks.

'Tell Andy that it wasn't Cynthia's fault,' said Cynthia, the wren.

'Sorry you missed it,' said Bessie, sympathising.

'He's had me standing waiting outside the Caradoc most of the day; could have been picked up at least half a dozen times,' said the unhappy Cynthia.

The newly married couple spent the night in a little hotel along Lord Street, Southport. It was pleasant to get away for a few short hours together. The evening meal was nothing special but the full English breakfast made up for it. It came as a welcome change to eat an egg each, a slice of bacon, sausage, piece of fried bread and a fried tomato, after a generous bowl of porridge. Though everything on the plate was meagre, it was the first proper cooked breakfast that Emily had eaten since her visit to Glasgow. Back in Bootle, they settled in as man and wife for the rest of the week. Andy was now striving to be a competent father and not just an uncle to the girls. A week later he headed back out to sea aboard the Buzzard. Near as it was to the end of the war, there were still battles to be fought on the ocean.

Chapter 24

End of the War

'There never was a good war or a bad peace.'

Benjamin Franklin, 1783

Bessie kept away from Emily's home till Andy returned to the sea.

'I didn't want to ruin your honeymoon.'

'You couldn't have done that, even if you'd tried.'

'You've been busy,' said Bessie. 'So have I. I've taken on young Colin. Given him a home. He was at his auntie's in Widnes but he never settled down. He said it brought back memories of his evacuation to Ormskirk.'

'That's great, Bess,' said Emily. 'I'm sure you'll do a good job. He is a decent lad, just a shade slow off the mark.'

'Yes. So I'm laying down some firm rules straight away. He's to finish school and go on to technical college. I'll get him started in a good trade. No more working for peanuts in the pub. I've told Gordon Penn he's finished,' Bessie said seriously.

'What did Gordon say?'

'Wasn't much he could say.'

'Get him a trade with some money attached,' suggested Emily.

'I've made him join the choir, that'll get him to church.'

'Better than all the foul language in the pub,' said Emily.

'Oh ... And I've finally joined the choir myself. To keep an eye on him.'

'Great, Bess. That's great. Andy will love it when he returns.'

'I've set down the rules, like the programmes on the BBC. No lies, no swearing and sex will play no part in his adventures.'

255

'He's okay, here. We don't have sex in Bootle. We just have kids.'

'For all that won us wings to clear the tops of grief, My friend who within me laughs Bids you dance and sing.'

Cecil Day-Lewis

The war ended on 8 May 1945, exactly four years after the worst night of the Blitz in Bootle. Every other month, and eventually every week since Christmas, people had said the war had ended and put the flags out, only to have to take them back in quickly, when it turned out to be a false rumour. On the afternoon of the eighth it was announced by Churchill, so this time it must be true. And it was.

The church bells rang out and more and more flags hung out on the houses and more and more people poured out into the streets. Everybody was just glad to be alive and everybody was everybody's friend. People laughed. People danced. People got drunk. Bessie popped into the pub, went over to the piano, plopped herself down on the stool and played spontaneously. She powered herself through the chords, hammered away with relish and sang out strongly:

'Now thank we all our God, with heart and hands and voices, who wondrous things hath done, in whom his world rejoices; who from our mother's arms hath blessed us on our way with countless gifts of love, and still is ours today.'

The hymn boomed out on to the street. Amazingly, the reception was cordial. Some of the drinkers joined in and many of the drunks cried gallons of tears. After all, everybody in Bootle had lost someone or something in the war. Bessie ordered herself a stout and sat on her piano stool with a big smile on her happy face.

'Well, I didn't know what else should be my first song in peacetime. That reprobate Hitler has paid in full for bombing me out of house and home, twice.'

'How do you know the words to the hymn?' asked Gordon Penn.

'You'll know I'm in the choir now and we've been practising the hymn for the Sunday services,' said Bessie.

'How did the vicar know it would be needed?' asked the publican.

'The vicar always seems to know the facts behind the news. We've been practising for the end of the war for weeks. He had the bells serviced, too.'

'Let's have it again,' insisted Gordon. 'First hymn I've ever heard in here apart from carols. Then go straight into a sing-along, so we all can join in.'

So Bessie played the hymn again. The drunks joined in, drank their beer and cried out of happiness at the same time. It was the greatest day that most of them would live to see. Then Bessie played some of the wartime favourites: *We'll Meet again,* and *The White Cliffs of Dover.* She played the *Hokey-Cokey* and they all joined in and danced a 'conga' out into the street. People danced with people they didn't know. They returned to the bar to replenish their drinks and sing *Auld Lang Syne.* Bessie was pleased when everybody got legless and unable to sing any more because she was exhausted. She slipped away to see Emily sitting out in the street with Ada. The whole neighbourhood was out in the street planning a huge party for the next day.

'Heck, I'm tired of hammering the piano. At times like this I wish that there were others who could take over the keyboard,' said Bessie.

'You'd be out of a job then,' said Emily.

'Where's Andy?' asked Bessie.

'Oh, he's still out in the Atlantic.'

'He'll know the war's over. Won't he?'

'Be-hopes.'

The Battle of the Atlantic raged from the first day of the war on the 3 September 1939 until the last day of the conflict, 8 May 1945.

The next day there was a large party in the street. Flags and bunting, saved from the Coronation, festooned the street. Trestle tables from the mission were arranged down the centre of the road. The party was mostly beef-spread and tomato sandwiches with some made of cheese and pickle to offer variety. There were cakes and bags of biscuits, followed, of course, by jelly and custard. The giant cake had been made two months previously when the first false alarm had been sounded for the end of the war. This had sent Mrs Cooper into a cooking frenzy. She'd collected all the spare dried fruit, flour, eggs, fat, coupons and money from the neighbours and made one giant cake, which had stood in readiness in her cupboard, covered in white icing with the word 'Victory' in red and blue. It was the biggest cake the kids had ever seen. Everybody received a huge slice to take home, wrapped in a serviette. An old piano was dragged out into the middle of the road and there was dancing and, of course, everybody joined in the *Hokey-Cokey* and *Knees up Mother Brown*.

There was a mile-long civic parade through the town a few days into peace. The soldiers and sailors all had smiles on their faces, as opposed to the serious faces when Andy had read the lesson in 1943. Jackie, from three doors down, returned from prison-of-war camp, looking thinner than when he had left. He had been taken prisoner at Dunkirk, where he'd only had a shovel to fight with. He had been held in a camp in Germany ever since. He smiled and laughed with his family and friends in the street but never ventured outside again.

Emily was happy but missed her new husband, Andy. She joined in the dancing, women mostly dancing with women. Bessie performed on the old piano, hitting some bum notes. She tried to play *Cruising Down the River* and *We'll Gather Lilacs* but hit all the wrong notes.

'When did you last get this tuned?' she asked the owner.

'The front room was Blitzed.'

'Sounds like it, too,' said Bessie struggling on manfully but getting some good laughs out of the audience at the expense of the piano.

'It's not as bad as all that,' said the sorry piano owner, not appreciating the joke.

Celebrations went on for a week and, after a further three days of chaos and confusion, Andy returned home. Emily and Andy kissed and cuddled for a long time inside the house before going outside, finding the little girls and carrying one each around the street and showing them off.

'Just nice to be a family again.' Emily tried not to cry.

Andy had been in the Atlantic for the week after the war ended, accepting the surrender of U-boats. The Buzzard had accompanied over thirty-five of them to Londonderry, the nearest port. There had been over two hundred U-boats operating up to VE Day. Now most of them had been herded into Irish and Scottish lochs, anchorages and ports, where they surrendered.

'Good, Emily. Now you can have a second honeymoon,' said Bessie.

'We haven't had the first yet.'

'You and Andy go and have it now,' she suggested. 'I'll look after the kids.'

Emily and Andy vanished back into the house. Ada and Bessie stayed outside, joined in the dancing with the kids and had another drink.

'One thing about the war. We never forgot how to celebrate.'

'We never had anything to celebrate.'

There was yet another party the next day, after locals who had been away years finally made it home, to finish up the left-overs. There was further dancing, singing and drinking around a bonfire with an effigy of Hitler burning on the top.

Percy the parrot had a new catch-phrase: 'The war in Europe ...' but he never could remember the 'is at an end' part.

Chapter 25

The First Weeks of Peace

'I sometimes think that the price of liberty
is not so much eternal vigilance as eternal dirt'

George Orwell

Everybody's life changed in 1945. For Emily it changed at the end of
the second week of peace. Andy received new orders when he was on
leave, at his new Bootle address. It came as a shock. He was seconded
to the Royal Canadian Navy and his new unit was stationed in Montreal.

'Wartime seems to be one shock after another,' he said to Emily.

'I thought this was peace,' said Emily. 'But why send you to
Canada? You are due to be demobbed,' said Emily.

'One thing I've learnt since 1939 is that nothing makes sense any
more.' They'd been together in the same house for just a week.
They'd watched sailors, soldiers and even POW returning home.
Andy wondered what would be in store for him in Canada.

'Suppose it doesn't change our plans. We're going to emigrate to
Canada when it all ends. So I'll be there in Canada when they find out
they've no further use for me. I'll just have to see if I can get myself
demobbed out there. Then I can set about finding somewhere for us
to live. Even if they make me return home to get demobbed, I'll have
a good idea of how the land lies in Montreal.' Andy thought deeply
about the whole affair. 'At least they haven't posted me to the Pacific,'
he said.

The disappointing thing about the posting was that Andy had to
leave and travel down to Southampton by the end of the week. They
threw a small party on the Friday night, just to say their farewells to
Andy. By now they were fed up with parties.

Andy left from Lime Street on the seven o'clock train on the Saturday. While Andy was leaving Liverpool, men, women and children were returning home. Returning evacuees, servicemen and women were returning to their families, often to bombsites and derelict streets that they did not recognise and to loved ones who had changed beyond recognition. After six years apart, children had changed from toddlers to children and from children to teenagers. Fathers didn't recognise their children, and mothers had survived six years without their kids and the menfolk. It was back to austerity, back to rationing and make-do and mend. Finding food was the big problem. Some people were more unhappy than when they had been apart. Once the dancing in the middle of the road and bombed site was over people found that they had nothing. Everything was old, worn out, full of grime, over-used but made-to-do during the long years of war. Fixtures and fittings were falling apart. Buildings were grey and grimy. Luxuries were nonexistent. The country was exhausted, Liverpool was wrecked and Bootle was still in a coma.

The story of Mary and Kitty Headley demonstrated the host of predicaments that people found themselves in. They were owners of the local corner shop. They'd eaten well during the war, and their dog, Ben, was the only fat dog in a road of skinny mongrels. They never needed ration books, except for clothes coupons. Kitty was always well dressed when everybody else struggled. Tom, her husband, had gone overseas to Malaya and been reported 'missing believed dead'. At the end of the war they waited. Tom never appeared. All three, Mary, Kitty and Ben, the dog, sat in the kitchen and were found, eventually, gassed by the open oven door. A neighbour had smelt the gas seeping out of the shop and called the police.

Emily's life had been changed by the war. She hadn't had her babies evacuated, they were too young. They were now seven and five and at school. She had avoided the trauma of being separated from her kids but she'd lost her first husband and was now separated from her second. Things would never be the same. Emily passed new fresh faces and old faces that knew her but she didn't recognise them because they had been six years away. She walked up the hill towards the vicarage and passed the gang of German prisoners of war from Walton Jail clearing one of the bombed sites and laying concrete footings for the soon to be erected pre-fabricated houses. Small crowds gathered to watch, saying such things as, 'They knocked them down. Let them build them back up.' However, the same week a local woman had given one of the prisoners an apple, been taken to court and fined one penny and severely reprimanded about her appalling behaviour.

On arriving at the vicarage, Emily set about preparing some tea and biscuits for the two clerics. They were both in the study scanning through the newspapers for news and indications as to where the current events were leading.

'Remember when we first met in this study in 1940,' Emily said to the father as he scanned through the news.

'Indeed, I do, Emily,' said the father. 'You thought I looked like Dev.'

'The older he gets, the more he looks like de Valera,' said the vicar.

'Me or Dev?' asked the father, smiling at his little query.

'Both of you,' said the vicar. 'It's the silvering of your temples.'

'So Andy has been sent to Canada,' the father changed the subject.

'Yes. He's on his way from Southampton.'

'Suppose it's too much to ask if we are okay for a meal?' asked the Vicar.

'Yes, certainly. We've been saved with those spuds from Pilling.'

'Excellent. Excellent.'

'Y'know, Vicar. Most people are worse off now that it's peace and a lot less happy than they ever were in the war. Things are scarce and the city is a horrendous mess. There's bombed sites and damaged property wherever you turn. Even the weather is rubbish since they started broadcasting the forecasts again,' said Emily.

'Folk have been celebrating in the ruins of their previous existence, with fathers not recognising their own kids. There's nothing left. Families are finding it impossible to stay together but they still have to soldier on,' added the father.

'Yes, the Yanks went into the war rich and came out rich. We went in reasonably rich and came out very poor,' said the vicar.

'The poor went in poor and came out destitute, without two ha'pennies to rub together,' said the father.

There was a period of silence, then Emily said, 'Doesn't the old song go "The rich get rich and the poor get children"? The war has singled out the poor to bear the burden. There's more unwanted starving children in the world now than before the war,' Emily added.

Silence prevailed.

'Yes, Emily, but don't forget that life is the greatest gift of God and we should not return it unopened,' said the father, and the silence again awaited takers.

'Even if we can't feed them,' said Emily.

'It makes me wonder,' said the vicar. 'Didn't St Benedict say that "the strong have something to strive after while the weak should not be weighed down with burdens too crushing to bear"?'

'He did indeed,' answered the father. 'That's what people always say, but St Theresa wrote that we should stay far away from all that is brilliant. Let us love our littleness, love to feel nothing.'

'People are certainly used to nothing,' said Emily.

'Gandhi says "We must learn to live simply, so the poor can simply live",' the father said, thinking he'd brought the discussion slap up to date.

'How long has Gandhi been a Catholic, father?' asked Emily.

There was a long silence while they all absorbed the thought that purer life was to be found in poverty.

'Let's all enjoy the next hotpot dinner; probably the last for a long time,' the vicar ended the sticky debate. 'Besides, the war in the Pacific will soon be at an end.'

'What?' said Emily. 'We've already had six years, how can you say "soon"?'

'Soon, none the less. The Yanks only have one enemy now.'

It was a special hotpot supper. Many of the usual guests had vanished. Some had been demobbed, some had been killed in action, some had been killed for no apparent reason, while others had simply moved back home. There were gaps at the table and Emily and Bessie were invited to fill them.

'The potatoes and carrots are delicious,' decided the vicar.

'Pilling is renowned for them,' said Emily. 'Mary next door fetched them back from Blackpool over the weekend.'

'It's okay, if you're not washing them,' said Bessie. 'The water was as black as the ace of spades. I had to change it four times.'

'It's the famous black volcanic soils that give the potatoes their special flavour,' said the vicar, who had read up all there was to read on the subject of vegetables. 'Indeed, they're as good as my Scottish Piper.'

After the supper Bessie and Colin perfomed a small recital. Colin's singing had developed with Bessie's extra attention and musical ear. He sang *Where 'er You Walk* and *What is Life to Me Without you*, while Bessie sang *We'll Gather Lilacs in the Spring Again* and *I'll Walk Beside You*. The vicar was very proud of the performances and suggested that it was he who had taken Bessie's singing out of the public house and into the church, which he had in a round-about way by giving her a cleaning job in December 1940.

Emily felt in the background for a change, thinking of Andy and wondering what the future might hold for her and the kids. Surely events would start unfolding once Japan was defeated.

Eventually VJ Day arrived and there were considerable celebrations again. Peace was proving to be rather boring, all this waiting around for something to happen, while there were wild, drunken parties in the street. *Hokey-Cokey* seemed to be a weekly event in which everybody was expected to join. The dance got rowdier and more and more physical as peace broke out.

Emily need not have worried. She received a letter from the Cunard Line, Liverpool, telling her to visit the offices down by the Pier Head to collect her tickets and documentation. Andy had set the wheels in motion as soon as he had arrived in Canada.

Emily collected her tickets and other papers. She was amazed to see the name 'Mrs Emily Ritchie' on everything and Andy's name followed by the phrase 'Serviceman applied for Citizenship of

Canada'. It was news to her but if it sped up the process then she was all for it. She was now what was called a 'war bride' and the passage was assisted to Montreal, aboard the Aquitania.

Emily had lots of questions and most received the answer 'Ask your husband'. Within a week there was a letter from Andy explaining everything. He'd arrived in Canada and found himself behind a desk in much the same sort of job that he had been posted to in Glasgow at the start of the war. He'd looked into arranging his demobilisation in Canada and been told the quickest way was to apply for Canadian citizenship. This he had done. Then, as soon as the war with Japan had come to an end, a regular Royal Navy officer out from the UK had been brought in to take over his desk. He had found himself being demobbed by the same fellows he'd been working with in the office. He was now living in Montreal looking for suitable housing.

The only thing left for Emily to do was sell off the furniture or give it away. It didn't take long to convince Ada that she should follow as soon as she could arrange a passage.

'I'm only sixty after all,' she said. 'I've years ahead of me. Colin can have Percy to look after. They've been friends ever since he brought him down off the roof.'

Emily told Bessie of the sudden move and she cried her eyes out so much Emily thought she'd never stop.

'So you are going,' sobbed Bessie.

'Of course, daft 'ead. I'm booked on Cunard. Don't cry, Bessie. I'm happy.'

'I'm crying 'cos you've got what you want and are happy at last.'

'We'll throw a party in the empty house. You've always wanted the sideboard and one or two other things, like the double bed. So I can leave you the keys and you can clear the place out after we've gone.'

The house was choc-a-bloc at the party, standing room only, and the guests crowded out into the street. Eventually, the pubs let out and the gathering exploded, until even the bobby on the beat asked questions.

'What's going on here?'

'It's Emily; she's emigrating to Canada in the morning.'

'Some people have all the luck,' said the constable.

Emily stowed her hand luggage in her assigned cabin on the Aquitania. She remembered what Father Deegan had said about his cabins on the troopers; they could not have been any starker than this one, which she and the two girls were sharing with a middle-aged couple and their elder daughter. The whole liner had seen better days and survived the war. There were eight berths but just six people in all. It would still be a tight squeeze. She took the girls back down to meet her friends on the landing stage.

Ada didn't like the accommodation but she said, 'I suppose it's free.'

The vicar was a busy man. He was seeing more people than just Emily off.

'Thanks for everything, Emily. Helping out at every turn during the long days of war, which I thought would never end. I'll always be indebted.'

'I shall always be indebted to you; because the job was my security.'

'I can't think of anything clever to say,' said the vicar. 'Just that you'll find Canada is a glorious place. You and Andy will be happy there.' Then he excused himself. 'I have to go and see a young curate who is going out on the same boat as you. He is bound for the Inuit settlement at Resolute.'

'Your old stomping ground.'

'Yes. He's young and eager, just like I was in the 1920s. He just needs some encouraging from me. Father Deegan will be impressed when I tell him. The young man was in the desert with the Inniskillings.'

'The father will be thrilled,' said Emily, close to tears.

The vicar went looking for his charge from the Bishop of the Arctic. This was the signal for Bessie to come across with Colin. Bessie's face was plastered with tears.

'There's no rationing in Canada. Will you be able to cope?'

'We withstood the bombs. We'll cope.'

'Will you miss us?'

'Silly question, Bess. Bootle taught me to be thankful for small mercies.'

'How do you know being prosperous will make you happy?' asked Bessie.

'I'll risk it,' Emily decided.

'Need to make tracks now,' decided Bessie, with tears in her eyes. 'It's getting late so much earlier since the blackouts.'

Bessie would survive as a wordsmith.

'Bye-bye, Emily. I'm close to tears even though I'll see you soon,' said Ada.

'See you soon, Mum,' Emily said, as she climbed the gangplank.

They waved from the side of the liner till they could see each other no longer.

They passed the line of docks and Bootle on one side of the river and New Brighton Tower on the other as the liner edged its way into Liverpool Bay. Emily couldn't see much because of her tears.

Epilogue

'The great oceanic battlefield still lies to the west of these islands, yet it bears no record of those whose bones lie beneath its surface and is troubled only by the great winds that scour its surface.'

Richard Woodman, *The Real Cruel Sea*

There was only ever going to be one winner of the Battle of the Atlantic – the ocean. Meanwhile, Emily sailed the Atlantic like so many men she had known and loved, for the first and last time, met up with Andy on the quayside at Montreal and, with the two kids, set out for Ladysmith on Vancouver Island, British Columbia.

Halfway across the prairies, aboard the long train, she discovered that she was pregnant with their first child, a boy they christened Andrew James.

.oOo.

Bibliography

Many of the historical incidents in the novel are referenced in all or many of the works below, with the exception of *Mrs Beeton's Cookery Book.*

References:

Nicholas Monsarrat – *The Cruel Sea* – Cassell – 1951

Nicholas Monsarrat – *Three Corvettes* – Cassell – 1975

Richard Woodman – *The Real Cruel Sea* – John Murray – 2004

Andrew Williams – *The Battle of the Atlantic* – BBC Worldwide – 2002

Richard Hough – *The Longest Battle* – Cassell – 1986

Max Arthur – *Lost Voices of the Royal Navy* – Hodder – 1996

Roy Jenkins – *Churchill* – Pan Books – 2002

D.E.G. Wemyss – *Relentless Pursuit* – Cerberus – 1955

Jim Fitzsimmons – *8th Irish Regiment* – Starfish Multimedia – 2004

John Hughes – *Port in a Storm* – Merseyside Port Folios – 1993

Liverpool Women's History Group – *A Different World* – Bluecoat Press – 2002

John Davies – *Coping with the Blitz* – The Catholic History Society – 2000

Derek Whale – *Lost Villages of Liverpool* – T. Stephenson & Sons – – 1984

Liverpool Echo and Bootle Times Archives – 1939 – 45

Houlston and Wright – *Enquire Within upon Everything* – London 1863

Mrs. Beeton's Cookery Book – Ward, Lock & Co – London & Melbourne

Bernard Griffiths – *Macnamara's Band.* – Severn House – 1960

Henry Elliot – *Presbyterian Hymnal* – 1879

Hymns Ancient & Modern – Canterbury Press – 1983